# Kiss Me Twice

Thomas Maxwell's novels

Kiss Me Once (1986)
The Saberdene Variations (1987)
Kiss Me Twice (1988)

# THOMAS MAXWELL

# KISS ME TWICE

A NOVEL

THE MYSTERIOUS PRESS
New York • London • Tokyo

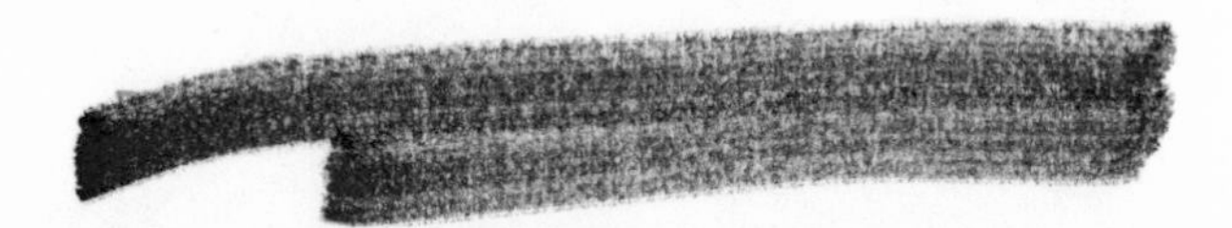

The Mysterious Press, 129 West 56th Street, New York, N.Y. 10019

Printed in the United States of America

First Printing: October 1988

10 9 8 7 6 5 4 3 2 1

**Library of Congress Cataloging-in-Publication Data**

Kiss me twice / Thomas Maxwell.
p. cm.
I. Title.
PS3563.A926K5 1988
813'.54—dc19 88-14138
ISBN 0-89296-164-3 CIP

for Elizabeth

Either it's love or it isn't.
You can't compromise.

—Coral Chandler to
Warren "Rip" Murdock

# KISS ME TWICE

# Chapter One

Lew Cassidy's wife was back from the dead and the idea of seeing her was scaring hell out of him.

He had driven north to Westchester in his 1940 Ford convertible with the top down and the sun putting a final September crisp on his tan. His bad leg was giving him trouble so he knew it was going to rain. He was out of town, out of patience, and just about out of luck. But he'd followed the summons to the vast estate hoping that maybe it was all going to work out, maybe it was going to be okay. He'd driven for another mile once he'd passed through the high iron gates and he wondered if any visitor ever got lucky in a place like this. It seemed unlikely.

Cassidy waited by himself in the unfamiliar room, a rich man's library, smelling of leather bindings and club chairs and generations of cigar smoke. He'd been shown in by a young Army officer who called him sir and said they'd been expecting him. Colonel MacMurdo would be with him in just a moment. Fifteen minutes had passed and he'd had a look at the massed bookcases, thousands of volumes, the empty fireplace, the bowls of flowers, the neatly arranged accessories on the immaculate desktop, the portrait over the mantelpiece of a long dead robber baron who'd once owned a railroad as well as this house, the rolling acreage of the estate.

The oppressive September heat was getting him down and the hour-long drive from Washington Square had given him too much time to think about all the craziness. Through the years of playing football, college and pro, he'd never felt so much on edge. He went to the mullioned casements and wound one set wide open. The breeze wasn't much and what there was was heavy, wet, and hot. A couple of wasps darted in the bright shafts of sunlight an arm's length away.

Cassidy took a deep breath, felt sweat running down his back, fusing him to his shirt beneath the seersucker jacket. He looked out across the stone terrace, past the heavy balustrade with its enormous cement urns. The flowers had packed it in, dry stalks bent haphazardly, like old bones. Somebody hadn't been attending to the watering.

The lawn sloped away in gently layered terraces to a massive stand of weeping willows shimmering green and gold like priceless wall hangings. The sky above and beyond them was smudged with low purple clouds, full of impending rain. You could feel it coming. You prayed it would hurry.

Lew Cassidy was still contemplating the skyline when he caught a flicker of movement at the corner of his vision and when he looked she was there. She was standing alone, wearing a sundress that showed her arms and shoulders and a broad-brimmed straw hat with a band that was a bright blur, that turned into a ribbon and dangled softly on her tanned back. She was turned away from him, watching the same dark clouds, but he didn't have to see her face. He knew. Then she turned slowly, her profile the same.

He hadn't seen her in nearly six years.

She'd been killed in the bombing of Cologne back in 1942.

And she'd come back from the dead, as if she'd risen from the ashes of the Third Reich, somehow immortal.

Karin.

Lew Cassidy's late wife. A stranger now.

• • •

He met her at the winter Olympic Games in 1936. The football season had ended and his father, Paul Cassidy, the movie producer, had put him on the payroll as a talent scout and they'd gone to Europe with the idea of finding a French leading man to bring back to Los Angeles to play the lead in an escape-from-Devil's-Island picture. They couldn't land the actor as it turned out and Adolphe Menjou finally signed to do the role and then the picture fell through because two others just like it beat them to the theaters. But it was no big tragedy, Paul Cassidy said, because Menjou was a horse's patoot and, anyway, if they'd signed the frog they might never have gone on to Germany and found Karin Richter and then all their lives would have been different and what the hell, the last thing the world needed was Menjou escaping from Devil's Island. Dying on Devil's Island, maybe, but escaping, no.

They were staying in the swanky resort town of Garmisch-Partenkirchen where the games were held, enjoying the excitement and getting a firsthand look at the Nazis people were beginning to talk about back in the States. The Germans seemed to think this Hitler character was the answer to their problems which, God knew, had been pretty all-encompassing. There were posters of the mustachioed face with the burning eyes everywhere you looked. The Charlie Chaplin mustache didn't seem funny once you were standing in a crowd of blond, pink-cheeked German athletes who weren't laughing. He seemed to have the country revved up and out of the dumps and everyone in Garmisch was having a hell of a fine time.

The Führer was said to have high hopes for the young skater, Karin Richter, who was nineteen and, the Germans kept saying, a threat to dethrone the twenty-four-year-old Norwegian girl, Sonja Henie, who'd won gold medals at Saint Moritz in 1928 and at Lake Placid in '32. In the end Karin Richter skated well and captivated the crowds with her youth and determination and beauty, but she didn't win a medal, let alone dethrone Henie, who won again.

The first time Lew Cassidy saw Karin Richter he was having breakfast in the hotel dining room and she was skating on the rink outside, just beyond the long windows where he sat. He watched her move like a snow queen emerging from the morning mist and fog, gliding across the ice, the skirt molded to her thighs, her face held high, eyes fixed on some distant point. Her concentration was almost palpable, like a protective coating. He couldn't take his eyes off her.

Paul Cassidy thought maybe he was on to something when Lew dragged him out to the rink to watch the gorgeous girl working on her figure eights in the fog. Paul Cassidy liked to insist that he was the first one in Hollywood who thought of making Sonja Henie a movie star. He'd come up a brick shy of a load in the money department but, then, that was show business for you. If you were in the movie end of things, giving up on a good idea never even crossed your mind. If somebody else came up with the same idea, then it meant you did, indeed, have a good idea—unless it had anything to do with Adolphe Menjou and Devil's Island.

Karin Richter was certainly a good enough skater to build a lightweight movie career around and, to be frank, Paul had never seen her as Lady Macbeth or Desdemona. He was, however, looking past strictly ice-bound pictures, past her legs, which were unusually long for a skater, past that cute little fanny. Paul was looking at her face. He might not know a damn thing about skating but he sure as the devil knew about movies. He knew it was the face that mattered. The face did all the heavy work in the movies and one look told him that Karin Richter had the face, all right.

Cheekbones higher than Mont Blanc, a nose just short of unapproachable, level eyebrows over solemn, oddly pale brown eyes, dark brown hair cut short with a kind of triangular wedge at the nape of her neck. Her upper lip was thin, the lower full, hinting at a pout. Lew said he couldn't get her face out of his mind. Paul knew exactly what he meant.

Lew dropped like a stone into those brown eyes. He followed her back to Cologne after the games, met her austere scientist father and faintly dismayed mother, and convinced her to marry him. They came back to the States together, Lew and Karin and Paul. There was some traipsing back and forth to Germany. Paul had to convince Herr Doktor Josef Goebbels, Hitler's propaganda genius in Berlin, that it was useful to have a beautiful German girl starring in American movies. When Lew and Karin were married up at Lake Placid in January of 1938, Goebbels sent them all the roses in town. Karin said the gesture proved that the Nazis had no taste, no sense of restraint. She found the Nazis intolerably vulgar and common, from their manners to their obsessive attention to their uniforms to their torchlight rallies. "They are trying to manufacture a myth," she said, "and they are so hopelessly small. They have the meanness of unworthy people who quite rightly have never gotten anywhere on merits of their own." She once told Lew, referring to the air ace of the Great War, Hermann Göring, "The only one I ever liked was Fat Hermann. He bounced me on his knee once when I won a children's skating competition. He pinned the medal on my blouse. It must have been 1927. . . . I was ten. He wasn't so fat then." That was the only good thing he'd ever heard her say about the Nazis.

By the autumn of 1939 she'd made three movies: *Murder Goes Skating* with George Brent and James Gleason, *Murder on Ice* with Tom Tully, and *Bless Your Heart*, a Christmas story in which she only skated once while playing a young nun at an orphanage. Dick Foran had been the priest. Then she'd found out that her father was very ill. It sounded like cancer. It sounded like he needed his daughter. His wife, her mother, had died a year before.

Hitler was lopping off chunks of Europe, but a lot of people were saying that now he had the *Lebensraum* he'd been yelling about for years. The sooner Karin went home for a visit, the better. And the sooner she'd be back in New York.

She sailed one bright and chilly fall day from Pier 42 on the Hudson, the American Export Line bound for Lisbon where she'd catch a Lufthansa flight for Berlin, then on to the family home in Cologne.

There was only one problem once she got there.

They wouldn't let her leave.

Her father needed her to nurse him while he kept working in the special laboratories the Reich had built for him and, maybe, she would have the time to make a movie or two for the German audience. She'd be staying for a while. And when the time stretched on Lew said he was coming to get her. She wrote him begging him not to do anything rash. She pleaded with him to stay in New York. She said that there were old family friends who had become Nazi sympathizers: not monsters, she wrote, just friends of the family, people she'd known and trusted all her life. They assured her that there were no plans for a wider war, that it was all over, that peace in Europe was at hand.

The only thing she had to worry about, they told her, was an impetuous American husband who didn't understand the way things stood in Germany. Keep him back home, these old friends of the family said, and the time will fly and you'll be together again. But if he came barging into Germany making a fuss, well, they couldn't be responsible for the consequences. They clucked and shook their heads and peered through their monocles. They were full of good advice.

So Lew didn't go.

He waited and played football and read the papers and watched the Nazis club Europe damned near to death. He watched the Blitzkrieg and Dunkirk and the Battle of Britain and eventually not even Karin's letters were getting through. And World War II finally murdered her in 1942 when the largest bombing assault in history turned the city of Cologne to smoking rubble. She and her father, who'd clung to life so steadfastly, were reported dead.

• • •

He watched her strolling slowly, her hands clasped behind her, the full skirt catching a breeze and billowing like a sail, her head down, the long slope of her neck with the ribbon blowing. The breeze worked its way up across the terrace and he felt it on his face. The coming rain smelled earthy and fresh.

He remembered the first of June 1942, the way he'd learned that she was dead. The huge headline—a three-decker—had spread the width of the *Times*, proclaiming the end of the city of Cologne. A thousand bombers—Lancasters and Halifaxes, Stirlings and Manchesters—had unloaded bombs for ninety minutes, one every six seconds, and had left seven-eighths of Cologne, a city the size of Boston, a flaming inferno. . . .

Berlin radio had called it a "terror attack" and had listed the prominent scientist and his movie-actress and Olympic-skater daughter among the dead.

And now, more than three years later, he stood in a stranger's library watching her strolling on an unfamiliar lawn, as if he were still locked in one of the dreams of her that had come so often through the years since her death. So many nights she'd come alive only to disappear into the shadows when morning came and there was another day to be faced. Lew Cassidy had fallen in love with another woman in those strange years since he'd said good-bye to Karin on Pier 42, but she was dead, too. He knew that she, Cindy, would stay dead because he'd watched her die, had held her dead body in his arms. But Karin was something else. . . .

• • •

The news that Karin was alive came by way of his father, who served as a major in a documentary film unit and had gone to France shortly after the D-Day landings. As the war in Europe ended, Paul Cassidy had been seconded to the team collecting the looted art treasures that were turning up all over the German landscape. In the course of preparing a filmed record of the discoveries he was summoned for an interview with an OSS man, Colonel Sam MacMurdo, who informed him that his daughter-in-law had been found alive and, more or less, well. MacMurdo said it was a complicated story he was only just beginning to piece together himself but the upshot was simply that the young lady, who was now twenty-eight, was in a position to do a great service for her country. He referred, of course, to the United States of America. He didn't go into detail since the whole business was very hush-hush at the moment but the idea was to get her back to the States and reunited with her husband, Paul's son Lew. MacMurdo needed Paul's help.

Paul couldn't see any particular problem with Lew, though it was bound to come as a shock, a wife coming back from the grave.

"Well, Major Cassidy," MacMurdo said, puffing his pipe and running a huge hand through his dark blond, curly hair, "there is a problem or two. Hell, the truth is, this is one very delicate matter. She got the *merde* bombed out of her in Cologne, pardon my French, and most of her memory went with it. Now three years have gone by, she's had the best medical care the Reich could offer, and physically she's okay. Absolutely okay." He sounded like a man trying to reassure himself. "But she does have this memory problem. . . . The girl has some pieces missing." MacMurdo seemed lost in thought, staring into the bowl of his pipe. They were sitting in an old Luftwaffe hangar that had become a kind of vast museum warehouse. Paintings were being catalogued, photographed, inspected by experts from Paris, London, and New York, then carefully crated for storage. On the wall behind MacMurdo hung a framed photograph of Reichsmarshal Göring that no one had bothered to remove. Painted on the wall next to Göring was the depiction of the ubiquitous big-nosed chap peering over the fence, his legend carefully inscribed below. KILROY WAS HERE.

Paul Cassidy waited, thinking about Karin and what she'd had to endure in the six years since he'd seen her. The war had proven that people were, among other things, almost infinitely resilient.

"And, too," MacMurdo said at last, "there's the question of Herr Moller." He sucked the pipe but it had gone out.

"I don't know the name," Paul Cassidy said. It was hot and still in the tiny office in the corner of the hangar.

"No reason why you should, none at all. That's what I'm here to tell you. Somewhere along the way, after the bombing of Cologne, your daughter-in-law picked up another husband."

"Give me another crack at that one—"

"She has another husband, Major. That's the problem insofar as your son goes. Husband Number Two is a man named Moller." He smiled sympathetically at Paul Cassidy. "So, you can see, the plot thickens, Major."

Paul Cassidy hadn't known quite what to say.

Two weeks later he was back in New York telling Lew that he had good news and bad news.

Now, in late September, Lew had been told that she was back and they wanted to brief him. It was still terribly hush-hush and he wasn't sure who *they* were or what the great service was that Karin could do or how he fit into what everybody had been calling the big picture ever since there'd been a war to talk about. He didn't give a damn about the big picture. He wanted to get the whole story about his wife and get it straight. That was a plenty big enough picture for the moment.

There hadn't been any effective way to prepare himself for the first sight of her. Somehow he thought she'd be different, that the war might have worked some sad magic on her. But there she was, trim and girlish, moving slowly, solemnly, almost floating across the deep green lawn. The willows swayed behind her. Then she stopped and turned back, one hand up to hold the straw hat in place. She said something and then a man came into view. She reached out and took his hand. Lew Cassidy flinched at the sight, as if someone had dug a knifepoint into his ribs.

The man was tall, wore a brown suit and a Panama hat. He stood with her, their backs to the house, looking at the darkening afternoon sky. Two people talking about the weather.

Then Lew Cassidy heard the door opening behind him and right away he smelled the pipe.

• • •

The library was a huge room. It had to be twenty-five feet square with seas of Oriental rugs, eighteen-foot ceilings, furniture from the den of the Mountain King. Yet it seemed too small to hold the man who'd just come in. Cassidy had once known a gangster's iceman called Bennie the Brute who had been a very large man in anybody's league, but this guy seemed to have six inches on Bennie in every direction. He was wearing full warm-weather officer's kit with enough ribbons on his left breast to stock the notions counter at Macy's. He was the biggest damn thing on two legs Cassidy had ever seen. He crossed the room in a couple of huge strides.

"Hiya, pard," he said. "Good to see you. I'm Sam MacMurdo, sorry to keep you cooling your heels this way. Take a pew. You must wonder what's going on and I don't blame you one damn bit. I won't waste your time with a lot of bullshit, but listen, pard, I gotta tell you I was at the Polo Grounds on December 7, 1941, when you got your leg torn up. I was sitting next to DiMaggio. Said he'd never seen anything like it." He placed the buff folder he was carrying on the leather-edged blotter and sat down behind the massive desk. He still looked like he was standing up. An immense black pipe was stuck in the corner of his mouth.

Cassidy sank into a club chair with cracks of age in the burgundy leather arms. "Well, he was right. I'd never seen anything like it either."

"How's the leg now?"

"Okay most of the time. Sometimes I use a walking stick, not often."

"But you're still in the detective business with your pal Leary?"

"Sure." Cassidy shrugged. "But Terry owns Max Bauman's old nightclub now—"

"That would be Heliotrope, right? Story I heard is that Leary shot Bauman full of holes and Bauman left him Heliotrope in his will. That true?"

"You've done your homework," Cassidy said, wondering what MacMurdo had on his mind. Some birds were twittering beyond the open windows, warning of the coming rain. Was Karin still watching the darkening sky? Was she still holding the man's hand? MacMurdo slowly filled his pipe from a yellow oilskin pouch.

"Now, when do I see my wife? And what's Leary got to do with this—"

"All your questions will be answered, Mr. Cassidy. We got a real situation here and I'm going to have to beg your indulgence. Couple things I've got to find out, get the lay of the land." He struck a wooden match on the side of a pewter holder and slowly sucked the flame down into the bowl. "So," he puffed, "you and Leary, you've still got Dependable Detective. . . ."

"Terry's still one of the owners, if that's what you mean."

"Interesting man. All those years he was a cop he was Max Bauman's boy. . . . That's a man who can walk a tightrope." He smiled easily. "I like that in a man. Enlightened duplicity. He'd have been right at home with the rest of us in OSS."

"Terry's the best friend I've ever had."

"I hear you've got another partner—"

"Harry Madrid. Another ex-cop."

"Sure, Harry Madrid goes way back. I heard Bat Masterson taught him a thing or two when Bat came back to New York to be a newspaperman. Good teacher." He smiled again. The large-featured face had a boyish cast, signifying a man who was used to being liked and trusted. "Harry must be sixty."

"Harry doesn't worry much about his age." Cassidy felt the sweat running down his face again. "But what has this got to do with Karin and me? I don't have much patience these days."

"I know. I'm sorry." MacMurdo smiled calmly through the wavering pillar of smoke. It was a clean, woodsy-smelling English blend. His eyes were narrowed, blue as summer's best skies, his nose long and fine with flared nostrils. His teeth were so white they looked like bad dentures but somehow you knew this guy was all original equipment. His skin was pale, with a slight flush of color in his cheeks. He looked like the biggest graduate in the history of Groton. He was trustworthy, loyal, helpful, friendly, courteous, and kind, at the very least. Cassidy had done some research of his own. He'd felt somewhat humbled because, according to those records that were not classified Sam MacMurdo had a shot at Most Valuable Player for World War II. Paul Cassidy had asked around and Clem Witt, who was close to Wild Bill Donovan at OSS, said Sam MacMurdo was the bravest son of a gun he'd ever known. MacMurdo had spent two years working with the Norwegian, French, and Greek resistance fighters. He'd spent the better part of a month in Berlin being a Wehrmacht officer and came out with a German rocket man who'd been one of the Peenemunde bunch working on the V-bombs. "He doesn't have ice water in his veins," Clem Witt told Paul who told Lew, "He doesn't have veins. He's all muscle and brains. No emotion, no fear, no blood to spill. He just goes in and does the job. He's the only hero I've ever seen who never takes a day off. Thank sweet Jesus he's on our side."

MacMurdo pressed a flathead nail down on top of the ash in the bowl, puffed slowly, deliberately, then applied another match. Halfway through the operation Cassidy was nearly overcome by an impulse to leap across the desk and make him eat the goddamn pipe, no matter how big and brave he was. He wisely fought off the inclination.

"I'm not going to pose as something I surely am not," MacMurdo drawled, "which is a doctor. I'm not going to talk about your wife's condition. We've got someone here who can do it in detail before you leave. Believe me, you'll see her, you'll talk to her, and you'll get the whole story. Here and now. Today." He looked down at the contents of the file folder and for the first time Cassidy got a look at the top of his head. A wide white scar slid like a knife's path from the hairline through the thick hair that was layered in waves back from his forehead. MacMurdo raised his eyes from the papers and noticed Cassidy's stare. He tapped his pipestem against the huge white slabs of teeth.

"I'm here to brief you on the military situation. I'm running something called Operation Hangover, a name you probably won't hear again because code names are boring and silly. I'm working for Allen Dulles and Bill Donovan, who has been my boss at OSS for a long time. The other fella I'm working for is President Harry S Truman himself. I met with him a week ago at the White House and I'm telling you this because you're supposed to get the idea that my mission is damned important, as important as the atomic bomb. More important because I'm of the mind that we've just dropped the only two atomic bombs anybody'll ever drop on anybody else.

"*More* important. So you wonder what could be more important than the old atom whammy? Well, some folks say the commies over there. I myself had dinner with General George S. Patton not long ago and you know what he said? He said we've spent all these years beating the shit out of the wrong enemy—he believes we should have just kept on fighting over there and whipped the Russians while we were at it. Well, I'll tell you, Lew, I'm not so sure we could whip 'em unless we took the bomb to 'em and damned if I don't think that'd be a bad habit to get into. So, what's more important than the bomb and the reds? The damn old Nazis, that's who." He flashed the sincere, disarming, boyish smile. "That's my job. The Nazis. I'm in charge of catching the bastards and it's looking like a hell of a big job, I promise you.

"They're coming to America. They're coming in through this whole Northeast corridor. They're coming in to Florida, smuggled in from Cuba and the Bahamas and you name it. The Tortugas, for all I know. They're coming in from Martinique, coming up from the Gulf Coast. Some will try to stay here, in New York and in the backwoods country in New England. Some will head for safety in Texas, damn big place Texas. Some will go to California. There'll be escape routes from the West Coast fanning out to Central America, South America. Argentina, Brazil, Peru, anywhere they can lose themselves among folks who agree with their politics.

"Now, there are two kinds of Nazis. . . . First, there are those who want to forget the war and what they did, who want to take up ordinary lives, never pay up for their crimes, and pray to God no one ever finds them. Lots of them will succeed for a while but when you and I are old men, forty, fifty years from now, in the 1980s and 1990s, there are still going to be Nazi war criminals turning up, potbellied old duffers in Waco and Dubuque and Waltham who've lived all those years in total anonymity, and some fine day they're gonna come out of the hardware store or the cigar stand and they're gonna bump right into some other old duffer, probably an old Jew who can't ever forget the face of the Devil who killed his wife and kids, and there's gonna be one of those moments of recognition . . . and that rheumy old Nazi is gonna have to face the music, pay the piper for what he did back in 'forty-two at Auschwitz or Treblinka or Belsen . . . the world ain't never gonna forget these old guys. . . .

"And I for one," MacMurdo said, tapping his pipe on the blotter and sprinkling dead ash, "frankly don't give a hoot in Hades for these guys. They've pretty near done all the bad stuff—the real villainy—they're gonna do. From now on they're just harmless old farts who had their day as monsters. . . . Lew, m'boy, it's the other ones I'm after. . . ."

"'The other ones,'" Cassidy said. The breeze had freshened at the window. He was still stuck to his shirt but the clouds had blocked out the sun. Where was Karin? Was the man in the brown suit her husband . . . ?

MacMurdo reached behind his desk chair and tugged at a cord dangling beside the heavy drapery. The door opened almost at once and the soldier who'd welcomed Cassidy brought in a tray with bottles of tonic, a bottle of Gordon's gin, a gleaming ice bucket, glasses, and a plate of sliced limes. Everything perfect, the way it always was at Terry's place on Park Avenue, or in the movies.

MacMurdo got up, built two drinks in the tall glasses, handed one to Cassidy, and said: "Chin-chin, Lew. Here's to doing our job together and doing it right!"

"About this job," Cassidy said, but MacMurdo held up his bear paw of a hand.

"I'm just about there," he said, moving back behind the desk, sitting down again. "You've been very patient, Lew, but this is all necessary, the big picture, y'know."

"I've heard about that."

"Ain't we all, pard, ain't we all." MacMurdo was shaking his head. He took a pull on the gin and tonic. "I want the ones who are trying to keep the Reich alive . . . the Fourth Reich. These guys are already laying the foundations for the Fourth Reich. I've just come from Germany, Lew, and we've got to accept some hard truths. We've got to rebuild Germany, we've got to have a strong Germany to stand up to the reds . . . it's the frying pan and the fire over there. A new era has already begun. We're in the postwar world already and old George Patton had a point, we can't let the reds swallow up Western Europe. And the only way to rebuild Germany is to use a whole wagonload of the guys who were running it before. Which means we've got to use the Nazis, get right into bed with some of 'em. Oh, we're trying to sanitize them, delouse them in a political sense, lie about 'em if we have to, but facts are facts and we need 'em. We need 'em to make the country start working again—judges, industrialists, scientists, politicians, police officials, academics, civil servants. We need them and they need us. You read me on this, Lew? So these Nazis are just part of the new equation and we're all gonna have to look the other way. We let them survive and they do what we need them to do. They're scared of the reds and so are we. . . . Funny old world, pard, but there it is.

"And then there are these other Nazi coots who are filtering into our country—*our* country, damn it—and these are the ones who don't want to just disappear and be forgotten, and they don't want to run their own country for us . . . they're the unreconstructed Nazi bastards who honest to God think they've just suffered a slight setback. And they're organized, they're financed, they've got networks backing them up. The Condor Legion operating out of Madrid . . . Die Spinne, do you know German? Well, I do, I spent some time in the Fatherland during the recent hostilities." He fixed Cassidy's eyes with his own and the little smile played across his wide mouth. "I saw you sneaking a gentlemanly peek at my little scar. Let me digress for just half a mo' and I'll tell you how I got it. It's a long story which I may bore you with some other time if we wind up in a foxhole together, but sufficeth to say, I was deep inside the Reich a while back trying my hand at kidnapping and, hell, look at me, I look like Hitler's perfect Aryan asshole, right? So I cut a pretty wide swath over there, pulled a lot of hijinks, as my daddy used to say. So I was up to my hind end in Nazis, lyin' my ass off, all fitted out with phony papers, the works, but like a jerk I did something dumb and an SS officer realized I was not quite what I seemed . . . well, hell, it looked pretty dark for the Mudville nine all of a sudden." He smiled at the memory, relishing it. "So, this SS guy got his Luger out and told me the jig was up. His hand was shaking like a little old widder woman in a cyclone and I made a move he didn't like and he squeezed off a round, point blank. . . . He'd have missed me entirely if I wasn't the big economy size, but as it was he shot me in the head—the one place he couldn't hurt me!" His laugh suddenly boomed through the room, a physical kind of thing. A deaf person would have felt it. "Lew, you should have seen the look on that kraut's face when he pulled the trigger again and nothing happened! Luger jammed. . . . I'll never forget his face. He suddenly realized it was just him and me, there I was, this big blond bastard, face covered in blood, and I was unhappy with him—man, he was lookin' his destiny right in the eye! Well, pard, when I finished him off there wasn't enough left to wipe up. . . ." His hand momentarily went to the scar on his scalp, stroked it. "I call it my dueling scar." He looked away for a moment, staring out the window and bringing himself back from Nazi Germany to Westchester County.

"Just another war story. The world's full of 'em, better ones. Hell, I got better ones myself." MacMurdo flashed the wide grin. "Now, back to these Nazi diehards coming our way. There's a whole lot of money involved here, Lew. Hell, these people *looted* Europe . . . you wouldn't believe how much money we're talking about."

He leaned back and his weight brought a squeak from the chair. He stared at Cassidy, his pipe engulfed in one hand. "Now we're getting down to the short strokes, Lew. I stumbled onto one of these escape networks during the course of some researches I was carrying out a few months ago—it's like God having his say, pard, putting the right man in the right place at the right time. It isn't big, not like the Condor Legion or Die Spinne, but it's real and I've got a handle on it. I've made this one my own private preserve. I found it, I don't think we'd ever have known of its existence had it not been for Sam's sheer dumb luck . . . and it all happened mainly because I'm a movie fan, Lew, if you can believe that. History gets made in funny ways. Now this network, this modest enterprise I'm intending to bring to grief, with your help—hell, look at it this way, Lew Cassidy's finally gonna get his chance to win World War II . . . this one's got another funny name, it's called Ludwig's Minotaur. Y'know, it was Allen Dulles himself who gave it the name. Ludwig's Minotaur."

Cassidy had found himself wrapped up in MacMurdo's story, almost against his will. For a moment he'd forgotten that there was a point to it, that it was coming back to himself, and to Karin. "So how *do* I fit in? Do I have any choice about any of this?"

"Oh, I'll leave that up to you, Lew. You remember King Ludwig, the Mad King of Bavaria. Fella who was Wagner's patron, same fella who built himself all those fairyland castles and whatnot. I saw a movie about the old boy once and now I know more. For instance, I know he had this minotaur statue, like something in a movie. Sometimes I get the feeling I'm *in* a movie . . . like that time with the Luger jamming. This minotaur makes me think about *The Maltese Falcon*. You catch that one at the Bijou, Lew?" Cassidy nodded. "Well, Ludwig had this Italian craftsman sculpt a minotaur out of gold—then Ludwig had the whole statue encrusted with diamonds, emeralds, rubies, the works; then he just put it on a table and looked at it. Who knows what he was thinking? But Wagner saw it, mentions it in some of his correspondence . . . then it wound up in a museum in Munich, then the Kaiser glommed onto it for a time, then it turns up again when Reichsmarchal Göring got hold of it. When he built Karinhall, to memorialize his first wife, he made a big show of installing the minotaur there. . . . And then once it began to look really bad last winter—the Battle of the Bulge, the Breakout in the Ardennes, whatever you call it, it didn't fool Hermann into thinking the outcome of the war was gonna be any different, he knew they were whipped. So Göring wanted to set up his own private, personal, first-class escape route. He figured that America was the place to go. He figured that no one could use the Jewish thing against him because he'd smuggled Jews out of Germany, friends of his wife Emmy's from the theater, and he thought what the hell, maybe his old pal Lindbergh could take care of him. Well, he was nuts and full of drugs by then, but that was his idea."

MacMurdo leaned back, took another long drink, and went back to the tray of fixings. The heat had melted the ice in Cassidy's and MacMurdo freshened both drinks. "Don't ya just love this stuff, Lew? Here we are, two old boys sittin' around bustin' our gums about Göring and King Ludwig and Charlie 'Lone Eagle' Lindbergh. . . . Well, Göring decided to finance his escape route with plenty of do-re-mi, some real, some forged from plates the Nazis had, all in dollars, and something else negotiable anywhere . . . the Ludwig Minotaur.

"And he picked an SS man he happened to like, to trust, a man he knew could build his escape route. He gave the money and the statue to Manfred Moller. One very tough galoot who'd been around, all over Europe for the last ten years, a swashbuckler, used to hang around with Otto Skorzeny—Skorzeny's the only guy in the war big as me!" He chuckled at the improbability of such a thing. "So, anyways, Manfred Moller took off across the North Atlantic by U-boat on his special mission and the Reich collapsed and Göring never got to make his escape . . . and Manfred Moller was out there somewhere with his money and the minotaur and no Reichsmarshal. . . .

"Now that brings us back to yours truly, scoutin' around the Germany that was left. Found myself up in the mountains, pretty little village, birds singin', I'm just pokin' around, followin' up on some hints we'd gotten about this Moller character. I thought I might see if I could dig up his brother, a respected doctor, name of Rolf Moller. Maybe Manfred might have told Rolf about what he was doing for Göring . . .

"It was no problem to find Rolf. He had a nice little clinic in this village, sort of a rich man's retreat. . . . Turns out Rolf was a head doctor, a psychiatrist as well as a surgeon, and he had a staff of other doctors, nurses, a damn nice little setup. Some of the Party leaders had gone there for everything from face-lifts to happy pills to clap cures. And his brother in the SS was a pal of Göring's and when you looked at his clinic and went out to the house, one of those gingerbread chalet places lookin' out across this beautiful peaceful valley, damned if you'd ever think there'd been a war on. I hated to leave. I *didn't* leave for a few days—most particularly after Rolf invited me to stay with him. So I bunked there in the lap of luxury for a spell and had me some long talks with Rolf and on the second, third day I met Mrs. Moller and I just knew I'd seen her somewhere before.

"Then one night, I woke up like a scared rabbit, twitchin' my nose, floppin' my ears, blinkin' my eyes—I knew where I'd seen Frau Moller.

"*Murder on Ice. Murder Goes Skating*. I'd seen the movies and this woman, Frau Moller, was the star! The skater. Karin Richter." He grinned, watching Lew stiffen. "Your dead wife."

• • •

Cassidy was alone again, the smell of MacMurdo's tobacco lingering behind him like evidence in the case. He stood at the open window watching the rain beginning to patter on the empty lawn. Karin had gone somewhere and soon he was going to see her again, look into her eyes, search for a sign. He took a deep breath, fixed his attention on the willows drooping heavily in the rain. Summer was suddenly shedding its heat, turning into fall. He tried to imagine that summer day in the Hartz Mountains, tried to get a picture of Sam MacMurdo's face, the eyes narrowing, when he looked at the unexpected woman and knew that somewhere he'd seen her before. . . .

The galloping Colonel had been doing his homework since he'd got wind of Manfred Moller's mission, stumbled across Karin, and put two and two and two together.

He'd begun by knowing that Moller had set off across the North Atlantic by U-boat with Ludwig's priceless minotaur and the money to pave Göring's escape route. Since then he'd learned that the U-boat had made landfall in Nova Scotia. It had limped the final two hundred miles with mechanical problems, no hope of going back or, indeed, of going much of anywhere. They'd come the final hundred miles in a typically dense March fog. Nobody noticed their arrival. It was dark and icy and bitterly cold on the Cabot Trail when the crew finally stumbled across some dumbfounded local lawmen and insisted they be taken prisoner and given someplace warm to sleep and maybe a bowl or two of soup. By that time Manfred Moller had slipped away into the fog with the Ludwig Minotaur and a backpack full of money.

Then a man answering Moller's description had engaged a private plane, flown by a known German sympathizer of Irish lineage, who had confided to a mechanic that he was taking a passenger to the States and then coming back, to hell with the fog. The mechanic had told MacMurdo, who had flown up from Halifax himself, that it was a big old seaplane from the early thirties, great puffy pontoons; he'd shown MacMurdo a photograph of the beat-up old crate that made MacMurdo glad he hadn't been a passenger. It didn't take a genius to figure out that he was heading into one of those hidden backwoods lakes deep in the Maine wilderness.

But the pilot never came back. The plane had never been found. As far as anyone could prove, Manfred Moller was no more.

"I don't believe it," MacMurdo had said. "That son of a gun is alive. He's out there with the king's minotaur and all that money and he's either setting up Göring's network . . . or he's setting himself up to be one very rich Nazi survivor. My bet is he's a good soldier, he'll try to fit himself into the Nazi networks. You know what I think happened, Lew? I think they flew in through the fog and rain and wind, they came down outa that fog, I can feel that old rust bucket quiverin' and shakin' and rattlin' and they're thinkin' where's all this fuckin' fog end, for God's sake? And all of a sudden, real quick like, they're sittin' right on top of them old Douglas firs, pontoons just skimmin' along and up ahead there's a piece of lake about the size of your thumbnail, like landin' a beat-up old jeep on an aircraft carrier in the middle of the Battle of the Coral Sea. . . . Well, maybe one of the firs clipped a pontoon, tore it up, or the wind comes up like your Great-aunt Fanny on a tear, and you just barely stagger onto the lake, everybody bangin' around inside that old tin cockpit, old Manfred holdin' on to his damn minotaur for dear life . . . and they make it by the skin of their teeth and they're sittin' there thankin' God for small favors and Manfred takes a deep breath, gets out his Luger, and bags himself one prop jockey, bang. Then he gets the lifeboat out, does whatever he's got to do to wreck the pontoons, and paddles like a mad bastard for shore while the plane sinks. . . . Now all Moller has to do is find a way to survive and, pard, he's one resourceful old boy." MacMurdo had been pacing the library, acting out all the roles including that of the plane. Now he came to rest, half sitting on the desk. "He's been in the States I figure six months, hiding, waiting . . . he's out there, pard, and I want you to find him. You and your pal Leary and Harry Madrid. I can't do it, Lew. I'm in charge of lookin' for all the Nazis in America . . . now, don't gimme that look, we got ourselves an edge." He smiled. "We've got Karin to use as bait."

Cassidy shook his head. "Wait a minute. That won't hold water. Why should he come out for Rolf Moller's wife?"

"Oh no, no, think again, pard. I don't think I said Karin's married to Dr. Rolf, did I? No, no, Karin's husband—present company excluded—is *Mandred* Moller. And he's gonna be mighty glad to know she's right here waiting for him! Beautiful, ain't it?"

When MacMurdo left the room Cassidy stood at the window trying to pull himself together. He knew what was coming next and he wasn't sure he was ready for it. He didn't have much time.

He heard a soft knock on the door and he said, "Come in."

# Chapter Two

In one sense he felt as if he'd seen her yesterday on Pier 42 with all the gulls around them. In another it was as if he were meeting her for the first time, meeting someone he'd heard too much about. She came into the library and hesitated, still as one of the glum oil portraits, looking for him; then she saw him over by the window but seemed not to know quite what to do about it. His throat was suddenly very dry. When he tried to swallow he ran into some trouble making the mechanism work. He was trying to take her in all at once, the sight of her, but the flood of memories kept getting in the way, bouncing him along like a cork, a man struggling for survival in the tide of the past.

Her eyes drew him in first. They were intelligent, of course, alert, and still seemed to glow, the unusually luminous pale brown he'd never seen in anyone else. Huge eyes, something like tan, as if darkness had been bleached out of them. The wide straight mouth, the faint hollows beneath high Nordic cheekbones, the broad shoulders, slim hips, long willowy legs. Her hair was different. It hung straight down one side of her face like a curtain, almost obscuring her left eye, and was tucked behind her ear on the other. She moved slowly into the room, like an explorer who wasn't about to do anything stupid, watching him as she came.

Memory was lapping at him, drowning him. He searched her

expression for any glimmer of recognition, felt a flush spreading across his face at the memory of her body, the ways she'd revealed to him that she wanted sex, how much he'd enjoyed learning the secrets of her needs, striving to satisfy them. . . .

Now he was seeing her, knowing she was indeed back from the dead, seeing in her face that she had no real notion of who he was. All the memories of them together were now only his memories and that fact, knowing they had shared the moments but now only his could reflect on them and treasure them and smile at them and keep them alive—that fact made him feel more desperately alone than he'd ever thought anyone could be. For her, their shared past had never happened and he was just another man, a stranger.

• • •

The man in the brown suit followed her into the room. He had a schoolmaster's bearing, ramrod straight. His eyes looked larger than life behind thick circular lenses, gold-framed. His pale brown hair was cut short. His mouth was small and his lips were delicately shaped, almost bee-stung. The suit was a well-cut country tweed, brown with a faint red line, and he wore a vest. He must have been very glad the temperature was doing a nosedive. The suit bore the stamp of Savile Row, which certainly made it prewar. He crossed the room and extended his hand. "I am Dr. Rolf Moller. This is Frau Manfred Moller."

"I'm Lew Cassidy." The two men shook hands.

Karin came closer, put out her hand. "How do you do?" She didn't sound quite the same. Probably she hadn't spoken much English for a long time. He took her hand, fought off the hope of some kind of gentle, knowing squeeze, and then her hand was gone. She'd put a bulky cable-knit cardigan on over her sundress. She'd pushed the sleeves up and tortoiseshell bracelets clicked on her wrist.

Rolf Moller was speaking to her in soft, precise English with a vaguely British accent. He'd spent time in London. "Karin, Mr. Cassidy is the man Colonel MacMurdo has been telling us about. Mr. Cassidy is going to find Manfred for us—"

Karin looked up quickly, the curtain of hair swaying, her eyes fixed on him. "Oh, will you find him?" She was almost breathless. Cassidy heard her concern and anxiety. There was a resonant crack of thunder and the wind came up noisily in the dried remains of the summer flowers. "Can you promise us, Mr. Cassidy? Do you know where he is?"

Cassidy shook his head. "No, no, I don't know where he is." He couldn't stop looking at her. For a moment she returned his stare with a puzzled expression, self-conscious. Finally he looked away, embarrassed. "I'll do everything I can."

"You must find him." Her voice wasn't as steady as he remembered it:

she sounded as if she'd been wounded. And, of course, she had. It was dawning on him that she was no longer the same person he'd known and loved. "You must understand, it's . . . it's a matter of life and death."

"I understand," Cassidy said. "Believe me, I do. But you must realize that Manfred Moller may very well be dead." Her fingers flew to her mouth as if in uncontrollable panic at the thought of Moller dead. She turned toward the window. The rain slanted past, blown in tattered sheets across the lawn. "You must be prepared for that possibility." He waited, watching her silent, eloquent back as she wrapped her arms around herself, tiny fists clenched. "Mrs. Moller?" He forced himself to say it.

"No, he must be alive . . . somewhere. I'm sure." She turned back to the room. "I'm sure he's alive. . . . You don't know him, but he—he . . . it's the kind of man he is. . . . I'm not putting this at all well. I'm sorry."

"Well," Cassidy said, "Colonel MacMurdo seems to agree with you. Prevailing opinion seems to be that your husband is a hard man to kill—"

"Oh, he is, he is. Mr. Cassidy . . . you *must* find him. . . ."

Rolf Moller said: "You can understand what a nerve-wracking experience this is for Karin—"

Her voice was breaking. "He's more important to me than you can possibly imagine . . . more than I can tell you . . ." She shook her head in frustration, brushed the veil of hair away from her eyes, pulling it back behind her ear. She wiped a tear from her cheek, turned away again, and made a soft noise in her throat. When she raked her fingers through her hair he saw that her nails were bitten, the paint chipped. She wasn't the same. She threw herself down in one of the leather chairs, pulled a lace handkerchief from the pocket of the cardigan and sniffled into it. Her hair had swung loose again and she yanked it back savagely, pulling it away from her temple.

It was Cassidy's day for scars. Now he saw one like a pale pinkish-white zipper disappearing into her thick hair. He flinched at the sight of it. Dr. Moller leaned down and put his arm around her trembling shoulders. He was shaking his head at Cassidy.

"Now, now," he murmured to her, "it's going to be all right, *liebchen*. You've had a long day. She's exhausted, Mr. Cassidy. She really should get some rest before dinner. Karin?" He stood back, looking at her like a keeper waiting for his beast to perform.

"Please forgive me," she said, glancing up at Cassidy. "I'm behaving like a child."

"Nothing to forgive, I assure you."

"And you're too kind," she said. She stood up. "We'll speak again soon, please?"

"You can bet on it."

"Find him as quickly as you can. Please."

Cassidy nodded. Rolf Moller took her arm, escorted her to the door where he stood speaking softly into her ear.

Cassidy could see the problem, the big problem, already; like a neon sign outside a tough private eye's office window. It was flashing in his face and somebody was playing a saxophone, or would have been had it been one of his father's pictures. MacMurdo and Karin both wanted him to find Manfred Moller. But for very different reasons, which was where it all got very complicated. She wanted her husband back. The Galloping Colonel wanted to destroy him and demolish his escape network. She couldn't know. Could she? Maybe she knew it was the only way of finding him. Maybe she'd solve the rest of the problem once they found him . . . or maybe MacMurdo had lied to her. . . .

Karin. She seemed to have split into two people, right in front of him. Which was his Karin? Which was Manfred Moller's? Hell, did Lew Cassidy's Karin even exist anymore, anywhere but in his own memory? They might have been husband and wife a million years ago on another planet.

Rolf Moller cleared his throat and Cassidy realized he hadn't been paying attention. Karin was gone and Moller was fitting a cigarette into a black holder. The cloudy darkness outside had plunged the library into a funereal gloom. Flame sprang from a gold lighter and Moller inhaled. "I said, perhaps we should have a word. You must have questions, Mr. Cassidy." He crossed to the desk and turned the lamp on. A yellow glow spread warmly.

"Questions," Cassidy said. "Sure. What shape is she really in? What does she remember, how far back? What the hell is that scar on her head? She and MacMurdo could put their heads together and make a matched set."

Moller pursed the bee-stung lips. The light reflected on the thick lenses, turning them flat, opaque, as if he had no eyes. Smoke curled slowly from his nostrils.

"What she remembers," Moller mused. "Forgive my being utterly frank with you—but obviously you can see that she has no memory of you. Which, I must assume, is your primary concern. You were frank with her about the possibility that my brother is dead." He shrugged. "I am frank with you, eh? What shape is she in? She is physically quite well, healthy, alert, good reflexes, the brain functioning normally. You understand, Mr. Cassidy, it is a miracle that Karin is alive at all. Do you know how I found her?"

"I know nothing about any of this. Until a couple of weeks ago I thought she was dead. For three years plus I've assumed my wife was dead—"

"Your *wife* is dead, I'm afraid—"

"And then I found out she's alive, married to this shadowy SS officer, and doesn't know me from Adam. That's what I know."

Moller carefully lowered himself into one of the wing-backed club chairs, crossed his legs at the knee, and adjusted what was left of the crease in his tweeds. "Please don't think I'm not sympathetic to your unhappy plight, Mr. Cassidy. It's just that we in Germany have had our own problems. We tend to be self-involved these days. But you have had a great shock, too, and the fact that it's a question of amnesia"—he sighed heavily—"makes it all the more unpredictable. Amnesia is uncharted territory to a very substantial degree. . . ." Then he took Cassidy back to Cologne with him and it was 1942 again.

It had all been a matter of purest fate, the way Rolf Moller saw it. He had been called to Cologne to treat a prominent party official whose heart had just about given out. He was walking back to his hotel when the bombing began. A bomb landed a block away. The front of a building cracked open to reveal a sheet of flame bursting through a cloud of brick dust, then crashed down on a black Mercedes that seemed almost human, straining to outrun it. Rolf had dashed for his life, ducked into a commercial office building, and prayed for all he was worth. The bombing lasted forever, went on and on, the street shaking as if suffering an interminable earthquake, the din pounding and pounding and pounding until he thought he was screaming, hammering at his senses until he could no longer hear even his own voice or the phantom scream welling within him. The city seemed engulfed in fire and the explosions kept racketing away and it took a while for him to realize that the bombs were no longer falling and he was more or less alive.

"I finally went out into the street," he said, "and it was beyond belief, bomb craters and smoking piles of bricks and stone, wrecked cars with bodies spilling out like entrails, bodies sprawled in gutters and hanging from windows, draped over the sills where fire and smoke got them, broken glass underfoot, fires burning everywhere, a searing kind of heat as if the sun had rushed closer to Earth. . . . I wanted to see what good I could do as a doctor—what was needed, of course, was a thousand doctors, a triage team trained to put the hopeless victims out of their agony . . . but if a triage unit had found Karin, well, I'm very much afraid she would have been considered hopeless. . . . I found a woman wandering in the rubble, firelight reflected in her eyes, covered with dirt and blood, dress stiff with blood, eyes glassy, unfocused, stumbling as if she were sightless, unable to respond when I called to her. By the time I got to her she had fallen to her knees and was crawling, cutting her knees and hands. . . . She pulled herself into a sitting position and the street, I'll never forget it, the street was both burning and flooding, fire everywhere but water spewing out of broken mains, she was leaning with her back against a dented, undetonated bomb, yes, a bomb . . . and she'd dragged a woman's severed leg with her, as if it were somehow worth saving. . . . The ground kept shaking with random explosions and there were sirens going off, firefighters here and there, ambulances trying to get into the streets past the mountains of smoking debris, hearses were being used as ambulances, there were horse-drawn delivery carts, people were staggering around moaning or screaming from the pain of their wounds, creatures stranded in Hell. . . .

"I went to the woman leaning against the bomb; I was thinking I had to get her away from the bomb. . . . When I got to her, when I took her arm, I realized that I could see her brain. . . . She was moaning in a kind of singsong voice, staring straight ahead, her face covered with mud and blood, her dress torn, it was a pretty summer dress but it was stiff and sticky with blood from her own wounds and from clutching the severed leg, and she'd lost her shoes and she kept reaching out and touching the leg beside her as if she were afraid it might walk away. . . . I believed she would certainly die from the head wounds, I nearly left her to go in search of someone I could actually help . . . but do you know what saved her, Mr. Cassidy? I'll tell you. Even as she was—and I'm sure my description fails to convey the condition she was in—but even so horribly brutalized, I could see how beautiful she was. . . . Odd, that she should be saved because her beauty was still visible and drew me to her. . . . People are not born equal, you see, and the will to survive was still alive within her inextinguishable beauty. Well, I helped her to her feet, I couldn't take my eyes away from the broken skull, that bit of living matter beneath the white and bloody shell of bone. . . .

"I got her to a hospital, she didn't need one of those doctors who was drowning in a sea of victims because she had one of her own, me, I was her personal doctor and that saved her. I knew some people at the hospital and with the help of a dear friend of mine, another brain surgeon who had his hands full, but with his help I operated on her and we did what we could. . . . We reconstructed her skull. . . . Her recovery was a perilous business, she didn't or wouldn't or couldn't speak for months, in the end she was capable of speaking but was clearly choosing not to, I'm quite sure of that, but she slept an enormous amount, almost comatose, and then miraculously she seemed to be curing herself from within, locked inside her womb of silence.

"Eventually I thought she was well enough to take her to my clinic and there she began to flourish. By September of 1942 she had begun to speak—now, I wonder, how can I make you see this? See what I felt when at last she spoke? I'd grown so accustomed to her silence, but I had been speaking normally to her right along, treating her as if she were normal because I knew by her physical responses that she could hear, that she was waiting until the time was right, she would nod and smile at one of my stuffy little jokes . . . She read, mostly the classics, she would never read the newspapers, nothing about the war. . . . Then one day I brought her a cup of tea, she was sitting at a table on the balcony outside her bedroom, looking out across the valley—she was living in her own room in my home by then—and she glanced up at me shyly and smiled very gently and said, 'Danke, Herr Dr. Moller.' I cried, Mr. Cassidy, I was smiling at her, but the tears were streaming down my cheeks, and she took my hand in hers and squeezed it. . . . She was coming back to the real world. It was unfortunate, of course, that the real world was blowing to pieces but, then, what would life be without irony?" He frowned at the crack of thunder, louder, nearer the house. Lightning tracked across the purple sky. "What would a German be these days without a sense of tragedy? And irony?"

"Not only Germans," Cassidy said.

It was at Dr. Moller's mountain home that Manfred Moller met Karin, there that they slowly—during his intermittent appearances—fell in love. They were married at the Catholic church in the village at a time when the groom was serving as SS liaison for Göring and knew that nothing could turn the tide of the war. Within a month of the marriage, in May of 1944, the Allies had invaded Fortress Europa, creating a second front in the West. By then no sane man in Germany was thinking about anything but the best possible terms of surrender. When the following winter the German army had made the final violent breakout in the Ardennes, Manfred had come home to spend Christmas with his wife and brother. Then he'd gone back to Berlin to lay the plans for and subsequently undertake the desperate final mission for Göring. They had never seen him again.

And then one day Sam MacMurdo had turned up looking for a line on Manfred and, as Rolf Moller said, "Here we are. Sometimes it's difficult for me to comprehend all that has happened since Colonel MacMurdo entered our lives. . . . Imagine what it's been like for Karin who remembers only fragments of her past, who doesn't know she was married before. . . . I don't know how I could have handled that utter void were it my own life—it seems impossible!" He clicked the cigarette holder and the butt dropped like a forlorn refugee into the ashtray. He took a white handkerchief from his sleeve—another Englishism—and polished his glasses. There were deep red indentations on the sides of his nose. "None of us knew who she was until MacMurdo recognized her. . . . It's all come in a rush, don't you see?"

• • •

"Amnesia is a kind of conjuror's trick," Dr. Rolf Moller observed. "Something is made to disappear. Amnesia is a very deep mystery."

Lew Cassidy sat in one of the matching leather chairs, rubbing his eyes, willing his brain to keep track of everything he'd heard during the long afternoon. The rain had become a steady, determined downpour. It rattled in the eaves and lead gutters and downspouts.

"Some of us pretend to know more about it than we actually do. I've been fascinated by the whole study of mnemonics, but in the course of a doctor's practice true cases of amnesia are very rare. Short-term shell shock, yes, in a century that has become one long charnel house—but this kind of amnesia, no, very rare. I've studied it with Archibald in London, with Wolff in Geneva, with Kruger in Leipzig, and I can assure you that the mystery is only beginning to render its answers. Of course, the more difficult the mystery is to solve, the more interesting it becomes. . . . The Enigma Syndrome, as old Kruger liked to call it. Amnesia stems from many different causes, but the only ones that concern us in this instance are actual injury to the brain, a physical cause—and shock of a psychological nature. There are as well different types of amnesia, primarily anterograde, which refers to the events *following* the trauma being lost in the mind of the patient—clearly not what we're dealing with here, and retrograde amnesia, in which events that occurred *before and during* the trauma are lost." He coughed again and cast an accusing glance at the cigarette, which was the ninth he'd lit since they'd begun talking. "In Karin's case, her entire history before the bombing of Cologne is gone." He snapped his fingers. "Utterly gone."

Cassidy said: "Was it the injury or . . ."

Moller shrugged, pursing his lips. He passed a small hand over his thinning light brown hair. He had bags under his eyes, dark pouches of worry partially hidden by his spectacles. It occurred to Cassidy that Moller was exhausted, worn down by the advent of MacMurdo. "I wish I could give you an answer, but whether it is traceable to the brain injury or to the shock"—he shrugged, a small, helpless gesture—"we cannot be absolutely sure. But we do know that what she has lost are the personal memories—that is, her identity, her personal history, by which I mean, as our friend MacMurdo would say, 'She doesn't know her ass from her teakettle, pard.' We've told her who her father was, some things of that nature, but she has no recollection whatsoever. She has, for example, no memory of having skated in the Olympic Games, nor of living in the United States, nor of making movies, nor of having married you. That which is less personal—how to drive a car, how to speak English, how to cook certain favorite dishes, indeed even how to ice skate—all that is intact.

"As a brain surgeon, I can understand that there may be a physical cause. Her brain sustained terrible trauma, but it is not easily measurable. There is also the possibility, which I see while wearing my psychiatrist's cap—which I hasten to add is much like a dunce cap, tall and pointed"—he permitted himself a small smile at his joke—"there is the possibility of psychoneurotic amnesia, retrograde, which causes a person to escape or deny those memories that are too painful to bear and remain sane. We would say that those memories are repressed, that is to say they are repressed or forgotten *intentionally*. . . . We call that motivated forgetting. In Karin's case, the bombing of Cologne would have desperately *needed* forgetting."

Cassidy said: "You mean if she remembers the bombing she'll remember just how godawful it was . . . but she might also remember the rest of her previous life, good and bad? Is that it, more or less?"

"More or less."

"Do you think her memory is gone for good?"

"Ah, there is no way to know. Sometimes the amnesia lasts for weeks, sometimes for years, sometimes forever. Karin has developed a whole *new* life, a whole new pattern of life. This condition is called a fugue state. Oddly enough, when the individual recovers the lost memory of the pretrauma past, the events of the new life—of the fugue state—are almost always forgotten."

"My God," Cassidy sighed. "Isn't there anything you can do to push her? Can't you drag that memory back to the surface?"

"Mr. Cassidy, think of what you're saying—you're suggesting a very dangerous game. What if she is dragged back, against her subconscious will, from the snug harbor of a place we call Forgetting. Suppose we force her all the way back to the here-and-now and she remembers what she's been trying to escape. Who's to say she won't crack at the remembered horror? Who's to say she won't simply go mad? Who's to say she won't escape the next time by killing herself? Would that be preferable, Mr. Cassidy? Did she survive the fiery hell of Cologne in 1942 only to kill herself in a world at peace in 1945? No, I think not. Better to just let nature work . . . let time have the chance to heal the scars. If she comes back under her own power it will be because somewhere deep within her wounded, battered psyche she has decided to return. . . .

"And then she will be Karin Cassidy again. Only then, I'm afraid . . ."

• • •

Cassidy and MacMurdo were standing under the roof of the portico at the side of the house. The rain was beating down and bouncing off the driveway. It was dark and the lamps on the columns glowed through the murk. You could see your breath in the cold. Fall had arrived. They were waiting for Clyde, one of MacMurdo's aides, to bring the Ford around. When it had looked like it was about to rain, sure enough, Clyde had gone out and pulled the rag top into place.

"Well, you've got the whole story now, Lew. The girl's had a tough time. Like lots of other folks." MacMurdo shrugged his massive shoulders. "Now about the job I've got for you, whattaya say?"

"I'll do what I can."

"Your country will owe you one, Lew."

"That's very reassuring, Colonel."

"Call me Sam, for Christ's sake."

"Well, you're a determined guy, Sam. I'll ask some questions, talk to some people—"

"That's right, pard. Gossip of the Rialto, as the Bard or somebody once said. You can get a line on the Nazi symps in New York. Let 'em know you've heard about the priceless minotaur, how it's been smuggled out of Germany and how it just may be on the market—hell, you know what to do." He took his pipe from his pocket and tapped the bowl on his heel.

"I've got an idea or two."

"Then there's the Maine situation. A plane goes down in Maine, somebody must have seen it or heard it. It's only been six months. And, look, we know these things cost money. Cost of doing business, you might say. You'll find a satchel in your car. Twenty grand."

"Come on, Colonel. That's way too much. Sounds like a bribe out of taxpayers' money—"

"Believe me, it's on the up and up. An operation like this, for the good of the state, has to be funded. What you do with the money is your affair. It's out of my hands. You may have to hire operatives, charter planes, pay some people off—look, you know what you're doing, pard." He began to fill the pipe. He'd never get it lit in the cold wind.

"I know what I'm doing," Cassidy said, "but I wonder about you, Colonel. What do you want out of this? What do you really want?"

"No mystery about that." He stopped fiddling with the pouch and pipe and stared at Cassidy. "I want Manfred Moller and the Nazis he's working with and for—I want 'em all in the hoosegow, pard, or at the end of a rope, where they damn well belong."

"That's all just fine," Cassidy said as Clyde pulled the rain-shiny Ford under the roof, the wipers sliding back and forth across the glass. The rain stopped bouncing off the white top as the car eased into shelter. "But has anybody told Karin? You may have noticed that what you want is decidedly not what she wants. She wants her husband, her other husband, back. You have a problem there—"

"Not me." MacMurdo shrugged. "She may have a problem a ways down the road, but that's life. Look, in the first place, she's got no complaints comin' so far as I can see. She was crawling around the gutters of Cologne with her brains runnin' out—hell, the way I look at it, she's way ahead of the game. And in the second place, Manfred Moller is an SS bastard who simply galls my ass, *pardonnez-moi*. I want him, pard.

And in the third place, if we take Manfred out of the picture that reduces by exactly half the number of available husbands for the lady. Puts you in the catbird seat, Lew. Think about it."

Cassidy was thinking about it as he got into the car and saw the leather briefcase on the passenger seat. Twenty thousand dollars. If he told Terry Leary about that much untraceable money floating around, Terry would want to split it, forget declaring it as income, and maybe that was the thing to do. But it ought to go into the Dependable Detective account. Cassidy wasn't sure but Terry would be. Terry knew how to deal with moral dilemmas. He laughed at them.

But he was thinking about Karin again by the time he had the car in gear and had slowly pulled away into the rain. Did he want to be the only available husband for Karin? Did he want this woman, the strange and distant creature Karin had become? It was a question that made him forget the twenty grand.

He was passing the front of the immense stone house when he slowed to a stop and dropped the briefcase over the back of the seat. The rain drummed steadily on the fabric top. He looked up at the house.

She was standing motionless, staring out the window at him. A chandelier shone brightly through the rain.

Slowly she lifted her hand like a little girl and waved at him. MacMurdo was right. It was just like a movie.

He felt as if his heart would break.

# Chapter Three

"In cash?" Terry Leary whistled softly, under his breath. "Twenty grand in cash in a briefcase? This is like it was back in the old days, right?" He grinned raffishly at Lew Cassidy, then turned to the thickset man on his left. "Like that time at the Shore in Jersey with Rocco's boys? Bless me, those were the days. And old Markie washing up on the beach roped to that sailor boy, a crab crawling out of his mouth . . . and Lew wound up with all the money that time, too. . . ." Terry Leary shook his head at the wonder of it all, his eyes glittering, as if to say *How did any of us get out of it alive?* "This MacMurdo," Terry said, swirling the ice in his Rob Roy, listening to it clink, "I like the man's style. Unorthodox, you might say. This money— it's a lot like a bribe." He chuckled with pleasure.

"Well, you sure as hell know a bribe when you see one," the third man said, just loudly enough to be heard. He had a habit of always speaking just loudly enough to be heard. A waiter came to the table, leaned over, and the man said just loudly enough to be heard: "Dickens martini, Charlie."

"Of course, the usual. And you, Mr. Cassidy?"

"Rob Roy'll be fine, Charlie."

Charlie went away and Cassidy remembered the first time he'd heard the other man order a Dickens martini. That had been a new one on Cassidy and he'd asked for an explanation. "No olive or twist," the man had said.

They were sitting at Leary's regular table, where Max Bauman had once sat most nights, well off to one side at the edge of the dance floor, near the exit to the hallway that led back to the dressing rooms or in the other direction to the office where Max had held court for years, running the club and his whole ugly empire. Now it was Leary's office because, as MacMurdo had already known, after Leary had killed Max the gangster's will had left Heliotrope to him. It was, indeed, a funny old world. Cassidy was reflecting on just how funny it all was when Terry handed him an eight-inch Havana. Cassidy savored its aroma, rolling it beneath his nose. Charlie came back with two drinks on a tray, set them down, and struck a wooden match for Cassidy's cigar, letting all the sulfur burn away first. It was funny about the cigars, too. Max Bauman had bequeathed his entire stash, which had been kept in the humidor room at Dunhill, to Terry Leary, whom he had, in his own way, before the brain tumor had ravaged him and turned him into a killing machine, loved like the son he'd lost in the South Pacific. Cassidy drew on the cigar until it was going nicely, then nodded to Charlie, who disappeared again.

The dance floor was filling up and when Cassidy glanced up at the bandstand he saw the afterimage that always lingered there for him. The blond girl with the English accent singing "The White Cliffs of Dover" and "Where or When." Cindy Squires. She was always there in his mind and he could hear her voice and he never spent any time at all in Heliotrope without remembering the night he'd met her, Max's new singing discovery, his songbird. Cassidy had come out of the men's room and had heard some jerk making a pass at her in the dressing room and he'd gone in and taken care of this clown and he'd met Cindy Squires. But that was another story, a long time ago, and there was no point in dwelling on it anymore.

A lot of the people from those days were dead. And today one of the dead ones had turned up alive and that was what he should be thinking about now, not a dead English singer. He was enjoying the cigar and the Rob Roy and Cindy wasn't up there anymore when he took another look. Will Eldridge and His Band were playing "Georgia on My Mind" and "Cabin in the Sky" and "Dancing in the Dark." It was a good black band and Will himself, who must have been seventy and was the son of slaves, could do more than front. He could step up there with his clarinet and still give Artie Shaw a run for his money if he were in the mood. Almost every man in the room was wearing a tuxedo, except for the guys in uniform still and there were a lot of those. The women were splendid in sleek low-cut dresses, lots of diamonds and pearls and ivory shoulders and satin-smooth backs, as they swayed and clung to the music.

Terry Leary had always looked a little too slick to be a cop, even when he'd been Gotham's darling, the most highly publicized homicide dick. Even then he'd looked more like one of the robbers than a cop. On the other hand he was perfectly cast as a nightclub owner. George Raft liked to hang out at Heliotrope and he was always trying to con Terry Leary into revealing the name of the tailor who did his evening clothes. Terry Leary would just stand there flipping a quarter until Raft couldn't keep a straight face. Sometimes Terry Leary said his tailor only ran up threads for real tough guys, not movie stiffs, and sometimes Raft's face went a little white and his smile got pretty tight. Leary's dark blond hair was slicked back and shone like the handle on your hairbrush. His tan was as even and creamy as your favorite starlet's. He was nursing his drink that he could make last all evening and enjoying his Havana and listening while Cassidy told him what had happened that afternoon with Sam MacMurdo and Rolf Moller and Karin. While he listened his eyes ceaselessly roved across his domain, registering who was in the night's catch, who was with whom, what was going on in his joint and what it meant especially if it meant trouble. Every so often he'd catch Cassidy's eye and grin. There was a secret language between them, some kind of sixth sense they had for each other. They went back a long way, the football hero and the cop, and they'd very nearly died for one another more than once.

The third man at the table, drinking the Dickens martini, looked vaguely uncomfortable in his tuxedo, as if he'd considered it objectively and concluded that deep down in his soul it was a betrayal of his code. It was also a little snug across the thighs and shoulders. He was by many years the oldest of the three, maybe sixty. His face was heavy and impassive, his eyes were shiny and alive and cold, like anthracite, long vertical lines that might have been carved deep in stone framed his mouth, and his dewlaps looked heavy as concrete. Somebody once said he looked like he was halfway to being a statue already and he'd replied, just loud enough to be heard, that the first bird who shit on him had better move fast. He wore a wing collar and a pale gray carnation that just about matched his hair, which was cut short and combed flat with water and sometimes Wave Set and a couple of stray strands stuck up in back no matter how much Wave Set he used. He'd once been a New York cop who thought Terry Leary was too crooked to live. But times changed and so had his mind. He came to revise his opinion the night Terry Leary put enough slugs into Max Bauman to render him unfit for a dog's breakfast. That night had been a kind of crucible of blood, with Max and Bennie the Brute and Cookie Candioli and Frank Erickson all going down for the last time. Out of that crucible Cassidy and Leary and he had come bonded together in a way that maybe only killing the bad guys can do. They hadn't made it to the war but by God they'd laid some very bad men in their graves.

He looked like everybody's Dutch uncle and sometimes people called him "Dutch." Under the table, when you ran out of trouser leg, you'd see that he still wore heavy black lace-up ankle-highs and white socks because there were some things a man just couldn't change. His name was Harry Madrid and a long time ago he'd learned a thing or two from Bat Masterson. He ran Dependable Detective for Leary and Cassidy as a full partner. Terry Leary had also made Cassidy a partner in Heliotrope but hardly anyone knew that. Walter Winchell had once written in his column that they were three rogues who could only have gotten together in New York, in the lights of Broadway.

"Did you see anything in her face?" Leary had known Karin, had helped arrange Goebbels's flowers at the church up in Lake Placid. "Did she know you? At all?"

Cassidy shook his head, explained the amnesia.

"Might come back, might not." Leary frowned. "That's mighty helpful. So," he let out a lengthy sigh, "how do you read this MacMurdo?"

"He's used to giving orders."

"Ha! Big deal! Does anybody pay attention?"

"I'd say so—"

Harry Madrid said, "You mean he ain't *asking* us to risk life and effing limb to find Manfred Moller and his fancy thingamajig?"

"He *expects* us to help," Cassidy said.

"He knows how to construct an argument," Leary said. "He starts with twenty grand. I respect this man."

Cassidy said, "He's smart. He's put a whole lot of pieces together to get this far. And he can't stand the idea of this guy getting away. He's got the guts of a burglar, he had to be damn cool to go into Berlin like he did—"

"Even cooler to get out." That was Madrid.

"He seems to know everybody from Truman," Cassidy said, "to Wild Bill Donovan. And I figure he's lucky. Lucky to be alive, lucky to find out about this Göring escape route, lucky to recognize Karin, lucky to connect her with us . . . lucky and smart."

Leary nodded. "I'm not so sure he's all that smart. Looks to me like he's invested twenty grand in a lot of empty blue sky. Unless he *knows* Manfred Moller is alive— What do you say, Harry?"

"Sounds to me like he's too big for his britches. He's only got the one angle to play with us. The woman."

"And the money," Leary said.

"Money's not an angle. It's a given. The woman's the angle, the sharp edge of the wedge." Madrid cocked an eye at Cassidy. He'd never met Karin. "She *is* the woman you married? She's not a ringer?"

"Jesus, Harry, what a question," Cassidy said.

"Look, son, no disrespect intended. But I've lived a long time and seen a lot of shit come down—and you haven't seen her in six years. Long time. She doesn't remember you, she doesn't recognize you. . . . Is she the same woman? It's an innocent question, sonny. And more important than anything but breathing. We don't *know* these people." Harry Madrid finished the martini and fixed Cassidy with a baleful stare.

"She's the same woman." He sounded surer than he felt. "I mean, she's changed in some ways, sure, she's been bombed to pieces, damn near killed, had a brain operation, lost her memory, got married to a man she's worried as hell about—yes, she's changed. She was the Queen of the May once; she isn't anymore. But it's Karin."

"Of course it is." Leary looked over at Harry. "He'd know in his gut, Harry. Don't be so cynical."

"Just asking, son. Just a thought. Somebody's got to be a real pro in this half-baked operation. When you're my age you sometimes aren't as trusting as you once were." He flicked a finger at Charlie, who nodded. "Dickens," Madrid said.

"He's got another angle," Cassidy said. "But you're not going to be impressed. He says he's giving us the chance to get a piece of World War Two. We can be patriots, we can do our bit."

Harry Madrid blinked his heavy-lidded, glittering eyes. They were always expressionless, as if they were Harry Madrid's antennae, uninvolved and feeling out the situation, getting word back to Harry. "You're right, son. I'm not impressed." Charlie arrived with another martini. Madrid might as well have been pouring them in his shoe for all the difference they made.

"What do you think, Lew?" Leary was smiling.

"I guess I'll see what I can turn up. Give it a little time."

"We can't let this lad loose on his own, Harry."

"True. He might do himself an injury."

"Well, then," Leary said. "What's our opening gambit, Lew?"

"I figure if I want to know about Nazis, Walter's the guy to go to."

Harry Madrid grunted in agreement. He slid his chair back and went through the arch under the exit sign. He was heading for the john.

"How was it, seeing her again?"

"Just about lost my lunch. So damned nervous. And they were feeding me all this information and all I wanted to do was look at her, think about her. You know."

"Do you want her back?"

The question lay between them like a ticking bomb because in the end it was all that mattered. The layers of meaning were waiting to be peeled away. The point was, they weren't in it yet. They could give the money back, take a hike. Cassidy could tell MacMurdo that the woman was no longer his Karin, that he figured he'd leave her to her new life. Cassidy could say that it was just none of his business, not anymore. They could say to hell with this phantom Nazi, they could tell MacMurdo to get lost.

The band was playing Gershwin and the customers were dancing and Lew Cassidy was looking past them into the clouds of memory, trying to sort through his emotions, trying to locate the moments in the past that had become indistinct, like blurred outlines on an old treasure map. Where was the damned treasure buried? Where was Karin's memory? Could he ever find it again? He looked back at Terry Leary.

"I'm damned if I know," Cassidy said at last.

Leary nodded.

• • •

The three of them came out of Heliotrope just as dawn was coming up over the Atlantic, over Long Island, the first fingers of sunlight reflected in the wet streets. The rain had stopped and the puddles glistened like fool's gold. The awnings still dripped and the doormen were long gone. The morning was crisp and clear. Steam drifted up from the manholes and somewhere trashcans were clattering and banging as haulers emptied them. From the Onyx down the street you could hear somebody still blowing a saxophone as if in mourning for the night just past. The doors of the clubs stood open and old black men were whistling while they swept the sidewalks.

Harry Madrid carefully placed his black snapbrim squarely on his big head. He yawned. "Well, gentlemen," he said, breathing deeply, "I'm going to ring a friend of mine up Portland way. Old cop. Ask a question or two about any mysterious aeroplanes. Got to start somewhere, unless they changed the rules while Harry Madrid was out for a piss." He frowned grumpily. "I'm too old for these long nights. Still, not a shot was fired, for which we must always be thankful." An old cop's benediction.

"Sleep tight, Harry," Cassidy said.

"Night, Harry." Leary clapped Harry Madrid's shoulder.

They watched him go, a bulky, dignified old gent with a rolling, listing walk, heading for home. As he went he touched the brim of his hat to a cop on the beat near the corner of Fifth Avenue.

Terry Leary stroked a knuckle along his thin mustache. "I wonder where Manfred Moller slept tonight, Moller and his minotaur and his bag of money . . . Does he dream of the good old days in Berlin with Göring and the boys? Does he think about the escape route Göring's never going to use? Or does he dream of Karin—and wonder where she is? Is he afraid he'll never see her again?"

Lew Cassidy was watching a garbage truck coming down the street like a tank.

"Hell," he said, "he's dead as a doornail. You know that as well as I do."

"Well, in that case," Leary said, "we'll go through the motions, take a look around, spend some of MacMurdo's money." He shrugged. "A fool and his money, after all. But listen to me, amigo. This thing isn't about Manfred Moller. It's about you and Karin. MacMurdo's pissing in the wind. He's the world's biggest Boy Scout and he just doesn't want his war to end. Guys like MacMurdo, they're lost without a war. . . . No, whatever this is about for Sam MacMurdo, for you—for the three of us—it's really all about you and Karin."

As he often did after long nights at Heliotrope, no matter how tired he was and he'd never been a hell of a lot tireder, Cassidy turned right and walked all the way down Fifth Avenue to Washington Square where he lived. It gave him a long time to think.

# Chapter Four

When Sherman Billingsley met him just inside the door at the Stork Club, Cassidy was immediately reminded of Terry Leary's observation that while Billingsley might be New York's most famous club owner he still looked like an undercooked bowl of day-old oatmeal and had a personality to match. Sherm shook Cassidy's hand with no great enthusiasm and mumbled something in his customary word-swallowing manner. "How's that, Sherm?" Cassidy inquired. Outside, the night's eleven o'clock crowd of would-be Stork Clubbers waited. Very few of them would ever gain entrance to the hallowed halls on Fifty-second Street off Fifth where, as Leary remarked on another occasion, "the world's most boring man is treated as if he's fascinating." Cassidy didn't think Sherm was all that bad. Just dull. Terry liked to plug the rivalry because he figured it was good for business. A feud.

Billingsley repeated himself from the corner of his mouth and Cassidy figured the hell with it.

"I said Walter's expecting you," Billingsley finally said sufficiently distinctly. "You know the way. How's your smartass partner?"

"Why, he's all right, Sherm. I'll tell him you asked." There was a lot of rhumba music going on, which reminded Cassidy of the night Walter, who was a damn fine dancer dating all the way back to his days in vaudeville, had tried and failed to teach him that particular step. Cassidy wasn't much on the dance floor, particularly since the Giants had torn his leg up that long-ago afternoon at the Polo Grounds. Walter had contended that his failure to learn was no fault of the teacher's, which was basically true.

"Don't bother," Billingsley muttered and turned away to shake hands with Doug Fairbanks, who was wearing enough medals to sink a lesser man.

Cassidy went to the Cub Room. At table 50 in the left-hand corner was the great man himself. The fact was simply that Walter Winchell dominated both newspapers and radio as no one else ever had. His column was carried in a thousand newspapers and his weekly broadcast was always in the upper reaches of the Top Ten. His audience, according to the people who measured such things, was over fifty million. He was the highest-salaried man in America that year, maybe in the world; he made a million dollars a year. There were those who also said he was the most powerful single individual in the country and, when it came to molding public opinion, Cassidy supposed he was. He could be a league-leading shitheel, of course, but he also had some pretty good instincts. He'd have laid down his life for Franklin Roosevelt. Arnold Foster, who had been an important force behind the Anti-Defamation League, once said in a group where Cassidy found himself: "Winchell has done more to light up the dark corners of bigotry in the United States than any other individual. He is read, heard, and admired by millions. His readers and listeners believe him. If he says bigotry is wrong, then it is automatically wrong. He is Mr. America." Arnold Foster was the kind of man who could say things like that quite unself-consciously and the speech was in Cassidy's mind as he stood watching Winchell at table 50—holding court, hearing the inside stories, collecting bits of paper from his legmen, making eyes at a starlet, winking knowingly to a famous senator, scribbling bits of information and quotes on the back of a proof of the day's column as was his habit. While Cassidy watched, Elliot Roosevelt loomed out of the crowd and slid in beside Winchell, leaned over and behind a cupped hand whispered something to him. Slowly a smile broke across Winchell's features, like a dog getting his teeth well and truly into the postman's ankle. He was wearing a dark blue suit, a white shirt, a white handkerchief in his breast pocket, and a latticework tie of blue and cream. He was drinking a glass of milk. He was just shy of fifty and his hair had been white for a long time. His cheeks were pink. Like a lot of men who were good dancers, he was short and compact. You had to admit he kept his tan in good shape.

That was how he and Terry Leary had come to know each other, by getting their tans at the Terminal Barbershop. Winchell had later convinced Terry that the Dawn Patrol Barbershop was the place to go and Terry had switched allegiance from the Terminal and the Hotel Taft's shop. Winchell had also been quick to pick up on Terry as the celebrity homicide dick, particularly at the time of the Sylvester Aubrey Bean case. He'd met Cassidy quite separately as the football hero who went to Germany and wound up marrying Hitler's favorite ice skater. One column painted Cassidy as the man who stole Karin Richter from under the Führer's nose, which was all a lot of malarkey but it made good copy, in a cheap kind of way. When Cassidy had been badly injured on December 7, 1941, in a football game at the Polo Grounds, Winchell had used the incident in his column in some vaguely symbolic way, along the lines of "the boys' games are over, the Big Game is just beginning and with God and FDR on our side, we'll see it through to the final victory."

Friendship with Leary and Cassidy had not, however, lured Winchell away from the Stork's Cub Room. He and Billingsley were chums, and besides, he had hated Max Bauman, the original owner of Heliotrope. Winchell figured Bauman for a bad actor and in the end had been right. When it came to robbers and cops, Winchell's favorites were Frank Costello and J. Edgar Hoover. They made an interesting trio. Winchell and Costello had become friends primarily because they were neighbors, both living at the Majestic, 115 Central Park West. Winchell let Costello know that Hoover, the Director of the FBI, was a fanatical horse player. Frank Erickson, the nation's most important bookie, reported directly to underworld boss Costello. As a favor to Winchell, Erickson would occasionally tip Costello to a sure winner at one track or another, New York to Florida, and Costello would pass the word to Winchell, who would then get on the phone to FBI headquarters and tell Hoover, who would get his bet down in the nick of time. It was one of many reasons why Hoover looked upon Winchell as the most effective way to communicate with the American public. Walter knew everyone and everyone listened to him.

In one of those curious coincidences that tend to give life in New York its unique texture, Winchell had also known Harry Madrid for ages. The connection there had been, way back in '33, the Nazis. It was Harry Madrid who'd taught Winchell how to use a gun, and ever since Winchell, at Harry's direction, had slept with what he called his "equalizer" in a slipper beside his bed. Winchell's mother had been terribly upset that her boy was carrying a gun so Walter told her he'd quit. Anyway, the gun stuff had begun the night Winchell got mugged near Central Park and Harry Madrid happened to be passing by.

It was a funny thing but Winchell had been entangled in the Nazi business longer than almost any other American in public life. It had begun back in early 1933, right around the time FDR went to Miami as President-elect to make a speech at Bay Front Park. While Roosevelt was speaking a drifter by the name of Joe Zangara, standing thirty-five feet away, opened fire in front of twenty thousand people and managed to kill Mayor Anton Cermak of Chicago. Winchell was in Miami at the time, had just filed his column at the Western Union office, and was about to leave when a messenger burst in with the news of the shooting. Winchell took off on foot, raced to the jail, bluffed his way inside, and listened in on the interrogation of Zangara. He wired the story to the *Mirror* in New York immediately: the result was his first international scoop.

While the attempt to assassinate FDR was all over the front pages, German Chancellor Adolf Hitler was observing in regard to the coming election that even *if the German people should desert us, that will not restrain us! Whatever happens we will take the course that is necessary to save Germany from ruin!* The endless night of the Nazis had begun but Winchell's first reaction—based to some degree on Quentin Reynolds telling him, "Winch, Hitler's nothing but a fag"—was merely scornful. But he laid on the scorn with a trowel. And quickly it turned to revulsion, more quickly than it did for Secretary of State Cordell Hull, who characterized the Nazis' campagn against the Jews as "mild." Winchell took to the air with one of his battle cries: "The Hull you say!"

He persisted, even in the face of protests from his two employers—the National Broadcasting Company, which was afraid the German authorities might cut off their correspondent in Berlin, and William Randolph Hearst, who was both adamantly anti-British and fearful for his news service, which flourished in Germany. Still, Winchell carried on against what he called "the Ratzis" and by the autumn he could barely contain his delight at a front-page report in Hitler's *Völkischer-Beobachter.* Underneath a photograph of himself Winchell saw the caption: "A New Enemy of the New Germany."

Buoyed by this recognition he turned his attention—while never lessening his coverage of the Broadway doings of chorines and playboys—to the activities of a certain Fritz Kuhn, whom he described as "Hitler's secret agent in the United States." Herr Kuhn was in fact the leader of the German-American Bund, a propaganda unit for the Third Reich that was financed by Nazis both in Germany and the States. These revelations came at the end of '33, and early in '34 Winchell further announced that the Bund was composed of seventy-one units throughout the country, including twenty-three in the vicinity of New York City. While the rest of the press ignored the Bund, Winchell kept after Kuhn and his organization. On one occasion that had passed into Stork Club mythology Kuhn arranged to sit at a table near Winchell's in the Cub room and subsequently tied one on, observing to his friends that Winchell was no better than FDR, both of them damn dirty Jews.

Winchell's attacks motivated his friend J. Edgar Hoover to turn the FBI loose on Kuhn, an investigation that uncovered illegal financial manipulations and led to Kuhn's indictment for grand larceny and forgery. Kuhn was subsequently tried, convicted, and imprisoned. Which was all to the good, but not long afterward Winchell was set upon by Nazi thugs near Central Park. After commenting on Winchell's parentage at length and in thick accents, they proceeded to blacken an eye, split his lip, and break a tooth.

Which was where Harry Madrid entered the picture. He had known Winchell for years, from his coverage of the gang wars in the twenties and thirties. This particular night he'd noticed Winchell up ahead and was quickening his step to catch up and join him in his stroll. Then he saw the two figures come from the shadows. At first he thought they were fans paying respects and then he knew they weren't.

He lumbered onto the scene like a battle wagon and laid out one of the mugs with a hamlike fist, then broke the other's ankle with his foot. Winchell, spitting blood, said, "What the hell took you so long?" He proved appreciative as only he could. The event was memorialized in the column and Harry Madrid was depicted not merely as one of New York's finest but as a warrior in the fight against Hitler. No mention was made of the rough but simple justice Harry Madrid had administered later that night in the back room of a Broadway police station.

Now Cassidy saw Elliot Roosevelt slide out of the booth and for a moment Winchell was alone, sipping his milk, jotting notes on the back of the folded column. Jack Spooner, the maître d' of the Cub Room, appeared at his elbow. "Nice to see you again, Mr. Cassidy. What can we do for you this evening?"

"I need a word with the Old Scrivener."

"Of course, right this way. Tonight's your lucky night."

"And why's that, Jack?"

"Mr. Billingsley's sending a bottle of the bubbly to table fifty. Who knows why?" He shrugged. "A Lanson 'twenty-eight. *He'll* probably stick with the mild"—nodding at Winchell—"but you'll enjoy it. You know what they say about gift horses, Mr. Cassidy."

Winchell looked up and grinned. "Mr. Touchdown," he said, his customary greeting.

• • •

"So, whattaya think of the suit, kid?" His raspy voice was as familiar as FDR's had been. He patted the lapel with a perfectly manicured hand, flicked at the white handkerchief. He was left-handed and still held the note-taking pencil. "It's new. New today. You like it?" Winchell was always showing off his new suits. He had a rule, new suits and old shoes. He had another rule that had to do with girls: have as many as possible, as often as possible. He kept his family safely tucked away on his sixteen-acre estate up in Scarsdale, and he had a peculiar relationship with his wife June, who knew how he carried on in town. Apparently they had a deal. On the one occasion that Cassidy had seen them together June had dominated the great man completely. She raised the children, who included, as well as their daughter Walda, two Chinese girls Walter had insisted on adopting. June was a pretty good hand at spending money, to hear Walter tell it. It was rumored that June had an iffy ticker but Walter never used that as an excuse for his affairs. He simply couldn't get his fill of what he invariably referred to as pussy and enjoyed holding forth on the precise anatomical details of movie stars he'd slept with. He used to say that he had a regular exercise regimen—bending, stretching, and coming. Well, that was just Winch being Winch. Cassidy had never quite understood his penchant for girls he really didn't give a damn about, but then it was none of his business. Socially Winchell had once introduced him to Polly Adler, whose "house" catered to the high and mighty, including a Rockefeller who was a regular patron. It was just the way he was and Polly had told Cassidy to drop by any time and she'd see that he was treated better than right.

"It's a nice suit," Cassidy said.

"Aw hell, you're just saying that." Winchell chuckled.

"So who was the blonde?"

"Madge Starling, for chrissakes. You been living on Mars or someplace? She's a model—get it?" He winked, cocked an eyebrow. "Don't even give her a thought. She's busy tonight." He gave a raspy laugh. "Anyway, she's been on more laps than a napkin." A tall man with elegant gray hair combed back in wings over his ears came to the table, leaned down, whispered something into Winchell's pink ear. Winchell frowned. "Yeah, yeah, okay, okay—can't you see I'm talking here? Later. Lemme breathe here, Erwin." The man flushed as if he'd been swatted with a rolled-up newspaper and backed away. "Guy's a big producer, got a hot tootsie, want to impress her, get her into the column. I tell you, keed, it never stops. Everybody wants a piece of Winchell." He sighed wearily, coping with the burdens of fame.

"Well, Madge Starling is safe from my advances. I'm not really in the market these days, Walter."

"Sure, sure, you're a Boy Scout. An *Eagle* Scout, you always have been and you can't say I've ever held it against you—"

"The thing is—well, I don't quite know how to say this . . . I need your help. I'm working for Uncle Sam all of a sudden and . . ."

"So? And what?"

"Well . . . and Karin is back." He hurried onward. "She wasn't killed in the Cologne raid after all, she's alive, they've brought her back. . . . I saw her yesterday—"

"You wouldn't shit me, Lew?"

"No, I wouldn't do that to you, Walter."

"So what's she got to do with Uncle Sam? You're sure, I mean, you're sure she's back—you're not having some kind of fit or hallucination?"

"Listen, Walter, it's a pretty involved story. It's all mixed up with the Nazis, for one thing. That's why I've come to you. . . ."

"Well, I'll be damned." Winchell was staring at him, eyes wide, appraising. "I'd say you've come to the right man, then."

Spooner personally arrived with the Lanson '28. He uncorked it with a flourish and a pop like a pistol shot. Heads turned but then people were always aware of Winchell and the action at table 50. "Mr. Winchell?"

Winchell pushed his glass of milk away. "For a change, John." Spooner poured for both of them, then screwed the bottle down into the gleaming ice bucket and departed. Winchell lifted his glass and Cassidy saw that his eyes were suddenly full, glistening. Once in a while sentiment grabbed Winchell by the ears and shook him. "To your beautiful Karin . . . and her return home." They drank and he plucked the handkerchief from his breast pocket, dabbed his eyes. It was a nice effect.

Cassidy smiled. "And to Mr. and Mrs. America and all the ships at sea!" He tried to mimic Walter's staccato delivery, the opening of the Sunday night broadcast that every American had come to know so well.

"I'll drink to them," Winchell said. "Now what's the story, Lewis?"

"Can you keep a secret?"

"You know me, keed. I was good enough for FDR. I'm good enough for Hoover. Secrets are my game."

Cassidy made it as quick as he could but he told most of it. MacMurdo and Karin and the Brothers Moller and the Ludwig Minotaur and the submarine and the flight from Nova Scotia and how Maine might figure in it and how no one ever saw Manfred and the plane again.

Winchell listened intently, said: "You want to help this MacMurdo bird? He's on the level?"

"Terry Leary checked him out today and I called Dad. He's the real McCoy. Certified hero and Nazi hunter."

Winchell kept himself tightly coiled; it was his nature. But now he leaned back and gave Cassidy another long look. "One thing I have to ask you—are you in this thing to get Karin back? I'm telling you, love is a pisser and you can quote me. Love fucks up a man's thinking, his judgment."

"I simply don't know, Winch. She—this woman she is now—she's never even seen me before, doesn't know me—"

"So what? You look at it that way, she's only three years old, for chrissakes. We're not talking about her, we're talking about you. Do you want her?"

"But I don't know her either. . . . That's the point. We're strangers. Period."

"Okay. Then you want to catch Nazis. And think the Karin thing over . . ."

"And I want to give value for money. Don't forget the twenty grand."

"Hell, I make that much a week." Winchell sighed and sipped champagne. "So what do you want Winchell to do?"

"Nazis. Put me on to the Nazis around town. The top of the heap. I've got to get a jump start."

"You want to know who's likely to be in on this escape-route business. Funny. I've been wondering about that myself. I hear things, doncha know. Mainly it's got to be some of the old Bund supporters, the men I call the Reich's American Bankers . . . the Unknown War Criminals." For a moment he sounded as if he were hunched over the microphone, hand poised over the ticker he kept chattering throughout the broadcast. "These people even I have to be careful about. Me! Winchell! Sure, sure, I'm not afraid of the bastards, Winchell's afraid of no man, but"—he shrugged—"some you gotta be careful with. . . ."

"Such as," Cassidy prompted.

"Such as Karl Dauner—"

"Dauner? You pulling my leg?"

"Never. Never when it comes to the Ratzis, my young friend. Karl Dauner. Financier, member of half a dozen boards, art collector, you name it—if there's money in it, Dauner's up to his ass in it—"

"But he was an outspoken foe of the Nazis, as they say. He was front man for some of the War Bond drives. . . . He got movie stars to go out on the road, sell bonds, he's got a piece of some big studio or something. . . ."

"All protective coloration. He was also the German American Bund's biggest money raiser, so far behind the scenes that only Winchell knows for sure. Probably not more than a handful of men in the world knew that and I guarantee you I'm the only one who isn't a Nazi. Believe me, Lew. Let me see what I can do. Come by the studio for the broadcast Sunday night. I'll try to have something for you." Winchell was tapping his pencil on the tablecloth. He had to get to work. Cassidy stood up and

Walter stuck out his hand. "I'll keep 'em crossed for you and Karin. You made a good team there for a while."

"Thanks, Winch."

"Now get the fuck outa here. I'm a newspaperman. And, Lew? Love to Terry. And Madrid, too. Ya gotta love Harry Madrid." He was laughing, beckoning to the tall man called Erwin to come join him, when Cassidy called it a night.

# CHAPTER FIVE

The next morning, a Friday, Cassidy went in to the Dependable Detective office in the Dalmane Building near Grand Central and spent a couple of hours distractedly shuffling papers and looking out the windows at the dull gray end of September, absentmindedly snapping his suspenders. The Yankees had petered out and were finishing a disappointing third so there wasn't a World Series to look forward to. It was still a wartime season and any chances they might have had to win it had been dealt away in midseason when pitcher Hank "Blisters" Borowy, with a ten-and-five record, was traded to the Cubs. He went eleven-and-two with the Cubs and led them to the National League pennant. Without him the Yankees floundered. Snuffy Sternweiss, the second-sacker, had led the league in batting with .309 but it had been a skeleton team and Cassidy hoped things would get better with the return of DiMaggio in '46. But for now not even baseball could distract him from his own life and, oddly enough for a former star, he'd never had much interest in following football. Playing it was bad enough. It had never really caught his imagination the way baseball did.

Dependable employed six full-time operatives and there was plenty to keep them busy but nothing for him to do that morning unless he wanted to check expense accounts. He didn't and Olive nodded understandingly.

She'd do it. Harry Madrid was the operations officer of the firm and he'd taken over, organized things. Harry and Olive didn't really need either Cassidy or Terry Leary to keep things humming on a daily basis. Cassidy and Leary were there mainly to use their connections to bring in clients. And Sam MacMurdo at twenty thousand dollars was a pretty heavy sort of client. Nevertheless, there was nothing for him to do about the office. Every time he went out into the reception area he felt as if he were disturbing Olive. "You hear from Harry lately?" he asked.

"Oh, sure, Lew. I thought you probably knew." She pulled a piece of notepaper from a spindle. "He's up in Maine." She thought about that. "Lew, why is Harry up in Maine? We don't have a case in Maine, do we? What should I tell people who call for him?" Cassidy liked Olive. When Max Bauman had decapitated Bryce Huntoon with the undercarriage of the elevator in the Dalmane Building, Olive, poor kid, had been the first one in, the one who'd pressed the button and torn Huntoon apart. Long time ago. Olive said she sometimes had nightmares about it still.

"Tell 'em he's up in Maine," Cassidy said. "He didn't happen to say when he's coming back, did he?"

She looked up again, this time from the columns of figures in the weekly expense reports. "The weekend. He was going to try to be back this weekend."

Cassidy nodded. He went back into his office, took his suit coat off the hanger and put it on. Blue chalk-stripe. He took the satchelful of money and went to see Bert Higgins at the bank.

There was a cold mist in the air. Wind currents slashed it around and he turned up the collar of his trench coat like Charles Boyer in the movies. It was the damp, chilly kind of weather that got inside his bad leg and made him remember running back that opening kickoff at the Polo Grounds. The weather had been coming on ever since that rainy day at the estate in Westchester. So warned, he'd brought his heavy stick with him, the one Terry had given him back in '42. It had a heavy knob and a little button beneath the knob's collar. When you pressed the button the knob lifted up into the palm of your hand. The knob was part of the handle of a ribbon-thin, razor-sharp sword. Now, standing at the corner of Forty-second Street and Fifth Avenue, he was simply leaning on it, waiting for a cab to pull over out of the early afternoon traffic.

But when he arrived at the massive arch in Washington Square at the foot of Fifth, he paid the driver, got out, and realized he didn't want to cage himself up in the apartment. He started across the park, kicking his way through the first big harvest of autumn leaves, and suddenly felt very tired, as if the weight of the past that had been loosed by seeing Karin had finally come crashing down on him. He sat down on a bench, pulled his trench coat tighter, tugged his hat brim down on his forehead, and plunged his fists deep into the pockets. He was looking through the trees toward the black windows of his apartment. It might have been the day Cindy Squires, one startlingly beautiful autumn day, had walked all the way down Fifth Avenue from the Plaza and made love with him for the first time in that same apartment that had changed so little since. She had been unlike any other woman he'd ever known, as beautiful as Karin, but shrouded in her own fatalistic vision of her life. When he remembered Cindy—and he did, still, every day of his life—he saw her as if she were standing alone, her fate clinging to her like a cloak, as if she had always known how it would end. He could recall everything about her, the ash-blond hair, the tiny breasts and solid, wide hips, the low husky voice, the way she'd had a final burst of hope near the end, hope that maybe her life—their life—could endure happily . . . but at the end, the very end, with Max Bauman's gun pressed up under her chin, she had known it was a frail, hopeless dream, and she had said good-bye to him with her eyes. . . . And the memory of her eyes had never dimmed for him.

That day she'd met him at the Plaza and taken the long walk down Fifth . . . it seemed a lifetime ago. . . . It *was* a lifetime ago. Hers, Max's, Bennie's. Lifetimes ago.

Cassidy shook himself out of the reverie and stood up, feeling the needles of mist in his face. Slowly he set off to circle the square, still in the grip of the past, listening to the tapping of his stick on the damp sidewalk, a wet leaf occasionally adhering to the ferrule.

He crossed the street in front of his apartment, pushed through the black wrought-iron gate, and went inside, accompanied as always by his platoon of ghosts.

• • •

He was sitting in the twilight of a cloudy afternoon, nursing a scotch on ice, and he hadn't bothered to turn on the table lamps. There was a steady throbbing in his leg, annoying, like waking yourself up by snoring. The window shades were drawn and he yanked the cord to pull them open. He was looking out at the square. The fallen leaves were glued to the sidewalk and he wasn't really seeing the square, he was seeing Cindy and Bennie and Terry Leary and the news from Europe wasn't so good and Karin was dead and it was a long time ago. He was stuck in the clouds of memory and he hadn't been paying attention to the view across the square because he hadn't seen anyone, but now the doorbell was ringing.

He got up, set the drink on an end table, went to the front hall, and opened the door.

She was standing in the doorway wearing a green trench coat and a black beret at a cocky angle, at variance with the huge tan eyes, which didn't look cocky at all. She wore tight leather gloves that stretched across her knuckles. She let her hand drop from the buzzer.

"Mr. Cassidy . . . it's just me." A smile darted across her mouth, as if she'd remembered how to do it and then as quickly forgotten again. She looked back at the square as if trying to fix the coordinates so she'd remember the place. "I'm very . . . confused." She turned back, searching his face as if an answer might be hidden there, like one of those "What's Wrong with this Picture?" puzzles.

"You'd better come on in," Cassidy said, standing aside. They'd lived in the apartment together for six months before she'd gone back to Germany to see her sick father. He watched her like a laboratory attendant watching an animal in a maze, wondering if she'd remember the course. She pulled the beret off and stood holding it, looking into the darkness of his living room. She was a stranger in an unfamiliar room. He closed the door behind him, followed her in, switched on a lamp. She looked at him as if she needed instructions. She ran one hand, the glove off now, through the curtain of her hair and he saw the scar again. She saw him looking at the scar and nodded, slowly letting the hair fall back into place. "My souvenir of the war," she said tonelessly. "I was lucky."

"Can I get you a drink? A Sea Breeze? It's the latest thing."

"No, thank you. I don't quite know what I'm . . . doing."

"Are you all right? How did you get here?" She suddenly put out a hand and steadied herself on the back of an overstuffed Morris chair. "You'd better sit down." He took her hand and she sat down, sat staring out the window. A car went past and as it did the driver turned the headlights on. "How would a cup of coffee suit you?"

"American coffee—" She looked up, innocent expectation. "Of course, it would be American. . . ." She was speaking softly, as if she were reassuring herself. "I'm *in* America. My God, I'm so tired and confused. Forgive me. I'd love some coffee."

He went to the kitchen, loaded the basket, and put the percolator on the gas ring. "So how did you get here, Karin?" Her name almost stuck in his throat again. He was going to have to get over that.

"Why, I . . . I drove." Her voice coming from the living room carried a note of surprise, as if she'd said she'd just trekked across the Sahara. "I just walked out the door and got into one of the cars and no one was around, I think Colonel MacMurdo was having a meeting—he's a great one for meetings. . . ." She sounded as if she were recounting a dream.

"You drove. How did you know where to go?"

"Well, I looked in the telephone book. . . . I've been so worried, we hadn't heard from you since you were at the house, I had to talk to you—" She was unbuttoning the trench coat, stood up and slipped it off. She was wearing a gray flannel dress, a jumper with a blue and gold blouse under it. "Then, when I was in the car, I drove into the city. . . . I suppose I was following road signs. And then it was all so strange, I can't explain it, Mr. Cassidy—"

"Call me Lew."

"Lew," she said softly. "Lew. Don't be angry with me—"

He smiled. Behind him he could hear the bubbling of the percolator. "I'm amazed you didn't get lost." She moved toward the window, turned to face him with the faint light behind her.

"I was, too. I just seemed to *come* here, it was as if the car . . . well, knew the way. I came here, there was a place to park, I got out of the car. I was in a fog, I just came to this building, this doorway." She clasped her hands at her waist in a characteristic gesture that had once indicated something like girlish excitement.

"You saw the number on the gate, that's all." He turned back to the coffee. The hair on the back of his neck stiffened. Had memory overtaken her? He took cups and saucers from the cupboard. They rattled like a Gene Krupa riff and he put the damned things on the counter. He took cream from the icebox and sugar from the cupboard, put them on a silver tray that they—*they*—had received as a wedding present.

He took the tray into the living room and put it on the coffee table. She was staring out the window chewing on a knuckle, eyes narrowed to slits. He went back and brought the percolator and a cast-iron trivet, set the one down on the other on a little Duncan Phyfe table she had seen and bought on Madison Avenue one day. There were tears trickling down her cheeks. He poured two cups of coffee, put cream and sugar in his own, just sugar in hers, without giving it a second thought. She wiped the tears away with her fists and sniffled, looked at the tray. "Sugar, please," she whispered.

"It's already in," he said.

She nodded, took a sip. "Just right."

"I know."

She held the cup in both hands as if it didn't have a handle. He watched her blow the steam across the surface as he had a thousand times before. "I felt as if I've been in New York before. I felt like I'd been possessed by the spirit of another person. . . ." The cup began to tremble in her hands, some of the scalding liquid sloshing over the edge. She put it down and dabbed her fingers with a napkin. "Oh my God, what if I'm going mad? I don't know how to handle all this." She couldn't stop the overflowing tears again.

There was a cool breeze fluttering the venetian blinds. All the streetlamps were lit and night had slouched into Washington Square.

"Have I been here before?" He could barely hear her. She looked at him, imploring. "You can't imagine what this is like. . . . I've lost so much of my life and I sometimes have visions, like a crazy woman, it's so frightening, I wake up screaming. . . ."

Cassidy took her hand in both of his and held her still.

"And I felt like I *know* you." She swallowed hard, concentrating on looking anywhere but at him. "It's just a flash, then it will be gone."

Cassidy shook his head, reached thankfully for his coffee. Something to do. Anything.

"I had a dream about you, after you left the house that day."

"What sort of dream?" He wondered if he should be asking. No, he probably should have shut up.

"We were just talking somewhere. There was a huge ship, like an ocean liner, sea gulls flapping around. . . . You were talking to me, I could see your lips moving and the gulls swooping but I couldn't hear anything, I couldn't hear what you were saying, and then you kissed me and I was crying and I hugged you. . . . It was just a dream, I know that, but why? I'd only just met you and I was dreaming about you. . . . It was so real . . . so very real . . . and then I woke up and I was soaked with sweat and I'd been crying into the pillow and I felt faint, I couldn't remember where I was . . . Do you know how terrifying that is for me? Not remembering, even for a few seconds? They seem like hours and I think it's all happening again, that I'll never remember anything again. . . ." She shook her head and made a face to banish the fear. "What's happening to me? What's going on inside my head? Look at me, I'm exhausted, I've never been so tired. . . . I can't sleep, I have these flashes. . . . When I saw that huge arch out there," she pointed out the window where it loomed in the lights, "I . . . I thought I'd seen it before. I thought I had been there, standing under the arch in a snowstorm, looking up at the snow swirling all around it, blowing down from the sky and there was a Christmas tree. . . . I'd seen all that, the lights bright on the tree and the snow and a choir of kids singing carols. . . ."

She was right, of course. Everything she had just described had happened. They had walked down Fifth Avenue in the snow and watched the arch and the Christmas tree lights come into view and then heard the piping, trilling voices of the children singing "O Come All Ye Faithful." Christmas of 1938, almost seven years ago. It was the last Christmas they'd spent together. And it had come back to her, like a tableau seen by lightning flash, as if the lightning were ripping at the shroud surrounding her memory. He had no idea how to handle it. He was afraid she might shatter if he weren't careful. Rolf Moller had said it was so dangerous to push her. He didn't know what the hell to do.

But *this* woman, this was Karin. His Karin. Behaving the way Karin would behave *being* Karin. It wasn't some other woman they all called Karin.

"You poor man," she said. "I'm so sorry. I shouldn't have come here bothering you this way. Sometimes I panic. I realize I have no memory of my life and it's like being closed within an unanswerable question, a room without a door and only some bad magic could put you there. So, I panic, I cry, I can't breathe. . . . Rolf says it's hysteria and I have to learn to overcome it . . . and I try, I do try, but it's like being an orphan, adopted by nice people who give you a good life but you desperately want to know who you really are. . . ."

Standing by the window in the darkened apartment, she turned toward him, whispered: "Why do I think I knew you once?"

"I don't know why." He smelled her, felt the warmth of her breath, saw the tears dried on her cheek, and there was nothing he could do but kiss her. This Karin was as much his wife as anyone else's and he turned her face toward him and put his mouth on hers, as gently as if he were making a wish. She trembled, then parted her lips and he tasted the tip of her tongue and she clutched him, kissed him hungrily before turning away, still in his grip.

She was gasping for breath, shaking her head, eyes closed. "What am I doing? What's going on here—"

"Don't talk. Just wait."

"No, no, I can't. What's happening to me? I've done all this before—" She pulled away and he let her go. "I'm doing this because I'm thinking about you the way you think about someone you know, someone from a previous life . . . like the sleeping princess in the wrong fairy tale. . . . Why do you want to kiss a madwoman? I'm like Frankenstein's monster, I'm not even human, I'm a woman without a life, most of me, all of me that should matter is missing."

"Well, maybe you're right about one thing. Maybe we knew each other in another life."

"But we're stuck with this life, aren't we?"

"You never know—"

"And everything depends on you, depends on your finding my husband—"

"That won't bring back your past, Karin."

"I'm worried just as much about the future. My future depends on finding him—"

"Why? You have a future whether I find him or not—"

"No. No, I don't."

"What are you telling me?"

"I—I can't say any more than that. But believe me, if you don't find him, I—I—you must find him. Elisabeth . . . no, no . . ." She came back to him, huddled against him, and he put his arms around her again.

"Elisabeth? Who's Elisabeth?" He stroked her hair.

"Oh, I don't know . . . no one. I don't know what I'm saying."

"Don't worry," he whispered. She was shaking. "Don't worry. I'll find him."

"Oh, thank you," she whimpered, as if she'd been beaten. "I believe you."

He was still holding her when the telephone began to ring.

• • •

"Jesus, pard, I'm glad you're home." It was MacMurdo and he wasn't happy. His voice sounded like somebody was rubbing a raw nerve. "This is gonna sound funny but, ah, is Karin with you?"

"She's right here. We're having coffee."

MacMurdo made what Cassidy figured was some kind of rustic cry of relief. "Jesus, Mary, and Joseph send their thanks, pard. Honest to God, they do! She just wandered off like some old kitchen mammy hankerin' for the bright lights. She all right? She didn't wreck the car? Hurt herself?"

"No, she's just fine. Parked right outside. She wanted to find out if I'd made any headway—"

"She remembers how to drive a car—is the telephone too tough for her? I ask you. We're all going crazy up here. Believe it. Then old Rolfie says maybe seeing you sort of . . . She can't hear this, can she?"

"No."

"Well, Rolf, he was thinking that seeing you might have poked a hole in the curtain between Then and Now. One smart kraut, Rolf. So how is she? You know what I mean—"

"She's all right. You want to talk to her?"

"Christ no, I might yell at her. Was Rolf right? About her memory and seeing you?"

"She's just worried about finding her husband. She wondered if I'd turned anything up. She found me in the phone book, couldn't get an answer, said everybody up your way was in a meeting so she just drove on down—"

"Jesus wept," MacMurdo murmured.

"Everything's fine." Cassidy smiled at Karin. She was carrying the tray of coffee things back to the kitchen. He'd seen her do precisely that a hundred times but, of course, for her it was the first. MacMurdo was saying something and Cassidy was sure he wasn't going to tell the Colonel about Karin's dreams and questions.

"The woman has the guts of a second-storey man. The brains of a pigeon, however. Well, you must think we're a bunch of assholes up here, lettin' her wander away—well, won't happen again, you can bet the farm on that. Look, my man, I've got something new to tell you. You think you could drive her back? I'll have one of my men take you home. Could you do that?"

"Sure. I'll bring her back." Karin had gone into the bathroom. "By the way, Harry Madrid's on the case. He's up in Maine."

"Damn! That's good news, Lew. None better than old Harry." Most of the tension had seeped out of MacMurdo's voice. "You guys, you're aces with me. See ya soon."

Cassidy hung up and Karin was standing behind him getting into her coat. "I'm so tired," she said softly. "I get headaches when I'm tired." He helped her with the coat, wishing he could kiss her again. Something told him it would be all wrong. "You're so kind to me," she said.

She curled her feet beneath her on the front seat of the car and Cassidy got some dance music on the radio. Pretty soon she was sound asleep.

He looked over at her every so often, wondering. Was he falling in love with her all over again?

# Chapter Six

MacMurdo and Rolf Moller were standing outside on the long stonework terrace that ran the width of the library and the long parlor across the front of the house. The lamps on top of the poles every few hundred feet of driveway were glowing through the mist and the house was ablaze with lights, as if it were a landing field Cassidy might miss or overshoot in the night. Wisps of autumn fog clung close to the damp earth. Cassidy pulled to a halt in the portico and waited for the welcoming committee to reach them.

MacMurdo came to Cassidy's side and opened the door. Moller headed straight for his patient, who was just waking up, groggy. Cassidy watched her yawn, patting her mouth with one hand, then stretching. She'd always awakened the same way, the same stretching and the same faces and head-shaking. She caught his eye before she got out, blinked, smiled tentatively, and was gone. Cassidy was remembering kissing her an hour before, but what was she thinking?

"Come on inside and let me pour you a stiff one." MacMurdo's huge hand clamped down on his shoulder. He was wearing a heavy oiled sweater, black, and dark corduroys, so that only his face and hands were entirely visible in the darkness. A little lampblack and he'd be ready for a sortie behind enemy lines. Cassidy was still wearing his dark blue chalk-stripe and trench coat. He felt like he'd come to the wrong party. "Thanks a million for bringing her back, pard. Goodness me, goes to show you you never know what's coming next." He chuckled to show you that, as far as he was concerned, you'd better be on your guard where women were involved. Cassidy nodded and followed him up the steps to the fieldstone terrace, on through the French windows into the library. "Name your poison, Lew."

"Scotch on ice." Cassidy was staring back out into the darkness that lay deep and damp beyond the penumbra of light. He heard the clink of ice in the heavy tumblers. "So, who's this Elisabeth, Sam? You didn't tell me about her."

More ice clinked and MacMurdo said, "Beg pardon, Lew? My mind was somewhere else. Who's this *who*?" He turned from the sideboard and handed Lew a glass heavy as a paperweight.

"Elisabeth."

"I'm not following you, pard." He touched glasses. "Chin-chin." He wet his whistle and said, "What Elisabeth?"

"Karin mentioned the name. When she was telling me how important it was that I find Manfred . . . she said the name. Elisabeth. I wondered who she is."

"Damned if I know. Frankly, it's not always the easiest thing in the world to do, keeping track of some of the stuff Karin comes up with. At least, that's been my experience. Elisabeth. New one on me. Did she say anything else about her?"

"Just the name."

MacMurdo shrugged. "She's a mystery. Karin, I mean. And she's dangerous. A loose cannon rattling around the deck. A storm at sea. The joker in the deck. The . . . the—"

"I get the idea."

MacMurdo laughed. "Yeah, I guess you do, at that." He took another drink, threw himself down in one of the leather chairs, and draped a long leg over the arm. "Seeing you didn't, you know, trigger her memory?"

"Nope."

"No, I guess it's deeper than that. Well, if she starts showing any signs of recognizing you, you'll let me know, right? It could make a difference, she could come back in little pieces and you could find yourself playing Sigmund Freud. And, from Uncle Sam's point of view, it wouldn't be so hot if she lost her interest in finding Manfred."

"Don't worry," Cassidy said.

"Oh, a healthy worry level is part of my original equipment. Under this happy-go-lucky exterior lurks a fella who feeds on a certain benign worry level. Not anxiety. Just a kind of permanent worry buzz. Keeps me alive and well, has so far, anyway. Anything about Manfred Moller makes me buzz. I look at old Manfred and you know what I see? I see he's a regular Florentine donkey." He chuckled softly.

"I'm afraid that one goes right past me," Cassidy said.

"You serious, pard?"

"Hard to believe, maybe, but I know nothing of Florentine donkeys."

"If you say so. Hell, I thought everybody knew that old story—"

"You plan on telling me, sport?"

MacMurdo shrugged. "Ain't exactly a secret. Happened in the thirteenth century so it ain't classified." He took another big swallow of scotch, enjoying himself. It was getting late and Cassidy could see him having a drink in any of a hundred officers' clubs and telling a story. Or maybe in a foxhole somewhere or hiding out in a smoky, bombed-out basement out there in the gap, behind enemy lines. He was the kind of man who could always make himself comfortable. Cassidy saw him as a kind of Warrior King, huge, implacable, king of the rotting corpses. "Just a dim little corner of military history. Siena and Florence at each other's throats—bunch of nervous, crazy Italians. Some Florentine bigshot decided he was going to put paid to the Sienese once and for all. He built these big goddamned catapults—this guy was fed up. The plague had killed a helluva lot of his donkeys and—well, he must have been pretty desperate, ready to do anything to pull out a knockout at the bell. Do you know how important donkeys were to thirteenth-century warfare? We just finished a war using more trucks and jeeps than you can count. Back then donkeys were the trucks and jeeps. So you know right away that old Florentine was in deep shit; the donkeys were dead, diseased, and worst of all the plague was starting to kill his troops. Well, pard, he sat there thinking, knowing two things—he had to get rid of those donkeys and he wanted to kick Siena's ass once and for all. So, the other shoe dropped—catapults! He had some of his good ol' boys load the dead donkeys—lousy job, dead-donkey loader—had 'em load those stinking carcasses onto the catapults and right before your eyes—think of it—beautiful sunny day, the Tuscan sky bluer than your old granny's hair, and suddenly the air is full of dead donkeys, blood and guts hangin' out, donkeys flyin' every which way, over the walls—well, shit, pard, it was quite a maneuver—"

"Did it work?"

"Oh, hell, I forget. I don't suppose it turned the tide of European history. But my point is this, Manfred Moller is a plague-infected Florentine donkey. The plague is Nazism, Lew—oh, maybe I get a little melodramatic on the subject, but if you'd seen what I've seen—"

"I've got my own argument with the Nazis," Cassidy said. "If you recall."

"Oh, I know, pard. Forgive this ol' country boy. But you see what I'm drivin' at? Göring is my Florentine general, he catapulted his plague donkey all the way to America—only we can't find him and this donkey's alive and he could infect every damn one of us." He drained the scotch and levered himself up out of the deep chair and headed back for the liquor cabinet. "Damn me, but I know this bastard is alive, Lew. And we're gonna get him and turn him into one dead donkey." He laughed harshly and splashed more scotch into his glass. "So much for the history lesson. Lemme freshen that up for you." He brought the bottle back and filled Cassidy's glass again. "Chin-chin."

It was all so comfortable, so seductive, as if there were nothing wrong at all. Just pals sitting around having a couple of belts and shooting the breeze. Good scotch, heavy leaded tumblers, a gleaming ice bucket, portraits on the oak-paneled walls, half the books in the world, and a fair amount of the world's known reserves of leather furniture. It was a men's club with two members. And, of course, it was nothing of the kind.

MacMurdo withdrew two cigars of great length and circumference from the humidor and cut the ends with a gold clipper. He handed one to Cassidy and they lit up. They puffed with deep satisfaction, rolling the smoke with the lingering taste of scotch on their tongues, two gents. They sat without speaking for several minutes, smoking, waiting for the millennium. The only thing missing was an old duffer snoring beneath his *Wall Street Journal* in a dim corner. Cassidy looked at MacMurdo through the smoke and experienced a surge of fellow feeling. He couldn't really analyze it, didn't try. Maybe it was just that Sam MacMurdo was deep down a good ol' boy.

"So, you said you had a piece of news for me. Of more recent vintage than the flying Florentine donkeys."

MacMurdo smiled. "That was merely a scholarly digression. Yes, I do have something else. I got word from one of my people in Washington who has been talking to another of my people back in Germany. And we've learned a bit more about Göring's escape route. Turns out there was one man Göring trusted to help with the plan at this end. An American. The man Göring sent Manfred Moller to find and link up with . . . the good news is we have a name." He eased the ash into the cut-glass boulder beside his armrest.

"Well?"

MacMurdo sighed and grinned forlornly, the cigar stuck in the corner of his mouth. He looked like a man chewing on a stick of dynamite. "The bad news is it's a code name. Vulkan. Our friend Manfred had to find one man and that man was called Vulkan."

• • •

It was past eleven when MacMurdo consulted his watch and grunted. "What the hell's going on here," he muttered to himself. He grappled briefly with the telephone on the desk. He dialed while clearing his throat. Three digits. An internal number. He waited. "Aw, shit," he exclaimed softly, looked at Cassidy. "My worry buzz. You carrying a heater, Lew?"

"A what?"

"A piece. Iron. A gun, for chrissakes. Come on, what would Bogart think of you? Shame, shame." While he spoke he was going behind the desk, opening a drawer, and removing a holstered .45 automatic. He pulled it out of the leather and made sure it was game ready.

"Yes," Cassidy said. "I'm armed, old sock." He checked the .38 in his shoulder harness. "Why are we playing with our guns?"

"Sergeant Minnelli down in the gate house doesn't answer. And Clyde hasn't reported back to me from his rounds." He looked at his watch again. "Eleven twenty-four. Clyde should be back. I gave the other two guys leave until morning. So Clyde and Carlo Minnelli, they're probably having a beer and doing the perimeter together but . . ." He grinned. It was his response to danger.

"You keep four men here? Sam, what's the scoop?"

"Precious cargo, pard. We got two people here we've gotta protect."

"Who the hell from? This is a whole new part of the story, old sock. You haven't been leveling with me. I don't like that."

"Look, all that matters to you in this equation is Karin. Of course, she's in danger. You're in danger. We're all in danger. A whole shitload of Nazis may jump out of the weeds and bite us. You comin'? Let's go find Minnelli and have a beer." He dropped a hand like a shovel on Cassidy's shoulder. "Cheer up, pard. A-hunting we will go."

It was dead still outside on the driveway, the mist and balloons of ground fog clustering around the light poles. The driveway curved slick and black and wet like a river of oil. You could just see your breath in the chill. The wind moved like a stealthy culprit in the forested rise surrounding the great house. There was a sudden noise like a muffled foghorn and Cassidy stopped, surprised.

MacMurdo said: "That better have been an owl—"

"Sounded like the advance man of an Iroquois raiding party."

"Too many movies for you, old son." MacMurdo moved easily. The gun hung at his side, engulfed in the huge hand. "Wait'll I get my hands on Clyde and Carlo, they think this is such soft duty. 'Course it is, compared to what they've both been through. North Africa, Sicily, Germany . . . This must seem like a country club."

"It *is* like a country club, Sam."

The stone guardhouse was quiet, the gate looming in the darkness beyond. The owl hooted again and there was a flurry of movement in the woods, a thrashing in the leaves, a mouse dying.

The door, when they were ten yards from the guardhouse, was seen to stand open. The guardhouse was a squat stone shed, fancied up with a black-and-white gabled roof that made it look like an excessively large birdhouse. The windows shone yellow and a splash of light spilled from the doorway onto the black driveway. There was something wrong. It was too still, too quiet. Cassidy glanced toward the side of the driveway near the gatehouse, looked back, found no shelter at all. They were alone and easy pickings if there was trouble. The door standing open beckoned ominously, looking for a sucker. It was the door that was wrong. It should have been closed.

Together they moved quickly to the shadow of the shed wall, flattened themselves. MacMurdo leaned along the rough surface and looked in the window. He drew back, turned to Cassidy, whispered: "Empty. This feels like a handful of something wet and brown, pard. You ready to use that peashooter of yours?"

Cassidy nodded. "Why don't I take a little trip round the corner?"

"Okay. Let's try real hard not to shoot each other."

Cassidy edged along the wall, poked his head around, couldn't see anything out of the ordinary. But halfway along this second wall he stepped on something squishy that squirmed and croaked and Cassidy swore, leaped back, and had his gun ready. It croaked again.

MacMurdo said from the darkness: "What is it?"

Cassidy swallowed, waited, said: "Frog. I hate the country, damn it. I'm a city boy." He moved along the rest of the back wall, turned the corner to the gate side, and stopped. There was something on the ground, dragged up close to the wall. It was a soldier. It was the late Carlo Minnelli.

Cassidy knelt, felt for a pulse in the throat, and got his hand sticky just before he touched the piano wire that had pierced the flesh and sunk deep into the bloody pulp. Minnelli's head rolled toward him, both eyes wide open and staring, the whites clouded with blood as if they'd exploded. Cassidy looked at the eyes and then at his smeared hand. He fought off a wave of nausea and wiped his hand across the corpse's coat front.

The door creaked. Cassidy leveled his revolver at the corner and fortunately MacMurdo spoke before he came around. "It's me. Hold your fire. What the hell's—" He appeared, huge and enormously tall from Cassidy's crouch, and said: "Damn!" staring down at Minnelli's body.

"Garrotted," Cassidy said. "Piano wire."

"We gotta get back to the house." He nodded at the body. "How long?"

"Minutes. He's warm and the blood's still running."

"Come on. We need some cover."

Cassidy followed him, running hard across the driveway, across the slippery grass, to the edge of the trees. MacMurdo kept on, jogging along the tree line, branches flapping wetly. Cassidy was lagging, his leg bothering him. Soon he was limping, gritting his teeth against the pain. It was hard to remember he'd once made his living running into, around, and over men not too much smaller than Sam MacMurdo. He looked up at the house that sat apparently peacefully, the lights glowing from the library windows. He was losing ground, saw MacMurdo pushing on, fading in and out in the darkness. Then there was a crash up ahead and he pulled up, waiting in the wet branches, soaking himself with their accumulated dampness. MacMurdo was down. He slowly edged forward, waiting for another sound. Finally it came.

"Lew? Where the hell are you?"

"Back here." Cassidy hobbled onward, wiping the water from his face and eyes. "You okay?"

"I'm fine. Clyde ain't so good though."

Cassidy reached the big man, who was upright, leaning with hands on knees, staring down at the body of the sergeant who had greeted Cassidy upon his arrival a few days before.

"Tripped over him. He's walkin' the streets o' Glory, pard. Let's get to the house and pray to God we're not too late."

Cassidy forced himself to keep up as they went back across the driveway and fetched up in the cover of the portico where two of the cars sat side by side. The mist was turning to a fine rain. MacMurdo whispered, out of breath: "I'm going across to the terrace, have a look into the library. You cover me in case we got a guy who thinks he's a marksman, too. Figure I'm safe from the piano wire out on the terrace. If I draw fire, you get into the house and flush 'em out."

Cassidy said: "Not a great plan, but a plan."

MacMurdo laughed under his breath. "Ain't this the shits, pard?"

MacMurdo took off, loped to the terrace steps, and was up in two bounds. He waited for a moment, crouching on the fieldstones. Cassidy waited, watching the shadows behind him for a man with a third length of piano wire, flicking his eyes back and forth from the shadows to MacMurdo, back again.

Finally MacMurdo rose and ran along the terrace railing.

The crack of the shot from the house came as the huge target reached the large concrete planter at the center of the railing's length.

Cassidy saw MacMurdo take the slug.

He pitched forward with a loud oath and Cassidy fired at the general direction from which the shot had come. He heard the ping and splinter from the stone facing.

He waited in the silence, his breath short, heart pounding. Rain was dripping off the vines, spattering his forehead. MacMurdo lay still, barely visible in the shadow of the railing.

Then without warning MacMurdo was upright, hurtling over the railing to land with a mighty thud, a muffled *fuck!*, in the flowerbed.

It was time to go inside and Cassidy didn't like the idea. He was taking a couple of deep breaths, checking for the piano-wire man just in case they came in pairs, when the light snapped on in a bedroom on the second floor.

Karin, wakened by the shot, stood outlined in the window.

"Go back!" It was MacMurdo shouting like a hound baying at the moon. "Karin, go back! Lock your door!"

Slowly, as if she were still lost in a dream, Karin moved away from the window.

Cassidy couldn't wait any longer.

He went to the side service door, keeping his back to the wall, pushed it open, stepped inside, and hesitated so his eyes might accustom themselves to the darkness. The hallway was narrow, windowless, pitch black. Each step sounded like a cannon shot. He didn't know the house well enough, had to feel his way as he tried to remember the layout. The shot from the house had come from the row of parlor windows: the parlor had been dark. But as he reached the main hallway, then the foyer with the parquet floor and the wide staircase and the chandelier softly tinkling in a draft—as he heard it he realized that the light in the library had also been extinguished.

Somewhere in the darkness he heard a movement, someone somewhere bumped into something. Someone with a gun, who knew he was there . . . or maybe not.

He crossed the foyer, edging along the wall opposite the parlor, hardly daring to breathe, inching along, not wanting to knock over some goddamn little table full of flowers and get his brains blown all over the wall. He peered into the parlor. The draperies were drawn. Nothing moved.

He stood stock still, holding his breath, straining to hear another man's fatal inhalation. Nothing. He'd lost all track of time. He felt as if he'd been in the house forever. Finally he continued along the hallway.

The draperies in the library were open. The lamps on the terrace cast shadows across the one room in the house whose geography he knew.

Without warning, the figure of a man was silhouetted against the light.

Cassidy, unseen, raised the .38, about to take a shot to wound. It was like a shooting gallery, an instant when the figures jerk to a stop.

"Who's there?" The man had sensed a presence. Something stayed Cassidy's trigger finger. "Who is it? MacMurdo?"

It was Rolf Moller.

In the barest fraction of a second Cassidy shouted at the doctor to get down and heard an unidentifiable but very real sound, somewhere off to his left, somewhere over near the library liquor cabinet. He fell to his knees as a bullet whacked into the wall beside his head. A second shot shattered the glass front of a bookcase.

Cassidy swiveled and fired in the direction of the muzzle flash, getting his shot off nearly between the other two.

The man grunted. A side chair clattered over.

The gunman leaped across the room, adrenaline making him almost airborne, and Cassidy snapped off a second shot that went astray as he slipped. The slug burrowed into the plaster of the ceiling, dust sprinkling like snow.

The figure kept going, broke through the French windows, ripping through the wooden framework, carrying bits of wood with him, flailing his arms trying to get free, then sprawling onto the terrace.

Cassidy was on his feet, trying to get a bead on him as he scrambled back to his feet, frozen for an instant in a shroud of torn curtain. Which way to go?

Cassidy fired again just as he saw, heard, damn near felt the heavy sound of MacMurdo's .45.

The man was hurled sideways, somehow managed a few steps before tumbling forward like the man on the high wire losing his balance, plummeting.

Cassidy went past the desk, saw Moller on his knees as if he might be praying. Past the obliterated window, the man lay huddled on the ground.

All the noise was over. The wind in the trees, the drip and patter of rain, nothing else.

MacMurdo's voice rode on the wind: "We got him, pard—"

The explosion caught them unaware.

The crumpled body lifted off the ground, the clothing seemed to shred, the glass in another of the French windows blew back into the library, Rolf Moller ducked back under the desk.

Cassidy felt slivers of glass nicking his face.

Smoke drifted up from the remains of the corpse as if he were the victim of that most curious of fates, spontaneous combustion.

Slowly Cassidy stepped out onto the fieldstones, glass crunching underfoot. He stepped on something soft and looked down. It was what had once been a man's hand.

MacMurdo hobbled up onto the terrace.

His corduroys were torn at the thigh where a slug had removed a bit of the old piss and vinegar. He limped across toward Cassidy. "Gotta do more than get me in the leg to stop me. Nice shootin', pard. I'm proud of you." He grinned. Rolf Moller was venturing out onto the terrace, carefully opening one of the remaining French windows.

MacMurdo stared down at the mess.

"This dead fucker had a grenade, for God's sake. Pin pulled, gonna just lob it back in on your head, my man." He looked at Cassidy. "This, I'd say, was your lucky night."

They both began to laugh. Rolf Moller looked at them as if they had dropped in from Mars. Which made it all the funnier.

# Chapter Seven

Walter Winchell stood on top of the wooden table, knees slightly bent. He leaped into the air, landed with a bang that shook the microphone near his feet, and began screaming at the heavyset man standing by.

"The fucking eddie," he howled, "it's an ass-wipe, Herman! Shitting paper! You get me? Walter Winchell doesn't give Mr. and Mrs. America this crap, Herman!" He kept jumping up and down, banging the table, face red, fists clenched, the mike bouncing.

Herman Klurfeld was used to his boss's outbursts as broadcast time approached. It was ten minutes to nine, Sunday evening, and most of the people in America were getting settled to sit down with their radios and Walter Winchell. Klurfeld looked at Lew Cassidy standing in the corner of the studio. Terry Leary was smoking a cigarette, grinning at the scene. Klurfeld passed them on his way out, the script flapping in his hand. "He doesn't like the editorial."

"I got that much," Leary said.

"I'd better give it some mascara and pancake." He smiled forlornly and left.

Winchell's mainspring began to wind down. He wiped his forehead with a handkerchief. "What the hell am I doing up here, for chrissakes?

I'm getting old. A man could hurt himself." He muttered: "Gimme a hand. What the fuck am I doing on the fuckin' table?"

Lew helped him down. "Acting pretty much like an asshole."

Leary laughed.

Winchell frowned. "Just a little artistic temperament, boy. Keeps 'em on their toes. Fuck 'em if they can't take a joke, that's what Winchell says." He was puffing. "Shit, I'm getting so old I can't take yes for an answer." He peered around, looking for a laugh. "Just kidding, just kidding. That'd be the day, boys, right?"

Leary blew several smoke rings. "That'll be the day, Walter."

Winchell looked at his watch. "You can stay in here with me, boys. Get a good look at the best there is doing his job. Now where the fuck's Herman? Herman!" He bellowed the name like an oath and an engineer behind the glass panel made a face, yanked off his headphones. Winchell gave his curious barking laugh. "Don't worry, Lew. I got you all set up with a nest of Ratzis. I said I would, didn't I?"

Klurfeld came back in, pushing his glasses up on his nose, handed the script to Winchell, who put his hand on the writer's shoulder and began reading through the editorial, two or three hundred words that always fell in the middle of the broadcast and that required, in particular, the Winchell touch. "Better, Herman, better. Always remember, Herman, Walter Winchell may be an asshole but we have to keep our little secret from Mr. and Mrs. America."

Klurfeld nodded.

Cassidy said: "To say nothing of all the ships at sea."

"Fuckin' A," Winchell said. Then he seemed to slip into a trance state. Two and a half minutes to nine. Everybody in the control room settled into place behind a haze of cigarette smoke. The director looked tense and sweaty, his tie worked loose and his shirtsleeves rolled up to his biceps. Klurfeld appeared in the control room and began chatting with the ad men representing the sponsor.

Winchell carefully adjusted the plain wooden chair at the proper angle to the table. He placed the heavy mike in a well-worn spot. Very quietly a network vice president came in and sat down beside him, straightening a pile of script so he could feed it smoothly to the great man a page at a time. Near the mike was the telegraph key that Winchell pounded to give the show its machine-gun-like staccato sound effects. As the seconds ticked away he worked his tie loose and unbuttoned the collar of his white shirt. He slowly lowered the zipper of his fly a couple of inches, settling into a half crouch of anticipation, as if the chair were a launching pad. The opening commercial was nearing an end. Winchell tensed, about to pounce, eyes on the director's arm, waiting for the pointing finger. With only a few seconds to go he looked up at Cassidy, flashed a quick wiseguy smile. "Lewis, I wanna die doing exactly this—it beats screwing!" The commercial ended. A nation of listeners, living rooms and kitchens and automobiles full of his fans at the end of another Sunday—they were all feeling the little squirting jolt of anticipation.

"Good evening, Mr. and Mrs. America and all the ships at sea!" He snapped the words, precise, incredibly quickly, a volley across the collective consciousness of a nation. "Let's go to press!" And he was off and running, Hollywood and Broadway and Washington and London and Berlin and Tokyo. He was racketing on about the capture of Tokyo Rose, the girl from Los Angeles who'd been visiting Japan and been trapped there at the start of the war, who'd become the seductive voice reaching out from the Empire of the Sun to the worn-out GIs slogging through the South Pacific. She'd been arrested in Tokyo early in September and was being brought back to the States to stand trial and Walter was rapping out her story. Cassidy sat back, stretched out his long legs, and let the voice carry him along, a Niagara of words, dots and dashes, insinuations and accusations and plaudits, near slanders, sentimental appreciations, jokes, ironies, broad vulgar sarcasms, every word like a grenade. You could hear the explosions across the landscape of the nation he loved.

• • •

Things at the house in Westchester had been smoothed over, at least superficially. When you're Colonel Sam MacMurdo and you're working for President Harry S Truman and Allen Dulles and your job is catching Nazis, you've got ways of taking care of things. By noon the day after the fireworks two civilians had arrived from Washington, bringing a complement of four soldiers in uniform. The bodies of Clyde and Minnelli had been taken away in an Army van, well before dawn. Plasterers and glaziers came in and repaired the damage to the house. Not a single police official had been notified. MacMurdo had taken care of it his way. The doctor who attended to his leg wound had been an Army man.

MacMurdo, who seemed impervious to pain, and Cassidy had tramped through the woods that afternoon. MacMurdo used a cane so, together, they looked like a broken-down song-and-dance team, two men with canes staggering off on the road to nowhere.

Near a dirt road half a mile from the house they found a mud-caked Harley Davidson motorcycle. It lay on its side. Nearby there was a set of tire tracks where another cycle had departed the scene, spraying mud across tree trunks and shrubbery. There had been two men, then, and one had escaped. MacMurdo took out his black pipe and dipped it into the oilskin pouch. He was wearing a leather bomber jacket. It was cracked and the wool was gray and old. A steady cold mist fluttered in the leaves. Cassidy stood looking down the dirt road, which was scrolled with muddy ruts. MacMurdo struck a kitchen match on his thumbnail and lit the pipe. He kicked the Harley. "You want a motorcycle?" Cassidy shook his head. MacMurdo delivered another kick. "Leave the damn thing here, then. I'll have somebody collect it. Bastard won't be needing it anymore." He puffed a thick gray cloud into the mist and they walked back to the huge house.

They stood before the damage the grenade had caused. The French doors had already been replaced. The cement was chipped and scorched, the stones themselves bore scattered whitened spots. MacMurdo ran his immense hand over the pitted surface.

Cassidy said: "Karin isn't a secret anymore. She has to be the point of all this. . . . You wouldn't hold out on me, would you, Sam?"

"She's the point," MacMurdo said, standing back and surveying the front of the whole house. "For me she's the bait to lure Manfred Moller into the open. For you she is what she is. And she ain't no secret no more, no how." He applied another match to his pipe.

"So where did your security fall apart, Sambo?"

"Damned if I know." He didn't seem to take offense. "Could be anyplace; nothin' I can do about it now. What bites my behind is *who* . . . who are these people that come here with grenades and start killing my people? No palaver, no bargaining, no talk about swaps—who are they?"

They went into the study and stared into the space between them, warming themselves before the fire.

"Well, pard," MacMurdo said at last, "it could be some folks who hate Nazis and want to take some scalps. People who believe the government is working with Nazis—oh, hell, there are such folks, believe me. Then there are the Nazis themselves who wanted to *rescue* Karin and Rolf. . . . For all we know, this could be Manfred's work . . . or Vulkan's—"

"But how could they know? Any of them?"

"Listen, you can't trust anybody anymore. Somebody on my team, somebody in Washington." He shrugged the massive shoulders. "Hell, we don't even have a clue as to Vulkan's identity—could be anybody." "Who knows? We gotta forget all this. From now on, our plans stay with us. Inner-circle stuff, okay?"

"You don't have to tell me. I don't talk—"

"You told Winchell—"

"Look, I'm trying to do a job. For you. So don't start with me—"

"Lew, Lew, I'm just sayin' the walls have ears, that's all. You don't have to get your game face on with me. Now, listen up, there's another possible group who could've pulled last night on us. The Nazis who want Karin and Rolf to lead them to Manfred, the goddamn thingummy, the minotaur, the treasure . . ."

"Or maybe the Radio City Rockettes," Cassidy said.

MacMurdo's laugh rocketed off the portraits of the robber barons. "You can say that again, pard! The Rockettes!"

• • •

There was another explosion of sorts over tea in the late afternoon. Later on MacMurdo called it a "real teacup rattler" but it wasn't so funny at the time. Everyone was on edge and it didn't take much to light the fuse.

When Rolf brought Karin down for tea in the formal parlor she seemed to look at, then through, him, as if the time in his apartment had never happened, as if she'd never remembered standing by the ocean liner or the Christmas tree under the Washington Square archway. She spoke only when addressed directly and then her voice was soft and toneless. She ate some cakes mechanically, sipped her tea, stared at her cup. Rolf Moller was nervous, his comments clipped, terse. When Karin declined a second cup of tea he spoke to her; she nodded, rose, and took his arm. A shade unsteadily she left the room with him. Cassidy went to the doorway and watched them ascend the stairs. He turned back to MacMurdo. "She's doped. He's given her something."

"Keep your shirt on, pard. He's the doctor."

"I don't trust the son of a bitch."

When Rolf Moller returned to the parlor and poured himself more tea, Cassidy glared at him. "You might tell me, Doctor, what's the point of keeping her shot up like a zombie?"

Moller stirred his tea, the spoon clinking steadily, for a long time. He was wearing his brown suit and tie, neat as a pin. He slowly fixed his gaze on Cassidy, pursing his lips. He blinked behind the flat round spectacles. "She is in a very delicate state. Excitement of the sort we had last night could crush her. Like an eggshell. A simple sedative will keep her calm."

"Calm? She's dead on her feet—"

"Tell me, Mr. Cassidy, am I now answerable to you? Are you dictating the care of my patient?" He stared at Cassidy over the rim of the bone-china cup.

"She's not about to break. She's a grown woman who's lost a chunk of memory. You don't have to turn her into a walking corpse!"

"I?" Moller spat out the monosyllable like Helmut Dantine in a movie, the rotten Nazi in a Times Square theater. "I? Turn her into a corpse?" He stood up. His cup tilted in its saucer, spilled steaming tea across the tablecloth. "You say this to me after last night? With you incompetent imbeciles guarding her life, I'd say her chances of survival decrease with each passing day! Your laughable security was breached with ease, two of your men murdered . . . very nearly all of us blown to bits. . . . Listen to me, my American friends—if our aim is to reunite Karin with my brother, to uncover this Göring escape route, to find this fabulous

Vulkan—who may or may not exist at all—I suggest you try to do it without killing Karin or destroying her mind. . . ." He was stalking about the room, lacking only a swagger stick to whip against his thigh. "And leave her medical care to me!" He snapped around on his heel and made one hell of an exit.

MacMurdo leaned back and bellowed: "Go fuck yourself, kraut bastard!" He glanced at Cassidy from the corner of his eye. "Guess that'll show him."

• • •

The broadcast ended. It was like pulling the plug on Winchell. He sagged in the chair, sweat stains spreading from his armpits. The network V.P. straightened the stack of yellow sheets. From the control room several other interested parties were filtering into the studio, fingering very sincere ties and shooting their cuffs. They stood around the star as if they'd been granted an audience. They were old hands at the New York sycophancy game, waiting for the star to notice them, waiting for him to validate their existences, waiting for him to break the sepulchral silence.

"The eddie," he said at last. "Whattya think? Was it Winchell?"

The V.P. said it was great, just great, and one of the ad men nodded enthusiastically, great, great, rubbing his little paws together.

Finally Winchell stood up and signaled for a playback of the broadcast. He paced, his face intent as he listened for the touch of Winchell in the night. He always said that he more than anyone else knew how Walter Winchell should sound. "Hell," Cassidy had heard him shout, "I invented the bastard!"

He nodded abruptly at the end of the playback. It was okay. As was his custom, he placed a call to his wife up at the estate. He didn't see her all that often and sex between them was a faint memory, but he depended on her judgment and approval. He never missed calling her once he'd survived another broadcast. He came back beaming. She'd liked the show. Standing in the middle of the studio he ceremoniously zipped his fly, buttoned his collar, cinched up his tie, and slipped into his blue serge suit coat. He winked at Cassidy. "You like the suit, kid? It's new."

He led the way into the V.P.'s office, shooed him out, and closed the door.

"Ratzis," he said. "I got some for you. Big party, charity-ball kind of thing. Sag Harbor. Now, pay attention, you mugs, here's the plan . . ."

• • •

Harry Madrid sat at the kitchen table, his elbows resting on the oilcloth covering, and finished off the thick roast-beef sandwich with mustard and onions. Tom Hayes, a retired Boston cop he'd known since the days of the Blackwood mob back in '22, reached over to the countertop and switched off the Philco.

"That Winchell, he's some talker, ain't he?"

"He's full of baloney," Harry Madrid said, patting his mouth with a napkin and reaching for the little pot of toothpicks. "Celebrity," he snorted. "Ten pounds of manure in a five-pound sack."

Hayes laughed and slurped up the last of the milky coffee in the saucer. Mary, his wife, was cleaning away the leftovers from the early afternoon Sunday dinner that had provided the hearty evening supper. "He may be full of baloney, Harry," she said, "but he helps remind us here in Tuggle, Maine, that there's another world out there. Movie stars and politicians, and gangsters and those Ratzis of his."

Harry made a sour face. "In the first place, my dear girl, the only world anyone needs is right here in Tuggle. And in the second place, the man Winchell is constructed primarily of baloney. Trust me on this one, Mary girl." He probed with his toothpick, sucked a filling.

"You're a professional nay-sayer, Harry." She wiped her hands on the flowered apron. "Your bark's one thing, your bite's another." She reached behind her and untied the apron strings. Watching her, the comfortable byplay between Mary and Tom Hayes, Harry Madrid wondered what might have happened if his own wife had lived, if the stomach cancer hadn't wasted her down to nothing and then taken her away. Maybe he'd have retired like Tom and gone off to some peaceful little burg like Tuggle and been a chief or even a deputy, done some hunting, listened to the radio with the wife and had a good laugh over Jack Benny and Fibber McGee and Molly and paid attention to Walter Winchell. Well, it was a pointless reflection, he supposed, because the cancer had taken her and Harry had fallen in with Cassidy who was all right and Terry Leary, of all people, who couldn't help being what he was. Good God, you never knew, you surely never did.

"Man to man, smoke Roi-tan." Hayes held out the box of cigars. "Let's take a walk, Harry. The wife likes me to do my smoking out of doors."

Harry Madrid went to the dining-room archway. Mary was sitting at the table cutting out a dress pattern. On the sideboard behind her was a silver-framed photograph of young Tom, Jr., in his navy uniform. He'd died years before, killed in the North Atlantic, killed on what they called "the Murmansk Run." Twenty-three years old and all that was left was his picture in the dining room, all the memories and sorrow his parents would never be through with. All because of the goddamn Ratzis. "Wonderful meal, Mary."

"You're not done yet," she said, clipping away. "Apple pie and Vermont Cheddar when you get back. Work up an appetite."

It was a crisp autumn evening. Dry leaves rustled underfoot, the tang of distant woodsmoke hung in the air. Tom Hayes's Labrador ran ahead barking desultorily at the rolling leaves. The moon was nearly full, the night sky clear for the first time in several days. The cheap cigar smoke was harsher than Leary's cache of Max Bauman's Havanas but there was something in it Harry Madrid preferred, quite possibly the stirring of youthful memories, a simpler world. Looking around the darkened streets of the small town that had somehow been hollowed out of the surrounding forests, Harry Madrid felt like a foreigner on some kind of rustic moon. He wore his long black overcoat and a handsome derby he'd bought on the Lower East Side in 1919. He looked at Tom Hayes ambling along in his black-and-red wool plaid jacket with a hunting cap to match. "My Christ, Tommy, look at you! You've gone native!"

"So what? I'm gonna live forever, too. It's healthy country, Harry. Some day, you pack it in, you oughta think about coming up here. Buy a nice little spread, five grand."

"Well, I've never had a notion I'd live forever. Then when I lost the wife . . ." He shrugged. "I didn't much care what happened anymore. I've got to give Terry Leary credit—"

"Never thought I'd hear you say that. That boy used to be a thorn in your paw."

"Well, sometimes people change."

Hayes laughed softly. "That's for sure. Question is, you do the changing or did Leary?"

"Both of us, I guess. The kid gave me an interest in life again, and if you laugh you'll be eatin' that cigar, Tom."

"I ain't laughing, Harry."

"Cassidy, now he's what you'd have to call a peculiar sort of fella. Guts of a burglar. But he's been hurt down deep inside. Hurt bad, like a man who's been gut-shot. He's had some bad luck with women. I never had much to do with women. Never really got the hang of what the hell they thought was going on. I knew they were in there thinking, but none of it ever really made any sense to me, not so far as I could tell, anyway. The wife, God rest her soul, was as bad as any."

"Well, y'know what they say." Tom Hayes inspected the glowing tip of his cigar. "You can't live with 'em, you can't shoot 'em."

They walked on in companionable silence. The smell of the forest, the damp dark earth, the leaves; Harry Madrid rather missed the stink and roar trapped in the dark Manhattan alleyways where sun was unknown.

"I finally got hold of the fella I was telling you about, Harry."

"That's good work, Tom. Where is he?"

"That's his place up ahead. Little bungalow up there. He's gonna show you on his map right about where he heard the crash. It was night, y'see, he was camping out—poaching, to be blunt—and the Guv'nor takes a dim view of trespassing and such like. Fella's name is Seth Marson.

Poacher from way back. Well, he naturally didn't want to come forth and risk the wrath of the Guv'nor. But you know how it is, Harry, small town, I put the word out there might be something in it for him—"

"What's fair?"

"Up here? Fifty simoleons."

"I'll make it a hunnert."

"You'll spoil my sources," Tom Hayes said.

"Well, I may need him to do some guide work."

"I'll be doing the guiding, Harry. Seth don't want no part of this after he talks to you."

They turned in at Seth Marson's gate. The wind was whipping at the crisp leaves, Hayes's Lab dashing on ahead, tongue flapping, looking for something to retrieve.

# Chapter Eight

It was Claire Benn's party, she being the more charitably inclined of the couple, but the house at Sag Harbor had been in Liddell Benn's family for enough years to make them—and it—handsomely decorative details of the Long Island power-structure façade. The road was narrow, constantly winding among birches and elms that had pushed to the paving's edge and seemed ready to march across to meet their fellows. They brushed and scraped at the sides of Terry Leary's cream-colored Chrysler sedan.

Boulders two stories high and somewhat smaller security guards in smartly creased black uniforms flanked the gated entrance to the Benn estate. Far up the driveway a white house with plenty of white columns sat in a glow of self-satisfaction that threw shadows at the groves of oaks and elms and maples surrounding it. Halfway up the drive you could hear the music, Jerome Kern, Cole Porter, Vernon Duke, heavy on the strings, muted brass; in the shadows on the side lawn the caterer's trucks sat quietly, the drivers smoking, laughing among themselves.

Leary pulled up before the columns and one of the mess-jacketed kids ran over to open the doors and park the car. Karin looked pale and beautiful as she stepped from the car. Cassidy had questioned the wisdom of dragging her into the evening's strategy but Winchell had stopped him, said that Karl Dauner was the heart of the Nazi end of things: he, or his friends, would want some proof that Cassidy's side had a blue chip to bring to the table.

An hour later Cassidy reflected that she had never been more beautiful; painfully, soulfully beautiful. He stood near the doorway to the billiards room with its heavy oak doors and watched her across acres of Italian marble, lit by the pink glow of the candles caressing the peach marble columns. She wore a simple low-cut black dress, her breasts full and firmly rounded, the gown strapless and well off the shoulder, a pearl choker, her hair thick and tawny and unadorned. She was dancing with Terry Leary, her eyes downcast. Terry was staring into her face, as if he were searching for some hint of the past, or at least a hint of her memory of it. Terry had told him that there was something about her that didn't ring true for him. "She either remembers and isn't telling you," he'd said, "or she's holding back something else. . . . I don't know if it's Manfred Moller on her mind, or you, but there's more going on in there than the good doctor thinks there is." Now Leary seemed to be seeking a hint. From the looks of things, he wasn't finding it.

The band was playing on a balcony over the foyer that swept away into the ballroom. The women were in ball gowns and the men in full evening kit, most in white tie and tails. The evening's scam seemed to center around an auction of objets d'art, the proceeds for the benefit of European War Refugee Relief. Liddell and Claire Benn had lent their humble residence for the venue. Winchell had assured Cassidy that no one could have been straighter politically than the Benns. Liddell, Winchell said, would have shit a gold brick the size of Fire Island if he'd known that his pal Karl Dauner was a Nazi. "So for chrissakes, don't tell him, keed. Ignorance is bliss," Winchell had smirked. "The dumb fucker!"

"You coming to the party, Winch?" Cassidy had wondered.

"You never know," Winchell replied. "As you should know, Winchell is ubiquitous, he knows all, sees all, and tells Mr. and Mrs. America what they need to know. Benn has been informed that he's to make sure you get a chance to have a chat with Dauner. And remember, Benn thinks Dauner is as big a horse's ass of a Republican as he is!"

The music was just swell and the lobster thermidor and the beef Wellington hit the spot. European War Refugees would doubtless have enjoyed the spread but there didn't seem to be any on the guest list. The champagne flowed like champagne, Bollinger by the truckload, and the punch filled a Medici fountain. The house was full of good spirits, toasts to the victors, and twenty or thirty works of art—paintings and Russian eggs and bits of sculpture and even an illuminated manuscript or two—but Cassidy kept worrying about Karin. She was still on Dr. Moller's sedatives. She was reacting in a kind of slow motion as if she weren't quite getting the jokes. Her eyes had a film over them. She moved hesitantly, as if she weren't sure of her footing. She was only registering the general outlines of the scene and Cassidy wondered if she'd remember she'd been dancing at the ball. She floated on the dance floor like an angel, unaware, soft in his arms. But, the drugs aside, he wondered how fragile she really was, how much her mind could handle if the memory of the bombing of Cologne came swirling back at her from the booby-trapped past.

Would it crush her like Dr. Moller's threatened eggshell?

Cassidy thought the doctor might be selling her short: the Karin that Cassidy had married could have handled it, could have handled anything—but this Karin, wounded and scared, how could you be sure? Which Karin was he holding against him as they danced? The delicate shell that might crack or the resourceful woman, who had turned up at his apartment and begun seeing flashes of the past, *their* past?

Looking down at her as they danced—the shine in her hair, the faint smile, the curl at the corners of her mouth, Cassidy knew the answer to the questions Terry and Winchell had asked.

Cassidy knew he wanted her. He wanted her back, he loved her as he'd loved her before. She could fill the empty center of his life. He loved her . . . didn't he?

If she could survive the reconstruction of her memory, wouldn't she then be *his* Karin again? He'd never know until she'd recovered what was gone.

How to do it? That was going to be the hard part. What would it take to see her through that dark passage, to the safety on the other side where, almost as another man, he saw himself waiting for her?

• • •

The band had struck up "You Do Something to Me." Cassidy, watching Karin again from across the room, decided he was tiptoeing dangerously near the rim of obsession. It was time to stop watching Karin and pay attention to business. In the end, there was only one way to get her back, and that involved paying attention to business. It always came back to that.

Liddell Benn materialized at his side, bald and mustachioed, smelling of perfumed wax. "Enjoying yourself, Mr. Cassidy?"

"Enjoying the scenery," Cassidy said.

"You refer to the ladies? Yes. Remarkably beautiful women seem determined to do their bit for the survivors of the recent war. Well, damn me if I don't say it's a good thing!"

"How true."

"Take my father. A racing man. He'd have been glad the war was over. He'd have headed back for the English racing, the French season. He was a great admirer of horse flesh, doncha know? You didn't know Dad by any chance, did you? Short man, fancied rather boisterous hacking jackets—"

"No, I didn't know Dad."

"Well, let me tell you," Benn said, surveying the crowd, "I prefer mounting another kind of filly—that's where Dad and I differed!" His white eyebrows shot up. He made a face of surprise at this moment of confidence-sharing. He smoothed his white mustache with a bony knuckle. "Haw, haw," he said, "haw, haw. Now that filly you brought. Damn fine conformation, seems to me. Good breeding."

"You should take a gander at her teeth."

"Deep chest, good wind. A stayer." He sounded as if he might saddle her up at any moment. Or go on this way forever.

A waiter with a tray of champagne came floating past and Cassidy took two glasses. He handed one to Benn, said: "To all the fine and brave refugees."

The host nodded but amended the toast: "And to all the fine womanhood in support of wogs, kikes, frogs, bohunks, spics, wops, and assorted whatnot!"

They drank and Benn licked the fringe of his mustache. "Seems to me I was supposed to introduce you to someone. Ring any bells with you, Cassidy?"

"Why, yes, I believe it does."

"Now, Mr. Winchell told me I wasn't to let on, just arrange it. Said it was something to do with the national interest. Do you think that could be true? Damn me, but he's a wonderful man. Great humanitarian!"

"Winchell?"

"Winchell? God no, he's a jumped-up little git, a twister, to my way of thinking. No, no, I have reference to Karl Dauner—name just came to me. One of the unsung heroes of the war—"

"Just the way he wants it, I'm sure."

"A great man. Backbone of the country, let's face it."

"Without a doubt."

"Do I detect a note of sarcasm, young fella?"

"I don't even know the man."

"Sarcasm is for the birds, Mr. Cassidy. Well, come along into the billiards room, come along."

The billiards room was oak-paneled, wore an exhausted Persian rug, heavy brocade draperies, a couple of portraits of long-ago Benns with villainous eyes. Art-wise the rest of the room was strictly horses. There were a well-stocked liquor cabinet and wall sconces and several high chairs so you could watch the action on the table if it got too exciting to ignore.

Karl Dauner was tall and thin, a hawk-nosed aristocratic old party with a better tailor than anyone should be able to afford. He was playing what

Cassidy would call pool and Benn would inevitably refer to as pocket billiards. He had an elegant soft stroke, no flourishes, no frills, just the balls kissing one another with a kind of Zen delicacy, just hard enough to propel them off the edge. That would be his style. Just enough force to get the job done with the least amount of fuss.

He was probably only sixty but so spare he looked older. His face was deeply lined, as if chiseled out of some unyielding stone that would chip but not carve. He had an ageless look in his eyes and a stance that made you think of somebody who'd been standing on a pedestal in the park since the end of the War Between the States. His face was long and rectangular and thin and he wore a hearing aid, the wire stretching from behind his ear to the battery pack in the breast pocket of his dinner jacket. It was a common accessory among men who'd been in the trenches thirty years before. He slowly, methodically, ran six balls while Benn and Cassidy watched. The band was playing "Isn't It Romantic?" and the draperies were thrown back, the windows open to the faint breeze. The room was full of blue cigar smoke but nearly empty of human habitation, just Dauner and another man with a cue and a vaguely familiar face.

His run having emptied the table, Dauner looked up and smiled at Benn. The balls were clicking as the other man emptied the pockets. Benn introduced them while Dauner's eyes played across their mouths, as if he were lip-reading as well, not entirely trusting his hearing aid. "Mr. Cassidy," he said, "it is indeed a great pleasure to meet you. I had a season box in the old days at the Polo Grounds. I saw you play there. Business kept me away on that ill-fated day that will live in infamy . . . but I was sorely distressed at the way your career ended." He had a way of talking, as if he were listening for the echo from the box in his breast pocket. It gave him a slightly quizzical expression every few words. He might have been hearing Fred Allen doing his best material on that little box.

"Roughly a thousand years ago," Cassidy said.

"I'm sure it must seem so to you," Dauner said.

Liddell Benn interrupted: "Karl, we're counting on your interest in the choice little Tiepolo? Is that the one? Well, you know the one I mean—if it isn't a picture of a horse, I don't know one from another."

"My dear Helena will be handling the bidding, Del. She has no sense of economy, I'm afraid—"

"Which will be wonderful for the refugees," Benn said.

"The refugees," Dauner mused, "the storm-tossed, they are always with us."

They were standing near the drinks table. Dauner splashed some extra soda into his scotch. The other man with a cue had sunk two balls, then missed one badly, and muttered something in a language Cassidy had never heard before. Benn turned to him, introduced him to Cassidy.

"Jaroslav Harkavy, the Rumanian pianist," Benn said. "One of our most honored refugees . . . Lewis Cassidy. Jaroslav is giving a recital at Town Hall on Friday." Harkavy bowed from the waist, without offering his hand. He wore a patchy beard and heavy glasses that slipped down his nose every time he leaned over to take a shot.

Benn and Harkavy left the room speaking of Michelangelo and Cassidy stood watching Dauner line up a shot of his own while he went on chatting casually. "Are you a lover of art, Mr. Cassidy? Or simply one who wishes these poor victims of war well?"

"When it comes to art, I'm one of those people who knows what he hates. If it looks to me like a bull terrier could paint it with a nose and two paws, I say the hell with it."

"Aha, a traditionalist. Good. I'm with you there. I prefer traditional representational pictures. That is, people who look like people and so on. There is so much lying in the world, why should art lie to us, as well? Paint what you see, that's my view. Helena is a fan of this modern stuff, Picasso and Braque, Rothko and Pollock and so on, it's quite beyond an old-fashioned fellow like me." Three ball in the corner. Potted like a sitting duck. "Dali. Fellow with all the melting pocket watches . . . can't make heads nor tails of it. A Freudian nightmare." Seven ball in the side. Leaving himself the six in the other side.

Cassidy said: "My interest tends more to sculpture."

"Does it really? Classical? Modern? Or American, perhaps, Remington, all those bucking broncos—rather nice. I believe our host owns a lovely Remington or two." The six fell right on schedule.

"I'm more often drawn to the—oh, let's say the eccentric, the unusual."

"You don't say. Country pleasures, that sort of thing?"

"Pardon?"

"Erotica, the risqué stuff. Always a seller's market."

"Try mythological," Cassidy said.

"Mythological. How extraordinarily interesting. You do surprise me, Mr. Cassidy." Eight ball in the far corner. "My wife would find this fascinating. I'd greatly enjoy seeing your collection. Just what sort of thing, may I inquire?" Four in the side, two rails, a very nice shot. Dainty, but firm.

"Well, I'm on the trail of a piece right now, a very special piece. An acquisition I have in mind. It's a rather curious story—one of those bits and pieces of wartime rumor. I've been given to understand that a very mysterious piece has turned up here in the United States. Frankly, between the two of us, it is more than likely that it's been smuggled in from Europe in the last few months."

"Are you saying it's Nazi loot?" Dauner was lining up the nine ball.

"Possibly. Probably."

"Then I'd be very careful if I were you, Mr. Cassidy."

"Oh, you know how it is, the collecting mania. You find yourself hot on the scent and common sense goes out the window."

Dauner pocketed the nine ball with an utter economy of motion. He stood up and chalked his cue. "You must have some fascinating sources. May I ask, just what is this mythical piece?"

"Oh, it's real enough. Not mythical at all."

"Aha, point to you! But tell me, what is it?"

"Just between the two of us?"

"But, of course, Mr. Cassidy! Discretion is imperative in the art world."

"It's a minotaur."

"A minotaur," Dauner mused. "Of all things. Do you know the provenance?"

"In outline. Apparently it was sculpted by an unknown Italian—it was the patron who mattered. The Mad King of Bavaria. Ludwig. From one of Ludwig's own drawings. You can imagine how odd a piece it is. . . . I have a passion to see it, hold it, own it. You understand."

Dauner bent over the table, caressed the ten ball the length of the table where it hung, teetering, then plopped into the leather pocket. "It sounds like a tremendously esoteric work. Is it any good? What's it made of?"

"Solid gold. Completely encrusted with precious stones—"

Dauner smiled.

"Its value is nearly incalculable. So I admit that my interest is not solely in the minotaur as a work of art."

Dauner stood looking across the lush green table. "Are you quite sure such a thing exists? It sounds more and more mythical—more and more unlikely. The stuff that dreams are made of, as the man said. If I may say so. Who possessed it last?"

"Reichsmarshal Göring."

Dauner laughed sharply, shook his head. "Well, you are quite the boy, Mr. Cassidy. Quite the lad. You amaze me, by God, you do! I'm not at all sure we're not breaking the law by just having this discussion."

"Well, what's a little rupture of the law when you're talking about something like Ludwig's Minotaur? Göring's minotaur! As I've made my way through life, I've learned that certain risks plainly justify themselves. This just happens to be such a risk. Men have died for this piece."

"When men have died for something," Dauner said, "it almost always means that more men will die for it. But tell me, how much is this thing worth? Quite frankly, it's certainly out of my league."

"Oh," Cassidy said, spreading his hands in an all-inclusive gesture, "would anyone be rash enough to set a price? It's invaluable—no point in discussing it in terms of money. No, money has nothing to do with it."

"I don't follow you."

"I am prepared to offer something in trade."

Dauner's smile clung manfully to his long, lined face. He carefully replaced his cue in the wall rack. "You must have something of inestimable value, Mr. Cassidy."

"Oh, I do, I do."

"I congratulate you, then. I can hardly imagine what such an item might be."

"It's not a work of art," Cassidy said. "You might say it's more of a service I can perform for the man who holds the minotaur now."

"Indeed? Well, I say it again, you are a fascinating chap. It's indisputable. But . . . a service?" He laughed in a doubting, comradely way. "I enjoy your company, Mr. Cassidy. Perhaps you and your friends would like to see some of my collection." He turned, one finger to his mouth as if he'd just thought of something wondrously clever. "Also, I have a private source of my own, a dealer with the most amazing way of finding things—"

"Might he know about the man with the minotaur?"

"Who knows? But if you wish, we could inquire of him about this minotaur you have on your mind. I'd enjoy the opportunity of bringing you together, you and my friend and the minotaur. Why don't you and your party come by my home once this is over? However, you must excuse me for the moment, I must watch over the checkbook while my wife buys a Tiepolo." He was consulting a gold pocket watch on a gold chain. "Shall we say eleven o'clock? We're only a couple of miles from here." He jotted down directions.

"Very kind of you," Cassidy said.

"There's nothing more satisfying than bringing people together. And your minotaur problem, well, I can't resist. Tell me, Mr. Cassidy, since your minotaur seems to have had a busy war—did you see any service abroad?"

"My leg kept me out. A million-dollar wound, you might say. How did you spend the war, Mr. Dauner?"

"Oh, I tried to do my bit in Washington."

"You're too modest. You were one of the dollar-a-year men, weren't you?"

"That's what they called us." He chuckled in a self-deprecating way. "I'd say most of us were overpaid. But I did find my share of fighting in the Great War. Thirty years ago."

"Who were you fighting for?"

"Ah, you have a blunt way with a question! In those days I was a German, one of the dreaded Boche, the Hun." He shrugged as if to say, Can you believe such a thing? "Did my time in the trenches. Young, idealistic, fighting for the Fatherland, that was how I marched off to war. I came back older than my years, cynical about mankind, fighting strictly to survive. I couldn't sleep for years . . . I heard noises, artillery shells exploding in my head." He took a cigarette from a box on the table and lit it, tasting it reflectively. "To be a German in 1918 was to have a dim future at best. I was thirty. I became Swiss. It was better to be Swiss. Forged papers, bribes, an unhappy business but a necessity. I was a lawyer, banker, ski instructor—I always believed it was wise to stay near the money. Being Swiss made a good life. But I became an American citizen in 1926. So much for my vita, Mr. Cassidy." He was smoking, smiling tolerantly, a man with all the answers. "I have nothing to hide, you see."

"You certainly seem to know a winner when you see one."

"I learned the hardest possible way. I've certainly done what I could to aid my adopted country. A convert is always a zealot. Don't you find that the case?"

"If I ever convert to anything I'll let you know."

"Eleven o'clock then?"

"Bank on it," Cassidy said.

# CHAPTER NINE

For the first mile there was a lot of traffic on the narrow road, guests emptying out of the Benns' driveway. Terry Leary drove carefully. Karin sat between them, half asleep, her head resting on Cassidy's shoulder. The champagne mixed with the sedatives hadn't done her any good. Cassidy stroked her forehead, brushed the hair back from her eyes, felt the ridge of scar tissue just past the hairline. He squeezed her tightly against him.

"Is Dauner our man Vulkan?" Terry kept his eyes on the taillights ahead.

"Looks like a helluva candidate to me. He's a confident bastard, I'll give him that."

"Did he sit up and take notice when you dragged out Ludwig and his minotaur?"

"Rolled over and stuck his paws in the air."

Traffic began to thin out after the first major turnoff but Leary didn't speed up. "I'm a little worried about Sleepy here," he said.

Cassidy leaned down and kissed her forehead. "Ready for Act Two?"

She opened one eye. "Where are we going?"

"Fella's house. We're going to talk about statues."

She struggled to swallow. Her throat was dry. "Will . . . will Manfred be there?"

"No. But that's what we're working on. We're trying to find him."

She clutched his hand, nails digging into his flesh. A look of atavistic fear crossed her face, lingered in her familiar eyes, as if she were back in the nightmare, the bombs raining from the smoky sky. Terry Leary's head was half turned, watching her, then the road.

Cassidy stared into her eyes. "Karin, Karin, calm down. Everything will be all right—"

She interrupted, whispering insistently. "You've got to tell me." He could just barely hear her. "Do I know you from before?" She swallowed again, licked her lips. The sedative and champagne had dried her out. "Please . . . if I did, then you're part of the past . . . part of my life. One of the secrets I can't get to . . ."

"Is she okay, amigo?"

Cassidy put his mouth to her ear. "Yes," he said, whispering into the delicate shell. "You know me from before. We met years ago, at the Olympics. You were skating. So beautiful I just stood there with my mouth open."

"The Olympics." He thought that was what she said but he might have imagined it. She might have just been breathing.

Leary put on the brakes and made ready to turn. "Looks like we're here, ladies and germs."

• • •

Karl Dauner met them at the front door of the vast brick building with its pristine white trim and neatly clipped hedges. He came outside still in his evening clothes, a black cape draped over his square shoulders. With his long face and piercing eyes he was giving a passable impression of Dracula. "My wife," he said, "is having some friends in for a nightcap. I've asked my art dealer friend to join us down at the tennis courts where we can speak privately." His eyes moved slowly from Cassidy to Leary to Karin. "Perhaps your young lady would prefer to join my wife?"

"Miss Richter," Cassidy said. "And Mr. Leary. This is Karl Dauner."

Dauner's gaze stuck for a moment on Karin. "I beg your pardon?"

"Miss Richter," Cassidy repeated. "Karin Richter." Cassidy turned to her with a smile, took her arm. "No, she'll come with us."

Dauner took her free hand, bent over it and brushed it with his lips. He was the kind of man who could get away with it and not look like a road-company ham. "I am enchanted, Miss Richter. Your face has haunted me all evening. I feel almost as if we've met somewhere. . . ."

"I think not," she said.

"Wishful thinking, no doubt." He pulled the coat tighter and led the way around the corner of the house. "This way, then." He slipped her free arm through his. "Watch your step here, my dear. This can be dangerous in the dark."

The lawn sloped down toward a lily pond bordered by stones and dark conical shapes, trimmed evergreens. The wind ran like ghosts among the trees, carrying a wet chill. The gardeners had been at work. There were several teepee-shaped mountains of leaves dotting the lawn.

The tennis courts turned out to be enclosed, in a huge looming structure, like a gymnasium or hangar made of glass. A very high greenhouse. Karin moved against Cassidy, shivering. Terry Leary brought up the rear, constantly looking deep into the darkness, the dark whispering shadows. Cassidy felt the weight of the .38 in the shoulder holster rubbing against his ribs.

Dauner opened the door, which seemed like a tiny cave entrance beneath the mountain of glass. They followed him inside.

The air seemed to swirl, a tiny cyclone surging past them and out the door, and they were overwhelmed by the smell of cooped-up clay, stale air, and old summer sweat. It was like the secret hangar, the mysterious airfield, in a boys' story of adventure. It was colder than it had been outside, like walking into a crypt.

Dauner snapped on one set of lightbulbs, enclosed in dangling wire cages that swayed slowly, shadows moving. The net was still up. A couple of racquets lay discarded on the scuffed clay. It felt like walking into one of the vast mausoleums of the rich, an elephants' graveyard, the deepest recesses of King Tut's tomb. Cassidy stopped, drew Karin closer still. Leary settled into a comfortable slouch, leaning against the door frame. Slowly he bounced a stray gray tennis ball on the clay before him.

Dauner sniffed the dead air. "I've never been out here in the middle of the night before. Ominous, isn't it? Well, we won't worry about that."

"Where's your friend?" Cassidy shifted uneasily. Dauner was right. It was ominous and dark and scary. The perfect place for an ambush.

Dauner produced a cigarette case and offered it around. There were no takers. He walked back across the court, kicked a loose ball into the darkness, and stood in the doorway looking out toward the house with its welcoming glow of lights. "Here he comes now. Felix," he called, "so terribly kind of you to come."

A short, roly-poly man stood puffing in the doorway.

"Mr. Cassidy," Dauner said, "this is Mr. Heinz Felix. Late of Berlin, in the old days. Now a dealer of some repute in New York, Palm Beach, Los Angeles, and Zurich." He introduced him to Leary and Karin.

Heinz Felix blew tiny bubbles of saliva as he nodded, panting, his fat little mouth making a solemn little smile. He was florid, probably in his forties, wore a huge gold signet ring. His face was puffy and blotched. He was perspiring heavily and his collar had wilted. His long hair was plastered against his round skull, curled over the damp, bedraggled collar. His tie, flowered, bore traces of a recent dinner. He looked like a character actor, or somebody from the pages of Dickens. When he extended his hand Cassidy felt as if he'd been offered a plate of fat, wet sausages.

"I got here as quickly as I could, Karl. Not much notice." He wheezed slightly, like a man with asthma. "This is the man?"

"Indeed."

Felix looked up at Cassidy, his rubbery lips working against themselves while he thought how to begin. "I understand that you are interested in a minotaur, a very special minotaur." He had a thick German accent that made him sound very scholarly.

"Look, gentlemen," Cassidy said, "why don't we just cut to the chase here? It's late and we would all like to know what's going on. Why do you think I came to you two guys? I know exactly what you are—do you understand? Exactly." Felix stiffened, cast an anxious glance at Dauner, a faithful, frightened hound and his master. "I have no interest in politics, yours or mine or anyone else's, so there's no need to pussyfoot around the bog. You guys may be the two biggest patriots since George and Martha Washington or you may have Hitler and Eva Braun stashed in the basement—it's no concern of mine. I want the Ludwig Minotaur. Göring's minotaur. I'm a simple victim of the collector's obsession."

Dauner folded his arms across his chest, chuckled softly. "I'm not altogether sure that I trust you, Mr. Cassidy. Delightful fellow and all, disarming—but I guard my trust most jealously."

"Well, unless you've got the minotaur, I couldn't care less. In fact, I'll do you one better—I don't trust anyone at all. Ever. I just want the minotaur. . . . I know *who* brought it to this country and it turns out that I have something he wants—"

"I'm quite baffled by everything you say," Dauner observed, "but for the sake of argument perhaps you could tell us what you have that he wants, this trade you seem to propose—would that be possible, Mr. Cassidy?"

"His wife. I have his wife." She shrank against him for an instant, then steadied herself.

Dauner cocked his head as if needing to make sure that his hearing aid had not deceived him. "Do tell, do tell. Well, I should think he'd be very interested, indeed. . . . Whoever this man may be. If, in fact, he exists at all—then, of course, he might try to acquire his wife and keep the blessed minotaur. As I say, if such a man and such a minotaur exist—"

"Well, my friend, if your chums haven't told you about this man and his treasure, I'd say you've been rather left out of things."

"And I would advise you, Mr. Cassidy, to watch your step." The tolerant smile had begun to fade.

"How good of you, how kind." Cassidy turned to the fat man, who was wiping his face with a crumpled white handkerchief. "Now, Mr. Felix, if you can get yourself dried off and pay attention, you might tell me where I can find this minotaur or I can get the hell out of here and stop wasting time."

Felix was trembling, turned on Dauner. "Karl, you fool—this man, this *person*, he knows everything, he *knows* . . . the Göring minotaur . . ." He was beginning to babble, words tumbling over one another. "The escape route, the money, he knows . . ." He stared off into the emptiness of the tennis court.

"Calm yourself, Felix." Dauner made a face of distaste, waving his hand before him. "Pull yourself together, old man."

"No need to quarrel, lads." Cassidy smiled, a peacemaker. "Because the wife of Manfred Moller is not all I have to offer—"

"He knows, he knows!" The fat man's explosion of words was almost involuntary. "He knows about Moller . . . it's a trick, he's made a fool of you—"

"Be quiet!" Dauner looked at Cassidy through the veil of smoke. "What else are you offering?"

"In addition to Frau Moller I also have my pledge of silence . . . in exchange for the minotaur."

Dauner turned his back, walked a few strides away, into the tennis court. "This is a very, very dangerous game you've chosen to play—"

"You're the one in danger," Cassidy said. "You're the Nazi."

Dauner turned to look at him. For an instant, Cassidy feared a bullet, but Dauner was still, his gloved hands holding the coat together. He exhaled, made a cloud of smoke, the cigarette stuck to his lip. Cassidy had had about enough.

"Now, where's the minotaur?"

"Do you actually want the minotaur, Mr. Cassidy? Or are you in fact looking for this Manfred Moller you've mentioned?"

"Believe me, it doesn't make any difference in the world to you."

"Perhaps I can be of no help to you whatsoever." He shrugged. "What then?"

"I will kill you. Right now, on your own tennis court. Advantage to me."

"Oh, my God!" Felix threw up his hands.

"You may tell him, Felix."

"The piece," Felix panted, "the statue reposes in Boston. Ah, so I have been told. A man called Henry Brenneman . . . a dealer in antiquities of greatest value."

"You're sure we're talking about the same thing? So high, covered all over with rubies and diamonds and emeralds, that sort of thing?"

"I have never seen it."

"What's it doing in Boston?"

"Come, come, Mr. Cassidy," Dauner said. "Believe me, it doesn't make any difference in the world to you. Let us now turn to the matter of the woman, the wife . . . how can you assure us that you can deliver her?"

"Tell me, why should I prove anything to you? Are you acting for the present owner of the statue now?"

Dauner slid one hand from beneath the cape. It contained a Luger, black and shiny, reptilian. "Because I shall look very foolish in the eyes of the minotaur's present owner if—"

"Tell me, do you mean Moller? Or Vulkan?"

Felix's spotty cheeks were flushed with fright. "Vulkan . . . my God, Karl, kill him! Kill them all! They know everything. . . ." He seemed to totter at the edge of the abyss. For a long moment the only sound was the wind yelping at the chinks in the glass, nibbling at the structural skeleton.

Dauner stared at Felix. "Well, this *has* turned into an unpleasant evening. However, as I was saying, I need some proof of the lady's existence, our quid pro quo—"

Karin suddenly pulled free from Cassidy to face Dauner.

"I'm Frau Moller," she cried, her face pale, her fingers raking her hair away from her eyes. "I am, I am. . . . Where is my husband?" She bit at a bleached knuckle, turned between the two men, staring, then slumped back against Cassidy. "What game are you playing?" Her fingers worked at his lapel. "What's happening here . . . ? I'm Frau Moller. . . ." Her eyes pleaded with Cassidy again, in fear and sorrow and anger.

Dauner leaned forward, trying to hear. "What? What is she saying?"

Karin was clinging to Cassidy, all eyes fastened on her, when the sky fell in, a sky of broken glass and noise and rushing wind, pane after pane of glass exploding in a fusillade of bullets, tommy guns rattling in the night, slugs ripping into the support beams.

Karin screamed, stumbled backward.

Cassidy caught her, pushed her flat on the clay, covered her with his own body, fumbling to get his gun from the holster.

Felix dropped to his knees, his face melting with the heat of fear. Then he struggled to his feet, wobbling, and ran wildly across the court. Several slugs shredded his back, blowing chunks of him away into the darkness, and he plunged forward, into the net, hung suspended like a winner who'd miscalculated and failed in his leap.

Terry Leary was kneeling beside the door returning fire, his .38 a toy against the jittering fire of the tommy guns.

Karl Dauner had disappeared into the shadows.

Cassidy placed him when he saw him fire through the broken glass on the other side of the court. The attackers were firing in on them from both sides, glass filling the air like a deadly snowfall.

Something somewhere began to screech, metal on metal, a tearing, squealing sound. Voices were calling from the darkness outside. Cassidy sheltered Karin's body as best he could, looked around; what the hell was that noise?

The answer came with a rush.

Far above, Cassidy saw the framework holding the glass canopy start to twist. It seemed to have developed a will of its own, silhouetted against the moonlight, twisting, pulling, the metal crying out.

It began to collapse.

With all the glass below shot to pieces and the supports weakened the weight was too much. The roof was pulling apart. The tommy-gun fire had stopped and while the skeleton of the building tore itself to pieces the first glass panels from above began to rain down.

Cassidy grabbed Karin and rolled toward the end wall until they were huddled against it. When the roof finally collapsed the crash was deafening, long sabers of steel frame tearing loose, plummeting downward like a thousand javelins, driving home into the clay, broken glass in shattering, drifting clouds all across the tennis court.

There was a ghastly, ear-splitting scream.

Dauner had made a dash across the court, trying to get out before it all came tumbling down.

A six-foot section of framework had skewered him at the fault line where he lay screaming, twisting, struggling to pull the stake from his back. He reached behind him, spasmodically, trying to reach the metal, succeeding only in tearing the wound. Blood was pumping out, spraying a red rainbow over him, spraying across his hands. He lay ten feet from Cassidy, his life pooling around him on the clay, his dark eyes no longer shiny but round and dulled in a moment of terminal surprise. Then he seemed no longer to give a damn. His hands stopped fluttering.

Terry Leary, still crouched by the door, looked over at Cassidy and gave an elaborate comic shrug. "World War Three maybe? I tell ya, amigo, I'm gettin' old before my time."

Once the noise had blown away and the last fragments of glass had come to rest, Cassidy slid off Karin, who lay still, her hands covering her face. She was staring out from between her fingers.

"Where the hell is everybody?" Cassidy squinted through the dust at Leary.

As if in reply there was another crack, a pistol shot, and the bullet whined off the door frame. Then a rattle of machine-gun fire. There was no way out of this. Another spray of fire from the darkness chopped at the clay surface, grinding shards of glass to dust, plucking at the body of Karl Dauner.

The ensuing stillness, the soft whispers in the grass as the attackers came closer for the kill, was cracked open by the sound of an automobile engine, revving at high speed, racing, bumping across the lawn, the headlights picking out four men with guns advancing on the ruin of the tennis court.

A burst of gunfire came from the car and one of the men was blown ass over appetite into the lily pond.

The car exploded through one of the teepees of leaves, skidded wildly, sliding out of control on the grass, until it fetched up against the stones bordering the pond. The rear wheels spun, then caught, the car jerking forward. The machine gun in the car burped again and a man yelled, something in a language Cassidy couldn't understand, didn't recognize. Someone from the stand of birches returned fire and the windshield of the car went.

From the house came the sound of more shots. The lights went out.

The car turned, swept back toward the tennis courts, came slewing sideways toward the doorway where Leary stood, frozen, the gun in his hand.

"Come on, pards! We got 'em right where we want 'em!"

Sam MacMurdo, bad leg and all, leaped out of the passenger side, Thompson submachine gun in his hand.

Cassidy helped Karin to her feet. Leary was holding the rear door open.

"Better bring her, pard. They might have left one sleeper in the weeds. I think they just finished off everybody in the house."

"We've got two dead down here—"

"Dauner?"

"The proverbial doornail. Who are these people?"

"Same ones visited us the other night. Come on!"

In the car Cassidy got a look at the driver.

Walter Winchell was hunched over the wheel, holding on for dear life.

"Give her the gun, Winch," MacMurdo said.

"You're a goddamned brigand, Sam," Cassidy said.

MacMurdo laughed. "A highwayman. Bad Sam MacMurdo. Stand and deliver, you fuckers!"

Winchell gunned it up the slope. They burst through the shrubbery like a tank, leaped the curbing into the driveway. Ahead in the darkness, taillights were disappearing through the gates. Winchell, speechless for once, floored the accelerator and they took the corner on two wheels, taking one of the wooden gates with them, spinning it away into the darkness.

Winchell pulled the car out of the fishtailing swerve, floored it again. A gale was blowing where there had once been a windshield. Winchell's hat blew into the back seat and he swore. Karin huddled against Cassidy. She seemed to be disappearing into the nightmare, her face blank.

"There they are!" Winchell waved at the road.

MacMurdo rested the machine gun on the dashboard, the barrel jutting out through the windshield frame, the round magazine hanging below, and opened fire.

The car ahead swerved wildly across the narrow road. MacMurdo raked the road with fire and both rear tires went. They were closing now and MacMurdo gave it another burst.

The car spun out of control, bounced off a thick white birch, rolled back across the road, rolled over twice, bouncing like a toy, came to rest on its side. The hood had pulled away, lay on its back like a dying beetle. Steam blew skyward like a geyser, spewing from the radiator.

Slowly, painfully, a man appeared at the side window, levering himself up and out of the car. In the headlights his bearded face was streaming blood. The beard was long and black, matted with blood. He yelled something, that same language that meant nothing to Cassidy. MacMurdo held his fire.

Halfway out the window the man brought his right hand out, leveled the machine gun at them.

MacMurdo eased off a short burst and the man jerked sideways. The gun clattered onto the road. The man's arm flexed upward, then fell back, leaving him hanging awkwardly, a broken doll.

Another man who had crawled through the broken windshield made a staggering, tripping dash across the road, trying to fade into the underbrush and the trees.

MacMurdo swiveled, fired again as if he were an efficient killing machine, the gun an extension of himself. Suddenly the firing stopped and he swore. The gun had jammed. He was struggling with it.

His quarry turned, stepped back out of the shadows, blinking in the bright light, his eyes shining red with the reflection like a wounded, crazed animal about to be steamrollered by his fate. He seemed to gather his strength, then charged them, his tommy gun sputtering, slugs firing wild.

MacMurdo swore at his gun.

Leary's view was blocked from where he sat and time was running out.

Cassidy shifted Karin's weight, opened the door, and stepped outside. He knew it was all going very fast but it was desperately slow in his mind.

He took the .38 from his holster and waited until the man was close enough.

It was a face he knew.

The pianist from the billiards room.

Harkavy.

He was playing at Town Hall on Friday night. But right now he was trying to get the gun level as he ran forward. His face was contorted with hatred.

"Nazis!" He kept screaming at them.

Cassidy raised the .38 and dropped him where he stood.

Cancel the performance.

# Chapter Ten

It took the train forever to struggle free from the muck of the city. It was afternoon and Cassidy was headed for Boston.

The sky was gray, the window was grimy and misty, the view desolate. The guy across the aisle had a Motorola portable radio, very snappy in brown leatherette with a Bakelite pop-up handle. He was trying to get the Cubs and the Tigers in the World Series. The broadcast was fading in and out and it was going to fade in and out with lots of static all afternoon. The radio just couldn't make sense of all the metal in the club car and the constantly moving location. Virgil Trucks was pitching for Detroit and Cassidy was damned if he could hear who was going for the Cubs. It was driving him crazy.

Everything was driving him crazy.

He didn't really want to keep going over it all but he couldn't get his mind onto much of anything else. He was still shaken by the events of the previous night. They were all lucky to be alive and none of it had made any sense at the time.

• • •

In the aftermath Karin was a wreck, yet trying so hard to be brave. When they'd driven away from the devastation on the lonely country road, as if putting it out of sight might clear up the mess, Winchell had refused to give up the wheel. He'd jammed his hat back on his head and driven back to the Dauner estate where Leary, Cassidy, and Karin had transferred to Leary's car for the drive back to Westchester.

Rolf Moller took one look at Karin, heard the story, and blew a succession of fuses. He was desperately worried about her mental state, her fugue state, the danger of shock opening her head like a Pandora's Box for the horrors to emerge. At least he'd switched images, giving up the cracking of the eggshell. Cassidy didn't leave her side until she went to bed full of pills. She didn't have much will left, moving like a somnambulist, forming her words carefully, her tongue thick—but she kept reaching out for him, grasping his hand. He saw her into bed, told her that she wouldn't have to go through anything so bad again. With Dr. Moller waiting impatiently in the doorway, she squeezed Cassidy's hand. "You will find my husband. . . ." The idea never left her mind. It seemed to crouch behind her every thought, frightening her, driving her onward. He tried to connect it to her behavior toward him and gave it up, realized that madness lay that way.

But he was sure that Rolf Moller was wrong about her. She was worried and run down and frightened, but she wasn't about to crack. She was worried about finding her husband, afraid for his safety. She loved her husband. And she was confused by Cassidy's role in her life. But she wasn't about to let herself unravel. . . .

Or was that only his prayer?

• • •

MacMurdo arrived at nearly two in the morning. He was limping and trying to ignore the pain. Rolf Moller changed the dressing on his thigh and MacMurdo came down to the kitchen wearing a plaid robe. "Christ, a skirmish like this one tonight, fella works up an appetite." Terry Leary uncapped a beer for him and MacMurdo eased himself down into a chair, began building a Dagwood sandwich.

He and Winchell had given the Dauner place a quick once-over. Karl Dauner and Heinz Felix were dead, as billed. In the house Helena Dauner and another couple were dead.

The assassination team, of which the pianist Harkavy had been a part, made for ironic tragedy. MacMurdo had satisfied himself that they were Gypsies from New York—he knew there were such groups, avenging their fellows across Central Europe rounded up and exterminated by Hitler. How they'd gotten a line on Dauner and his colleagues, to say nothing of the MacMurdo operation headquartered in Westchester, was a mystery. "And destined to stay that way," MacMurdo said, "just one of those goddamn things." He chomped on the sandwich, wiped mayonnaise and mustard from the corner of his mouth. "We just can't spend any time worrying about it. War is full of things you can't explain. Hell, I worked with Gypsies behind German lines. Fierce bastards. Damn near as ruthless as your faithful servant here. And one thing I learned, what one Gypsy knows, all Gypsies know. They attacked us here and they did the job tonight. . . ." He shrugged. "We had no casualties tonight, praise God. We can't let this stop us." He turned to Cassidy. "Pard, you're on the trail, you're doin' a helluva job. Now tell me what you got up to with our late Nazis. . . ."

• • •

It turned out that MacMurdo had never intended to go to Washington the previous day. Working on the hunch that the enemy might be able to identify him, he'd planned the evening using Karin as the bait to attract the killers, with himself as the backup.

It was all seat-of-the-pants flying but it was the way he'd worked all through the war. You got the ball and you ran with it, you improvised, you never got bogged down inside the plan. The important thing was to start. Then once the game was going, hell, you picked your spots and hoped you could react faster than the other guy.

Once he'd set Karin, Cassidy, and Leary among the pigeons, he'd tailed them. Winchell had known MacMurdo from the old days, the phony war, when MacMurdo had run his own intelligence service out of London and Vienna, nominally seconded to the British and MI5. MacMurdo had fed Winchell information that kept him a step or two ahead of the competition. In return Winchell had leaked bits and pieces at MacMurdo's request. Winchell claimed that since he'd set up the introduction to Dauner he deserved the chance to ride shotgun. Instead MacMurdo had made him driver. He was going to handle the guns himself. You couldn't say no to Walter Winchell, though, and Winchell had liked the idea of being the wheel man.

At Grand Central, MacMurdo took Cassidy aside. "You were never in any real danger," he began, and Cassidy exploded with laughter. "No, seriously, we had the operation taped. Winch was in on it all the way. Hell of a guy, Winch. Of course, we didn't know the goddamn tennis court was gonna collapse—Jesus, what a mess!"

"Listen to me, Colonel. I don't care if you want to be a war hero every day for the rest of your life. And when I get tired of it I can tell you to go to hell. But you goddamn near got Karin killed. If she'd died and I'd ever found out how you set it up, you'd have wished you were behind enemy lines again. I'd have come after you—that might not scare you much today, but I'd have scared you sooner or later."

"Well, the way I figured it, if she got killed, you'd have gotten killed yourself. Come on, pard, cheer up. Only the bad guys get killed in MacMurdo's world. By the way, there were some of those grenades on the two stiffs at Dauner's place . . . same kind they used on us. I gave them to your pal Leary. To keep the maiden safe in the tower." He looked at his watch, shook Cassidy's hand. "Time for your train, pard. And I really am headed for Washington. We'll be in touch. You've got the number in D.C. Good hunting up there. Remember—find the minotaur, you find Moller. It's his passport to the future. That and the money. If the Göring escape route gets set up—well, find Moller and the minotaur and we close it all down. I wish to hell I were going with you, pard. You're gonna have some fun!"

• • •

Cassidy had a club sandwich and a beer as the train rocked and swayed northward and he thought about Sam MacMurdo. The crazy bastard really did wish he was setting off on the trail of the minotaur and Manfred Moller. He really would have looked upon it as having some fun. He had a way of making his plans your plans, his risks your risks. By the time Cassidy was rolling toward Boston his own reasons for the enterprise were being blurred by events. He was becoming one of MacMurdo's creatures, doing his bidding. Having some fun. He knew that none of his motives had actually changed: he was doing it for his country, he was doing it for Karin because he knew he still loved her. Loving her made it all the more necessary to find Moller, bring them together somehow, and unlock her memory. . . . Once Karin was whole again, life could lurch forward again.

But all that being true, MacMurdo still transformed the reality behind a smokescreen of action. The action was for MacMurdo the end in itself. And when the minotaur and Manfred Moller and the rest of them were history, Sam MacMurdo would be off somewhere looking for the action. And for the moment Cassidy knew he was being swept along with him. The problem, of course, was that while MacMurdo was indestructible, Cassidy wasn't.

• • •

The maiden in the tower, MacMurdo had said.

It was the best place for her. She was out of the game now. It was MacMurdo's game and the only way Cassidy would keep playing was to put the maiden in the tower and keep her there. Until it was over.

"But first you gotta find a tower," MacMurdo had said.

"No problem."

"That was the easy part, pard. You gotta have a scary kind of monster to guard her in the tower." He was grinning, enjoying himself. He was always in the game. "Where you gonna find yourself that monster?"

"*That's* the easy part."

That was when they tucked Karin away in Terry Leary's apartment on Park Avenue.

The maiden had her tower and the monster to keep her safe.

• • •

By the time they pulled into South Station the Boston papers were out with the World Series final on the stands. The ink was still wet and there were crowds around the newsies hawking them. South Station was full of travelers, lots of servicemen in uniform and mothers with tired, hungry kids who were setting up a dinnertime howl, and Brahmins still doing their bit coming from Washington and going to Washington. It was still the war and it would be for a while yet.

Cassidy hadn't been to Boston since the fall of '41 when the Bulldogs had come up for a game and he'd scored three touchdowns, bucking across from inside the one on the last play of the game. The Bulldogs were down by seventeen at the time so it didn't make much difference, except to the guys playing the point spread, which was a newish gimmick some smarty had figured out. But it was his last memory of Boston, grinding across the goal line, getting his face shoved into mud three inches deep at the end of a wet and very dark afternoon. As football went, it was a pretty fair memory. And it was ancient history, four years ago, a whole damn war ago.

He slipped a nickel into the kid's ink-black hand and got the ink smeared all over his own hands. Never mind, it was worth it. Fire Trucks had gone all the way at Briggs Stadium in Detroit and the Tigers had evened the Series at a game each, 4–1. Hank Greenberg's three-run homer off Hank Wyse in the fifth had decided it. Claude Passeau was going tomorrow for the Cubs against Stubby Overmire, which would close out the three games in Detroit. Then they'd move to Wrigley Field for however long it might take for somebody to win four. Cassidy was trying to figure out how the Cubs might win it and it always came down to the ex-Yankee Hank Borowy and Detroit's magnificent lefthander, Hal Newhouser, whom the sportswriters always called Prince Hal. He had this wonderful scar under one eye, wore it like a badge of courage and a warning, and sometimes it would half hypnotize a hitter. Borowy had pitched a six-hit shutout in the opener and Newhouser hadn't survived the third inning. The Cubs won that one, 9–0, but now it was all even. Borowy and Newhouser would probably go against each other again in the fifth game and it would probably be another rubber match. It was going to be close all the way, probably seven games, and it was funny how, even with the Yankees out of it and Karin and MacMurdo and Nazis and Gypsies with tommy guns all joining hands to fuck up his life, Cassidy still found himself caring about the World Series. It was the game. That was where MacMurdo was all fouled up. Baseball was the game. Murder and mayhem and the lady with the memory scared out of her, that was the dark side of life. For MacMurdo it was all a game, that dark side. He probably didn't give a shit about the World Series.

Somebody poked at the newspaper and Cassidy lowered it so he could see. Harry Madrid worked the dead cigar into the corner of his mouth. "How are you, Lew?"

"Damn glad to see you, Harry." Harry Madrid nodded and stood there like one of the pillars holding the train station in place and Cassidy had to smile. Once you really got to know Harry Madrid—and it wasn't easy, it had taken Cassidy a long, hard time—there was no one else quite like him. It was like going into battle with the last of the Wild Bunch on your side.

"I got your wire and here I am. I figure we both got stories to tell. So who goes first?" His hands were pushed down in the deep pockets of his black overcoat. The crowds swelling around him seemed to bounce off him and he didn't notice.

"Where did you book us in?"

"Parker House, where else? It's MacMurdo's twenty grand."

Cassidy folded the newspaper, stuck it under his arm. They shouldered their way through the crowds in the station and found themselves on the densely packed sidewalk. It was damp and dark gray and cold, the wet cold you were always running into in the Boston autumn. They climbed into a cab, one of the high step-up models from back in the thirties, with big round headlamps stuck up on top of the fenders. "You go first," Cassidy said.

Harry Madrid told his story as they inched along through the traffic, winding through tight, claustrophobic streets with those funny Boston names. Somebody had once told Cassidy the streets had been laid out according to the wanderings of sheep and cows a couple of hundred years ago. Cassidy figured it was the truth.

"I found the place where Manfred Moller's plane probably went down."

"Harry, that's great!"

"Yeah." Harry Madrid was unwrapping the cellophane from a thick, stubby Roi-tan. Then he licked the end and bit it and pushed it into the corner of his mouth. "It's on what would likely have been the flight path, it's way back in the bush on this very ritzy estate, fella with the asshole name—if you don't mind an editorial comment—of Tash Benedictus. So help me, Lew, that's his name. Mighty back-woodsy up there."

"Quiet, I suppose."

"Are you kidding? Lots of noises, and what bothers me is none of 'em are human."

"Is."
"What?"
"Is human. None is singular, Harry."
"Sometimes I do worry about you, son." He puffed smoke out the cab window. "Anyway, I suppose you're a reg'lar Natty Bumppo in the woods. Being a college man and all. Well, I hate the Boy Scout stuff. The woods, the animals, the snakes, furry stuff creepin' up behind you, Lew, little piles of their leavings everywhere—"
"You actually been out in the woods yet?"
"Oh no, I wouldn't leave you out of the fun. We'll go in together, get a merit badge."
"So we just walk in, have a look around, see the wreck of the plane—"
"Well, it's a little more complicated than that."
"Always is, isn't it, Harry?"
"Well, you know how things go, Lew. Things are always the same and they always get complicated. Somehow, sooner or later."

• • •

Locke-Ober or Durgin-Park. They flipped for it and took the longer walk down Scollay Square way to Durgin-Park and dined on turkey with all the trimmings. "It's like a holiday," Harry Madrid said, mopping up gravy with a hot biscuit. "This is a good place, Lew." They were sitting at a long table with a lot of other people. Cassidy waited while Harry drank a fourth cup of coffee and polished off a second helping of Indian pudding.

They walked back to the Parker House. It was raining and the drops made a popping sound, tapping on Harry Madrid's bowler. Cassidy told him everything that had happened the night before, the party at Benn's place, the old-fashioned shindig at Dauner's, the shootout on the road, all of it. Harry puffed on his Roi-tan, hands in pockets, his huge bulb-toed black shoes splashing through puddles. He was a good listener. Always had been. Secret of his success, if you'd asked him.

"There'll be something in the papers tomorrow," Cassidy said as they made way for a group of sailors back from the war. The oldest looked maybe nineteen. They were looking for a whorehouse. They didn't have far to go.

"So we're looking for this minotaur thing." Harry Madrid's brow beneath the hard rolled brim of his hat was furrowed. "I don't like this, Lew. What are we supposed to be doing, anyway? I'm heading into the woods looking for Manfred Moller. And now we're looking for this minotaur thing—"

"It's a minotaur, Harry. Not a minotaur thing—"

"Smells like vintage red herring to me," Harry grumbled.

"I want to know exactly how Henry Brenneman got it. If Dauner and this Felix character knew where it was, then Moller must have survived the flight in, must have made contact with Vulkan. Was Dauner himself Vulkan? I don't know. But somebody got that minotaur from Moller . . . or Moller himself got it out to Brenneman—"

"Maybe some poacher stumbled across the damn thing."

"Fate would not be that cruel, Harry."

"Ha!"

"No, I don't think so. Unless he was a poacher who knew about the Göring escape route, a Nazi poacher. That minotaur wound up in the Nazi pipeline. So, we're sniffing around for the Nazis—for Vulkan, for the connection to our friend Dauner. . . ."

"If Felix and Dauner knew about the minotaur thing," Harry said, chewing the Roi-tan to an unsightly shredded mess, "where does Brenneman fit in?"

"He's either in it with them, or he's an innocent bystander."

"Well, sonny, there are no innocent bystanders. So let's get to it. I'm looking forward to getting back to New York, where it's safe and sane. I'm a fish out of water in the woods. I hate the woods, Lew, nature, that stuff."

• • •

Henry Brenneman was at home to answer the phone in Cambridge. There was some Bach playing on the radio and Cassidy's mental picture fitted him out with an old wool cardigan, tweed slacks, carpet slippers, a roaring fire, and a glass of scotch handy. He sounded like a man with bushy eyebrows and a comfortable paunch. The names of Felix and Karl Dauner put a crimp in the comfy style and Henry Brenneman's voice dropped a tone or two.

"Could we discuss this tomorrow, Mr. Cassidy? I'm home for the night and . . . I'm not alone." The last three words were spoken in a whisper. "Tomorrow would be preferable." He covered the mouthpiece, spoke to someone else.

"I'm afraid time is of the essence," Cassidy said. "Felix and Dauner have very kindly assured me that you have a certain piece, a very special piece. . . ."

"Ah . . ."

"A provenance that goes all the way back to King Ludwig of Bavaria—"

"Oh," he whispered again, his voice suddenly brittle with tension. "I don't think I can possibly—"

"It's a minotaur, encrusted with diamonds and whatnot, a unique piece."

"Tomorrow, please—"

"Why don't we just stop out at your place now, take a look at it? We could be there in half an hour, Mr. Brenneman."

"Yes, yes, I have such a piece, yes. But no, you mustn't come here, it's . . . it's at my shop. It has come into my possession rather recently, but you must wait until tomorrow. I cannot possibly—"

"Tonight would be better," Cassidy said. He winked at Harry Madrid.

"But I couldn't possibly show the piece without speaking to Mr. Dauner. I would require some word from Mr. Dauner or Mr. Felix, I'm sure—"

"Well, that's going to be a problem," Cassidy said.

"Not for me, I assure you." Brenneman sounded stuffy and pleased with his own importance, thought he was winning the argument.

"Listen to me carefully, Mr. Brenneman. I don't care if the president of Harvard just dropped by with a couple of tarts—listen to me. Mr. Felix and Mr. Dauner were murdered . . . murdered, as in shot down in cold blood, last night. I was there. It'll be in the papers tomorrow morning. Are you with me so far?"

"Yes." His voice was barely audible.

"Dauner died practically in my arms. By nothing short of a miracle, I survived. Now listen very carefully—the last thing Karl Dauner told me was your name, that you have the Ludwig Minotaur. Now, I want to see it. Tonight, not tomorrow. Once certain parties learn that Dauner is dead, anything might happen. . . ."

"Murdered?" The voice was weak. He wasn't winning the argument anymore. "What are you implying—"

"All I need to do is verify the existence of the minotaur and ask you a few questions, like how it actually came into your hands—"

"There's no mystery to that." He was recovering some lost composure. "A commercial messenger service delivered it to me, I don't recall who. . . . But Karl Dauner told me it was coming, or it could have been Felix acting for Dauner, it's all the same. I've done a great deal of business with Mr. Dauner over the years. A wonderful man, a notable collector. I got the impression they—he, Dauner—wanted me to babysit the piece, keep it out of sight. . . . Mr. Cassidy?"

"Yes?"

"Who killed Mr. Dauner?"

"Can you keep a secret?"

"In my work it's a requisite."

"Some people who just hate Nazis."

There was a long pause. "Oh, my goodness . . . You can't possibly mean . . ."

"For your sake, Mr. Brenneman, I think I should take a look at the minotaur tonight. Don't you?"

"Just a look?"

"You have my word."

"All right. I have a town house on Beacon Hill. I sometimes use it as a showroom for special pieces. It's on Joy Street. Do you know it?"

"Just give me the number."

Brenneman did and said he'd be expecting them in two hours. "Until midnight, then."

"One more thing, Mr. Brenneman."

"Yes?"

"Do you handle much Nazi loot? Or is this piece an exception?"

"Don't provoke me, sir." He hung up.

Cassidy and Harry Madrid went down to the bar at the Parker House. Cassidy asked for a dry Rob Roy. Harry Madrid said, "Dickens martini."

The bartender nodded. "That'll be no olive or twist."

Harry Madrid smiled. "What's the point of just having a look at this minotaur thing?"

"None that I can see."

"So what's the deal, Lew?"

"Well, gosh, Harry, I'm gonna steal the damn thing."

"Why, Lew!"

"I know, I know."

"You lied to that man."

"Well, I didn't figure he'd go along with it if I'd told him my true intentions. That I was gonna steal it."

"Liberate it," Harry Madrid said. "Spoils of war. We're gonna liberate the minotaur thing."

"Then, by God," Cassidy said, "we'll have the two things in the world that mean more than anything else to Manfred Moller."

"He'll have to come after them," Harry Madrid said.

"You'd think so, wouldn't you?"

• • •

They stood at the corner of Beacon and Joy, which angled uphill in the general direction of Louisburg Square. The streetlamps cast long shadows. The damp wind made the deep covering of fallen leaves ripple like a rug with something big and scary under it. The streets were slick. They looked up Joy Street into the shadows. The wavering light behind the canopy of trees gave the scene the look of a stage set. It was two minutes to midnight. The gold-domed statehouse glowed faintly against the night sky. Behind them the Common stretched far away, a long slope into darkness, dotted by occasional lamp poles.

"This is a lot like a movie," Harry Madrid muttered. "Now we go to the dark house and find the art dealer murdered and the minotaur thing gone. It's always the same. It can be Tom Conway or Bogart or John Garfield or George Sanders, it's always the same. Did you ever see Lionel

Stander and Edward Arnold in the Nero Wolfe movie? Well, it would be the same with them, too. Or William Powell and Myrna Loy and that dog? No matter who's in it, I'm tellin' you, Lew, the art dealer's a dead duck, a goner." He sucked his cigar and the smoke was whirled away.

"Harry, you interest me strangely," Cassidy said.

"Now don't get weird on me," Harry Madrid growled.

"I had no idea you were a movie fan."

"It was the wife in the first place. She enjoyed a movie, two, three times a week, Bank Night, best dishes we ever had the wife won at the Orpheum one night back in 'thirty-five." He sighed philosophically. "Chinese scene on 'em, all in blue. Well, when she passed on, I kept going to the movies, beat stayin' at home reading *Collier's* and *Bluebook* and listening to the radio."

"Well, let's go see if life imitates art," Cassidy said.

"Oh, hell, the movies, that's just entertainment."

They walked up Joy Street and stopped in front of a brownstone town house. "See," Harry Madrid said. "It's not dark. Fella standing in the window looking for us. He's the killer—"

"Harry, he's Mr. Brenneman, for God's sake."

They climbed the steps and didn't have to knock. The door swung open and a tall man in a worn corduroy jacket and crepe-soled shoes asked them to come in, come in.

Cassidy stood in the dim hallway with the tile floor and iron boot-scraper. Two more narrow glass-paneled doors led into the foyer. "Good of you to meet us, Mr. Brenneman."

"Please excuse me—is it Cassidy?"

"And this is Mr. Madrid," Cassidy said.

"I see. Well, I'm not Mr. Brenneman. My name is Andrew Folger, Mr. Brenneman's assistant. I was spending the evening at Henry's, going over some inventory lists and—well, listen to me, what am I going on about?" He smiled self-consciously. He had a bushy head of hair and a straggly mustache that was damp at the tip from being chewed on. He had a way of speaking with his chin tucked down so that he was always peering out and slightly up when he looked at you. You couldn't see his eyes behind round glasses. The shy academic, the perfect assistant. "So," he said, clasping his hands almost daintily. "Mr. Brenneman is downstairs in our secret storage room." He turned back, smiling at the idea of such secrecy in such a gentlemanly profession, then led the way down the hall toward the rear of the house, Victorian splendor on view in the parlors, glorious Boston ferns on pedestals everywhere. "We keep the most valuable pieces there. Fireproof. Like a room-size vault. Oh, Mr. Brenneman takes great pains. Mind the step."

Folger led the way down to the kitchen level, opened another door down a flight of unfinished wooden stairs with brooms and mops hanging in clips on the wall. At the bottom in the dim basement with the cement floor and dusty basement smell, Folger said, "Right over here, gentlemen."

A wedge of light fell across the cement floor from a heavy vaultlike door. The special room seemed to have been hewn out of Beacon Hill itself. "Mr. Brenneman," Folger called. "They're here." In a low voice Folger said: "He asked me to show you in and leave you alone with him." He added fussily: "He gets that way sometimes."

Cassidy smiled at the old-maidishness.

Folger pulled the heavy door open, out into the cellar. It swung soundlessly, well oiled. "Go right ahead."

Cassidy went in first, followed by Harry Madrid.

Brenneman was sitting in the shadow, a pool of light from a gooseneck lamp illuminating a ledger on the desk. He didn't look up or speak and Cassidy felt like an intruder.

With a faint movement of air the door closed behind them.

Harry Madrid said: "Lew, I don't like—"

Unmistakably there was the sound of bolts being shot.

Cassidy was behind the desk in a flash, shaking the figure of Henry Brenneman.

Harry Madrid turned and rammed his whole two hundred and thirty pounds at the heavy door and knew they'd been had.

Henry Brenneman slid forward in the chair, his head striking the wooden desk smartly. He didn't say a word. Cassidy turned the gooseneck back, lay the hot bright light across Brenneman's face.

The eyes were wide open. The gold-rimmed spectacles were awkwardly skewed. His shirtfront and tan cardigan sweater were soaked with blood. His throat had been cut none too cleanly. The weapon, a heavy scissors worn smooth by handling, had been driven with considerable force into his chest.

Harry Madrid observed the scene with a certain calm detachment. "Just like the goddamn movies," he said at last.

• • •

Cassidy felt good about being up the creek with a guy like Harry Madrid. The old bastard just unwrapped another cheap cigar, lit it, and sat in a slipcovered armchair, puffing. Cassidy wondered how long he could survive without a change of air. Harry Madrid looked like a man waiting for an idea to come to him.

The room was paneled in what seemed to be dark oak, a most civilized room considering its location just off a normally shabby cellar. Obviously it had been put to the use described by the perfidious Andrew Folger, who had just taken over the top spot on Cassidy's list. Cassidy sat on the edge of the desk, swinging his good leg. He was twirling his walking stick like a big loser in the drum majorette sweepstakes. He contemplated how much he would enjoy unsheathing the sword and sinking it into Andrew Folger.

"I don't suppose anyone could hear us yell," he said.

"You gotta doubt it, Lew."

"Somebody might smell us if you've got enough cigars."

"Naw. They'd just think some old cat crawled in somewhere and croaked."

Cassidy nodded.

"That Folger the fella I think he was?"

"I don't know. Spent some time in England—"

"He did?"

"He said 'mind the step.' Never heard an American say that."

"No German accent, though."

"Well, his brother Rolf doesn't have a German accent either. Or not much of one."

"So Folger could have been Manfred Moller. . . ."

"It figures." Cassidy shrugged. "Maybe he was stopping in to check on his minotaur. Damn. I can't begin to figure it out. But Folger knew we were coming. Brenneman obviously knew him, there's been no struggle here. Brenneman came down here to get the minotaur—either for us to steal or for Folger/Moller to reclaim or inspect. With us coming, Folger/Moller knew *somebody* had traced the minotaur. . . . Well, he wouldn't have to know *who* to know he damn well wanted to keep it for himself." Cassidy sighed. "Harry, you don't seem very worried, and I'm glad about that. So, how the hell are we gonna get out of here?"

Harry Madrid leaned forward, eased himself up out of the chair. It was getting hot in the tightly closed room. Beads of perspiration dotted his forehead. He squinted through the smoke, eyes deep and dark beneath the brim of the bowler. "Think of it, Lew. This Manfred Moller, he's sort of captured my imagination. Here, give me your stick a minute." He took it, tapped it against his chin, his eyes far away for the moment. "SS man, the fella Göring picked for the secret mission to set up his escape route, probably knew Hitler personally . . . storybook stuff, Lew. It's all a part of history. Now, cross your fingers, son, 'cause I'm just about to play the only card I've got." He took Cassidy's stick and went to the wood-paneled wall behind the desk, opposite the bolted-from-the-outside door, and began tapping the heavy head against the oak.

Cassidy watched, mopping his face with his handkerchief. Harry's turning out to be a movie fan had taken him by surprise and now he'd started thinking along the same lines. He wasn't thinking about Nazis. He was thinking about those goddamn submarine pictures, everybody cooped up in a tiny space, drowning in their own sweat, either depth charges going off all the time or some nitwit yelling *Up periscope! Up periscope!* or *Mayday! Mayday!* and *Crash dive! Crash dive!* The more he thought the hotter he got and the smaller the room seemed and he felt like he was trying to get inside the Tokyo sub pens and end the war for Warner Brothers and the gang in the second balcony back at the Orpheum.

Harry Madrid was still tapping the wall, his ear cocked, listening. He stopped and looked back at Cassidy, crooked a finger, beckoning him. "C'mere. Listen along here." He resumed tapping.

"You're looking for a secret compartment?"

"Secret passage, you mean. Tunnel. This sound hollow to you, Lew? Your ears are younger than mine."

"Shot in the dark, Harry?"

"Never take a shot in the dark, son. Might hit a friendly, then where the dickens would you be? Shit, wish I hadn't said dickens; I'm thirsty as hell. Sound hollow there, Lew?"

"I don't know." He listened. "Tap again, Harry, tap again."

"I'd say it sounds hollow," Harry Madrid said. "It better sound hollow. How d'you get the sword out of this thing?"

Cassidy released the knob, felt the heavy pressure leap into his palm. He handed the sword to Harry Madrid, who looked at it with overt disapproval. "A queer's weapon. Thin cold steel."

"Bullshit, Harry."

Harry Madrid tested the sword tip with a blunt fingertip, snorted. "Pig sticker." He then began to wedge it in between the molding and the sheet of paneling proper. "This blade ain't gonna snap on me, is it?"

"Finest Sheffield, Harry."

"Finest, finest," he muttered, prying at the molding, chipping at the fine oak. "What we're looking for here is your subterranean passageway. You'll find them hither and yon and thither all over Beacon Hill. Fairly honeycombed with 'em. You may ask yourself, what does Harry Madrid know about such things?"

"Crossed my mind, Harry."

"Goes back to the old bootlegging days. I came up here on an investigation or two, some of my mick colleagues showed me the ins and outs of Beacon Hill. The leggers used to make regular deliveries in the middle of the night. Pull their big Pierces or Maxwells up a block away, in some alley, disappear down a hole and—Bob's your uncle!—there's good booze on old Joy Street tonight." A strip of molding tore loose and Harry Madrid leaned against the panel, shoved. It gave, flopped to and fro in its frame.

There was a squeaking, the flash of a tooth, the glitter of an eye, a fat rat clumsily tripping in the light, falling onto the floor. It limped hastily under the cover of the desk.

"Smells like the grave." Cassidy peered into the darkness.

"Won't be a cakewalk," Harry Madrid said. "It's like one of those penny dreadfuls of my boyhood. Lots of spiders and slugs and stink and webs and the rest of that rat's kinfolk."

"Christ. You go first. It's dark in there."

Cassidy made another check of the room where Henry Brenneman still sat in his desk chair.

No wondrous minotaur.

The walk to freedom was more of a crouch and it was far worse than Harry Madrid's prediction. But in the end, ten minutes later, they emerged through an ancient wooden door into an alleyway with a streetlamp at the end and Beacon Street cresting twenty yards away. The bootleggers had known what they were doing, all right.

# Chapter Eleven

Harry Madrid was laughing softly to himself when Cassidy walked into the coffee shop at nine thirty the next morning. He was soaking up egg yolk with a piece of toast from a silver toast rack. His Parker House linen napkin was carefully tucked inside his shirt collar and hung like a semaphore flag across his chest. His dark blue suit had been brushed but a bit of cobweb from the night before clung to the back of one sleeve. He mulched the egg and toast around in his mouth and told Lew to take a chair.

"What finds you in such good humor this dark and dreary morning?" Cassidy had slept fitfully, coping with Harry's snoring from the other bed. But it was his own overburdened mind that had held sleep at bay. The questions just kept multiplying but they never came with any answers to match.

"Well, son," Harry Madrid said, shifting his bulk in the chair and arranging three more slices of crisp bacon on his plate, "it's like this. I've been a copper a long time, now I'm a private copper, and I seen a lot of dead crazy situations—things you just couldn't explain. Ever. Things that just wouldn't yield to investigation. Or to imagination." He picked up a piece of bacon and daintily placed it in his mouth. A forkful of fried potatoes followed, then a half of a broiled tomato. "And I got to thinking about the Boston coppers, they're gonna get around to this thing up there on Joy Street and, well," he chortled, "they've got the beginnings of a legend on their hands. They're eventually gonna find a dead guy, prominent art dealer, behind a bolted door in a basement vault . . . and an old bootlegger's tunnel used for an escape route—but who by? The murderer? Why wouldn't the murderer have left the vault and bolted the door behind him? He would have! So who was locked in the vault with the stiff? Who bolted the door? And what's been stolen? There's no way they're gonna know about the minotaur thing. . . . You get it, Lew? They're lost on this one and that's why I'm laughing and in such good humor. They're gonna have to call on Dr. Fell to figure this one out. Remember the old rhyme, Lew?

*I do not like thee, Dr. Fell,*
*The reason why I cannot tell,*
*But this I know and know full well,*
*I do not like thee, Dr. Fell.*"

Harry Madrid shook his head, his broad chest quaking. Cassidy got a fresh cup of coffee, ordered pancakes and Canadian bacon, and wished he could share Harry Madrid's outlook. Instead, he felt like a man trying to battle his way out of a room full of cotton wadding. He didn't seem to be landing any punches but he was getting tired and losing every round on points. He couldn't even keep his metaphors under control.

While he waited for breakfast he began working his way through the morning newspapers. Two of them carried the story of the murders at Dauner's Long Island estate. They were long on Dauner-as-Patriot but otherwise botched, sketchy accounts, reflecting the kind of uncertainty Harry Madrid had seen in the future of the Boston police force. The New York papers that had reached the Parker House weren't much more in the know. The connection between the dead assassins on the grounds of Dauner's home and the dead men on the road was mentioned only as a possibility, one theory among several. The pianist Harkavy was properly identified but there was no mention of Gypsies. It was going to take them forever to straighten out the angles and when it came to explaining why a bunch of Gypsies—if they were ever identified as such—should conduct the massacre of an American superpatriot like Karl Dauner, his wife, their guests, well, the law was going to wind up sitting on its collective thumb.

Cassidy didn't know whether to laugh or cry.

After breakfast he called New York and got Terry Leary out of bed. To satisfy Cassidy he went and checked on Karin. He came back to the telephone yawning, lighting a cigarette. Karin was sound asleep. She hadn't been too lively ever since the Long Island business, but then Cassidy knew all that. Something he didn't know was that Rolf Moller had decided he could not, would not, allow his patient, for whom he continued to feel the responsibility of both a doctor and a brother-in-law, to be removed from his care. Therefore, Dr. Moller was moving in on Leary. He didn't sound overjoyed at the prospect. "There's something about the kraut bastard," he said. "Gives me the creeps. I don't trust him."

• • •

Cassidy wanted some maneuverability for whatever lay ahead of them in Maine. He had left the Ford convertible in the garage back in New York. It had a clutch problem and a certain eccentricity in the brakes. And now they needed a car.

"Well," Harry Madrid said, "this is just the sort of eventuality MacMurdo had in mind for the twenty Gs. Special transport. We simply lay it on."

"Buy a car?"

"Why not, son?"

It took less than an hour for Cassidy to find a dealer with precisely what he had in mind. The Packard man had a mint-condition 1936 gunmetal gray Packard convertible. With a rumble seat, a separate trunk box fixed to the rear end, a radio in first-rate working order, ditto the heater. Balloon white sidewalls, set of snow chains, tool kit, the works. Been in drydock all through the war and the owner had died on Bataan in the Philippines. He'd been a Boston lawyer and his mother had held on to the hope that he might return. Now there was no more hope. The dealer said she didn't really need a car anymore but she was keeping the '31 Cord and the '36 Cord.

In the end Cassidy peeled off twelve hundred bucks and the Packard was his. "Pretty penny," Harry Madrid said, stroking the gray leather seat.

"Pretty car," Cassidy said.

"That, my boy, you can say again."

• • •

They were on the road, heading north from Boston, a dirty wet sky pushing down on them. The wind gathering strength from its trip across the ocean whipped at the Packard, looking for a chink in the fit of the fabric top. It couldn't quite find one and whined like a motherless child about it. It was cold, much colder than when Cassidy had left New York.

Up here, north of Boston, summer was a faded memory of lost youth and it was going to be a long winter.

The heater was trying to cope. The man on the radio between the afternoon serials said there was a winter storm that was carrying snow but it might stay up in Canada, then swirl on out to Nova Scotia and beyond. Then again it might slip down as far south as Boston. Of course, it might not happen at all. "This," Harry Madrid said, biting his cigar, "has more suspense than 'Helen Trent.' Crazy weather, Lew. They say it's all the bomb, this crazy weather. I don't know, I guess I'm a relic of another age, like a dinosaur. I belong to a simpler time. The crossbow and vats of boiling oil."

"You, my friend," Cassidy said, "exist outside of time. Like . . . oh, I don't know, like General Patton. You're a warrior, Harry."

"That's a very nice thing of you to say, Lew."

"This fucked-up world always needs a Harry Madrid," he said. "There's never enough of 'em to go around."

Rain began picking at the windshield.

"So where the hell is Tuggle?"

Harry Madrid began struggling with the cleverly folded map from the gas station. "It's up northwest of Bangor, over that way, toward the Blue Mountains. I'm here to tell ya, Lew, it's winter up there. Colder'n a witch's tit, right now and right on through mid-June. My, my, I'd love to get hold of the fella designed this map. I'd have his manhood for your aerial, Lew. It'd be a pleasure. You just take a left at some place called Abner. That's right, town called Abner. I'll bet it's a little place, too. Left for Tuggle. Lew, what are we doin' up here, rootin' around for Nazis in Tuggle, Maine?"

"Doin' the Lord's work, Harry." Cassidy smiled.

"I don't know. Everything's crazy. Maybe they're right. Maybe it's that goddamn bomb."

• • •

The radio was powerful and he had no trouble picking up the World Series. The rain had grown sleety. It was hard to imagine a sun-washed diamond, the crack of the bat in the crisp autumnal breezes, the fly balls floating against the pale blue sky. It was crazy. Maybe Harry Madrid was right, maybe it was the bomb.

Claude Passeau was pitching in the enemy's ballpark but through five innings he'd held the Tigers hitless. He was marching toward baseball history, yet Cassidy's mind kept wandering. What the hell was he doing, going to Maine in some damn storm, searching for a man who wasn't there . . . ?

There was no point in worrying about Andrew Folger who was

probably Manfred Moller. Now that he had the minotaur again it was impossible to know what he might do. Would he try to reach Vulkan?

Well, what if Karl Dauner had been Vulkan? Was Manfred Moller therefore alone and friendless? What then would be his state of mind? He could go back to ground somewhere . . . but where? It all depended on Vulkan. And if Vulkan was still alive, if he was still out there, could Moller be sure he could trust him?

When it came to that, why did he take the minotaur back? Why did he kill Brenneman?

That would make you think someone else had seen to Brenneman's getting it. Manfred was reclaiming it. But who would have taken it from Manfred and transferred it to Brenneman?

Had Dauner and Felix given it to Brenneman? It sounded like Brenneman thought they had . . . but that didn't make sense. And it didn't make it true. The minotaur had been in Boston, not New York. Which made you think somebody else, someone with Boston as the hub, had made sure the minotaur had stayed there . . . which made you think it wasn't Dauner's work. But Dauner had known about it, had done business with Brenneman before.

Had the minotaur been *stolen* from Moller?

Oh, for God's sake!

Who knew he had the damn thing? How could somebody steal it?

Had Vulkan or someone else betrayed him? But, then, how had Moller known where the minotaur had been taken?

Did the killing of Dauner somehow set Moller in motion? Did the killing of Dauner mean Brenneman was about to die? Had to die?

Well, add it all up and that was why Cassidy and Harry Madrid were going to Maine.

Cassidy saw only questions and nary an answer.

They had no choice but to go back to the beginning, back to their first idea: find out where Moller had come into the United States and then reconstruct his trail. It wasn't much, but it was all they had.

• • •

The afternoon wore on and the dark day had turned to a bleak twilight. Out in Detroit Passeau had finished up a masterpiece, marred only by Rudy York's single in the sixth. A one-hitter and the Cubs left Detroit leading the Series two games to one.

Try as he might Cassidy couldn't remember hearing York's hit.

Harry Madrid had been napping for a while but roused himself by some internal alarm system.

The headlights probed at the night. The sleet had turned back to rain and then slacked off until the night was left with only the wind shrieking out of the forested hills they could no longer see.

Harry Madrid blew his nose and pointed at the weather-faded road sign. TUGGLE.

"We're here," he said.

# CHAPTER TWELVE

"Could be worse," Tom Hayes said, sucking on a corncob pipe that he was smoking upside down so the steady light rain wouldn't dampen the tobacco in the bowl.

"I'd like to know how." Harry Madrid, covered in one of the khaki-green all-weather coats Hayes had dug out of the attic, was sitting on the brown pine needles under the towering tree where they were taking a break. He had his bowler determinedly clamped down on his huge head.

They had left Tom's pickup truck back on the dirt road that cut through the vast estates belonging to Tash Benedictus. From the roadside Hayes had pointed out a thin column of gray smoke rising from the forested hillside about four miles away, across a deep valley nearly black with pines. Hayes handed Cassidy his field glasses, pointing toward the smoke. Cassidy had focused the lenses and through the rain he'd made out the slate roof and single high pointed turret of the Benedictus castle, called—Cassidy hoped whimsically—Last Bastion. Hayes had said the idea was to steer well clear of the castle, given the owner's attitude about strangers, poachers, and trespassers. So, for two hours, they had slogged through uncomfortable, nearly impenetrable country that scratched at them, lay traps and natural tripwires for their weary feet, and sucked wetly at them when it had the chance, pulling them toward the underworld. But old Seth Marson was the one who had the line on the crash and Seth said it was the Keyhole Lake area they needed to search. And it was toward Keyhole Lake that they were struggling.

"Could be worse," Tom Hayes said again. "Could be summer. Nothing a whole lot worse than summer in these woods. A man can be out there on the lake having the time of his life, fishing up a storm, working the silveriest trout you ever seen, but you can't stay out on the water forever. And when you come ashore—you got a bag full of trout or salmon or bass, whatever, you're a happy man—and then, Mother o' God, the blackflies got you." He sucked on the pipe, took it out of his mouth, knocked the dottle out on a flat stone. He ground the ash under his heel. They were all wearing green wellies from the attic stock. "And when the blackflies get you, you'd know just how much worse it can get." He grinned from Cassidy to Harry Madrid, both of whom were sweating like pigs in the forty-degree weather. "Blackflies, they're hellfire, they get at you, up your nose, in your eyes, damn things can get inside your clothes, make a beeline right for your arsehole. . . ."

"Shut up," Harry Madrid said. "Just be a pal, Tom, and shut up."

Hayes laughed, tucked his corncob back into his pocket.

Cassidy looked at his watch. It was just past noon. They'd be playing ball in Chicago in a couple hours. They might as well be on the moon. "How much farther to Keyhole Lake?"

"Coupla hours," Hayes said.

"Big lake?"

Hayes shook his head. "Not so big." He picked up the rightly rolled bed kit. "Might as well be on our way, gents."

They were each carrying a bedroll and a small packet of provisions for overnight. Hayes also carried a cooking kit, nothing heavy, all useful. "Funny thing about blackflies," he said. "Folks used to say they never bothered pretty women. Just a superstition. Cheap whore probably safest of all. Damn blackflies won't go near perfume. Stronger the better." He chuckled and set off, leading the way single file. "Blackflies can kill a man. They just start chewing on you, they can just keep chewing until you're dead, y'know."

"Shut up, Tom," Harry Madrid said.

Cassidy couldn't stop sweating. The exertion of fighting the thick, grasping undergrowth, coupled with the terrible humidity, was drenching him, soaking every stitch inside the rubberized coat. He tried to pull as much air into his lungs as possible, he tried to will his heart to slow its heavy thudding. He had to hand it to Manfred Moller if the son of a bitch made it through this alive.

• • •

The two hours dragged past, turned into three, before they collapsed on a spiny ridge looking down toward a narrow sand beach spotted with bits of wood, charred remains of campfires from the summer, a fireplace crudely built of stones. Keyhole Lake.

The light was beginning to fade, the low, dark gray clouds turning purple, ripe with more rain. Hayes pointed down at the lake, a hundred yards away, where a tiny inlet flowed under the boughs of several giant pines.

Hayes sighed, stood stretching his back. "Make camp down there, get a fire going, take the damp outa the bones. Come on, gents."

Hayes had a gift for building fires out of what seemed to be waterlogged pine boughs and blowdown and undergrowth. He got the flames licking up through the brown-and-green brush and the smell of burning pine needles swirled around them like the smoke caught in the lake breeze. The surface of the lake was quiet but for the rain that blew across the water like a gossamer curtain. Cassidy had seen the same mesmerizing effect from the tunnel under the stadium, with the leather pads beneath his jersey soaked with rain and heavy, had seen the rain blowing in sheets across the field, blurring the white yard stripes, the fans huddled under blankets and umbrellas in the darkening stands. Here it was as if the giant pines, rising in the tiers on the hillsides surrounding Keyhole Lake, formed the stadium and he was looking out from a tunnel formed by the heavy, drooping branches above him.

"It'll be dark soon enough," Cassidy said. "Whattaya say, Harry? Let's have a look."

Harry Madrid grunted, dumping water from one of his wellies. A rock dropped out and he grunted again. He tugged the boot on again. "It's a fool's errand, Lewis."

"Well, that must be us. Let's look around."

By six o'clock they'd battled their way through several hundred square yards of pine forest bordering the northeast quadrant of the lake. Seth Marson had been very specific on the detail map as to where he'd been, where he judged the crash to have taken plce, where he'd smelled the oil fire though he'd not actually seen it. And by six o'clock they hadn't seen anything either. They trooped back to the inlet where the flickering campfire burned a bright red-orange hole in the darkness.

Hayes was squatting beside the fire frying slabs of ham in a folding frying pan. He looked up, eyebrows raised, corncob pipe clamped between his widely spaced teeth. "Any luck?"

"Ha!" Harry Madrid sat down on a rock cushioned by his bedroll. It was not a mirthful laugh.

By the light of the campfire Cassidy unfolded the map Marson had marked for Hayes and Harry Madrid. They had just finished searching about a tenth of the area Marson felt so sure of and it had been hard work. They were trespassing, for one thing, and the lake was awfully inaccessible, for another. How much could they do the next day? Then they'd have to fight their way out and load up on more provisions, then fight their way back in again. The whole idea seemed hopelessly difficult and desperately quixotic. It was no surprise that the plane had never been found. If it was there at all. And if it had gone down in the thick forest, the idea that Manfred Moller survived the crash seemed farfetched. It all seemed farfetched and the preternatural calm of the drenched forest added to the feeling that this, here, was real, while the hugger-mugger of Boston and New York was make-believe. What would Winchell have made of the forest, the campfire, the rain, and the severely dropping temperature?

"Wha'd I tell you, Lewis?" Harry Madrid was rubbing his hands together. They were pink, chapped by the damp and cold. "Colder'n a witch's tit. My God, how I hate the country life. This would just never, ever happen to a man in the city. Any city. Only out in the godforsaken wilderness."

"Soup's on." Tom Hayes pointed to the tin plates.

There was ham, fried bread, white Vermont Cheddar, apples, Black & White scotch and a measured amount of water.

"It's funny, but I always thought camping out like this would be sort of cozy." Cassidy frowned. "Mainly I'm stiff and cold."

"You get that warped view from reading *The Open Road for Boys*," Hayes said.

"If I don't make it through the night," Harry Madrid said, "just fix me up with a Viking funeral. Right here on this miserable fucking lake. Your reward will come in Heaven."

They swigged at the scotch whiskey and nibbled on cheese and then they rolled out their sleeping bags. Things occasionally moved in the underbrush, cracking a fallen branch, bumping into stumps. Loons or some damned thing called across the lake and from time to time there was a splash in the lake, a cry across the water.

"Are we safe out here?" Harry Madrid looked up from his quiet contemplation of the fire. He sprinkled it with more twigs and smoke billowed out at him. He fanned it away. "It's awful damn noisy around here all of a sudden."

"We're pretty safe, I guess," Tom Hayes said. He was nursing scotch from a telescoping tin cup. "Only thing that's likely to hurt us is a bear."

"Well, my God, Tom, that's a relief," Harry muttered. "I was all set to get worried there."

"Or a moose. I suppose a moose gets all riled up he could do a man some damage. Catch you in the nuts with those big antlers mebbe. Worse, a moose could fall on you. Now that'd be a horse of another color."

Harry Madrid groaned. "Lew, what am I doing here? No, don't bother to answer. There is no answer, son."

• • •

By his watch, in the low light of the campfire, it was only half past seven, but Cassidy's bones were weary and aching. His eyelids dragged him down like anchors and he kept yawning. Harry Madrid was already snoring, an immense bulk inside his sleeping bag. Cassidy was sprawled on top of his, warming himself as close to the fire as he could get. Tom Hayes had wandered off into the shadows to relieve himself. The splashing sounds continued erratically out in the lake. There was a dull grayish-silver glow behind the clouds and the rain had stopped as the temperature fell. One night out in the elements was one too many so far as Cassidy was concerned, but how the hell else could you find the plane? And unless you found the plane how could you retrace the path of Manfred Moller?

Still, he felt like an idiot. A very cold, very uncomfortable idiot.

Tom Hayes came back into the penumbra of firelight, carefully buttoning his heavy gamekeeper's trousers. "Get tired real early out in the woods," he said. "Old Harry's sawing wood." He chuckled. "You better knock off. Don't worry about the fire, I'll keep feeding it." He set the tin camping dishes he'd just washed down at the lake on a bed of pine needles near the fire. "Got some good country sausages for breakfast," he said almost to himself. "Now get some shut-eye. We'll find your airplane in the morning. If it's around here, anyway, we will."

Cassidy closed his eyes but when he came awake he couldn't remember falling asleep. Blearily he looked at his watch again. It was only a quarter past eight.

But something was wrong.

He leaned up to see what Harry Madrid and Hayes were doing and his head bumped into something. Something hard.

He spun his head and the hard thing got in the way of his cheek and the damn thing hurt. He forced his eyes open. A very large shape was standing over him, quite literally blocking out the moon.

"The jug can bump the stone," it said, "or the stone can bump the jug, but no matter how you cut it, it's bad for the jug. Why don't you just sit still, friend?"

The hard thing was the business end of a double-barreled shotgun that was pressing against his nose and mouth, forcing his head back down. He couldn't move his lips, couldn't have spoken if he'd had anything pertinent to say. And he didn't.

A blinding light hit him head on. It was like he imagined a needle would feel, driven into your eyeball. He squeezed his eyes shut. All he could see then was a glare, bright red.

A voice that wasn't coming from the man with the shotgun came from somewhere else, off to the side, a different voice. Whoever it was seemed to be an Englishman.

"I say, you chaps," the voice said, at ease, laconically. It was like a parody of someone in a novel by P. G. Wodehouse. Bertie Wooster, maybe. Perhaps the man with the gun was Jeeves. "You awake, old man?"

Cassidy tried to nod.

"Come, come, Porter," the voice said. "No need to actually *insert* the weapon." Cassidy felt the gun's twin muzzles withdraw. He heard Harry Madrid and Hayes rustling, coming awake. "Now, you chaps are in the soup, I'm afraid. Which is to say you're off limits." Mercifully the light slid away from Cassidy's face and pinned Madrid and Hayes to their sleeping rolls. One of them was spluttering with indignation.

The large shape—Porter by name and possibly by occupation—moved away to point his shotgun in the general direction of the others. Another man stepped into view, above Cassidy, whose eyes were returning to something like normal. This new visitor was stocky, wore a cap and a tweed hacking jacket with a heavy scarf wrapped around his throat. His left sleeve was empty, tucked into his jacket pocket. His right arm was partially extended, a gloved hand holding what looked like a Colt .45. He wore jodhpurs and lace-up hightops.

"What's going on?" Cassidy's mouth was dry with sudden fear.

"Well, how to put it? You've been nicked in the act of trespassing, old dear. You've no business in the world being on my land."

He came closer. He had a round, almost cherubic face, full-cheeked, the tweed cap pulled low on his broad forehead. He was smiling, his mouth the bottom half of a circle above a dimpled chin that became a couple of chins in no time at all. The pleasant aspect of his face, seemingly made for smiling, was marred somewhat by the fact that he only had one eye. A black patch was strapped to his left eye, the black band bisecting his forehead and crossing a curled lump of tissue where his left ear had been. Something very bad had once happened just to his left. Very, very bad. "Come along, lads. Collect your bits and pieces. We're going for a ride." He never stopped smiling. But the .45 didn't waver either.

Cassidy stood up slowly. He heard Harry Madrid and Hayes getting up. The former was grousing. "Be careful with that gun, young man," he said, "or I might have to wrap it around your neck." It occurred to Cassidy that Harry Madrid wasn't kidding.

"By the way," the smiling man said, "my name is Benedictus."

"And I'm one of Snow White's dwarfs," Harry Madrid muttered.

Benedictus laughed lightly.

"Grumpy, I presume," he said.

# Chapter Thirteen

"You're right, of course, the torches are a nice touch," Benedictus observed, his footsteps echoing on the cold stone floor of the entrance hall. The walls were constructed of immense blocks of what appeared to be stone. They looked so heavy, so real, that Cassidy doubted their authenticity. He'd seen so many movies that featured such elaborate castles, frequently presided over by a gaga scientist in the familiar person of Lugosi or Karloff. His father had also taken him to visit movie sets when he was a boy and he had seen more when he'd been in Los Angeles with Karin while she worked on her own pictures. The more real things looked the more likely they were to be made of papier-mâché.

Boulders and dungeon walls and castles. Nothing was the real McCoy out there, you couldn't be sure of anything. You could lean against a castle wall in Verona and fall headfirst into a Dodge City saloon where Hoot Gibson was twirling a six-shooter.

Cassidy put his hand out, touched the wall. He felt a faint pang of disappointment when it was cold and unyielding and unquestionably real. "It's all a nice touch, Mr. Benedictus."

"And what does that mean, precisely?" He'd taken off his cap to reveal a thatch of thinning reddish hair. His one eye was green as an apple. He wore a well-tended sandy Guards mustache.

"It looks like a movie set," Cassidy said.

"Ha! Top hole, old man! Most people come tottering on in and say something banal. Nice castle you have here, they say. But a movie set! And how bloody true . . . *too* bloody true. It *is* a movie set. I had Jeremy Frere design it. Right after he did that pretentious bit of rubbish for Korda. *Lord Ugly's Castle*, happily chopped to pieces by Gainsborough and released in three small theaters in suburban Bucharest."

"My father hired Frere once. He's a drunk."

"And that's the best thing about him," Benedictus said. "Just who the hell are you, Cassidy? And your father, too?" He turned to the huge Porter, who was proving to be the strong silent type. "Take their coats and things, Porter. Get a move on."

"My father makes movies, bounces around. Or he did before he started making movies for the War Department. I suppose he'll get back to it eventually. His name is Paul Cassidy."

"Never heard of him."

"Why should you have?"

"I'm Pinnacle Pictures," Benedictus said. "That's why."

"Are you joking?"

"Alas, no."

"Alas?"

"Oh, business is good. *The* business is a zoo. That is a bear, Mr. Madrid."

Harry Madrid was standing before a stuffed bear preserved forever reared up on its hind legs, front legs extended like the arms of a lethal lover, about to hug someone. Its glass eyes stared down at Harry Madrid from a couple of feet over his head.

"I sort of thought that's what it was." The bear stood in a corner of the entrance hall. Its counterpart thirty feet away was a suit of armor. "What did it take to stop an animal like that?"

Benedictus laughed and shook his head, his green eye reflecting for a moment the flames flickering in the wall sconces. "Damned if I know. My checkbook, I guess. I bought it from a taxidermist in Los Angeles. It's a Kodiak, I think he said. I daresay it never saw Maine during its lifetime. Casts a certain spell, though, don't you agree?"

"More than a suit of armor," Cassidy said.

"Oh, that old thing. My wife did a picture with Fairbanks years and years ago and she kept the armor. Said it was better company than old Doug." He turned to Tom Hayes, who seemed dumbstruck by the dimensions and nature of the surroundings, probably because he didn't see enough movies. "Come, come, man. Your mouth's open. You're Mr. Hayes? Well, Mr. Hayes, what do you make of Last Bastion?"

"Last what?" Hayes asked, lifting the knight's visor with his forefinger, letting it clang noisily back into place.

"Last Bastion. That's the appellation I've applied to this great damp pile of rubble. It's only twenty-five years old, with no expense spared to give it just the right medieval patina."

"Damnedest place I've ever seen." Hayes stroked his chin in amazement.

"Well said! You'll do the part of the Local Rustic." Benedictus turned back to Cassidy. "Shall we start the revels, then? I mean to say, you're more or less captive to the Lord of the Manor. Though you'll be a damn sight more comfortable here tonight than out there in the muck. I'm not such a terrible fate, after all." He clapped Cassidy on the arm. "Come on, chaps, come in by the fire. We'll tell stories and tie one on. I want to know who you are and what the devil you're playing at in my back yard. I would be within my rights to plug you varmints. . . ."

"You've seen too many movies, Mr. Benedictus."

"Ahhh, thrust home! Call me Tash, Mr. Cassidy. We're going to be pals, I'm sure of it."

"What is this Tash business? Odd name."

"I was born in a remote part of the world called Tashkent, in the year of our Lord 1895. Turkestan ring a bell? Samarkand? Well, Tashkent is the leading city of the Uzbek region of what we must now think of as the Union of Soviet Socialist Republics. Soviet central Asia. My parents were off on some grim sort of lark, I suppose, rather dim my parents, both of them, and they thought it would be romantic to name their baby son, me, Tashkent. It has not been an easy burden to bear." He was leading the way through a thick keystone arch. "But enough about me. I want to hear about you, all about you. . . ."

• • •

When Benedictus and Porter had rousted them out of their first sleep they had discovered they were only fifty yards from a road that Benedictus had laid out, one that did not appear on any map. Porter had noticed them earlier, had reported intruders to the Guv'nor, as he and most of the neighbors called Benedictus, who had decided to pick them up. It was, after all, good sport and made for an evening's entertainment.

On the way back to the castle in the truck it had begun to snow, a fine, almost sandy snow driven by an increasingly hard wind. Now as he settled into a deep wingback chair Cassidy heard the wind in the chimney, heard the rattle of the snow on the long windows. Harry Madrid sat closer to the fire, which burned, a conflagration, in a fireplace the size of a room with a mantelpiece big enough for a Busby Berkeley chorus line. Lions crouched on either side of the grate. The walls were hung with ancestral portraits in heavy frames. Harry Madrid stared at the painted faces, then looked back at the round face and red hair of his host, as if seeking a resemblance.

"No need to look at me," Benedictus said. "I don't know who those blokes are. I bought 'em in a job lot at Sotheby's. I daresay they're somebody's ancestors. But surely not mine." His demeanor was boyish for a man of fifty, as if it all were a game of let's pretend: the bogus castle, the jodhpurs and the empty sleeve and the eye patch and the hearing aid jammed into his right ear. He was five nine, must have weighed two hundred pounds, but he moved lightly on small feet, like a dancer. He somehow managed not to be dwarfed by the gigantic scale of the room, which must have been seventy feet long, forty feet wide and twenty-five feet high. Everything was out of any human scale, as if the place had been built to be committed to film with bubbling test tubes and a whirling cyclotron in the laboratory next door.

Once they were all settled, spread out around the crackling fire, and Porter had supplied them with bottles of Irish whiskey and siphons of soda water, Benedictus stretched his booted legs out before him, crossed them, and fixed Cassidy with his sparkling pale green eye. "Now, tell us your story, old man. And don't try to fob off some tedious poaching tale on yours truly. Let's have a real story."

Half an hour later he scowled and splashed water on top of half a tumbler of Bushmill's. He stood with his back to the fireplace and glared at his guests.

"You mean to tell me that some damnable Hun, a Nazi, actually used my land—*my land*—as a point of illegal entry? Some bloody saboteur? Some swinish war criminal? An SS man?" The scowl deepened, his face flushed. "Is this what you're telling me, sir? Well, let me tell you—"

"That's not exactly it," Cassidy said. If he wanted Benedictus's help, the continuing opportunity to search for the plane, to reconstruct Manfred Moller's adventures, he had to level with the eccentric Guv'nor. "He's not a saboteur, he's not a war criminal so far as we know . . . he *is* a sort of advance man for escaping Nazi leaders, those who've slipped through the nets, those who'll never stand trial, those who are making off with loot and art treasures and their own skins—in short, those who want to survive in a new world."

"But surely," Benedictus said with a thick air of outraged propriety, "the point is this man's a rotter, an emissary of an evil empire." He fumed and stomped around in a circle, in the shadows of the flickering fire, like the dwarf or the troll in the story about Rumpelstiltskin. "We'd have known how to handle his sort at school, I promise you."

"And where was that?"

Benedictus's head snapped up. "What? What?" He tapped the hearing aid, stroked the wires. "Oh, school. Winchester." He started to speak again and a tinny whine seemed to emanate from his chest. He banged on the pocket of his shirt inside the hacking jacket and pulled the hearing aid from his ear. "Bloody thing!" he shouted. "Goes off on its own—rogue, y'know—starts screeching in my ear. Bloody nuisance at the ballet! I'd be better off with an ear trumpet! Well, well? What's supposed to have happened to this Nazi swine? By God, I'd have liked to get him in my sights, I'd have put paid to the bastard!" His voice sank to a whisper as he worked the earpiece back into place. "By God, I would." He looked slowly from face to face. "And you chaps are seconded to the Secret Service?"

"Not Hayes. He's our guide. Madrid and I are, shall we say, draftees? Willing, very willing. We want to find this man, destroy his network." Cassidy was beginning to feel like a righter of wrongs, a character from "Captain Midnight" or "Don Winslow of the Navy."

"Good for you, young Cassidy!" Benedictus took a long drink and shook his head vehemently. "My land, you say. You believe he landed his aircraft out there somewhere." He swung his good arm around in an arc, indicating the estate beyond the walls. Whiskey splashed his hand. "But how could I not know? No, no, I would have known! Damn me, lad, you're on a snipe hunt, I'm afraid. When do you think his plane went down?"

Cassidy told him.

Benedictus stared into space, calculating. "I wasn't here!" he cried. "I was in Los Angeles. . . . It's just possible, I suppose, the man could have come down where this poacher of yours says. . . . Well, blast! Who'd have thought such things could happen!"

In the silence that followed the fire snapped, the huge logs settling in on themselves as the flames ate them away. The gritty snow tapped at the windows.

"I want to have another look tomorrow," Cassidy said.

"Yes, old boy, of course, you must. Perhaps we can all go down there and beat the bushes." He strode across the worn Persian carpet, which was landing-strip size, and stood staring out into the darkness. "Snow," he mused.

Harry Madrid heaved himself to a standing position and stumped stiffly across to join him. He was smoking a Roi-tan, carrying his heavy glass in his meaty right hand. "Not a damn thing we can do about that. No point in worrying about it."

Benedictus nodded. "Right you are," he said. He swung back to Cassidy and Hayes, who seemed to have lost his powers of speech in the opulent surroundings. "Well, it's time for a bit of chow, what? Perhaps my lady will join us if we are fortunate."

Cassidy stood up and drained his glass.

Benedictus looked back out the window as if he'd heard a cry in the night. "My God, how I hate the bloody Germans," he said softly.

• • •

"I was just telling our guests, my darling, how much I hate the bloody Germans." Benedictus was sitting at the head of the long table. The furniture in the dining room was so huge and so ornate, so laden with a kind of Grinling Gibbons carving, that it seemed to anchor the castle in case it began, like so many dreams, to float away. As Benedictus spoke to his wife, she leaned over his plate cutting his meat, several slices from the large roast leg of lamb. He finally grew impatient, shooing her away. She dropped her eyes, began to unfold his napkin for him. "Enough, for Christ's sake!" He spoke sharply, the words stinging, bringing a flush to her almost artificially pale cheeks.

Cassidy watched her walk the length of the table, like a banished countess leaving the presence. She carried herself straight, with grace, as if to say that she could take the spear in the back if it came. "Yes," she said, her voice deep and slightly hoarse, a smoker's voice. "Tash certainly has good reason to hate the bloody Germans." She reached the end of the table, where Cassidy rose and held her chair. "Why, thank you, Mr. Cassidy," she said. "How kind you are." She looked up, her eyes black as an inquisitor's sins, outlined in thick black paint, the lashes long, like tiny wings or whips. Her wide mouth made a faint smile. Cassidy felt as if he'd been blindsided out of bounds. He felt as if the breath had been blown clean out of him.

It was all about the movies, because of the movies.

Mona Ransom had made her first picture at the age of sixteen, in 1923. She was the flip side of Mary Pickford, her hair jet black and cut in a kind of gleaming helmet with Dutch-boy points curling beneath her ears and seeming on the verge of piercing her ghostly white cheek just above the line of her jaw. She was, professionally speaking, a Very Bad Girl. She was a vamp, a tramp, a golddigger, a whore with no heart at all; she sang a siren song in one movie after another and danced and kissed and put her nipples on display and made rolled stockings and low-waisted flapper fashions a symbol of sex and licentiousness and evil in every home across the land. She inevitably came to a bad end in the last reel, coughing her life away in a barren tenement or tied to a stake by the Indians or strangled by a jealous husband she'd taunted all the way through the picture or . . . Well, whatever she got she damned well deserved. She made the move to talkies without missing a beat, maturing into womanhood and giving the hairstyle that swept the country her name. The Ransom. A King's Ransom, they said, or Pay the Ransom, it's worth it. There were lots of lines about Mona Ransom and her hair and her style and the white face and the eyes burning like coal. Then, in the late thirties, when she herself was just past thirty, she was gone. It wasn't something you sat up and noticed. Bad Girls weren't quite the hot tickets they'd once been. They seemed a little corny, to tell the truth. The great comediennes were replacing them and by the time you'd lapped up Claudette Colbert and Myrna Loy and all the rest, Roz Russell and Carole Lombard and Norma Shearer, you tended to forget about a Mona Ransom. She'd been there for a long time and then she wasn't there anymore. Now Lew Cassidy knew where she was. She was married to Pinnacle Pictures. She was Mrs. Benedictus.

Tash Benedictus was staring at Cassidy as if he were privy to the quick biography playing a limited run in Cassidy's mind, the rush of emotion that had come at the first look into her eyes, the first whiff of her perfume and the sound of her voice.

"Are you two quite through down there?" The sarcasm was too thick for the provocation. Cassidy realized that Benedictus was losing the battle with the Bushmill's.

"I believe we are, my dear," she said. She smiled at Cassidy. Hers was the widest mouth he'd ever seen. Everything about her was exaggerated. Her white, white shoulders were unusually wide, the black dinner dress unusually severe, the strand of pearls perfect, with a hint of pink. Her lipstick was so dark a scarlet that it was another color that didn't have a name. Her fingers were extraordinarily long and delicate as they curled around the Baccarat stemware. He could imagine her touch. He realized that Harry Madrid was watching. When he returned the look Harry glanced at Mona Ransom, then slowly rolled his eyes heavenward. Mona Ransom's gaze slid from Cassidy to her husband. "You were about to tell our guests why you hate the bloody Germans, weren't you, dear?"

"Ah," Benedictus said, chewing on a piece of lamb, halving a roast potato with his fork, "was I, indeed? Thank you for reminding me, my darling. It's odd, isn't it? The way she thinks that because I'm physically crippled I'm mentally impaired as well. Ah, Cassidy, what's one to do with women? Yes, I do hate the bloody Germans." He ate the potato, then drained off half a goblet of a heavy claret. "Germans did this to me." He reached across his thick chest and flapped the empty sleeve of his jacket. "In the Great War. Battle of the Somme. Same old story. Up to my arse in blood, death in the trenches, rats dining on my buddies, I'd have been overjoyed to die with them . . . make a rat's dinner of old Tash. . . . But I didn't die. Great awful shelling, direct hit down the line . . . Lost my arm, lost my eye, made mince out of my ear, rattled my brain around like a pea in a bucket, but you know what damn near killed me? It's a true story, I damn near drowned in Lance Corporal

Hixon's blood. They thought I was dead, see? And Hixon's chest got blown out through his bung and he landed on top of me and I took a deep breath and drank about a gallon of his blood. . . ." He grinned across his plate, speared another slab of lamb, and began chewing. He lifted his glass. "I give you the bloody Huns, may we kill 'em until we run out of 'em!" He finished off his wine and poured the goblet full again.

"But that's not the worst thing they've done to me. Oh, not by a long shot. They killed my son. Not, let me add, Miss Ransom's son—my son by my first wife. Battle of Britain, summer of 'forty. Over the Channel. Spitfire pilot." Benedictus rubbed his nose, sniffed. "Watery grave. Asleep in the deep. Nineteen years old. I hate the bloody Germans. And, gentlemen, I wish you good hunting. If you catch the bastard, spill some blood for old Tash Benedictus." He belched softly into his napkin. "And spill some more for his son, the late Crispin Anthony Benedictus."

He wiped his eye with the napkin, then looked around the table with a defiant expression on his round face.

• • •

Then, later on, there was the unpleasant business of the serving girl and the teapot. Cassidy guessed that there was a staff of at least five. Porter, the chauffeur and jack of all trades; a kind of butler who had served the lamb, carved it, presented the wine, and supervised the two girls who did the rest of the serving; and somewhere there was presumably a cook. It was the younger of the serving girls, who seemed to be twenty at the most and probably just out of high school, she of the spotty complexion and the washed-out mousy brown hair, she of the starched gray uniform and stiff white apron—it was she who ran afoul of the teapot, which in this event contained the coffee.

The butler had brought the Hennessy cognac to the table on a silver tray. He had warmed the snifters over a flame. He had brought the cheese tray. All was well. There wasn't a bloody German in sight and the Guv'nor was in his cups.

The girl, who had a cold and a red nose to prove it, brought the coffee. Mona Ransom shook her head, said it would keep her awake. Hayes, Harry Madrid, and Cassidy all accepted and she poured carefully.

When she got to the head of the table where Benedictus slouched in his chair like a latter-day Richard III on his throne, she hesitated. "Sir?" she said.

"Of course, you daft girl," he snapped. She began pouring and something displeased the Guv'nor, who sat up, said, "Don't take forever, for the love of Christ!" He jabbed at her arm, urging her on, and the coffee overflowed the bone china, sloshing into the saucer.

Benedictus exploded.

"Here, you silly cow, give it to me. We'll make a proper job of it!"

He grabbed the pot in his right hand, pulled it out of her grip. His hand was clasped around the body of the pot and suddenly his face was contorted with the pain, the heat of the pot burning his palm. He gave a wordless cry and stood up, pushing the huge chair backward, and hurled the pot across the room. It shattered on the floor, boiling coffee splashing the wall.

The girl stood stock still, trembling, her eyes wide with fear, full of the hopeless realization of generations of serving wenches who have always known they will bear the anger and the blame no matter whose the fault.

Benedictus turned on her, holding his burned hand before him as if it were Exhibit A. "You hopeless, idiotic bitch," he said, his voice steely and under control, the drunken slur just below the surface. "You will clean this up and then you will get out of my sight. You're a sow, a slovenly sow, do you understand?" He watched her shake until she seemed to burst, to split apart at the seams. She began sobbing hysterically, unable to move. "Clean it up!" he screamed. He was turning a rich, plummy crimson. He took one step toward her as if to strike her when Mona Ransom's deep, hoarse voice froze the scene.

"Oh, Tash, you are such a drunken sot!"

She didn't speak at all loudly but it was as if she'd driven the exclamation point through his heart. "Now you've made poor Dora cry. Really, Tash. It's a good thing you have only one hand." She'd gone to the sobbing Dora and put her arm around the quaking shoulders. "With two it's difficult to imagine just how much hell you'd raise." She led Dora down the room toward the serving entrance.

"Porter!" Benedictus bawled. "Porter, you wretch!"

The immense figure materialized in the doorway leading God only knew where. "Yes, Guv'nor?"

"Well, come here, man! Lead the master, who seems to be a bit under the weather, not entirely himself . . . to his bed."

Benedictus turned back and made a drunken bow to the three men rooted to their spots at the table. "I trust you've all enjoyed our bit of cabaret. We do aim to give satisfaction." He threw back his head and laughed, a high piping sound, like a boy soprano. Porter came in and Benedictus threw his arm over the big man's shoulder, was led away like a battlefield casualty.

Porter looked back from the doorway.

"Give me a moment, gentlemen, and I'll get the Guv'nor tucked in. Then I'll show you to your rooms."

• • •

Cassidy wondered how many fireplaces Last Bastion contained. There was a honey of a fireplace in his bedroom. The ashes were banked, glowing red from within, and the stacked coal hissed softly. He took off his hiking clothes and slipped into a white terrycloth robe that had been waiting for him on the turned-down bed. Away from the fireplace the room was cold. The windows were set into the wall several inches and faced out onto a wide stretch of lawn just barely discernible a couple of stories below. It had grown a stubble of snow and the grainy flakes still filled the sky. It was past midnight. He turned away from the unsatisfying glimpse of the night, wrapped the robe tight, and climbed into bed.

He was bone weary but wound up by the evening, the performances of Tash Benedictus and his wife. He'd watched enough of the moviemaking process to have the feeling that he'd stepped into some kind of show tonight, something that was both real and simultaneously a fake. Still, Benedictus couldn't have faked the last bit, the rage at the girl, the exposure of his own pathetic ego. He hadn't faked the missing arm and the missing eye and the ugly balled-up piece of pulp that had been an ear. Cassidy simply didn't know what to make of it, of him. But he sure as hell hated the bloody Germans.

And then there was Mona Ransom.

Cassidy thought he was beginning to have a dream when he heard the slight squeak, saw the door slowly come open, the shadowy figure step into his room. When it dawned on him that it wasn't a dream he leaned up on one elbow, tried shaking the cobwebs loose, said: "Harry? What the hell's—"

"It's not Harry."

He recognized the deep throaty voice, still hoarse.

"It's me." She stood beside the bed. "I'm cold."

"I'm not surprised, walking around a castle in the middle of the night. It's cold work, Miss Ransom."

"I'm also lonely, Mr. Cassidy."

"Me, I'm just cold."

"I can make you warm." Cassidy had never heard a human voice with less humor in it than hers, just then.

"You sound like you're trapped in one of your old movies. I'm sure you've delivered these lines before."

"A thousand times before. Believe me. Will you take a hand in solving my problems?" She was standing next to the bed. He could smell her. The wool robe brushed his face as she untied the belt.

"Oh, my. Which problems are those?"

"Cold. Loneliness. Move over. I've got something I think I should tell you." She pulled the blankets back, put one knee on the sheet, hesitated, reached out and put her fingertips to his mouth. "Do I worry you?"

"I'm not sure I'd call it a worry."

She pulled the robe open and carefully stroked his mouth with her right nipple. "Suck it," she said softly. "Do I have to tell you everything?"

"It might be fun."

She slid down beside him, her laughter low and rich, her breath warm on his face. "I'm just like I was in the movies. You thought about the movies when you first saw me, didn't you? Well, I don't blame you. I wasn't acting, I'm afraid. At least not much. Do you mind if I take advantage of you? I rather like being in charge . . . setting the pace, would that be all right with you? Does your poor leg bother you?"

"That's not my leg, Miss Ransom."

She giggled against his face. He kissed her neck while she stroked him until her fingers were slippery. She licked her fingers while he watched.

"What was it you had in mind?"

"A very expert fuck, Mr. Cassidy. You can really just stay as you are, phone in your performance. I'm going to do all the work. I just love to do all the work. . . ." She slid down and began and for a while she couldn't talk and he twined his fingers in her thick black hair, leaned down to kiss it. Then he heard himself gasp and she coughed quietly, her fingers squeezing him, and he pulled her up and kissed her for a long time while she worked her body against his thigh, leaving his leg wet, then crawling on top of him, then riding him, her head hanging down above him, trembling. It all went on for a long time until they were both dripping wet and hot, the covers thrown back. "You must think me a slut. Well, I expect you're quite right. But I haven't always been, you know."

"I'm sure. You're really . . . ah, indescribable."

"It's my theory that it's a man's world—what do you think of that, Mr. Cassidy?" She nestled against him, her long fingers flat against his chest.

"A widely held theory, I understand."

"I look upon it as my job to redress the balance. I take the lead when it suits me—"

"May I say that it suits you?"

"And I observe the behavior of men. I study men. I do not study Tash anymore. I know all I care to know about my dear husband. He frustrates me in every imaginable way. As you may just have discovered. Tash did not describe to you this evening the full extent of his war injuries. He had no son, Mr. Cassidy. He will never have a son. It is a fantasy, a game he sometimes plays. . . . No man was ever more suited to the movie business. Tash is all a fantasy, while you," she cooed darkly against his chest, "are all too real. I'm quite warm now. And not as lonely as before. You have behaved very decently, Mr. Cassidy."

"I try to do my part, of course."

"And you do it very well."

"What was it you said you had to tell me?"

"Oh, that." She kissed him. "Maybe I'd better not."

"I wonder what you could possibly know to tell a complete stranger."

"I think you'd be utterly amazed." She looked up, sucking her knuckle, then wiping it across his mouth.

He sat up, took her broad shoulders in his hands, held her firmly. "Then tell me, Miss Ransom. Pay the piper."

"You're hurting me."

"Believe me, this isn't hurting. Now speak up."

"You're not being nice at all—"

"It's a man's world, remember?"

"He knew all about you, that's all—"

"Who knew what? This is no time for obscurity."

"Tash," she whispered. "He knew you were coming. That's why he was on the lookout for you."

"Impossible—"

"Nothing is impossible with Tash. He knew you were coming. He's been waiting. . . ."

Cassidy heard a soft but insistent tapping at the door.

He got out of bed and slipped into the robe.

"Oh, damn," she sighed.

"Is this going to be Tash with an elephant gun?"

"No."

Cassidy opened the door a few inches. "Yes?"

It was Porter, still fully clothed.

"Excuse me, sir. I've come to see Miss Ransom back to her room. If she's ready, of course."

• • •

Tash Benedictus was remarkably sober. He sat in his study, listening to the snow rattling on the glass. In his own way he was a rather romantic soul. To prove it he was listening to a recording of *Swan Lake* on his Victrola. His hearing aid did the best it could, prodded his memory of the music. Most of his listening had a lot to do with memory.

The rap came at his door and Porter entered.

"I've put her back to bed, Guv'nor. House is all quiet now."

"Well done. Now toddle." He watched Porter retire, closing the door behind him.

Benedictus looked at the ormolu clock ticking on the mantelpiece. He'd let his fire die down.

He picked up the old black telephone, an upright model, and slid it to the middle of his desk. He lifted the earpiece out of the prongs, leaned toward the mouthpiece, and placed his call. He waited until it was patched across the miles and the storm. Finally he heard someone lifting the receiver at the other end.

After a few seconds a voice said: "Yes?"

"I'm calling from Tuggle," Benedictus said.

The line broke up with static as if the wind and snow were chewing at the telephone lines. He waited for what seemed like an eternity.

Finally the voice spoke again.

"Vulkan here."

# CHAPTER FOURTEEN

The household, the castle, Last Bastion, was quiet when Cassidy awoke. He'd slept late. It was nearly ten o'clock. He wandered down the hallway, hoping to God he didn't run into his bedmate of the night before or, for that matter, her husband or her incurious keeper, the remarkable Porter. He found the bathroom before anyone discovered him and had a shower that parboiled him. It was wonderful. He rubbed himself dry, slipped back into the robe, and padded quickly down the freezing passage to his room. He dressed in yesterday's hiking clothes. He went down the stairs and heard a radio voice talking about the storm from a station in Bangor. He followed the voice until he heard a low murmur of conversation, passed through a wide double doorway into the dining room.

Porter, Harry Madrid, and Tom Hayes were having breakfast and discussing the weather. Harry Madrid looked up. He had grown a white stubble and his steely hair was slicked straight back with water. "Morning, Lew. Sleep well?"

"You should have been there." He looked at Porter who nodded a good morning. "You should have gotten me up, Harry."

"No need, is there? What we're looking for ain't going anywhere. Plate for you over on the sideboard there."

Porter said: "Coffee's on the table, sir."

Cassidy went to the sideboard, took one look, and realized how hungry he was. There were kidneys in a thick brown sauce, sausages, scalloped potatoes, scrambled eggs, broiled tomatoes, bacon, all in chafing dishes. He loaded up, came back to the table, and Porter poured him a large mug of coffee, pushed a long silver toast rack toward him, followed by silver pots of jam and marmalade. "You guys go right on talking," Cassidy said. "Pay me no mind." He dug in like a starving man.

"Worked up an appetite, did you?" Tom Hayes said. "Well, this is a sight better breakfast than you'd of gotten from me out there." He motioned with a jerk of his head toward the long windows where the drapes were tied back and it was still snowing, thicker than last night.

Porter had finished eating, leaned back with a toothpick. "I was out having a look-see at first light. Only a couple of inches, real dry, but that's changing now. Flakes are getting big and spongy, heavy as cement." He stood up and went to the windows and stared out, getting a handle on the day. "Temperature's up, about forty. Take a look at those big pines, see how they droop, how white they are, like frosting on a cake. Heart-attack weather." He laughed harshly. From where Cassidy sat the world looked like last year's Christmas cards.

The other three men kept thinking of things to say about the weather and Cassidy ate and tried to remember that the visit from Mona Ransom had actually happened, hadn't been some weird, out-of-left-field dream. He felt vaguely foolish, as if he'd somehow been used, an easy lay. He regretted the whole thing. In anything approaching a normal human being her behavior would have been absurd, laughable, but that was the point: *she* was Mona Ransom. And Cassidy wasn't laughing.

He didn't want to see her again. He was afraid of the effect she might have on him, embarrassed by what he might do if given the opportunity. He was just too old and too hurt for that kind of stuff. Although at thirty-three he was five years younger than Mona Ransom. It occurred to him that what the World Series was to him visiting strangers' bedrooms was to Mona Ransom. If she'd been telling the truth about the extent of Benedictus's war injuries, she was terribly ill-suited to the marriage. But she was as involved in her performance as her husband had been. Nothing seemed quite real in the castle. Anyway, if he was no good to her sexually, what had he offered? Money, sure, but she'd probably had a good deal of her own. And her career had ended with the marriage. Security, maybe? The knowledge that the money would always be there . . . and someone to take care of her, too? But then what was he getting out of it if sex wasn't part of it? Maybe he was one of those wounded and embittered men who enjoyed crippling someone else in a subtler, more malevolent manner. From what he'd seen of it, their marriage had a good bit in common with a carnival House of Horrors.

When he went back to the sideboard for a refill he saw that the coffee stains had been cleaned away from the wall where the old Winchester man had pitched the coffeepot. But there, behind a leg of the sideboard, he saw a triangular chip of china. He bent down and picked it up, seeing a small corner of the design, blue paint. He brought it back to the table where Porter was pouring himself another cup of coffee. He put the chip down beside Porter's mug.

"Just in case you're trying to reconstruct the pot."

Porter looked up solemnly. "Thank you, sir, but I doubt very much if that's quite on."

"No, probably not. Won't our host be joining us for breakfast?"

"I think not. They have not yet arisen." He gave Cassidy a wintry smile. There wasn't a hint of his middle-of-the night errand, returning Miss Ransom to her rightful owner, as it were.

• • •

They were all standing around in the wide driveway, their waterproofs rapidly being covered with the clinging wet snow. The world had been enveloped in a pristine, pure, and innocent whiteness. Porter was putting the chains on the truck. Tom Hayes hunkered down beside him, lining them up as Porter backed up on them. It seemed to be understood that their search for the remnants of Manfred Moller's plane would continue, the snow notwithstanding.

They piled back into the truck and Porter put it in gear. It shimmied slightly, settling its weight down into the virgin snow, then crunched forward, spoiling the day's perfection. The road sat on a ridge that the wind naturally tended to sweep. It lay like a white satin ribbon, die-straight, like a narrow fairway surrounded by one hell of a deep rough.

When Porter braked to a halt he pointed out the window on the driver's side. "Keyhole Lake's right down there, past the pines about fifty yards in, then down the hill. Now, unless you gentlemen are professional mountaineers and trackers, let me warn you not to get in there and overdo it. You can get all heated up, sit down to take a rest, and just die. Mark my words. Synchronize your watches. In five minutes it will be noon. It's going to keep snowing and the temperature will be going down with the sun. The snow will sneak up on you, it'll be deep before you quite know it, and you'll have the undergrowth and the snow to contend with. Keep all this in mind. Pace yourselves." He sounded like a scoutmaster or a very gentle top kick. "You can see the road's straight as a string. Take your time when you start back and you'll get there. Now, if you're not back by five or six I'll drive down and wait for you. Are we all clear on that, gentlemen?"

• • •

The landscape didn't look treacherous, which only went to show you how looks could deceive.

Within the first ten yards Cassidy had wrenched his ankle in the hidden undergrowth and pitched forward, sprawled flat on his face. He struggled up to his knees and heard Harry Madrid moving slowly but surely, chortling. Tom Hayes moved ahead, more practiced, more of a woodsman. Cassidy waited on his knees until Harry Madrid drew even with him.

"This Seth Marson, you think he knows what the hell he's talking about?"

"Well, I must say, Lewis, that's how he struck me. He's done a lot of poaching and I'm told that poachers—and this is quite understandable if you think about it—I'm told that poachers will always know the lay of the land better than anybody, better even than the gamekeeper. So, I've been figuring that our friend Seth knows whereof he speaks."

"That's a yes, then?"

"You could say that, Lewis."

They forged deep into the pine woods but it was still a world of blinding whiteness in which you instinctively squinted, shutting out as much of the glare as possible. The snow fell steadily, slowly drifting, silently making things disappear. Tiny anonymous birds flitted from tree to tree but kept civil tongues in their heads. A squirrel peered out of a hole in the snow, looking somewhat disgruntled. The storm was four or five weeks ahead of schedule.

Pushing past boughs so heavily weighted that they lay exhausted on the ground, Cassidy loosed an avalanche from boughs above and was suddenly swamped by a billion icy crystals, snow down inside his collar, soaking him, turning his sweat into ice water. "Ah, goddammit!" he bellowed, brushing himself off, causing another avalanche.

Harry Madrid said: "What'd I tell you about nature, Lewis? It's a bad and scary place. Reminds me of the old Jack London story, fella down to his last match, then all the snow slides down on him and—"

"Harry, for chrissakes, I know the story, everybody knows that story."

"You think so?" He smiled benignly at Cassidy's distress. "You're so beautiful when you're mad, son." His cement jowls shook with mirth.

"Thank you, Harry." It had never occurred to Cassidy that Harry Madrid had a sense of humor. He'd thought Harry was remorseless, a throwback, not much of a laugher. You lived and you learned.

They reached the snowy shores of the lake where Tom Hayes was waiting for them. He'd found the remains of the camp they'd made the night before. It was colder by the water, as if the lake created wind. They wrote off the area they'd traversed previously and sorted out where each would set out now. Harry Madrid got the first chunk of land, Cassidy the middle third, Hayes the farthest. They set out from the lake, relying on their eyes, searching the whiteness, stopping, blinking at the glare, trying to see past the glare and find the prize.

And hour passed, then two, then three and the sun was drooping toward the pointed pine tops in the west. They had all worked their way toward a central clearing hewn for no visible reason from the middle of the forest. They straggled around the edge, thankful to be out of the pressing trees. Cassidy was as wet as he'd ever been outside of a swimming pool. Sweat ran into his eyes, sweat mixed with the constant drifting snow on his face. He was breathing hard. Harry Madrid found a stump and looked out across the clearing. It couldn't have been more than fifty yards, maybe less, across the waving scrim of snow to the trees on the other side. They looked like something from a fairy tale, deep in the Black Forest of the Brothers Grimm.

"I'm too damn old for this." Harry Madrid wiped his face with a blue bandanna. "Put a fork in me, Mama, I'm done."

Cassidy nodded. "Looks like we've just about had it. Fucking snow . . ."

The snow had reached a depth of a foot in the clearing, where there were no trees to break its fall to earth.

The quietness was like nothing Cassidy had ever experienced. The isolation coupled with the muffling effect of the snow was too much. He realized it was frightening him. You could cease to exist in such a place, die so easily, just give up, give in. You could drown in the quiet, slip beneath the waves of snow, give up on trying to resurrect your life and bring your dead wife back from the grave. . . . It had looked like a pisser of a job going in and then there'd been that little shock of hope, the touch of the icy fingers up and down your spine, when she'd known how to get to the apartment on Washington Square. When she'd remembered those scenes, the gulls and the huge ships at the pier, the Christmas tree in the snow under the great archway at the foot of Fifth Avenue. There'd been hope all of a sudden. And then nothing. Nothing except watching her dance and realizing he still loved her. . . . So it was still a pisser and he knew damned well something would go wrong. He wouldn't get the girl, and in the dark pit of his gut, for the first time in his life, he felt the premonition that you spent a lifetime trying to avoid.

He had the feeling that he was going to die over this goddamn Manfred Moller thing.

• • •

"Hey, you guys . . . Jesus, you guys! Look!"

Hayes was standing out at the edge of the trees, twenty or thirty feet along the circle, staring out into the falling snow, his voice a supercharged whisper. "C'mere, over here." He was beckoning to them, waving his arm.

Cassidy picked his way through the mounds of snow growing like crazy fungus on the clots of underbrush, came to stand beside Hayes. Harry Madrid was puffing along behind him. Hayes pointed across the clearing, through the snow. "There, through the snow, see where I'm pointing. Jesus, he's big as a house. . . ."

Cassidy strained to see through the snow, looking along the rim of stubble and pine boughs. "What the hell are you talking about?" He breathed the words, knowing that it was time to whisper.

Harry Madrid said: "Well, I'll be a son of a gun. I see it. Big ain't the word!"

Then Cassidy saw it. Just inside the trees edging the clearing, camouflaged against the dark boughs mottled with clumps of snow.

A moose, looking about the size of an elephant.

There it stood, its great spread of scooplike antlers, its long nose-heavy face: it stood quietly in the snow like the world's only big moose statue. It was staring throughtfully ahead, almost in profile from where they stood. The antlers were blotched with snow. It turned slowly, just its big drooping head, to have a look at the three of them. The moose did not seem overly impressed. The massive head turned back to what had engaged its attention in the first place.

It took several minutes of standing there peering across the clearing until the thing, the object, took form like something in a puzzle. Cassidy saw the truth of it first, realized what the moose found so fascinating, and he smiled.

The snowy fuselage and tail section of an airplane, its nose squashed down into the earth.

The moose seemed to be chewing on a broken, dangling piece of pontoon.

The plane hadn't quite made the lake.

• • •

It had been an old crate to begin with and a spring, summer, and early fall out in the elements hadn't done it any good. Most of the paint had peeled away and the metal had rusted in spots. The rivets had been worked loose when it had hit the ground. There were streaks of blackened, burned oil traces where the engine housing had burrowed into earth. Some broken, browned pine boughs, a few lopsided trees indicated the downward path as the crash had occurred.

The pines were so high, so full, that they must have cushioned the impact, creating a kind of slide-chute effect as it settled down to rest. Some faint words painted on the door over the wing said & HAL FAX, N A SCO . The one pontoon had been ripped clear off, nowhere to be seen. The other—the one the moose had been pushing about with its nose—hung sideways, dangling by a metal strut. One wing had been crumpled back and sheared off, lay twenty feet away in the snow. The other wing had torn loose from the fuselage, held only by a couple of rivets, wedged against the scarred trunk of a pine that was rather the worse for the encounter.

The moose had ambled away as if it had sensed it had nothing to fear from these men, two of whom at least had no business whatsoever in the middle of the woods.

They had to work fast. The light was going, long purple shadows slumping down on them from high up in the trees. The wind had come up, whistled in the pines, and the snow kept falling, heavier yet. Tom Hayes had a flashlight in his pocket but none of them wanted to be stranded short of the road in the dark with nothing but a flashlight.

Fortunately the fire during the crash hadn't amounted to much, which made looking around considerably simpler than it might have been. Cassidy climbed up onto the loose wing, ducking the dangling pontoon, and prized back the door on the pilot's side of the cockpit.

The pilot himself was still strapped into his seat, a ramshackled bucket with stuffing coming out and the frame showing. His head rested forward on his chest; or rather the skull, which had lost most of its flesh and skin and the entire complement of eyes. The flight jacket was torn, also the trousers. Animals, birds, all the little carnivores who lived in the woods, had made a feast of the pilot. His fingers were stripped of skin and one thumb had simply disappeared. But the animals of the forest hadn't killed him. Neither had the crash. What killed him was the bullet that had entered the right temple and blown most of the left side of the cranium away. The bullet had kept on going through the fuselage.

Cassidy climbed down, went around the tail section, and found the door on the passenger side of the cockpit hanging open, stiff and set with rust on its hinges.

Harry Madrid surveyed the scene.

"Doesn't take Sherlock Holmes to figure out what happened. Our man Moller's a hardy little fart. They crash-land, pine trees cushion the impact and save their lives. Moller kills the pilot. . . . Pilot was a dead man from the moment he agreed to fly him in, I guess, doncha think, Lewis?"

"I think absolutely anybody who gets in Moller's way is a dead man."

Harry Madrid nodded. "Göring picked the right man for the job. He's a man who gets the job done. Kind of your killing machine . . ." He harrumphed. "Well, I've run up against lots of killing machines in my time." He spat into the snow. "They all get dead somewhere along the way."

Tom Hayes flicked on the flashlight and handed it to Cassidy. "I'd advise you fellas to think about heading up to the road. It's nearly five."

Harry Madrid said, "How time flies."

Cassidy shone the light around the interior of the cockpit, looking for something that might prove that Manfred Moller had been there, had killed and survived. Snow and dead leaves and a bad, rotting smell, that was the interior. To hell with it.

He climbed down and stood looking at the wreckage.

Then, as a last thought before packing it in, he dropped to his knees and looked for a compartment in the belly of the fuselage that might have been used for luggage.

He found the handle but it was locked. He gave it a tug to no avail. Of course, Moller wouldn't have survived the crash and then neglected to take his minotaur with him, his minotaur and whatever else he might have had.

Harry Madrid grunted and knelt beside him. "Here, use this to pry it open." He handed Cassidy a heavy bit of broken strut.

Cassidy took it, handed the flashlight to Harry Madrid. Their breath blew out in thick visible clouds. The temperature was diving again as night fell. He fit the flattened end of the strut into the narrow gap and pushed. The door popped open easily, like a toy. Harry Madrid leaned up, pointed the light into the compartment.

Nothing.

Cassidy hadn't been expecting anything, had only hoped. He leaned back on his haunches and looked at Harry Madrid.

"Well, Lewis, we found what we came for. Cheer up."

As he stood up the flashlight slipped from Harry Madrid's hand, dropped to the thin snow covering the leaves beneath the plane's belly. The flashlight hit something just dusted by the snow, something bright that the light had picked out.

Cassidy dropped to his knees again and dug his nails into the snow and leaves, looking for the flash of something shiny and green in the wet mush of dead leaves. He found it and brushed it off, held it up. Tom Hayes was looking over Harry Madrid's shoulder at it and gasped.

A broad smile crossed Harry Madrid's normally impassive monolithic face. "Musta dropped off that minotaur thing during the getaway."

Tom Hayes wiped his mouth with one hand, took off his red-and-black cap, and ran his other hand through his hair. "Well, I'll be a monkey's uncle, damned to hell and back if I won't."

In his hand Lew Cassidy was holding one very large, very green emerald.

• • •

They reached the road and stood calf-deep in the snow by its side. Cassidy leaned forward, hands on knees, breathing deeply. The wind blew across the road's surface, kept it smooth, the snow not as deep as it was in the gullies and the shoulders that slanted away.

Porter hadn't come down with the truck yet and it was just past six o'clock.

Harry Madrid was puffing, looking up the ribbon of road. "I hate to face it, but I think we'd better start walking. If he comes for us he can pick us up on the way. This stuff is only six or seven inches deep."

Darkness was landing on them with a terrible thud.

It was a long hard walk and Porter never showed.

Harry Madrid was puffing like a steam engine.

Cassidy kept thinking about Manfred Moller, tried not to think about how tired he was, how cold his feet were, how brittle and numb his hands felt. All right, so Moller made it to Maine, survived the crash, killed the pilot . . . lost an emerald . . .

But where had he gone? There he'd been, out in the middle of the Maine woods, probably pretty badly shaken up, carrying his treasure on him, looking for the man code-named Vulkan. What had the poor lost son of a bitch done?

One thing Cassidy knew for sure. If Tash Benedictus had found him he'd have been one dead bloody German.

• • •

They straggled the last hundred yards to the castle with the wind howling at them, the last survivors of the lost legion, back from the far side of beyond.

They had the very hell of a time raising anyone. Finally the butler opened the heavy door, stood in his cardigan and carpet slippers, mouth agape as if the three men in the night had entirely slipped his mind. "My goodness," he said, standing back as they tramped in, dripping in the huge echoing foyer. "You must be exhausted. Are you all right? You'll be wanting toddies. Hot buttered rum?"

The fire was roaring in no time. The butler brought the boiling water, the butter, the rum, sugar cubes, bitters. And the news.

There was no one to tell of their find.

The Benedictuses, with Porter in tow, had decamped for parts unknown. Twenty-one pieces of luggage, by actual count. No, the butler didn't know where they were going and that really wasn't so unusual; Mr. and Mrs. Benedictus were an impulsive couple—it could be Palm Beach or the other castle, the one in Killarney, or Beverly Hills or the mountain place, or even just down to New York for a few weeks. There was just no telling. When it was relevant for the staff to be informed, Mr. Benedictus would certainly inform them.

"The man's got a passion for castles," Harry Madrid said.

"Well, only the two, sir," the butler said. "This one and the one in Ireland. Mr. Benedictus is very fond of castles, collecting his art, and riding. Riding to hounds and . . . well, just plain riding."

"And very fond of Mrs. Benedictus," Cassidy said.

"And all with only one arm and one eye," Harry Madrid said. "What a guy!"

"Mr. Benedictus is a remarkable man." The butler was dropping the butter into the hot water and rum.

While they warmed themselves at the fire, finishing the drinks, the butler reappeared with trays of cold roast beef, bread, mustard, pickles, steaming bowls of beef-and-barley soup. They ate with a certain devotion to the task.

"How's the World Series going?" Cassidy asked.

"I beg your pardon, sir?" The butler was clearing the trays.

"Baseball. The Tigers and the Cubs."

"I'm afraid I'm not a baseball enthusiast, sir."

Cassidy looked over at Harry Madrid, who had lit up a Roi-tan. "You know, Harry, I was reading this article about this new process. Television. This article said someday people will be able to watch the World Series—watch it, like a movie, Harry—right in their own homes. Baseball, football, movies. Think of it, Harry—"

"Wise up, Lewis." Harry Madrid chuckled. "It'll never happen. A sucker's scheme, get people to invest or some damn thing." He yawned.

"You think I could call the newspaper in Bangor or some place, find out the results?"

Tom Hayes said, "No luck on the phone, I'm afraid. Just tried to call the wife. She must be worried sick. . . ." He threw up his hands, his face forlorn. "Phone lines are down. Always happens, every damned storm we get, bang, down the bastards go. . . ." He shook his head at the perfidy of the phone lines. "The lights'll go next, mark my words."

Half an hour later the lights flickered and went out.

Fortunately the wall sconces, the nice Hollywood touch, were oil-fed and burned on. Tom Hayes said, "Wha'd I tell you guys?"

They slowly stumbled off to bed carrying candles the butler provided. "We're used to this sort of thing. It's the country, after all, isn't it? No electricity at all in the Killarney castle. No telephone either. Well, sleep well, gentlemen."

Harry Madrid knocked on Cassidy's door ten minutes later. When Cassidy opened the door he said, "Go to sleep, Harry. It's late."

Harry Madrid was chewing on the dead Roi-tan. "Lemme see the rock again, old son."

"I was just admiring it myself." He went back to the bed and picked it up from on top of the blanket. He flipped it to Harry Madrid.

"It's Nazi green, Lew. As I live and breathe." He placed it back on the blanket. "Sleep tight, son. We are most definitely on the trail."

"Are we, Harry?"

"Bank on it."

Harry Madrid left and Cassidy crawled back into bed, the emerald under his pillow. *Nazi green.* He smiled to himself, blew out the candle, listened to the wind at the window.

He was thinking about Mona Ransom. What was her number, anyway? Was she just a goony adventuress? A head case, a Section Eight? An old-fashioned nympho?

He remembered her calling Tash Benedictus a drunken sot. He remembered her comforting the poor girl, Dora. . . .

She had seemed very much in control then, able to dominate her drunken sot of a husband. And, God knew, she'd been totally in control when she'd come to his room. And she'd got precisely what she'd come for.

But what had she meant: *Tash . . . He knew you were coming. . . .*

# Chapter Fifteen

Cassidy decided that Tuggle, Maine, under the blanket of snow, looked like a Hollywood construction on a backlot somewhere, the setting for one of those romantic comedies with a moral that would show Cary Grant or William Powell or Ronald Colman to good advantage with Loretta Young or Irene Dunne. Maybe a Pinnacle Picture, though hardly a Mona Ransom vehicle. All the sounds were muffled and you could hear the chains clinking as the wheels rolled through the snow. The café at the corner had grown a patina of ice on the plate-glass windows and everybody was smiling the way folks do when they're drawn together by the elements having a go at them. It was all just the way a small town up in the piney woods was supposed to be, even with a castle nearby and the wreckage of a plane with a corpse in the cockpit providing a hearty repast for the local insect population.

The Packard convertible, wearing its chains, moved in stately grace toward the corner café, Harriet's Kitchen, and settled up against a drift half obscuring a mailbox. Harry Madrid got out and stretched, taking deep manly breaths. Cassidy stepped into the drift and hobbled out to the sidewalk. He was stiff but happy to be leaving simple little Tuggle, where he had yet to find anything that made much sense.

They had left the castle at first light, showered and cleaned up the best they could, full of hot coffee, shivering in the cold. The butler had driven them until they'd located Tom Hayes's truck, one of the larger drifts on the road where they'd left it two days before. They declined Tom's invitation to join him and his wife for breakfast. Cassidy couldn't face a family get-together and said they had to try to get to New York in one shot and you never knew how bad the roads might be.

Once they drove away from the Hayes house, Cassidy turned to Harry Madrid. "But first, my good companion, we have a breakfast fit for men hitting the road. And I find a newspaper."

It was positively steamy in Harriet's Kitchen. It was eight o'clock and the booths were mostly full. It was like a surprise holiday and you had the feeling that the morning regulars had been joined by fellows who'd normally have been doing something else. The boisterous holiday quality mingled with the steam and the aroma of coffee and frying bacon and hot toast and maple syrup and the sound of snow shovels scraping along the sidewalk outside.

Cassidy saw newspapers in a stack by the cash register, newspapers from Bangor and Portland for the last few days. He slapped the change down on the counter and led the way to the last empty booth. "Harry, order breakfast for both of us and don't spare the horses. It's a long way to New York." He sighed as Harry Madrid began rumbling to the fat waitress with tightly curled hair like copper filings. He found the sports pages.

That first day out in the woods they'd played Game Four at Wrigley in Chicago. Dizzy Trout had gone all the way for the Tigers to beat a succession of four Chicago pitchers, 4–1. The Series was then even after four games. But yesterday, while they were wandering around out in the storm and finally finding the plane, Hal Newhouser had taken the hill for the Tigers and thrown a complete game at the Cubs, beating them 8–4. He struck out nine and benefited from Hank Greenberg's three doubles. Detroit had a three-games-to-two advantage and could win it all today behind Virgil Trucks. Claude Passeau, whose artistic one-hit shutout had won Game Three for the Cubs, would be trying to even the Series again. Cassidy prayed for the Packard's radio.

Breakfast was arriving at the table by the time he put the papers aside. Fried eggs, bacon, corn muffins, stacks of pancakes, pots of maple syrup, on and on it came. Cassidy had the feeling that he would never forget a single mouthful he'd consumed in the state of Maine. Harry Madrid read the papers while he ate. Cassidy fell to the feast but his mind kept turning back to Tash Benedictus . . . who had known they were coming.

Mona Ransom's conclusion utterly baffled him.

*How* could he have known?

*Who* could have told him?

And for God's sake, *why?*

It seemed to him that Benedictus—aside from his appalling performance while drunk, which was doubtless customary—had been a kind host. The man had obviously been through a hell of a lot, had suffered far more than his share. And he was a good if capricious host. So if he had been expecting his visitors, he hadn't made any special efforts for them . . . had treated them as he would have any other orphans of the storm. So what was the point in his knowing they were coming?

He felt as if someone were watching him.

Right then, in Harriet's Kitchen, he felt the hairs on the back of his neck rise.

As it turned out, someone was watching him.

• • •

She was sitting at the counter, a forlorn waif with huge eyes that seemed to be habitually widened, as if everything she saw surprised her and, for the most part, did so unpleasantly. She wore a plain light brown cloth coat that matched the color of her hair and was badly frayed at the cuffs. Her wispy, mousy hair escaped untidily from beneath a cheap woolen beret. Her gloves seemed to match the beret and couldn't have been much good against the cold. She stared at Cassidy over the rim of her coffee cup, clasped in both hands for the warmth. She dropped her eyes, then raised them again. He fixed them with his own. Her eyes were large, hazel, beautifully warm and passionate eyes that gave the impression of being strangers to passion, and they certainly didn't fit with the pale, almost gray complexion, the short, rather frightened nose, the mouth that seemed perpetually prepared to sob. At her feet she'd put her suitcase, one of those cardboard jobs from the five-and-dime. She'd strapped an old belt around it to hold it together when the cheap locks inevitably popped. She wore short boots with buttons and imitation fur ruffed at the top. One of her gray knee socks had a hole on the calf and her pale flesh showed through.

Cassidy slid out of the booth and went over to her. She quickly turned back to the counter, almost flinching. He stopped beside her and said: "It's Dora, isn't it? Why don't you join my friend and me for breakfast?"

"Oh, I couldn't, sir. I'm sorry if I was staring, I wasn't thinking. . . . I mean, I was thinking, but of something else. . . ." She looked up at the clock over the pie and pastry cabinet.

"Are you in a hurry?"

"This is where the bus stops, out front. I've got an hour."

"Where are you going? Is this your day off?"

"Portland. Back home." She suddenly sniffled and he realized she was near tears, her red-rimmed eyes about to overflow.

"Dora, I insist you come have a real breakfast." He gently took her arm and she came, so easily, almost weightless. Somebody, he thought, really ought to kick some manners into Tash Benedictus's fat ass. How much pleasure could there be in maltreating so manifestly defenseless a creature as Dora?

"Harry, you remember Dora," he said. "From the castle."

"Morning, miss," he rumbled from the newspaper.

Cassidy asked the waitress to bring more bacon and eggs and pancakes. Dora sat meekly in the corner of the booth, looking up at Cassidy. The windows next to her were sheets of ice and snow, opaque, which seemed to intensify the light from outside.

"It's Dora's day off, Harry. She's going to Portland. Your family there, Dora?"

"It's not my day off," she said. She pulled a crumpled hankie from her coat pocket and rubbed at her pink nose, which stood out like a cherry in a blancmange. "I've quit my job. My mother's going to kill me." Her cheeks were wet with tears. She hiccuped and looked up girlishly, shyly. "I couldn't go on working for that man. . . . You saw, you saw how he—" She broke off and let herself go, sobbing. Harry Madrid looked over the top of his newspaper.

"Come on, sister. It's not the end of the world. Benedictus is a jerk. World's full of 'em. I'll bet you a nickel your mother wouldn't work for him either." He went back behind his newspaper as if that should have solved her problems. Dora's breakfast came.

"Eat up," Cassidy said. The café was completely full now, booths and tables and counter. The two waitresses were running back and forth looking frantic. Somebody had turned on a radio. Somebody else yelled, "Hey, Harriet, shake a leg!" There was lots of laughter.

Harriet herself poked her head through the window between the kitchen and the counter. "Shorthanded, Arnie. Sally left for Bangor. Gettin' married, how's that for a laugh? Keep your shirt on!" The head disappeared. The waitresses dashed.

Dora had recovered enough to begin on the eggs. Once started she quickly got the hang of it.

"So, you gave notice," Cassidy said.

"No, I just left." She chewed and swallowed. "Serves them right. Serves *him* right. But he'll never notice I'm gone. Not much satisfaction in that, is there?" She took a forkful of pancakes, said: "You're very nice. . . ." She looked out of the corner of her eye at him. "What do you want from me?" Her wariness was sad.

Cassidy shook his head. "You were getting a bum deal, that's all. I don't want anything from you. Don't get a warped view of humanity, Dora."

"That's a good one," she said softly.

"You're not looking forward to going home."

"You can say that again—"

"How long have you worked at the castle, Dora?"

"Since February. I started on Valentine's Day. I thought it was a good omen. Lucky . . ." She shrugged.

"Why, then, you were there when the plane went down." Harry Madrid lowered the paper and began folding it as he joined the conversation. "You remember the night the plane crashed out there in the back forty—"

"What are you talking about? I don't know anything about a plane crash. . . ." She looked at them as if she'd discovered what they *really* wanted. She drew back, wary again.

Cassidy leaned forward, his elbows on the table, and smiled at her. "A plane did crash back there, but you weren't the only one who didn't notice—hell, nobody ever went looking for it. We've found exactly one guy who happened to hear it go down . . . and he was a poacher."

Dora relaxed again. "Well, good for him! The Guv'nor hates poachers. . . ." She grinned hesitantly and for the first time the huge eyes sparkled.

"So you're in good company, Dora—"

"What's that supposed to mean?"

"Dora, you've got to learn to relax," Cassidy said. "We're just buying you some breakfast. And you want to know what else?"

"What?"

"You don't want to go home to mother, am I right?"

She nodded. "I'll have to live at home then, see. I'm nineteen and a half. I'll go crazy if I live at home. She's worse than the Guv'nor. . . ." She sighed as if she'd had a lot of practice. "Guess I should have thought of that before I . . . well, who cares, hunh?"

"I'll bet I can even find you a job—"

"Doin' what? I won't—"

"Right here in Tuggle. How would that be? You like Tuggle? Got a boyfriend?"

"Well, sort of. I know this boy, Ned. . . . He worked on the shrubbery and stuff this summer, he helped the other man. He called me once. . . ." She slipped a dreamy smile across her face, like a gloved hand, then drew it away.

"Well, let me tell you something else that happened about the same time that plane nobody saw or heard crashed—"

"Look, I'm not kidding you, I never heard anything 'bout any plane! Now what kind of job are you talking about? How would you know anything about Tuggle? Are you planning to dash my hopes?" It must have been an expression she'd picked up somewhere else, her mother maybe. The family probably dealt in dashed hopes.

"Never fear. But"—he paused, wondering just how to put it, reaching, trying to make the shot in the dark—"maybe you could tell me about the man who came to stay at the castle toward the end of the winter, you know the man—you remember him, don't you, Dora? Had a foreign way of speaking?"

Harry Madrid stopped the match halfway to his Roi-tan.

The cacophony of voices, the swinging kitchen doors, the repartee between Harriet and the men having breakfast and the sweating waitresses: it all went on just as before. But for Cassidy it was silent as he waited for Dora to pay off. Or not.

"Oh, him," she said. "I remember him. That was Mr. Miller. Fred Miller. He didn't say much but he didn't seem foreign. He was an old friend of the Guv'nor's, I guess. He kept to himself most of the time. But he was nice. He liked to work in the gardens. Y'know Ned, the one I told you about, he and Miller used to work together on trimming all the shrubs. They did that all summer."

"Did Ned ever talk about him?"

"No, not much. Said he was a good worker, real quiet."

"Fred Miller," Harry Madrid said. He was grinning. He drew the flame to his cigar.

"Well," Cassidy said, "Fred Miller is exactly the guy I meant, Dora." Cassidy patted Dora's shoulder. "You'd say he was a nice fella?"

"Nice enough to me. Like I said, real quiet. He did have an accent, now I think about it. But not *foreign*, y'know? More like an Englishman. He said he'd lived in London for a while." She shrugged. "If you want to know how nice he was, the one to ask would be Mona. . . . Mrs. Benedictus, I mean. She knew him well. If you know what I mean." She patted her lips primly, washing her hands and mind of Mona Ransom.

"I don't know what you mean, exactly," Cassidy said.

"Well, Mona Ransom is just like those old movies of hers. My mom wouldn't let me go to them when I was little and then she wasn't in movies anymore. But I got the idea. She's a plain old whore, that's what she is. Everybody in the castle knew she was doin' it with Mr. Miller. Don't ask me why the Guv'nor didn't do nothing, but he just acted like he didn't know. Or care. Maybe he don't really care. . . . But Mona Ransom and Fred Miller carried on all the time. Just somethin' awful. Though I must admit she was always good to me."

"So what happened? I didn't see Mr. Miller around these past two days—"

"Well, you just missed 'im," Dora said. "He just wasn't there anymore one day. A day or two before you showed up." She shrugged her narrow shoulders. "Just gone. Like me, you could say. Nobody seemed to know where he'd gone to, but it wasn't none of our business." She nibbled at a crust of toast and finally flashed a smile at Cassidy.

"Well, you really have been very helpful, Dora," he said. "It was a stroke of luck we ran into you."

She nodded. "Now what was this you were saying about a job for me?"

• • •

Snowplows were working on the highway about forty miles south of Tuggle on the Boston road, and half an hour later Cassidy pulled off onto the shoulder and removed the chains from the tires. The snow was melting, the heavy pine boughs dripping, a million tiny waterfalls. Another half hour and you'd never have known there'd been a blizzard up north.

Harry Madrid looked over at Cassidy. "Maine seems like a dream—a fucking nightmare, you might say—that I never hope to repeat. Give me the city every time, Lew. Now, how did you fix little Dora's situation back there? She's going to work at Harriet's kitchen, I take it?"

"Well, you saw what a fix Harriet was in. Overworked and understaffed. Harriet saw the wisdom in my suggestion that another warm body with experience at the castle could do no harm. She offered twenty dollars a week and I got her up to twenty-five, plus tips, of course. Nothing to it."

"Nothing to it," Harry Madrid said.

"Well, I gave Harriet the first month's wages, just to give Dora time to prove herself. Won't cost Harriet a penny and a month later little Dora will have proven herself indispensable. I paid Dora another fifty for the information, a little cushion money. Fred Miller. Manfred Moller. Not very original."

"You're a generous man, Lew."

Cassidy smiled. "In this case it's part of expenses. Sam MacMurdo's money."

• • •

So, Tash Benedictus was a liar.

He'd known the plane was sticking like a dagger up to the hilt in his pine forest.

He'd given the survivor the run of his home—and of his wife, as well—for several months. Casual hospitality was one thing, but the red-carpet treatment for Manfred Moller was something else entirely.

But why? Why would Tash Benedictus protect one of those bloody Germans?

They listened to the sixth game of the World Series all through the afternoon and it was a honey. It kept Harry Madrid from his nap. The Packard devoured the miles like it hadn't had a meal since its owner had gone off to war and never come back. And Cassidy kept turning the questions over and over and over in his mind.

It was one of those games that no one who saw it at Wrigley or heard it over the radio would ever forget. Trucks was gone in the fifth. Passeau lasted into the seventh and departed with the Cubs hanging on to a one-run lead. But in the eighth the mighty Greenberg hit his second homer of the Series and tied it up. Then Hank Borowy, the ex-Yankee, came on for the ninth inning after going five in the previous day's start and didn't give the Tigers another hit, on through the tenth, eleventh, and twelfth. The tension was bubbling over, you could hear it in the announcers' voices, the continuing roar of the crowd at Wrigley where they had no lights and the sun was going down. And then in the bottom of the twelfth, suddenly, in an instant, it was over, Stan Hack ramming a hot smash past Greenberg to the wall and the winning run had scored. Cubs 8, Tigers 7. It was one of *those* games. Cassidy had played in football games like that, a couple or three in his career, and they made whatever else came after oddly irrelevant. At least in a certain way. The Cubs and an exhausted Hank Borowy had got off the floor and tied the Series at three games apiece. It was too bad there had to be a seventh game to decide it.

• • •

By the time New York was a pink-and-silver glow of lights up ahead and the night was warm as spring, almost balmy, Cassidy had begun to figure it out. Not make sense of it, mind. Just figure it out.

Manfred Moller and his airplane hadn't just crashed aimlessly in the woods, in the wilderness. They'd been trying to hit Keyhole Lake and they'd come pretty damn close.

They'd been aiming for the lake closest to the castle.

They'd been coming to see Tash Benedictus. Which led to one peculiar but inescapable conclusion.

Tash Benedictus was Vulkan.

Tash Benedictus had suffered and damned near died in the trenches, the work of the bloody Germans. His son—if he'd existed at all—had died in action during the Battle of Britain. Those bloody Germans again.

But Moller was heading for Tash Benedictus and Tash made him feel right at home.

So Tash Benedictus was Vulkan.

Sometimes things just didn't make sense.

"Wake up, Harry. New Yawk City. The end of the line."

# Chapter Sixteen

Harry Madrid sat on the couch looking out the window at Washington Square while Cassidy showered and got into his dinner jacket. He smoked a cigar and drank a Dickens martini he'd made for himself and then Cassidy came in straightening his tie, shooting his cuffs. Harry Madrid regarded him with a patient smile. "Never thought I'd get back to civilization," he said. "God, how I hate the country!"

Cassidy called Terry Leary's apartment up on Park.

Rolf Moller answered the phone, snapping: "Yes, yes, Moller here."

"Doctor, it's Lew Cassidy. We've just gotten back to the city. I'm wondering how Karin is."

"Are you sure, Mr. Cassidy? After what you've put her through, are you quite sure you care what happens to her? You have subjected her to more danger in a short time than the Allied air force did in all those—"

"Rolf, old sock, why don't you just button up the Teutonic bullshit and tell me how she's holding up? And may I remind you that your friend Sam MacMurdo is the creator of the master plan here. Now tell me how she is, let me speak to her, or I'll come over there and defenestrate you without a moment's regret. Got me, pal?" He winked at Harry Madrid.

"Yes, yes, of course. Threats come naturally to men like you, don't they? I didn't expect you to understand. Remorse is foreign to you—"

"How is she?" His voice was suddenly shaking with anger and he didn't want to argue with this irritating shithead. Just then it seemed to Cassidy that the Brothers Moller richly deserved one another.

"She responds nicely in a calm environment," Moller said. "She's worried sick—do you understand? Sick. She is worried about her husband's well-being. She is terrified about all the violence, the seemingly endless violence that clings to you, Mr. Cassidy. Her mental state is delicately balanced—and you persist in exposing her to the very worst—"

"I get the idea. I don't like it either. If you think I enjoy putting her through all this, then you're an imbecile. I'm trying to get this job done, to find her husband. . . . It's been difficult, Doctor."

Rolf Moller sighed, finally said, "Well, forgive me if I seem overly protective of my patient. It's her welfare that motivates me. Waiting, as we've been doing here, can be as difficult as being out on the front lines. Tell me, do you have any news of my brother? I take it you didn't find him."

Cassidy hesitated before speaking. He wanted to report to MacMurdo before saying anything out of school. "We found his trail. . . . We found the plane. We know he was there."

"Yes?"

"But we lost the trail in Boston. We're working on it. We'll find him." He hoped he sounded more certain than he was.

"And the treasure?"

"Don't expect miracles, Doc. One step at a time."

"Yes. A doctor, a psychiatrist of all people must be patient. I realize that." He was sounding sympathetic and Cassidy had a glimpse of what he was experiencing. They were all in the fire, every one of them.

"May I speak to Karin?"

"They're all at Heliotrope. It's her first evening out since . . . well, since your adventures on Long Island. She's medicated but I thought it would do her good. She's not to feel a prisoner but she's been having dreams that have disturbed her—don't bother to ask, she says she can't remember them when she wakes. Tonight I thought she should take a step back toward normal behavior."

"Who's in the party?"

"Mr. Leary and Colonel MacMurdo. He's just back from Washington today—"

Something struck Cassidy as odd. "Why aren't you with her, Doc? It's not like you—"

"Sometimes the doctor needs a night off, too. This is permissible, is it not?" He paused. "It seemed to me that she would be in good hands with Mr. Leary and the Colonel."

"You're doing fine, Doc. I'm sure you did the right thing."

• • •

Cassidy stood near the cigarette stand inside the door at Heliotrope. He felt as if he'd just returned from a year in the wilderness. His heart was doing a tanglefoot rhumba and he knew it was because of Karin and there wasn't a thing he could do about it. It was dark in the big room and the girl singer was bouncing through "On the Atchison, Topeka, and the Santa Fe." Harry Madrid headed back to the office to change into his tux. "Don't tell me," he muttered. "It's all a matter of setting the proper goddamn tone." Cassidy smiled fondly at the broad back retreating through the crimson curtains. His hands were sweating and it was all because of Karin.

"Lew, where the hell have you been? The Series is on; there's money to be wagered and you're not getting your share."

"Been outa town, Bingo."

"Game Seven tomorrow. Your timing's good."

Bingo Slattery was a friendly book who worked out of several of the clubs on Swing Street. He was always good for the Heliotrope crowd's wagers and back in the old days, back in the memorable autumn of 1941, he'd made himself a small fortune backing Lew Cassidy's astonishing string of touchdowns that had led the National Football League. He always said that Cassidy's going down for good on December 7 had been God's way of providing for him, Bingo Slattery. The string had run out, Bingo was up a hundred and fifty grand, and it was just too bad that it had ended the kid's career. Still, Bingo knew when to be thankful. Later on, he'd made a hell of a killing on the Battle of the Coral Sea.

"What are you quoting, Bingo?"

"You won't believe this but I got word outa Chi-town that the Cubbies are outa pitchas. Brace yourself—I got word they're coming back with Borowy tomorrow. To start."

"Impossible. That'd be three days in a row. Five innings yesterday, four hitless innings today . . . They can't start him tomorrow."

"That's the word I got outa Chi-town, Lew." Bingo lit an Old Gold and looked all-knowing. Bingo was a great one for saying things like Chi-town, pronounced Shy-town.

"Cubs better pray for rain. Tigers going with Newhouser?"

Bingo nodded.

"So what's the quote?"

"Two-to-one for you, Lew. Eight-to-five for the common rabble." He grinned through a smoke ring. His teeth needed a little work.

"I'll venture a grand on the Cubs in that case."

"You're bettin' with your heart, Lewis. The Tigers are a lock."

"No." Cassidy chuckled, patted him on the shoulder pads of his dark gray chalk-stripe. "I'm betting with someone else's money."

"Then you're talkin' about the smartest bet in town."

"I'll still pray for rain. You see Terry tonight?"

"Oh, to be sure. The publican is at his usual table, in the bosom of his friends. Say, you know who's in town? I saw him gettin' a shave and a trim at the Dawn Patrol. Damned piece of glass still stuck in his eye!"

"The monocle? You're kidding!"

"Not Me's back on Broadway, Lew. I haven't seen him since, well hell, before the war. 'Thirty-nine or 'forty maybe?"

"I'll be damned," Cassidy said. "I heard he was in the RAF or something. You're sure? It was definitely Not Me Nicholson?"

"How many guys you know wear a monocle and go by the name of Not Me? No, Lew, it was our Not Me. I gave him five hundred, even money, that Ike's got Patton back in civvies by the end of the year. I don't know, it's about even money, wouldn't you say?"

"Not Me Nicholson," Cassidy said. "I'll be a monkey's uncle. You see him again, Bingo, tell him to give me a call. I would positively love to see old Not Me. What an incredible fuck-up, what a helluva guy. Hey, did you fuck up again, Nicholson?"

Bingo Slattery snapped to attention. "Not me, no sir."

You had to laugh.

• • •

Cassidy waited until the singer's set was over and then he and Harry Madrid converged on the table where Terry Leary, MacMurdo, and Karin were finishing their steaks. There wasn't much conversation going on, three people in search of an elusive good time. Leary saw them first. He gave the impression that he'd never been so glad to see anyone in his life. He stood up, smiling broadly, running a knuckle along his thin mustache. He said that Cassidy and Harry Madrid were a sight for sore eyes.

"When did you get back, amigo? Where the hell have you been?"

"It's a long and involved tale," Cassidy said.

MacMurdo stood, shook hands with both of them. He was wearing a dark blue suit in the 52-Long range. "Glad you're back. Just got in from Washington myself. Listen, you'd better fill me in on things. We gettin' anywhere, pard?"

"Hi, Karin." MacMurdo's voice was oiling along in the background with the sound of chatter and ice in tumblers and the band playing something for the dancers. Cassidy was looking down into Karin's eyes. She was wearing a silver dress with a little silver jacket to cover her bare shoulders. She looked up at him, raked the hair away from her eyes. "How are you doing?"

She tried to smile, nodded. "I'm all right. Terry says the Mad Doctor keeps me on the rails and I guess he's right. Are you all right? I've been worried about what you've had to do . . . all because of me."

"Don't be silly," he said. "Didn't the Colonel tell you? I'm doing my best to make sure the good guys win the peace."

MacMurdo said, "You two kids can talk later. I want to hear your report, Lew. Time's a-wasting—"

"Keep your shirt on, Sam. And try to remember that you don't give me orders. You can make suggestions and you can ask favors—"

"And I can tidy up after you, too. You try to remember that one, Lew."

"Sam, don't get me to laughing. Go easy with me. It's been a weird coupla days."

"Please!" Karin reached up and took Cassidy's hand. "Don't argue. Please. Just tell me, Lew, do you have any news about Manfred?" Her voice was soft but he heard it better than anyone else's. It was so much like it had been in the old days, when she'd been the only one who mattered for him.

"Harry," he said, "you brief old Sam here. And, Terry, you blow a hole or two in Sam if he gets uppity." He grinned at MacMurdo. "We can talk later. Right now I'm going to take Karin away with me for a briefing of her own."

He took her hand as she got up, smelled her clean fresh hair and some scent he didn't know, saw the uncertain questioning look in her soft brown eyes. The band was playing "If I Loved You" from the big hit show *Carousel*. He followed her, moving among the tightly packed tables with the heliotrope lights burnishing the heliotrope walls. He pointed through the heavy velvet heliotrope curtains that led into the corridor. You turned one way and you went back into the past, you went down to the dressing rooms and you rescued Cindy Squires and you didn't know it but you signed her death warrant. You turned the other way and you hung on to the present, you took a step into the future, you kept on turning pages until you figured out a way to get your late wife back, to make your life add up to something again.

He opened the door to Terry Leary's office and she went in. He locked the door and when he turned back she was standing with her back to the desk, her hands clasped before her, looking into his eyes. She was biting her lower lip and trying not to show it. She was shaking slightly as if a low-jolt voltage were always rippling through her lean body. Her voice was so husky, so soft, that he had to lean toward her to hear.

"I'm embarrassed to tell you," she began, stopped. She squeezed her hands tighter, shivering. The silver dress clung to her. She forced her hands back so she was leaning on them. "I have been so worried about you. Wondering if someone was trying to kill you. Poor Rolf, he had a fit about what happened out at Sag Harbor—he acts like you planned it and I tried to tell him that it wasn't like that at all. He's so protective, he doesn't want anything to happen to me now that I've come this far." She smiled sadly. "I try to explain to him that the war isn't over for us, that we haven't gotten through it yet. He says he doesn't want me to risk my life—well, who does want to? Sometimes there are reasons . . . but you, Cassidy, why are you doing this? What am I to you? Are you a bounty hunter? That's what Rolf called you, a man in it for the money—"

"No, I'm not in it for the money. My reasons are entirely personal, Karin."

"But why? What are your reasons?"

"There's no point in going into that now."

"But I'm so curious about you. And I don't know why. . . . Do you believe in second sight? Telepathy? I had dreams about you again—"

"Karin, I came here to tell you about what happened up north."

"Why do I have these dreams about you? What are you to me, Lewis?"

"Have you talked to anyone else about me?"

"No. Well, just in passing to Terry. Did he know me, too? He seems to—oh, I don't know, I catch him watching me when he thinks I'm reading or listening to the radio. He watches me as if he's analyzing me, watching me give a performance and looking for mistakes. I don't understand . . . but I dreamed about you, on that pier, the gulls, you were talking to me but I still couldn't hear you—" He had moved closer to her, fighting all his impulses, fighting the past. He took her shoulders in his hands. She was short of breath, looking up at him. "Why do I want you to kiss me? I want you to put your arms around me. . . . I was so worried about you, Lew."

"Well, I'm safe and I would sell my grandmother to kiss you and hold you but I've got to tell you about the search for your husband—"

"Oh, my God! What am I thinking of? You see? You see how my brain isn't working properly? I forgot all about that—yet it was all I could think of when I saw you. . . . Did you find him? Is he all right?"

He lifted her up and set her on the edge of the desk. He poured two small cognacs from a decanter that had once belonged to Max Bauman. "To the past," he said. "May we go there soon." They drank and then he told her about the trip north.

• • •

So far as he could see it, she had paid a lot to hear the truth. It was bad enough, what MacMurdo was planning for Manfred Moller if they ever did find him. She wasn't going to get her husband back, not *that* husband, anyway. But Cassidy couldn't worry about that yet. There'd be time at the other end, somewhere in the last chapter, when they did find him. Cassidy wasn't much of a chess player. That's just the way it was. So he told her about the airplane with the corpse and the man who had stayed at Benedictus's castle and the killing of the art dealer in Boston and the disappearance of the Ludwig Minotaur.

"He might have killed you. . . ." She was staring at him, her mouth slightly open, the hair swinging forward beside her eyes.

"He had a kind of half-assed try," Cassidy said.

Suddenly she threw herself forward, her head against his chest, her hands clutching at him frantically, trying to get a grip, as if her life depended on it. He folded his arms around her, felt her fluttering against him. She tilted her face up, her eyes slightly glassy. "I don't want to die," she whispered. "I'm trying to salvage what I can of my life. . . . You're part of my life now, whatever you were in the years that are gone . . . and I don't want you to die. And that's why I'm this way, what I'm afraid of. . . . I'm afraid they'll kill you." Her body was trembling against him, in fear or in passion, he couldn't tell. "Does Manfred know who you are? Can he find you?"

"I don't know," Cassidy said. "I wouldn't think he'd want to find me. I'd think he'd want to get as far away from me as he—"

"Not if he knows you have me."

"There is that," he whispered into her ear, his cheek against the terrible scar beneath her hair.

"He will kill you if he must."

"Maybe I will kill him."

"He's brave and resourceful. He's fighting for his life."

"Do you love him, Karin?"

"He's my husband."

"That's no answer—"

"It's the only answer you'll get from me. He's my husband, I want him back. . . . MacMurdo told me he'd find him. He's got to find him. That's all there is, Lew."

"Why? Do you know what MacMurdo has in mind for your husband? Have you thought about that?"

"It doesn't matter. I trust MacMurdo. I have to trust him. He's the only hope I have . . . I must trust him. We'll work out something. I'll worry about everything then—"

"Why trust him?"

"No choice, that's—"

"Do you think MacMurdo's in this to reunite you and Manfred Moller?"

"I don't want to talk about it anymore."

"Well, he's alive, he's out there somewhere. He may know you're here. . . . We don't know what the hell he's going to do next—"

"Kiss me, Lew. Please, just kiss me."

He held her and kissed her and when they stopped he said: "See, nothing has changed. . . ."

Or had he only thought it?

She murmured: "Kiss me again, kiss me twice."

# Chapter Seventeen

Cassidy was touching her elbow, steering her through the crowd toward the table, when he noticed a rather bulky, shortish man standing behind MacMurdo, who was deep in conversation with Harry Madrid. There was something familiar about the man's back, the slightly tight fit of his dinner jacket, the way he listed slightly to port.

While Cassidy watched, the man, who had a cigar in one hand and a martini in the other, lurched unsteadily toward MacMurdo's back, reached out to steady himself, and poured his martini on the Colonel. All over the Colonel. It seemed to be a very large martini, a trick glass, bottomless, a joke in questionable taste.

MacMurdo leaped up, knocking over his own drink, turning, his face an empurpled mask of rage. Surprise. "What the fucking hell!" He was spinning around, tipping his chair over. People at nearby tables were noticing in a languid New York way, quietly, but beginning to stare. MacMurdo was grabbing his napkin and mopping at his coat front. "Jesus Christ, man, anything more you'd like to pour on me? A Thermos? Bottle of fucking wine? Goddammit!"

Terry Leary was regarding the scene with an amused detachment, his narrow mustache giving the effect of a man with two simultaneous smiles, one piggybacking. The drunk tottered toward MacMurdo, reaching out to assist him in some unimaginable way, the result being to add a sprinkling of cigar ash to the sodden clothing. He wore a tux with a stiff wing collar, still clutched the empty martini glass. "Look there, old man," he said, reached out and dislodged a large green olive from the breast pocket of MacMurdo's jacket.

"Get your hands off me!" MacMurdo bellowed. "Just back off, dammit."

"Well, really!" the drunk said, his back still toward Cassidy. Karin had moved away and taken her seat next to Leary.

Leary looked up and smiled at the interloper.

"Young sir," Leary said, "did you spill your drink on my friend?"

The drunk turned, drew himself up to his full five-eight, and composed his round pink face. He wore a shocked expression, his eyebrows arching toward the pale, straw-colored hair that drooped across his forehead. The light caught, flashed, reflected, in the circle of glass dropping from his right eye, dangling at the end of a black ribbon. . . .

With an awesome dignity, fumbling his monocle back into his eye, he spoke.

"Not me, most definitely not me! The fault is other than mine. Some other chap back there, a waiter d'you think? Some blighter bumped into me. . . ." He shrugged, the picture of slandered innocence.

Cassidy advanced, threw his arms around the drunk in a bear hug.

"Nicholson! You old bastard! So the Jerries didn't get you after all?"

"Jerries? Not me, not me! I daresay it was some other bloke they got. The good die young but Nicholson endures!" He blinked and the monocle dropped away again. "Why, Lewis, old fish! It's you. . . . Lewis!" He stuck the monocle back in his eye.

"The last time I saw you, Not Me, you know what you were doing?"

"Well, the old gray matter isn't what it once was—"

"You and P. J. Pilkington were pinching that vase from the Metropolitan—"

"Not me," he said, shaking his head. "It was Pilkington, if you recall. Old Pilkers. Frightful ass."

"Jesus Christ," MacMurdo muttered. "It's you. Nicholson. The last survivor of a gaudy and unnecessary age. I might have known. You know this asshole, Cassidy?"

"And we weren't actually pinching the vase, Lewis. I mean to say, I worked at the Met, I was doing, you know, *thing*. Research, that's the word."

"And I was driving the getaway car!"

"Back in 'thirty-eight, was it, Lewis? By gadfrey, I think it must have been. Seven long years ago, Lewis. Lots of water under the bridge since then. It's a different world, Lewis. A dashed different world, I'm sorry to say. We've entered the age of the extremely Common Man. Demoralizing and thing. Distressing. Both."

"Yes, Colonel, I do indeed know this man." Cassidy looked at Not Me. "We have heard the chimes at midnight."

• • •

Not Me Nicholson had made a career, a life, out of being a friend in need, a pal in search of a party, an absolutely fatuous ass with deep pockets, a ready smile, and an infinite capacity for taking pains to ensure he knew from where the next drink was coming. From early on, as he told the story, growing up the son of an English father and an American mother in London's Mayfair, he was a monumental fuck-up.

"I think my overall performance may have given rise to the term actually," he used to say. "I fucked up in my nanny's arms. In the nursery, I was always the little tyke who managed to get his shit in his hair. I fucked up in St. James's Park in my pram. I went on to fuck up at Eton, then further enriched my growing legend at Balliol—which is Oxford, Cassidy, you cretinous nit. It is not immodest, I think, for me to speculate that Oxford will eventually have my brain for scientific analysis. Assuming, of course, that it can be found. Well, there I was, always the one with the blotted copybook. Positively blackened was the old copybook, truth to tell.

"Well, dash it all," he would go on, "my sorry story is that I was quite naturally singled out for accusation every time the old soufflé collapsed. By the laws of nature, by the beard of Zeus, I was not literally responsible for most of the cock-ups which, I admit, would occur in my immediate vicinity with alarming frequency. No one, I promise you, was more alarmed than I. The words most often heard on my lips were, 'Not me!' Thus the appellation which has clung to these weary shoulders of mine. I wear it like a badge of courage. My constituency is the army of the falsely accused."

Thus, early on, Archibald Grandison Nicholson became Not Me Nicholson. Through the years the moniker had served him well. As Nicholson said, "Not Me has been a dashed fine ice-breaker with the available crumpet. And let's admit it, I can use all the ice-breaking assistance I can get."

Not Me was on the short side, impeccably tailored though he had a pronounced weakness for purple hosiery; he wore a monocle like his father and combed his dishwater blond hair with goo from Trumper. He was, on the whole, a bit of a toff though Cassidy had never actually seen him wear either a top hat or spats. He was well connected. He played polo with Royals, lost his share at Biarritz and Monte. Generally it could be said that Not Me Nicholson was a relic of another age.

Cassidy met him back in '37 at a party at the Metropolitan Museum where Not Me had somehow finagled a subcuratorial position thanks to his mother's family's longtime financial generosity. Opposites attracted, as it turned out, and the two young men had become good friends. Things had gone from bad to worse, culminating in the scavenger hunt that had involved the pinching of a Roman vase. All a lark, Not Me had explained to the proper authorities and, miraculously, with Terry Leary intervening, Not Me and Pilkers Pilkington and football hero Cassidy had escaped without making the newspapers. That had been in the summer of '38, when Karin had been shooting a picture on the West Coast.

Not Me returned to England in '39 because somewhere along the way Pilkers had taught him to fly a plane. "Maybe I'll become one of those fly-boy chappies," Not Me had speculated. "I'm made of very stern stuff. Deep inside, y'know. Stuff of heroes, in point of fact. There was a Nicholson at Waterloo, for instance."

Back in '40 or '41 somebody had mentioned Not Me, a rumor went round that he'd been killed during the Battle of Britain. Somehow it made sense, it was the kind of romantic, quixotic end you might have prophesied for a fellow cut from the cloth that had produced Not Me. Cassidy had reflexively thought of Not Me when Tash Benedictus had spoken of his son's death in the skies over the Channel. It was just one of those sad things. He hadn't expected ever to see Not Me Nicholson again.

• • •

MacMurdo had calmed down, recaptured his good humor. He had draped one huge arm around Not Me's shoulder and weighed him down into a chair Terry Leary had commandeered from another table.

"Dammit, Gizmo," MacMurdo was saying as Not Me smiled a trifle faint-heartedly, as if he half expected MacMurdo to turn violent at any moment, "it's just like old times." He looked from Terry to Cassidy to Harry Mardid, who seemed on the verge of having a snooze, said: "Not Me's drunk as a duck and I'm all wet. Jesus, it takes me back. There I was out in the drink, trying to get from France back to fucking Jersey in a goddamn Brit dinghy—I mean a dinghy, some damn thing left over from Dunkirk, I'm all by my lonesome, the outboard motor conks out, I'm takin' on water and I'm bailin' with a coffee can, contemplating an early and watery grave. I'm dressed up in honest-to-God SS kit, lookin' like the worst Nazi in creation, and it's foggy as a bitch. . . . I'm a man whose jig was up yet again. . . ." MacMurdo looked around the faces again, then back at Not Me. "When all of a sudden, through the fog comes this wimpy little spotlight and I hear another outboard putt-putting along. And this voice like something out of a musical comedy says, 'I say there . . . you drowning chappie . . . Is that you, Colonel MacMurdo? Oh, you, chappie . . . need a lift?" MacMurdo's laughter boomed. Heads turned. "And it was old Not Me! He was running the operation for

MI5, God only knows why, and get this—he'd drunk himself silly that night and got to wondering about two in the A.M. where the hell MacMurdo was, wasn't he supposed to be back by now? So, drunk as a lord, he staggered off and found a little boat and set out in the general direction of France looking for me! Well, I was a goner without Gizmo here stumbling across me. . . . He was feelin' no pain and I was frozen damn near to death, he pulled me into his boat and we watched mine sink, and then he looked at me, and he says, "Now, I set out from Jersey. You wouldn't know where it is from here, I suppose?" MacMurdo grinned hugely at the memory. "We were so damned turned around, we didn't know which way was up. So we hung on until morning and thank God the fog cleared off and there was Jersey, about three hundred yards away. . . . Nobody knew what the hell to make of us, Not Me with his monocle and flask, me in my SS getup. . . . By God, war is hell, Gizmo!"

• • •

The evening broke up not long after that. Harry Madrid had given MacMurdo a thorough rundown on the Maine expedition. MacMurdo had said he'd talk to Cassidy about their next moves tomorrow. Grabbing Cassidy's hand, pumping it, MacMurdo said: "Great work, pard. We're gonna get our man, I know it, sure as shootin'."

Harry Madrid was tired and heading home. Terry Leary told Cassidy he looked like he was out on his feet. Cassidy felt funny about leaving Karin: it seemed to him that they should go home together, back to the apartment on Washington Square, that life would then be normal. It only went to show you how tired he was. She was still Manfred Moller's wife. But . . . but he kept hoping that the Past was back there, trying to break through. . . .

Terry read his mind. "Don't worry, amigo. I'm taking care of her. We're gonna get this figured out. Listen, you okay? Harry was telling quite a story."

"It was quite a time," Cassidy said. "Is she all right?"

Leary shrugged. "Physically fine. Otherwise, who the hell knows? I catch her looking at me sometimes, I wish I could just grab her and shake her, say Karin, for chrissakes, it's me, Terry Leary, I was the best man when you married Lew—so cut the shit and tell me what's going on here. . . . But I don't, I know all about the rules. . . . But, Lew, why can't we tell her the truth? Oh, I know, I know. Rolf and I have talked about it, he's told me. . . . We've got to let her come to it herself, then it will be real, it'll mean something. He's the doctor. So I behave." He smiled. "So I'm keeping her safe, amigo. Don't worry."

"I want her, Terry."

"I know you do."

Cassidy leaned over her chair, told her he'd see her the next day. He kissed her cheek. She nodded. "I'm glad you're safe," she whispered.
Not Me sauntered up as Cassidy was preparing to depart.
"Got a bunk for me, old lad?"

• • •

Not Me Nicholson sat on the couch that would be his bed and swirled brandy in his snifter, yawning. He'd slipped his jacket over the back of a chair but his tie and wing collar were still presentable and his purple braces matched his socks.
"Awfully kind of you," he said through the yawn.
"I thought you were dead," Cassidy said. He was sitting in one of the big chairs, slumped low, ankles crossed far away. The windows were open to a balmy, damp night.
"Not me. It was Pilkers who died. He was flying off my wing. Gave me a big grin and a wave, silly old Pilkers. His cockpit was full of smoke then, I couldn't see him anymore, the Hurricane just peeled off, down he went. ME 109 got him. I got all sentimental and went after the swine, chased him damn near to France." He yawned again, shaking his head. The monocle came loose and he just let it hang there.
"You get him?"
"Not me. He got tired of my hounding him, he came after me with blood in his eye. We were both damn low on fuel so he put thirty or forty rounds into my fuselage, blew out the fuel line and all sorts of other things that are more or less imperative if you want to stay airborne. Well, I seldom knew what the hell I was doing. He finally tired of the sport and I went down out there somewhere . . . bloody cold and wet. Seems to me I spent the whole damn war cold and wet all the way through. Fisherman chappie picked me up. Turns out I was nicked up a bit. Ending the old dashing-airman routine for me. Somehow we still managed to win the war." He laughed. "What a farce it all was. Too damn bad about old Pilkers, though. That's the really shoddy thing about the war, I should think. All the good chaps dying that way." He took a long, slow puff on his cigar. "One doesn't cling to life quite so steadfastly any longer. So much of one's old crowd is gone."
"Was MacMurdo's story on the level, the way you found him in the fog?"
"Oh, God! More or less, I suppose. It was much deeper into the war, the tide had turned, and I'd been pretty drunk for quite some time. Ever since Pilkers went down. After that the only sensible course seemed to be to stay well into the netherworld until I got the all-clear. But MacMurdo's story had the ring of relative truth to it. He was a complete head case, of course. Psychotically brave, if you ask me, and lucky beyond imagining. The man actually believes he can control fate by *thing*, the power of his

will. He talks more utter rot than anyone I've ever known. With the possible exception of dear lamented Pilkers who was, as I am myself, a coward. That's what makes Pilkers so much more of a hero, don't you see? He was always scared, shaking so he couldn't speak, but he did what he thought he had to do. Fourteen kills, old Pilkers had. Paralyzed with fear the whole damn time. Fool like MacMurdo, he just keeps doing what comes naturally."

"You were really in MI5?"

"Well, Lewis, I had to do something, didn't I? Nothing much safer than being a spy behind a desk. Always the chance of tripping on the stair, I suppose, or getting eyestrain, but it's other chappies out there doing the dying. The work suited me." He sighed deeply, worked on his brandy. "Oh, what a beastly day I've had. By the way, I ran into your father in Vienna a couple weeks back. Top of his game, I am here to tell you."

"What were you doing in Vienna? Still a spy?"

"No, it was all the art commission to-ing and fro-ing. Some twit noticed that my dossier mentions my less than distinguished career at the Metropolitan. Ergo, I must know all about art. Hopeless, isn't it?"

"You still in the service?"

"I suppose so. Can't wait to get out. My demobbing will be a red-letter occasion." He yawned.

"So what brings you to New York?"

"Well, now that bit's just a trifle murky. But officially I'm liaising with some blighter in Washington. I'm sort of the lowest man on my totem pole and my chap in Washington has been off on the mountaintop communing and plotting. So I came up here to check on the old bunch, you and Leary, really. Now, Terry hinted to me that you are quite a story yourself. But he was exaggeratedly close-mouthed. Said you could tell me. . . . I gathered that he is no longer one of New York's Finest, you are utterly washed up as a footballer, and that your life has been rich with tragedy these past several years. Now can any of this be true? You look fit, a model of rectitude and sobriety—now what's been happening, Cassers. Do give us the word. . . ."

Not Me wasn't yawning anymore.

• • •

The story came back to life for him as he told Not Me. He had to fight off the emotion, had to take a page from Not Me's style book. Not Me listened, nodded, poured more brandy, slowly smoked his cigar. Finally Cassidy had come to an end, drained, and fell silent.

Not Me stirred himself, stretched. "You've had a terribly . . . terribly . . . well, *complicated* time of it. And here she is, she actually can't remember you? Extraordinary. Noël Coward could write a play, couldn't he? Perhaps he already has. Well, what are you going to do? I mean, you're trying to catch this appalling Nazi husband of hers . . . but if she's still stuck on him, old bean, it seems to me you've made matters worse. And then there's this fantastical minotaur! I mean, *really.* And you've actually met this Manfred Moller—"

"Well, we weren't introduced."

"Ah, Cassers, how true, how true. He was too busy trying to bury you alive. . . . My Godfrey, it is a thrilling story. And beautiful movie stars creeping into your bed—"

"Just the one, Not Me."

"Principle remains the same, I daresay. I certainly do wish you all the luck in the world, Cassers. What's your next move?"

"There you have me. I'm curious about Benedictus's role in it, why he lied to me, what he was doing playing the host to Manfred Moller—"

"Lucky you ran into the downtrodden maid."

"I want to know about Benedictus."

"How will you manage that?"

"I know just the man to ask."

The telephone rang. Cassidy jumped, surprised.

Not Me said, "Late for callers, what?"

Cassidy picked up the phone. "Hello?"

It was Terry Leary.

Dr. Rolf Moller was dead.

# CHAPTER EIGHTEEN

There was an olive-drab army blanket covering most of the lumpy shape on the Park Avenue sidewalk. A bare foot and a slippered foot stuck out at one end of the blanket. The bare foot was scratched and bent at an unpleasant angle. It could have been anyone, anyone who was dead. There was blood seeping out from beneath the blanket. It looked like a black stain in the light of the streetlamps.

Two police cars were pulled up at the curb. The medical examiner's meat wagon was parked behind the squad cars. There was a fine mist in the air. It was a warm night, the air thick and cloying. Staring down at the blanket and the blood Cassidy smelled the recent death and felt his stomach turning. Not Me stood behind him looking anywhere but down. He walked over to a potted plant in a cement tub and from its mulchy surface withdrew the missing slipper. He came back to Cassidy dangling the leather slipper from an extended forefinger. He dropped it on the sidewalk, not too far from the bare foot. Not Me looked up at Cassidy. "Funny," he said. "He looks so dashed cold, so pale and beastly cold."

Terry Leary, still wearing his tuxedo, was standing near the meat wagon engaged in conversation with a couple of uniformed cops. They were world-weary vets, guys Terry had known for a long time. They were not deeply moved by death although they would be—in the words of

Waldo Lydecker—sincerely sorry to see their neighbors' children eaten by wolves. They were both nodding as Terry talked to them, using his hands, pointing up to the windows of his apartment on the twelfth floor.

An unmarked car pulled up and a plainclothes dick Cassidy knew by sight got out and strode over toward Leary and the two uniforms, who'd been joined by a couple of guys in coveralls from the ME van. The suit said, "When did this character go off the high dive?"

One of the uniforms said, "We got the call about four hours ago. Got right over."

"Four fucking hours?" The detective looked up the side of the elegant façade. "Four?"

"They were trying to figure out where he came from," Leary said.

"I don't get it—"

"Where he jumped from, Murphy. Not what planet he called home. We weren't home, you see, and it was my terrace."

"You know the diver personally?"

Leary nodded. "He was a German, survivor of the recent hostilities."

"Kraut bastard," Murhpy observed. "Died of a guilty conscience, wouldn't you say?"

"Murph, you're one stupid mick."

"Takes one to know one, Terry."

Leary laughed, shook his head.

"Let's see the deceased," Murphy said.

Cassidy and Not Me edged closer. Leary winked at Cassidy and took his arm. "Murph, you know Lew Cassidy." Murphy nodded. "And this odd duck with the fruity monocle goes by the alias of Not Me Nicholson."

"Gotta be a con man," Murphy said.

"I say—" Not Me blurted.

"Something like that," Leary said. "In this case, an old friend."

"I want to meet this kraut," Murphy said. "Danny, the blanket, please."

"Grab your guts, Lew," Leary said. "Rolf has taken quite a turn for the worse."

One of the uniforms pulled the olive-drab blanket back.

Not Me peered down at the corpse. "Oh, I say," he said, a small gurgling sound bubbling in his throat. "Excuse me, old bean," he muttered, backing away. He got to the curb just in time. Leaning against the fender of a squad car he left his dinner and several drinks in the gutter. One of the men in coveralls went to him, spoke softly. The other laughed behind his hand. Not Me finished and leaned back, bracing himself against the fender. "Awfully sorry," he said, wiping his face with his handkerchief. "Christ. Caught me by surprise. Made a bit of a mess." The monocle swung from the black ribbon.

Cassidy stared down at the mess that had until four hours before been a civilized German doctor. He really wasn't seeing the remains, he was remembering his first view of the man, out on the terrace at the Westchester mansion MacMurdo had occupied as a kind of spoil of war. Karin had been standing alone, waiting beneath the gathering storm clouds, purple with black at the center like enormous flowers, and Cassidy hadn't seen her in so many years. She'd been wearing a straw hat with the colorful ribbon wafting in the wind. And then Rolf Moller had joined her, so straight and severe in his brown English tweeds, and within a couple of hours the man had told Cassidy the story of Karin's war, the details of her survival. He remembered how he'd heard of Karin's almost dying, the carnage and fire and smoke of Cologne, Rolf finding her in the street, well along the dusty road to death, her head broken open. . . . It was Rolf who had made her live, forced her to live. . . .

He thought of all the times he'd found the good doctor an irritating, officious prick, but always, *always,* Rolf's concern had been for Karin, for Karin's safety. . . .

Now the poor bastard had gone off the terrace head first and there he lay, skull split open like a cantaloupe, the features loosened, pulled out of shape, nearly obliterated, neck broken. The remnants of his face, bloody shreds, a kind of jelly running from the battered skull. Both of his eyeballs were gone. Just gone. Spilled into the streets perhaps, crushed and smeared by the passing cars.

It was pretty awful. He could see the headlines. GOOD KRAUT DIES.

Cassidy turned away, saw Not Me pale, sagging. He went to him. "Hell of a day," Cassidy said.

Murphy said: "Funny, this one is. Never saw a brain diver go by way of a swan. They usually go feet first, see. Or if they do a header they usually get their hands up to block the fall, you always get your broken wrists, shit like that, but here you got your world-class swan dive. So, you know the geezer, Terry?"

"Like I said, Murph. He was a houseguest of mine. He came by way of the express from my terrace, sad to say."

Murphy sighed, looked around at the passersby who couldn't help stopping for a look. It was the middle of the night but it was a warm and damp October and there were always people out for a walk, frequently with dogs. Dogs seemed to find a corpse at least as interesting as their masters did.

"Well, Terry, I guess we'd better have a chat."

"Let's adjourn to the drawing room," Terry said. "We could all use a drink."

• • •

The picture of the evening's events, which had culminated in the death of Rolf Moller, emerged beclouded by vagueness, uncertainty. Cassidy had the feeling that it was like finding yourself surrounded by a noxious gas, something you couldn't see or contain or identify, something that was going to evaporate before you ever traced it back to its source. But it was something that had left Moller in ill-matched pieces on the sidewalk.

Terry Leary, MacMurdo, and Karin had left Moller alone in the apartment. He'd been tired and edgy, had said he wanted a night alone. They went on to Heliotrope. Cassidy had called and spoken with Moller, learned that everyone else was at the club, and he and Harry Madrid had gotten to Heliotrope an hour or so later. Harry Madrid left the club early, then Not Me Nicholson and Cassidy had started talking and, subsequently, been the next to leave. By that time Rolf Moller had already been dead more than an hour, nearly two hours, in fact.

Leary, MacMurdo, and Karin stayed on at Heliotrope for another hour or so. Karin was enjoying the music, had wanted to prolong the evening. Terry Leary had taken this as a positive sign of her mental state; maybe she was putting some of the fear and tension behind her, that was the way Terry was looking at it. He had danced with her once and remembered that she'd been almost asleep, and when he asked her what she was thinking about she said she was just "trying to remember" and she'd smiled sleepily at him, her eyes nearly closed. Terry said she wasn't completely there but he'd thought she was as happy as she'd been since he'd known her. Cassidy knew he meant this time around.

When they'd got back to the building on Park Avenue they'd driven directly into the underground garage and taken the elevator, never having seen all the activity at the front of the building. In the apartment Karin had gone sleepily to her room, assuming that Moller was asleep in the other guest room. Terry Leary and MacMurdo had stepped onto the terrace for fresh air. It hadn't taken long to notice the crowd gathered on the sidewalk below, hadn't taken long to see the body.

The night doorman hadn't known Rolf Moller. The police had begun checking apartments. Terry and MacMurdo had looked in Moller's room and found him missing.

Karin had heard them, come out of her room, sensed the situation and, in her robe, accompanied them to the lobby. At the sight of her doctor's body, her brother-in-law's body, she had fainted. MacMurdo carried her back to the elevator, up to the apartment. Terry Leary had routed out his own doctor, Frank Carnochan. He'd come immediately, given Karin a hypo that put her out in moments. Carnochan was still on the scene, arranging for a nurse to come and spend the night with Karin. "Fainting, hypo, amnesia, you can't be too careful," Carnochan said.

How much could Karin take?

That was the only question that mattered anymore. Cindy's eyes had kissed him and said good-bye and now Karin had been given back to him and he was doing his best to put the good-bye look in her eyes, too, doing his best to kill her, too, and all he wanted to do, poor sap, was save her. . . .

"I say, steady on, old man." Not Me laid his hand on Cassidy's arm. "Here." He plucked his handkerchief from his sleeve.

Cassidy realized there were tears streaking his face.

"You need a stiff one, old bean."

Not Me slid another snifter along the bar.

• • •

The cops had gone, Rolf Moller had been scraped off Park Avenue and put in a sack, the nurse had gone to watch over Karin, and Carnochan had taken his black bag and bid them good night.

"Well, it looks like Rolfie got himself all depressed and chucked himself off the terrace." MacMurdo stopped pacing, lit the stubby black pipe he seemed to favor, got it going, and ran the fingers of his left hand through the heavy layers of wavy hair. "Anybody here believe he killed himself?" Nobody said anything. "Anybody have any ideas why he might kill himself? Has he been depressed? Frightened? Unstable in any way?" No one said anything. Not Me Nicholson was sitting on a beige couch, listing to his left, monocle wedged into the socket, eyes nearly closed. "Damn," MacMurdo went on. "I go away for a few days I lose my feel for everything. So now I'm back for the duration. We'll see this thing through. Excuse me if I'm a little obvious but I'm getting back in here, getting my feet wet. Washington always gets a fella all turned inside out. So, let's see. . . . If somebody got into the apartment, unseen by the doorman—which doesn't seem insurmountably difficult with the garage having no full-time attendant—and then pushed the doctor off the terrace, if all that is true, then Rolf knew the man who killed him. No sign of any kind of struggle, not even out on the terrace. 'Course he was probably dead before he went over, judo chop or some damn thing. So, pards, we gotta ask ourselves, who the hell did Rolfie even *know*? And, *why* would anybody want to kill him? He's a doctor, he's Karin's keeper—what could he have done to warrant getting killed?

"Yet, if somebody killed him, that somebody *knew* him enough to have a reason to kill him. Terry says the place is unchanged. Nothing messed about or rearranged, nothing stolen." MacMurdo puffed, walked over to the grand piano. The thick carpet seemed to be growing up around the legs. He picked out something that seemed tuneless until it resolved itself into "Deep in the Heart of Texas." "Well, dammit, he knew *us*. It's like one of those mystery novels I used to read back during planning days, when we were putting together the cross-channel invasion." It was like him not to call it by its code name and to assume you'd know he had a hand in the planning. "You get a small group of people in a snowbound English country house. Then Sir Godfrey Bindlestiff is found drowned in the mustard pot and all around the house the snow is fresh and unblemished—ergo, one of the houseguests did it. Rolf Moller knew us. But we're all accounted for. Yet someone he accepted dropped him off the terrace. Makes me want to wish to God he killed himself."

Not Me snored and woke himself up. He looked around with a false brightness on his round face, smiling confidently as if to assure everyone he hadn't missed a thing.

"Are you asleep?" Leary inquired.

"Not me."

Cassidy swiveled around on the bar stool. He'd been watching MacMurdo in the mirror behind the bar. Now he looked at all of them. MacMurdo puffed his pipe. Terry Leary was playing with a large black cat he'd picked up somewhere along the way. It was chewing on his thumb. "There's someone else he knew here in the states," Cassidy said. MacMurdo's head snapped around. "His brother . . . and we know his brother is a killer."

MacMurdo stared sourly at Cassidy. "His brother." He poked at the gray ash in the bowl of his pipe, yanked his finger back, burned. "His bloody damn brother. Why would Manfred Moller kill Rolf? Why would Manfred find Rolf and not stick around to see Karin?"

Cassidy shrugged. "Maybe he knows what you've got planned for him. I don't know why he'd kill Rolf. I don't know a damned thing."

Not Me Nicholson peered from face to face, covering his mouth with an open palm. "Dashed odd lot of chaps you run with, Cassers. A man feels not quite safe. Makes a fella's hackles rise and so on."

MacMurdo stared at him as if he were speaking a foreign tongue. He turned to Cassidy. "Manfred. I don't like it. But the hell of it is I haven't got a better idea."

• • •

Not Me had conked out full length on the couch. His black patent pumps were set neatly side by side on the carpet. He snored softly through his mouth, apologetically.

MacMurdo didn't feel like calling it a night yet. He asked Cassidy some probing questions, confirming things Harry Madrid had told him. Then he went back out onto the terrace, poking more tobacco into the black pipe. He looked down at the street again. Warm night breezes rustled the trees in their pots. Somewhere a clock struck three. The wind blew out a couple of MacMurdo's matches before he got the tobacco properly lit and then he paced back into the room. Cassidy decided he did indeed look like a character from one of those mystery novels. Detective Inspector MacMurdo of the Yard. It was a three o'clock kind of thought.

"Let me sorta run through this," MacMurdo said. He went to the bar and sniffed the decanter of cognac to judge whether it met his standards. He finally drizzled half an inch into a snifter. "I know," he said, "he hates those bloody Germans, but Benedictus-as-Vulkan is our best angle, it seems to me. And now he's gone. Well, we'll find him sooner or later, I suppose. We'd better.

"Manfred Moller. Somebody tipped him off as to what was going on. That there were people looking for him, namely us. Manfred went and got his minotaur from Brenneman, then killed him—the timing on this is all a little scary for Manfred. He very nearly killed both of you, as well. One wonders," MacMurdo said, sucking noisily on the pipe, "why didn't he kill the two of you straightaway? But we don't know the answer to that. In any case, like Tash Benedictus, Manfred Moller is gone. Whereabouts unknown. Unless he was here tonight and murdered his brother.

"How does the late Karl Dauner fit in? Benedictus, as the first one to make contact with Manfred, must have contacted Dauner, who was a link in the Göring escape network. Then somebody close to Dauner must have gotten word back to Benedictus and/or Manfred Moller about the slaughter of what we may without intending a pun call the Dauner Party. At which point, with Benedictus's approval or not, Manfred decided he wanted his minotaur back.

"I figure that Manfred gave up the minotaur the first time around because he's a good soldier and that was his job—to deliver the minotaur to Vulkan, to set up the Göring network.

"What happened was that Cassidy here scared Dauner shitless out on the old tennis court. Dauner saw the possibility of being exposed as a Nazi unless he played ball with Lew—he sure as hell didn't know a bunch of ragtag Gypsies were gonna have his ass. Leaving out Gypsies, Dauner would have gotten the word to Benedictus and Manfred, who would doubtless have killed you at their leisure, dumped you in the lake up there in Maine, and gone right ahead setting up their network. But the Gypsies killed Dauner and somebody got word of it to Benedictus and/or Manfred so when you showed up Manfred had probably decided the network was shot to hell and he'd better grab the minotaur for himself and go to ground. . . . He's hiding, one assumes, from Gypsies, from us, and from Benedictus, or call him Vulkan, who would probably want some of the minotaur for himself. . . .

"So, our work's cut out for us. All we have to do is find Benedictus and Moller, or just Moller. . . . I reckon Manfred Moller could lose himself real easy, but Benedictus is different. Don't forget, Benedictus doesn't know you got the true story from that maid, what's her name, Dora. . . . So Benedictus thinks he's safe so far as you're concerned. And he, too, may just be out there somewhere wondering where the hell Manfred Moller went. . . . Unless, of course, he already knows . . ."

# Chapter Nineteen

Cassidy woke late, fumbled out of the bedclothes, and staggered into the living room where Not Me Nicholson reclined still, softly snoring, black mask over his eyes. He threw the draperies open and blinked in a brightness that was deceiving because it was in fact raining lightly, whispering in the fallen leaves. The sun burnished the foggy haze, turning Washington Square old gold, like a hand-colored photograph from another age. Strollers in the square, walking their dogs, seemed to move slowly, as if they were not wholly formed, figments of a dreamer's imagination.

"I say," a voice from the couch said unhappily, "up awfully early, aren't we? Rather a long and beastly night . . ." The voice coughed and trailed off.

"Nearly noon," Cassidy said. He stood in his pajamas, stretching before the window. The Packard sat before him, rain beaded on the highly polished paintwork. It looked like the old Ford might be retired to stud. He wished that he had someone to share the cars with . . . a wife, touring the countryside, all that stuff. He turned to Not Me and clapped his hands. "Time to face the world. We are the quick, it's the others who are dead. Arise."

"Oh, Christ." Not Me threw his legs over the edges of the sofa and sat up, his head in his hands. He peeled the sleep mask from his eyes, moaned. "Did I have a bloody nightmare, old fish, or was it raining bodies on Park Avenue last night?"

"One body by actual count." Somebody had killed Rolf Moller. The thought surfaced for the first time since waking.

"Ah. It was real, then. I was afraid of that. I must say, this track you're running on, Lewis, is a bit fast, a bit tricky for the likes of this old cod. That fella really was dead, quite definitely dead, whoever the hell killed him. . . . You know, I'd have called it a suicide while whatever-it-is, while the balance of his mind was unsettled, or disturbed, you know the mumbo-jumbo. I mean, no evidence of anyone calling on him full of bloody intent." He yawned and coughed and took his cigarette case from the coffee table and stuck the Craven A into his holder. He flicked a tiny gold lighter, lit it, inhaled, gasped, and broke into a radiant smile. "Nothing," he coughed, "like the first gasper of the day."

"He didn't kill himself," Cassidy said.

"Well, whatever you say, Cassers, I'm sure. You know me, always looking on the bright side. Comparatively speaking, of course. Why don't you go perform the morning ablutions, old top, while I sit here and compose myself for the day. Never an easy task."

An hour later, showered and dressed, they sat down to coffee and a great deal of toast. Cassidy had spent some time on the telephone while Not Me had cleaned up. Then he had made the coffee and started the toast.

Not Me came in looking like a million pounds, all from the little overnight case he'd reclaimed from the Heliotrope checkroom the night before. He sat down, covered a piece of toast with strawberry jam, and dipped it in his coffee. "Learned this from my old dad. Used to make my sainted mother want to throw up. Actually I think that's why dad did it."

"I can appreciate your mother's point of view."

"Judging from what I've seen of your life in the past few hours, you can't afford to be overly squeamish, my son." He chewed meditatively, making little sucking sounds that involved little bits of decomposing toast.

"You ever get married, Not Me?"

"You mean, speaking of squeamish? No, not me. Who would have me? A wastrel. A varlet. Undependable. Given to public tipsiness."

"You're rich. And the rest of it is pretty much an act."

"Ah, would that it were so, vicar."

"You're well educated. Cute in a puckish way."

"After all these years, you're telling me I'm your type? You little jackanapes, you've hidden it under a bushel—afraid of being spurned, I daresay."

"I was thinking about that Balliol education—"

"Ah, the years the locusts ate."

"What's a minotaur, Not Me?"

"Say again?"

"Minotaur."

"Yes, the Minotaur. Well, a mythical beast. You know, the same old story, head of a bull, body of a regular chappie. It's all Greek to me, as the man said. You've heard of Daedalus, of course."

"Not lately. Refresh my memory. Just for the record."

"Yes, well, let me see. Daedalus built the well-known Labyrinth to house the Minotaur. But I get ahead of myself. I used to know a bit about Greek mythology, actually, before my mind began to go. Poseidon it was, sent a snow-white bull to Minos, head man on Crete at the time in question. This bull was for sacrificial purposes, as I recall. But Minos liked the bull and kept it alive, sacrificed some other bull. . . . There are those who say the story is all bull, ha-ha, my little joke. Poseidon was displeased by Minos's perfidy—I mean, he'd probably gone to a good bit of trouble to send Minos the bull. Anyway, Poseidon punished Minos by making Minos's wife Pasiphaë fall in love with the bull. Well, take that, Minos! There was as it turned out an offspring of this peculiar union between Pasiphaë and the white bull. . . . Yes, this is where the monstrous Minotaur makes his very first appearance. And Daedalus built the Labyrinth where the Minotaur was sequestered."

"Oh, those Greeks," Cassidy murmured.

"Oh, that's only half the story. It has all miraculously come back to me. We jump ahead a bit and we find some Athenians all in a snit killing Minos's son Androgeos. Minos had his hellish revenge, however. He required the Athenians to send him seven lads and seven maidens every ninth year—or each year, depending on who's putting you in the picture. He would then feed these young folks to the Minotaur, who was, we must assume, a carnivore. The third time the Athenians handed over the fourteen kids to be sacrificed, the Athenian Theseus volunteered—he was a sort of hero by trade, as I recall. Theseus joined forces with Minos's daughter Ariadne and together they killed the Minotaur. End of story. Did Theseus dance off into the sunset with Ariadne? I do not recall. But that is the tale of the Minotaur. Please, no applause."

Later, breakfast cleared away, Not Me took his leave.

"I really must get back to my own labyrinth, Lewis," he said. "I do hope you get through your present difficulties, find the bad 'uns, and get whatever you want from Karin. I'll drop it now because anything I could say would be even more fatuous than is my customary standard. But I do care, old chum of mine."

"I know. Where are you off to?"

"Up to the Metropolitan to take a peek at a Rembrandt which just may be the teeniest bit fake. Then it's back to Washington, make a report to men behind desks on this art-commission fiddle in Europe . . . A few things seem to have gone astray. Then . . . well, my dance card remains to be filled in." He smiled roundly. "Peace has broken out and Not Me must think of something to do with myself."

"It's been good to see you," Cassidy said. "Sorry I got you into last night's mess—"

"Poor blighter. Ah well, in the midst of life and whatnot." He turned at the door. "This," he said, "is Nicholson leaving."

• • •

Cassidy called Terry Leary. Karin was still asleep; MacMurdo had gone off on some business of his own.

"Nursie still there?"

"Nursie's on the job."

"You busy?"

"Not me, as our friend Nicholson would say. I was toying with the idea of stopping by our office—you remember Dependable Detective? Thought I might reintroduce myself to Olive . . . but then I thought it might put a crimp in my nap schedule—"

"I'll pick you up in half an hour."

• • •

Terry Leary was waiting on the sidewalk, not far from the spot where Rolf Moller had landed. A maintenance man was on his knees scrubbing the stain off the sidewalk. A photographer from one of the papers was taking his picture, cracking wise.

When he saw the gunmetal gray Packard he did a double take.

"Lewis," he said, admiring the grace and elegance, the high vertical grille, "this is *you*. Today, my son, you are a man! Look at you, chalk-stripe on charcoal, new trench coat, a Borsalino at a jaunty angle."

"Celebrating not being in the Maine woods," Cassidy said. "You're all spiffed up yourself."

"There comes a time when you're just about whipped, you're hanging on the ropes. We bottomed out last night, amigo, finding Rolf splattered all over the sidewalk. Karin cracking up, MacMurdo generally pissed off, you looking at Karin with that sorry lost expression . . . and you just have to do something, get the edge back. You dress up, get a shine on your shoes, pull your socks up . . . and here comes Cassidy trying hard to look like Gary Cooper, super duper, with a Packard, and you know what? We're coming off the canvas, amigo, we're making a comeback."

• • •

Walter Winchell's thinning white hair was sticking out, a shambles he'd tried to comb with his fingers. His face was even pinker than usual.

He was wearing a paisley silk dressing gown over a pair of dark blue pajamas. His feet were bare and pink with neatly trimmed toenails. He opened the door himself and led the way energetically across the carpeted foyer. There were a couple of huge Chinese vases in the corners, a houseboy in the kitchen making coffee, and, as it turned out, a blonde in the bedroom.

Cassidy had called Winchell on his private, personal, bedroom number while Not Me had been bathing. Winchell had listened carefully, knowing the number would never have been used frivolously. When Cassidy had finished talking Winchell had looked at the sleeping girl by his side and said to give him a couple of hours.

Now he was standing in the middle of the living room making what were for him early-in-the-day jokes. When he slowed down, he said: "I got the whole story for you, kid. You're gonna love it. Just fucking love it."

"Wal-*ter* . . . Oh, Wal-*ter,* hon-*eee* . . ." The girl's voice came from down the hall, right on cue, as if he'd wanted them to know what was in the bedroom. He grinned devilishly.

The girl came padding barefoot down to the living room, stood leaning against a glass-fronted highboy. She was short and very dark with long bleached blond hair that managed to look just fine and nicely tousled. She wore a man's pajama top, nothing else. Her thighs looked very firm. She had dimpled knees. She was licking her thumb, as if she were just about to start sucking it.

"Are you coming back to bed, Walter?" Her voice was thick with sleep. Cassidy wondered it she'd reached her eighteenth birthday yet.

"Not now, puss. You can go back to sleep. Or whatever. You want to go shopping?"

She shook her head sulkily, edging her thumb into her mouth.

"Well, do whatever you want. Just don't bother us. You get my drift? Get lost—"

"Sleep over again tonight?"

"Sure, sure. Why don't you take in a moom pitcha? Would you like that?"

"I don't know."

"Well, just stay the fuck away from me for a while." He turned to Cassidy and Leary once the girl had disappeared down the hall. "Costello—and I don't mean Lou, heh, heh—sent her to me with the highest recommendation."

There was a radio somewhere, a low babble of voices, and the houseboy was talking to himself in the kitchen. Winchell went to the French doors that gave on to the terrace overlooking Central Park. The moist breeze flutterd the curtains. A striped green-and-white canvas awning hung out over the flagstones and the fringe flapped lightheartedly.

The mist hung in soft vaporous clouds over the park, the changing colors of the leaves blurred behind them, everything softening into a kind of abstract beauty.

Winchell led the way outside, took a deep breath, and beat his chest. "So this is what morning looks like," he said.

"No, it's what three o'clock in the afternoon looks like."

"Seems earlier. What about the Series?"

"The houseboy appeared in the doorway pushing a rolling cart. "Raining in Chicago," he said. "Looks like they'll wait till tomorrow." He was about forty and had a flat, pugnacious face. Cassidy recognized him, one of those funny flashes. Jersey Allie Morris, welterweight, never a contender but in the mid-thirties and even before that a durable puncher who took four or five to give one honey. Somehow he seemed to have come out of it with his senses more or less intact. He gave the cart a once-over. "Anything else, Mr. Winchell?"

"No, kid, that's great. I'll ring if we need more coffee. You might look after Miss Congeniality in the bedroom."

"You bet, boss." He rolled the cart out onto the terrace and left.

It was nice under the awning, the mist occasionally blowing lightly in their faces. Winchell sat down on one of the wrought-iron chairs and pulled it up to the matching green table. "Siddown, siddown, Lew, Terry, I got a story for you guys. It's a real story, make a helluva book. Or a movie. Cagney, Jimmy Cagney, it's tailor-made for him. Think about Cagney, keep him in your mind. This is tough-guy stuff." He poured coffee and took the lid off a serving dish full of scrambled eggs covered with strips of bacon. Another bowl, under a heavy linen napkin, held warm Danish. "Come on, eat, eat. I haven't had a breakfast like this, out here on my terrace, nice misty morning—hell, in ages. Eat for chrissakes!"

Terry Leary spooned out a plateful of eggs and took a Danish. He poured coffee while Winchell clucked like a Jewish mother.

"I just ate, Winch," Cassidy said. "I want to hear the story. In your own words, Winch."

"In my own words," Winchell said, nibbling a bit of bacon. "Jeez, Lew. That's good. In my own words." He sipped coffee, tugged his robe tighter. "My story is about a guy by the name of Brian Sheehan. . . . But it all goes back to a man called Casement. Roger Casement. You remember him, right?" But Winchell went on to explain.

Roger Casement had been an Irishman, born in Kingstown, County Dublin, who served the Crown with great distinction until 1912, when ill health forced him into retirement, back to Ireland. He was forty-eight. By then he was Sir Roger. His great service, which had brought him worldwide fame, had come while he was a British consul out in

Portuguese East Africa, Angola, the Congo Free State, and finally in Brazil. He believed very deeply in the minimal human rights, that a man—any man, whatever the color of his skin—deserved to be treated like a human being. He saw the way white traders hideously exploited native labor in the Congo and he raised a hell of a row. He brought the spotlight of world attention to the atrocities the traders were committing daily. In 1904 his Congo report was published, resulting in an extensive retooling of Belgian rule in the Congo four years later. In 1912 his report on similar crimes against humanity in the Putumayo River region of Peru got him his knighthood.

Although he was a Protestant, Casement's sympathies had always lain with the anti-British Irish nationalists, who were for the most part Catholic. In retirement he threw himself into their cause. In 1913 he helped found the Irish National Volunteers. While he was in New York in 1914 on a fund-raising mission among the American Irish, war broke out in Europe. In his view it was Germany against the English: that was the part of the equation that mattered. By November of 1914 Casement had made his way to the high command in Berlin, making his pitch that the Germans would be well advised to aid the Irish independence movement as a sort of back-door attack against the English. It must have struck him as a perfectly sensible suggestion.

Yet it came to nothing. The Germans couldn't see their way clear to send an expeditionary force to Ireland. Even more disappointing was Casement's discovery that the preponderance of Irishmen held prisoner would refuse to serve in a brigade he envisioned fighting against the English.

But he didn't give up. It was 1916. He was back in Germany, this time asking for the loan of German army officers to lead the Irish rising planned for Easter. Again the Germans turned him down.

Suddenly desperate to get back and stop the planned revolt, he left for Ireland by German submarine. He made landfall near Tralee, County Kerry, where he was met by some of his Irish supporters. But he was also met by the Black and Tans, arrested, and taken to London where he was tried, convicted of treason on June 29, and sentenced to be hanged.

There was a flurry of serious attempts by prominent Englishmen to save his life in light of his distinguished career, but they came to grief.

Roger Casement was hanged on August 3, 1916.

• • •

"So, who's Brian Sheehan?" Cassidy had weakened and was nibbling a prune Danish and working on his third cup of coffee.

"Brian Sheehan was a young Irishman, did some university at Christ's, Dublin, got wind of Casement's Irish National Volunteers, figured it sounded like an adventure. He met Casement in 1914 when he was nineteen or twenty. Casement took a shine to him. Now, let me add," Winchell said, tweaking his nose with a forefinger, "it's said that Casement was queer as a three-dollar bill. Wouldn't surprise me, frankly. But I'm not saying that Brian Sheehan was his bumboy. May have been, but fuck it, if you'll pardon the expression, I can't know every goddamned thing!"

"Relax, Winch, it's a helluva yarn." Leary grinned at him. "Save your energy for your little thumb sucker. Does this story ever come to a point?"

"Oh, does it have a point! Gimme a Danish there and perk up this coffee. You're a mick, I'm teaching you some history."

"I learned about Roger Casement at my daddy's knee," Leary said. "But he never told me about Brian Sheehan."

"Because he didn't know, Sunny Jim. He wasn't Winchell!"

"So?" Cassidy said. "Casement liked this kid."

"And he took him to New York on the money-raising mission. They were there when war broke out in Europe. Casement took him to Berlin with him and by the time they got turned down by the heinies the kid was starting to grow up. He had a heart murmur, or that's the story I've heard, and he didn't have to spend the war in the trenches. Instead he served as a kind of aide, maybe even a kind of go-fer, y'know, a dogsbody . . . to Sir Roger Casement. He was up to his ears in the planning for the Easter Rising and, when Casement went back to Germany, Brian Sheehan was on the committee to welcome him back. Casement came back empty and the welcome he got wasn't quite what he'd expected. But you might say Sir Roger was the lucky one. Brian Sheehan was just a smartass little mick. Some of the interrogators had a field day with Brian and when they'd turned him into a bloody lump they dumped him by the roadside on the outskirts of Dublin. The Easter Rising was over and they figured the kid wasn't gonna be much trouble to anyone anymore.

"Brian Sheehan was a cripple by then. Helluva mess, by God. Somehow he got to the United States by 1920. He was always close to the cause of the Irish Nationalists, always working behind the scenes, everything from printing leaflets on a hidden press to running guns and raising money. In the United States he went to work on the money side of things, going from one Irish pub to another passing the hat, trading on the hatred of the English, workin' the speakeasies. New York, Boston, Philly, Jersey. Decided to make some money once he got to know the bootleggers. They trusted him—hell, they were all micks. Brian was a good boy, he worked hard. By the time he was thirty, along about 1925, he was worth a few million and he met a girl . . . Enid Mallory, just a kid really, but beautiful, and people were noticing her. Brian was taking a vacation in California, that was when he met Enid. He'd never seen anything like California and he'd sure as hell never seen anything like Enid. . . . And he was something new for her, too. A cripple! But he had some kind of inner character, something that showed through the wreck of his body. . . . A cynical man would say it was the glow of his money showing through. . . . But in the end she turned him down and he went back to Boston, back to making money. He discovered he couldn't get Enid Mallory out of his mind. And Brian was a very determined lad.

"Years passed, he went to California a couple of times, always made sure he saw Enid. One trip he discovered she had amounted to something, she was a real successful girl, but she'd picked up some bad habits . . . like a drug habit, for instance. She was in bad shape. She worked for this big company and they weren't happy with her. They kept her hidden away up in the mountains, they trotted her out to do a job, then they'd hide her again, kept her hopped up, didn't pay her, fiddled the books—hell, she was making a fortune for them and they weren't paying her in anything but dope. But they didn't count on Brian Sheehan. They were fucking with the woman he loved, they'd damn near killed her. . . .

"So Brian Sheehan went up to the mountain hideaway with considerable weaponry, all by himself. He killed the three men who were guarding her. He did it with two shotguns. I doubt very much if he felt the faintest twinge of remorse. He got poor Enid out of there. Saved her life, God's truth.

"Then you know what the crazy bastard did?

"He bought the company she worked for. He relieved certain men at the top of their duties and then he took them up to the hideaway in the mountains—or rather, he took them up to the mountains first, then he told them they were through, at which time some of his mick employees from back East came in and tied them up in uncomfortable little packages. Out came the gasoline, they soaked these assholes with it and somebody suddenly got careless with matches and—poof! Whole place burned right down to the ground. Brian Sheehan celebrated by building one very handsome vacation retreat on exactly the same spot. I know, I been to parties there. Enid's still beautiful and Brian—Christ, he's a piece of work. You'd swear he was an Englishman, the way he lords it around. He sort of became an Englishman with the end of Prohibition." Winchell broke into a loud, hacking laugh, staccato bursts. "Lemme tell you, boys, there's nobody in the world tougher than a tough mick. I wouldn't kid you."

Terry Leary waited, feeling the mist, looking from Cassidy to Winchell, both of them nodding sagely.

Leary said, "So what do Brian Sheehan and Enid Mallory have to do with all our problems, Winch?"

Cassidy looked up from his empty coffee cup. "Brian Sheehan is Tash Benedictus and Enid Mallory is Mona Ransom. And the company he bought is Pinnacle Pictures. And Benedictus doesn't hate those bloody Germans. He hates those bloody Englishmen who took off his ear and removed his eye—"

"And cut off his arm with a carpenter's saw," Winchell said, "and smashed one of his balls with a hammer."

"Which," Cassidy said, "makes him a natural ally of Karl Dauner. A natural ally of anybody who hates the bloody Englishmen."

Winchell leaned back, smiling. "Did I tell ya ya'd love it?"

# Chapter Twenty

The taxis were swirling through the wet leaves on Central Park West and rich women in fur coats, too warm for the weather, were walking bright-eyed, button-nosed poodles. One of the dogs had just cocked his leg on one of the Packard's rear tires. The bored woman, in black gloves and a sable jacket, held the leash and looked the other way.

Cassidy said, "Let's go for a walk, Terry," and headed across the street into the park. The humidity was making his leg act up. His stick made little round indentations on the path. Leary caught up with him. He carried his trench coat over his shoulder, wore a double-breasted gray suit and a collar pin and a gray homburg. To a casual passerby they would have looked like a couple of men-about-town from the pages of *Esquire*. The complexity of their lives, Cassidy reflected, would have sent that casual passerby reeling. But then everyone's life was complex when you came right down to it. It was the continual threat of violence that set theirs apart. In any case, it all seemed a trifle daunting to Cassidy, more complex than anything he'd ever tried to unravel. There were so goddam many people involved. . . . Tash Benedictus, for God's sake. *Brian Sheehan . . .*

"How does Winchell find out this stuff?" Leary shook his head, perplexed. "Well, I guess it's his business. He knows so much, it's amazing he's still alive."

"I suppose he's got the goods on so many big-timers stuck away in lock boxes, they'll do anything to keep him alive." The leaves were thick on the paths. The park was somehow insulated from the city's racket. They were alone. A red rubber beach ball lay in the grass. Cassidy kicked it into a pond where it floated, a last memory of summer.

"I wasn't up there in Maine, amigo. I didn't meet this character or his crazy wife—she actually came sneaking into your room in the middle of the night? I mean, this is a true story? This is movie stuff, you know that?"

"That's where she's from, the Planet of the Movies. I suppose you act in enough of them you begin to think they're real."

"You ought to know. Your father's a producer, Karin was an actress—"

"These are facts already known to me, shamus."

"Just a reminder. You're the one with movie stars creeping into your bed—"

"One, one movie star. An ex-druggie, hopped-up nitwit, and it's the husband that matters—"

"You mean he crept into your chamber as well? What the hell goes on up there in woodsy old Maine?"

"He made the earth move for me, Terry."

"That's disgusting. And you an old-time football star the kids look up to."

"Yeah, I know. This Benedictus thing—what a crooked, twisty life. You wonder if he ever gets confused over just who the hell he is—hero of the Somme, scourge of the bloody Germans, bereaved father of a son dead in the Battle of Britain . . . or is he the Boston mick 'legger who fell in love with the vamp and bought the studio and systematically iced the guys who'd run the studio . . . or is he the idealistic Irishman, follower of the martyr Roger Casement, and for that matter a crippled martyr himself at the hands of the Black and Tans, a professional Irish rebel. . . . The crazy bastard is a walking history lesson. What do you make of a guy like that, Terry?"

"That's easy," Leary said. He stopped by a boulder, dropped his trench coat, and dug a pigskin case from his pocket. He fished out one of Max Bauman's Havanas and lit it. "He's a liar, amigo. His whole life is a lie. Maybe not even Winchell has the truth. And he's a murderer. Not much of a parlay. We're going to have trouble with this man."

They walked on, up a rock-strewn, overgrown hill, down toward the bridle path. Horses moved through the mist, hooves thumping, flicking their heads, snorting.

Cassidy leaned against an elm, resting his bum leg. "I figure all of his political sympathies are with the Irish, which means they're against the English. And therefore with the Germans. Maybe he knew some Germans from thirty years ago, from when he went to Berlin with Casement. Maybe he maintained some friendships with guys who rose in the army after Hitler came to power. . . . Maybe some of those guys worked with Göring, flew with Göring in the Great War. . . . Maybe those guys were counting on the Göring escape route. . . .

"So Moller flew in, got all the way to the right man, Tash Benedictus. Now it all gets a little confused. The maid says Manfred Moller was sleeping with our Enid Mallory, better known as Mona Ransom or Mrs. Benedictus . . . and somehow Moller's priceless minotaur wound up with Henry Breeneman in Boston . . . presumably via Benedictus who was obviously involved at some level with Karl Dauner. Benedictus or Dauner, one of them has to be Vulkan . . . Vulkan's running the whole bloody thing. But maybe it doesn't matter who Vulkan is. . . ."

Terry Leary listened stoically, puffing quietly.

"Then," Cassidy said, "for some reason, Moller figured he had to kill Brenneman. He took his minotaur and disappeared—now timing and logic tell you that that had to be connected with Dauner's getting killed . . . but how? Did Moller just get spooked? Or is it something else? And then who killed Rolf Moller?"

Terry Leary was watching a beautiful woman with blond wisps trailing from beneath her riding hat canter past, leaning solidly forward in the saddle. "Women and horses," he mused, then turned back to Cassidy. "It seems to me what you've got boils down to three main questions. First, where is Manfred Moller now? Second, did Manfred kill Rolf Moller, and if so, why? And third, there's Benedictus: what is his game and where has he gone?" He turned back, watching the woman and horse out of sight around a bend.

The questions changed a little every so often but the more they changed, the more they stayed the same. And basically it had always been only the one question: where was Manfred Moller? That's why MacMurdo was in it, why Karin was in it, and finally why he himself was in it. Find Manfred Moller and everything would somehow be made clear, mysteries solved, fates resolved.

At least he could now explain Tash Benedictus. Terry wasn't altogether correct. Benedictus wasn't just a liar: he was a player, he'd been a player all along. And he was still in the game. Whatever he was doing, wherever he was, he was still in the game and still making up his own rules. Everything he was doing was based on two suppositions. He was Irish and he hated the fucking limeys. . . .

All the questions bothered Cassidy, like gremlins needling away at him. But there was another one that had his attention like a flashing red light.

Mona Ransom had told him that Benedictus *knew he was coming. . . .*

If that was true—well, he just didn't like to think about it. If Benedictus knew Cassidy was coming, then there was a traitor somewhere in the ranks. Was someone watching them from up close?

Then it occurred to him. Had Rolf Moller discovered the truth? And died for it?

• • •

Karin was in a fury.

There was nothing of the meek, frightened, confused piece of damaged goods she'd been ever since he met her again at MacMurdo's invitation. Then she'd been wispy, a haunting memory of the woman he'd married, as if she'd been clumsily erased, leaving an outline, hints of what she'd been before. Now, as if the on-switch had been flipped, she was all there, no wisps, no hints, no memory of the wounded victim.

MacMurdo was standing by the doors to the terrace, staring out at the buildings across Park Avenue. Leary was sitting on a padded leather stool at his bar, watching her reflection in the slatted mirror behind the rows of glasses and bottles. The mirror broke her into a thousand images and each one of them was in full cry. Cassidy watched her from a deep armchair with a date palm arching over his head.

"It's about time you all realized I'm a human being," she said, gritting her teeth. "I'm not a specimen in a jar or a skeleton dangling in the closet. Here I am, the real thing, an actual person." She was wearing tan gabardine slacks and a black silk blouse with the collar turned up and the cuffs rolled back. The nurse who'd spent the night with her stood at the entrance to the hallway. She wore a starched white uniform and looked worried.

"I'm sick of being kept in the dark! Some of you seem to know who I am, who I *was*. . . ." She stared briefly at Cassidy, her face softening for an instant. Then the resolve returned. "Some of you know the part of my life I can't remember. . . . Some of you lie to me—do you think I'm unaware of all that? Well, don't be so fatuous. You should know better. . . .

"And I'm sick of all the pills, sick to death of sleeping all the time and feeling groggy—"

MacMurdo said, "It was Rolf who kept you sedated—"

"Don't lie to me! Rolf, yes, but on your orders, Colonel. Rolf told me that, told me he had to do whatever you asked. He said you wanted me calm and slow-thinking, you didn't want me to be troublesome. Why lie, Colonel? Do you have another doctor who'll have to do what you say now that Rolf's dead?"

"No," MacMurdo said sadly. "Right now I wish I did, I promise you.

This is what I wanted to avoid—this hysterical bullshit from an unbalanced woman." He wouldn't look at her. He just kept staring out across the terrace from which Rolf Moller had gone to his death.

"And now," she went on, pacing angrily across the sunken living room, her fists clenched, "now this new lunacy! No, Colonel, my husband did not materialize out of the night and murder his brother! *Mein Gott*, the very idea! Every idea you have, every remedy you have—*Schlimmbesserung*—you know that word? *Schlimmbesserung!* It means a new remedy, a new solution—that makes everything worse! You're an expert, Colonel! The idea of Manfred killing Rolf is . . . it's preposterous! I'm sick of the whole idiotic business—"

"Karin!" MacMurdo's powerful voice, like his laugh, filled the room as he finally turned to look at her. "Frau Moller." She stopped, staring at him. "May I remind you of the deal you made? You agreed to help us."

"A deal with the Devil!" Her face was white, stretched tight across her cheekbones. "Yes, of course, I remember. I'm still here. Yes, I remember. . . ." She was trembling with either fear or rage. Cassidy couldn't be sure. "So just find Manfred . . . and try to keep at least a few of us alive!"

She stormed out of the room, back down the hallway to her room. The nurse turned to follow. Karin waved her away. "Leave me alone. Please." The bedroom door slammed.

"Women!" MacMurdo sighed and spat out the word as if it were spoiled and foul.

Terry Leary laughed.

• • •

Cassidy knocked softly on the bedroom door. MacMurdo and Leary had gone onto the terrace to watch the mist thicken over Park Avenue. Cassidy was fed up with MacMurdo, didn't give a damn about him or his plans just then. He knocked on the door again.

"Who is it?"

"Me. Cassidy."

Several seconds passed; then she opened the door. She turned, went back into the room. He followed her. She'd opened the windows and straightened the bedclothes. Now she stood with her arms folded across her chest, staring at him.

"If I can't trust you," she said, "I'm alone. Maybe it's best that I realize the truth. Can I trust you? Or not? Just who are you? What are you to me?" Her eyes ate him up. There was the fearlessness of the end of the tether in her eyes again. "I see you in my dreams. You tell me you met me at the Olympics in 1936. I don't remember the Olympics, I don't remember you . . . but I dream of you and the dreams are like memories. In 1936 I was nineteen years old, Mr. Cassidy. A girl. I'd never been away from home. . . . I remember things from childhood, tiny things. . . . I know I was a child in 1936. And you met me, you tell me I was beautiful. . . . What happened after we met? Did we see one another again?" She stared at him, her eyes narrowing, as if that might bring their meeting into better focus. "Why can't you tell me what you know about me? Why is it all a secret?" The anger had gone out of her voice but not the energy. He could see it: she was free of medication. "Can't you tell me even that?" She was Karin now. He couldn't let her disappear again.

"Because Rolf said I couldn't!"

"But why not? What harm could it do for me to know who I am?" She brushed the curtain of hair back from her eye. "What is the point? What has anyone to fear from me? I don't understand."

"It's not that. Rolf said it's you, you're the one in danger. Not physical danger, though you seem to have had nothing but that since you got here. . . . No, he meant psychological danger. Amnesia is an uncharted land, Karin. Rolf was afraid that forcing you to remember could drive you—could hurt you, could make you not want to live—"

"Could drive me mad? Could make me want to kill myself? That's what you're trying to say, isn't it? What's so awful, Lew? What memories would drive me to kill myself? What was he talking about?"

"He was talking about how you lost your memory. He didn't want it forced on you. . . . He said the amnesia was your way of protecting yourself from the memories."

"Memories of the war," she said impatiently. "The war, the war . . . trauma. Shock! Rolf acted as if I was the only person who had a bad war. Well, it's not true! Everybody over there had a bad war and they go on. So why can't I? Because Rolf brought me back to life—did I become his property? To be protected forever from life?"

"You didn't just have a bad war, Karin. It went far beyond that—"

"Well, I'm not having such a hell of a wonderful peace, either!"

Cassidy laughed aloud. "I know the feeling."

"You believe everything Rolf told you?"

"Why shouldn't I?"

"Because it's all ridiculous!" She spoke calmly, smiling enigmatically. "You don't know even half of it. Believe me."

"Who knows all of it?"

"That's the problem. No one knows all of it, we all just know some of it. Not even Colonel MacMurdo knows all of it."

"What part doesn't he know?"

She laughed, shaking her head, as if it were all a joke. "He doesn't know what I'm thinking. He wishes he did but he can't get inside my head so he can't be sure of me. That frightens him."

"And you," Cassidy said, "don't know what I know about you. It's like a Chinese box puzzle, isn't it?"

"Tell me what you know about me, Lew. Please."

"Wait a little longer," he said. "Then I'll help you put all the pieces together. Let's get Manfred found, let's get all that straightened out, then there'll be all the time in the world."

"All the time in the world," she said. "Aren't you afraid of tempting fate? No one who has lived through a war, even one she cannot remember, puts much faith in all the time in the world. But before anything else, we must find Manfred."

"Is Manfred the key?"

"I wouldn't be here if it weren't for Manfred."

"How much does he know?"

"He's the missing piece. And it's funny. He knows the least of all. Poor Manfred . . . I wake in the middle of the night, maybe from a dream about you, and I think of Manfred. I feel so sorry for him now."

• • •

Late that evening Cassidy sat in the darkened living room of his apartment. He had skipped dinner. He hadn't gone to Heliotrope with Terry. He sat in the dark, staring out at Washington Square but not really seeing it. He kept trying to put it all together but it was like playing chess out of your league, against somebody who knew all your moves almost before you did. He was losing badly when the ringing doorbell woke him up.

He rubbed his eyes and stood up, stumbling over an empty highball glass and a cushion from the couch. He felt like Robert Benchley in the movies, demonstrating all the ways to be clumsy and confused, set upon and brought to grief by inanimate objects that move when you're not looking. The bell kept ringing.

It was a Western Union delivery boy. "Just about gave up on you, mister." He looked down at the telegram in his hand. "Cassidy, is it?"

"That's right. I hope you're not about to break into song."

"What? Oh, singing telegrams? No, that's not my department. This is just your plain old regular telegram, sir."

Cassidy gave him half a dollar and went back inside. He turned the lights on and blearily opened the envelope.

It didn't make sense at first, all the little strips of paper with all the words in upper case and jumbled together. Then, in a flash of consciousness, it came together. It had been sent from Beverly Hills, California.

CASSIDY. IF YOU WANT THE MAN YOU CAME LOOKING FOR I'VE GOT HIM STOP NAME IS FRED MILLER STOP I'M READY TO MAKE A DEAL STOP I CAN DELIVER STOP GO TO OCEAN VIEW MOTOR COURT NORTH OF MALIBU STOP REGISTER AS BRIAN SHEEHAN STOP COME ALONE STOP I'LL COME TO YOU STOP JUST WAIT FOR ME STOP MONA

Cassidy read it through several times.

It was either real or it was a setup and he could think of only one way to find out.

# Chapter Twenty-one

The fog swirled in and puffed at the darkness as if it carried its own light, more fog than was needed, really, for setting the scene. Cassidy's father would have said the special-effects man was overdoing the whole thing. But, in the odd way things happen, this was real and you couldn't cut back on the fog. Cold and autumnal, it swept in off the Pacific and the coast highway disappeared and so did the Malibu cliffs and the rocky beaches stretching northward toward Santa Barbara. Somewhere in the fog, lost like an abandoned, derelict freighter, a rust bucket, sat the scarred relic from the Great Depression, the Ocean View Motor Court.

The sign had been painted over but the old name could still be seen, a palimpsest, faded gold lettering, each letter outlined in green. In the old days, it had proclaimed the El Dorado Tourist Cabins. Under the three light bulbs shining on the sign through the blowing fog the new red lettering looked gaudy and desperate. It had already begun to flake and peel in the damp salt air. It was not a Mona Ransom kind of place but it was the right place. When he'd checked in two days before, Cliff Howard, the owner, had sucked his toothpick, tilted his big straw cowboy hat back on his head, and said: "Oh, so you're Mr. Sheehan, we've got your reservation here. Guess your people didn't know when you were due in. Just told us to hold a cabin for you. Hard to believe," he chuckled sourly, "but it ain't been too tough to do. We're sort of betwixt and between here, nineteen cabins and you got your pick of seventeen of 'em. We're not actually on the celebrity tourist trail. Hell, one day, coupla years back musta been, I thought honest-to-God Alan Ladd checked in one day. Wife and I both love a good Alan Ladd picture. . . ." He shifted the toothpick and shook his head balefully. "Alan Ladd. Sheeee-it. Turned out to be an insurance salesman from Strawberry Point. That's Iowa, y'know. Boy, that man truly did look like Alan Ladd. Little short guy. Did you know that, Mr. Sheehan? Alan Ladd is about knee-high to a grasshopper. Lotsa people don't believe that when you tell 'em. But he is, little short guy." He blotted the signature with an advertising card that proclaimed that loose lips could sink ships. A grinning Japanese admiral with teeth the size of cakes of Palmolive watched an American battleship going down. There was a calendar for 1942 printed beside the slogan.

Cassidy had taken number 7 and he was heading toward the third night wondering if he'd been a sucker. He ate his meals at the celebrated EATS CAFÉ presided over by Alma Howard. He gassed up his rented Plymouth at the pumps in front of the café and Cliff checked his plugs and oil and swiped ineffectually at the windshield.

"You want to drive down to the water," Cliff Howard said, "you gotta go down about half a mile, take a sharp left, park the jalopy, and walk down them wooden stairs to the beach. Watch them stairs, they're all crumbly. This climate plays hell with anything metal or wood. Which don't leave a hell of a lot else, now I think of it."

Cliff spent most of the time bent over the fender of a rusted-out Chevy that had last seen better days in the Coolidge Administration. Right about now, the fall of '45, it looked a lot like Field Marshal Rommel had personally driven his tank over it. Cliff didn't seem to mind. He'd brought the Chevy out from Grand Forks in '39 when he and Alma had inherited the old El Dorado from Alma's late sister and he said the Chevy had whatcha-call your sentimental value. It was the only way he was ever going to get out of Grand Forks unless it was to move to Rapid City where his brother had a hardware store, so—what the hell—he took it and lit out for Sunny Cal. "Grand Forks, Rapid City," he sighed, "that whole part of the world. You ever go see the faces at Mount Rushmore? We used to see 'em once a summer at least. Pretty boring after the first twenty-five years or so. California, I says to Alma, that's the place to be! Damn right." He sucked a toothpick. His face was bright red—as if the sun had dyed it permanently—until you got to the middle of his forehead and then it had that fish-belly whiteness you saw in farmers and ball players. He'd put in his time in the fields, all right. Years and years of it. He'd never lose the look.

During the days Cassidy sat outside in the metal lawn chairs watching the stucco bubble, watching Cliff bent over the Chevy fully as intent as a brain surgeon trying to restore George Brent's sight or Bette Davis's whatnot. Cassidy finally caught up with the *Los Angeles Times* and learned that the Cubs had been demolished by the Tigers in the final game of the Series. Newhouser had gone the full nine in the 9–3 win. The Cubs had gambled on Borowy yet again, with only a day's rest, and the Tigers had shellacked him in the first. He hadn't gotten anybody out and at the end of an inning it was 5–0 and the Series was over. It was just as well he'd been flying to California and hadn't heard the stupid game.

His third dinner at the café consisted of meat loaf and mashed potatoes and a Coke and peach pie and coffee and Cliff Howard sat in the booth across the table and ate a Velveeta-on-white sandwich, washed down with about a quart of milk. "It's my ulcers," he said. "Bet you didn't know I got me part of a sheep's stomach. No lie, can you believe that, Brian?"

"Well, it's hard to believe," Cassidy said. "How long have you had these ulcers?"

"The war, man, the war. I got so goddamned worried 'bout Jap attacks along the coast here, I got me my ulcer. Used to go down and patrol the beach looking for those little two-man subs . . . kept hearing planes, thought every damn one of 'em was a Zero coming off a carrier out there. Silly damn fool that I was! Real dumb clodbuster from Grand Forks, I guess you could say. . . . And now we're gonna have a real war, Brian, you wait and see—"

"Didn't we just have a real war?"

"Just a preliminary, Brian. It's the Communists we're gonna wind up fighting. The Russians. They're the ones. They're coming after us, Brian. And you know what else? We're gonna rue the day we whipped the Nazis because we're gonna wish we had some of those old boys to help us fight the commies. My ulcer gives me a helluva time when I get to thinking about them commie bastards; are we tough enough to beat 'em? Old George Patton is tough enough, you can count on that. Those Nazis—well, they had their faults and I ain't sayin' they didn't, but they were tough, they saw the Russkies for what they were—"

"But the Russians beat the shit out of the Nazis," Cassidy said.

"Well, young fella, you can be pretty damned sure of one thing. Russians would of been nothing but a slick spot on the highway if the U.S. of A. had marched in arm-in-arm with the German army. Bet on that, young fella. Money in the bank."

After dinner Cassidy sat on the stoop outside the door to his cabin and waited in the fog. He heard gulls squawking above and Fred Allen on the radio from one of the other occupied cabins and he watched while the fog thickened and blurred the lights on the gas pumps, the lights in the café windows and glowing on the sorry sign.

He sat in the fog and thought about things and he waited for Mona Ransom.

• • •

Sam MacMurdo, eyes gleaming in anticipation of the kill, had been overjoyed at Mona Ransom's telegram. "This is it, pard," he said. "The balloon's gone up." He sounded as if Rolf Moller and his killer were all but forgotten.

He'd gotten on the phone to Washington and in an hour the word had come through that a DC-3 was laid on for the afternoon. MacMurdo would be serving as copilot and they'd leave from LaGuardia. MacMurdo had grinned widely. "Allen Dulles himself set this one up." He looked a little as if he expected applause for having the spymaster's ear.

The plane had been outfitted for the transportation of military VIPs. Cassidy thanked God for that, having imagined a naked interior and a ride of endless discomfort, three thousand miles across America.

MacMurdo was up in the cockpit. Back in the cabin Cassidy, Terry Leary, and Karin made themselves comfortable in padded seats with heavy olive-drab blankets, Thermos bottles of coffee, packets of sandwiches. They were scheduled to set down for fuel three times; at least that was what Cassidy thought he heard. It didn't really matter. Harry Madrid refused to join them. He wouldn't fly and that was all there was to it. On the other hand, he didn't want to miss the fun. He was off on the noon train after arrangements for what MacMurdo called "billeting" had been made through one of Dulles's contacts in Los Angeles. They would be staying at a house in the Hollywood Hills above Sunset Boulevard that had been used by the Army intelligence people since mid-1941. All of them, that is, but Cassidy, who would be waiting for Mona Ransom at the Ocean View Motor Court.

During the night with the engines throbbing and the air in the cabin thin and cold Karin had leaned against him, two army blankets over them, and he'd asked her what kind of man Manfred Moller actually was. She had sniffled and burrowed her fists against his chest and thought for a moment before she spoke.

"He likes jokes," she said. "That's what appealed to me at first. He was anything but the fearsome SS man, though he looked very nice in his uniform. He never talked about the war except to tell funny stories about himself and the other soldiers, the kind of stories that come out of any war, I suppose. People making funny, stupid mistakes . . . He always tried to cheer me up and tell me that soon the war would be over. He used to say that the Americans and the English were our natural allies, not our enemies. He would say that once we'd lost the war we'd join with America and face the Russians together. . . . He wasn't a monster, Lew. He thought about things, he tried to see what lay beneath the surface.

"He loves amateur theatricals, used to joke about playing Hamlet in German though he could easily have done it in English." She spoke with real affection. There was no denying that, no way around it. "He came back at Christmas and played Saint Nicholas for the village children, somehow made sure that there was a party, something to make everyone forget the war for a day or two. And he made me forget—odd for me to say, since I'd forgotten so much already, but you know what I mean. . . . He made me forget that I'd *forgotten,* he made me feel that I could still be happy sometimes. I'm explaining all this very badly. He was so good with children, they truly believed he was Father Christmas . . . all padded. . . . They loved him, he'd lead them singing with little Elisabeth bouncing on his knee. . . ." She seemed to drift away, lost in the memory of wartime Christmases.

"You mentioned Elisabeth once before," Cassidy said. "When I first saw you again—"

"Again?"

"You know what I mean. A few weeks ago." He looked down at her face tilted up, solemn. He kissed her forehead, near the scar at the temple. "Tell me about Elisabeth. What was her story?"

"Oh, no particular story. Just another war story. A sweet, lovely little girl, beautiful . . . no father, you see. And Manfred was so good with her, almost as if she were his own daughter. It makes me so sad, thinking about him now, hiding, running, afraid. . . ." She bit her knuckle. In the dim reddish light of the darkened cabin he saw the tears on her cheeks. The tears were never far away.

"I wouldn't worry about him too much. He's quite good at taking care of himself. He's already killed the man who flew him into the States, an art dealer in Boston, and quite possibly his brother—"

"Please, believe me," she sighed. "That's impossible."

"And so far as Manfred himself knows, he killed Harry Madrid and me up in Boston. You'd better face it, Karin, he may have been a helluva Father Christmas, but when it comes to murder the man is running up the score."

As the plane droned on he heard her crying softly in her sleep.

• • •

Middle of the night. An Army airbase in Kansas.

Karin was sleeping soundly and they left her under the blankets on the plane. MacMurdo went off to talk with a mechanic while the refueling was carried out. Terry Leary and Cassidy headed for the canteen where there were doughnuts and strong, brackish coffee. They stood by the window in the Quonset hut and watched the floodlit tarmac, the airplanes at rest casting shadows like sleeping pterodactyls.

Terry Leary wiped confectioner's sugar from his thin mustache and set the coffee cup down. He was wearing his serious face, which was on view less frequently with each passing year. The more serious life got, he'd decided some time ago, the more you needed to retain your sense of life's essential absurdity. It was all a comedy in the end and life was so short and nobody would remember you'd been here, anyway. He wasn't given to thinking too deeply because most of the things people worried about seemed beyond their control. The more they thought the worse things seemed to get. So he tried not to take it all quite so seriously.

But it was the deepest, darkest hour of the night. He was out in the middle of a place no man had ever gone before—Kansas was off the edge of Terry Leary's map—and he was worried. He had a tendency, against all his better judgment, to take Cassidy's life seriously. Cassidy's life in the years since Karin had disappeared into Germany had been just about the only thing that Terry Leary worried about. His own life he was content to deal with as a roll of the dice. Cassidy's life was something to worry about. Terry Leary wanted to make sure Cassidy's life turned out right, whatever that meant. And right now Terry Leary was wishing that Karin had died in the bombing of Cologne. The way God had probably intended.

"You're not going to like this, amigo," he said.

"I'm not?" Cassidy watched MacMurdo in another of his elements, shooting the breeze with the pilot and the mechanics. The moon was full and silver and they were laughing like kids getting to stay up all night.

"You listening?"

"Sure." Cassidy yawned. "Shoot."

"It's about Karin. I've been thinking."

"Me, too. What am I not going to like? I'm pretty realistic about her, Terry. It's all kind of a mess." He grinned tiredly. "You've been through a lot with me. And women. What's on your mind?"

"There's something wrong with Karin. I can feel it."

"Well, sure. That's not exactly a stop-press scoop."

"There's something all wrong with this memory-loss thing of hers." He took a deep breath. "I think maybe she's faking it . . . or faking some of it. Or it's different than we think. Jesus, I'm screwing this up. I'm sorry, amigo."

"What the hell are you talking about?" He smiled wearily at Terry. "Faking it? You can't fake amnesia, not over a period of time. And if you tried you'd have to have a hell of a reason. It seems to me she hasn't got much of a reason. Hasn't got any reason, so far as I can see. You'd better give this some more thought. What makes you think such a crazy thing?"

"Okay, okay. I don't know. But I had an idea, something that might help her. It could bring her back. It might be worth a try."

"She's in a delicate condition—" Cassidy stopped. "No, scratch that. That was Rolf's idea. I think she's about as fragile as cast iron. Aside from thinking she's faking it, what's your idea?"

"Omar."

"Omar?"

"Omar Popescu. Ring any bells?"

• • •

Later on, in the unreal white light of the dawn over the Rockies, Karin stretched and woke up and said that never in her life had she ever had such drastic need of a bathroom. He sent her off and when she came back her hair was combed and her face rubbed pink and shiny with cold water. She sat down, stared out at the thin stips of halfhearted clouds that lay like knife blades across the hazy pale sky. She leaned back against him and said: "What will happen in Los Angeles?"

He reassured her. "All our problems should be solved."

"What is it Terry says? Everybody's a comic?" She spoke without rancor. "What I mean is, what will happen to Manfred? Is Colonel MacMurdo going to kill him?" Her eyes were fixed on the view beyond the window. Her voice was calm.

"I don't think so. He's going to want to ask him a lot of questions, of course. Whatever he knows of the Nazis in America." He shrugged, wondering if he was anywhere near the mark.

"He'll be disappointed then. Manfred doesn't know anything about all that. He's a soldier, not a spy. You'd think MacMurdo would have more sense."

"Well, there's the minotaur. And some money he's supposed to have. Maybe even plates for printing money—"

"He must be driving a truck, then! MacMurdo is a man with secrets. He's good with secrets, isn't he? I'd worry about that if I were you—"

"He's had to be, the war he's had."

"We all have our secrets, I suppose. All of us. What's your secret, Lewis?"

"I'm an open book."

"Don't act so innocent. I know you're not. Are we going to learn the secrets in California? Is that really why we're coming all this way?"

"There's a man I want you to meet in California."

"What sort of man? Another doctor? Will I like him? Will somebody kill him?"

"No, not a doctor. Far from it. More of a magician. Or a charlatan. I've never been sure. But he's a nice man. An actor sometimes. Calls himself a mentalist. Most everybody else calls him a mountebank. I don't know—he likes to see himself as a kind of wizard. You'll like him. He usually smells of garlic. He says it's in his blood, the garlic."

"Keeps the werewolves away."

"Vampires, I thought. He played a vampire in the movies a few times. Terrible movies. You could always see the microphone booms. Monogram Pictures. My father knew him in the old days. Still does, I guess."

"Who is this man?"

"His name's Omar Popescu. Or so he says. Somebody once told me his real name is Murray Rosenblatt and he was born in Seattle. In Hollywood everyone is actually someone else. I knew him back in the thirties before I got—"

"Before what?"

"Before I got married."

"You're married? You never told—where is this wife? I've never heard you speak of a wife—"

"No, she's not with me—"

"But you are married?"

"Not exactly. It's a long story. I'll tell you about it someday. For the moment, don't forget it's *your* husband we're interested in right now. Will you answer one more question, Karin?"

"If I can."

"Are you in love with Manfred Moller?"

"Love." She turned slowly from the window so he could see her elegant profile. "Love," she said again. "Love didn't really play a part in it. I can't explain what condition I was in. . . . You'd have had to see me to understand. I was quite dead for a time, you see. I had no memory of anything, I couldn't talk, and then when I finally could speak I still couldn't think of anything to say. I don't mean to make a joke of it, I had nothing to say. And then finally I did speak. . . . Rolf was like a father, I knew he could give me life again . . . and then Manfred came and he was so good and kind to me. He fell in love with me. . . . I don't think I'll talk about it anymore now."

She leaned against him and closed her eyes.

• • •

He must have drifted off for a moment or two because when he shook himself and looked up he saw two huge headlamps shining through the fog, looking as enormous as movie-premiere searchlights. The car turned slowly, visible only in outline, a Rolls-Royce that made him think of the *Queen Mary* sliding up to its berth. It wasn't the sort of conveyance one associated with the run-down, pockmarked, beaten-up motor court.

Footsteps sounded on the gravel walk. A band was playing on the radio that Fred Allen had vacated. Stan Kenton live from Balboa.

Cassidy saw the figure take shape, the belted mink coat, a soft fedora pulled down, the whole thing blurred by the fog.

"Mr. Sheehan, I presume?"

Her voice was deep and smoky and by its nature insinuating.

"Oh, hell," Cassidy said. "I suppose so."

# CHAPTER TWENTY-TWO

"Let's take your car," she said. The obsidian eyes glittered beneath the hat's brim. "It's not impossible that my husband is having me followed. I didn't see anyone in the fog, but you can't be too careful when you're dealing with Tash Benedictus."

They slid into the small rented car with the cracked seatcovers and the smell of cheap cigars seeping from every crevice.

"Where am I going?"

"Take a left on the highway and I'll direct you." She was firm, all business, the way she'd been at dinner when she'd befriended Dora. Cassidy kept thinking about her, remembering the pressure of her thighs clamping around him, and he had the feeling he was the only one in the car preoccupied with those particular reflections.

The fog was too thick for any speed. He switched on the yellow fog light hanging on the driver's door frame. In half an hour they had crept along the road, hearing the surf below, its throb dulled by the fog that absorbed the sound like the beach soaked up the ocean, and turned into a defile between two boulders that worked its way down to a narrow strip of hard-packed sand. It was a perfect place for a murder, except you'd have to find it first. Cassidy felt as if he'd been there before, probably ransoming somebody's emeralds, and he *had* been there before but it was all in the movies he'd seen as a kid and William Powell was the one retrieving the lovely lady's gems.

"Pull in here," she said.

"Whatever you say." He braked and turned off the lights, left the motor running.

"Turn it off," she said. "I'm nervous, Mr. Cassidy. Let's get out and walk. It's funny about foggy nights. There's always plenty of light from up above the fog. And I don't want to be a sitting duck in the car."

She waited while he came around to open the door. She took his hand and got out.

"What do you mean, 'sitting duck'?"

"My husband knows men with guns. My God, my husband *is* a man with a gun. Look, I know what you're thinking, Mr. Cassidy."

"Well, good for you. Now, why the hell am I here?"

"My, aren't we testy," she said.

"You'd be testy, too, if you'd been sitting on your can all this time listening to Cliff Howard tell you how we'd just won the wrong war."

"Mmm. Cliff is a character. Central Casting."

"Where have you been?"

"I'm not a free agent. Tash is very watchful. The point is I'm here now and you've come all this way to make a deal—"

"Rescuing another maiden in a tower."

"To make a deal," she continued, ignoring him. "Everyone comes to California to make a deal. That's what California is for. You want a certain man. I've cornered the market on the man in question. I'll trade you, him for my husband—"

"Then I'd have both of them. I don't want your husband. I want Manfred Moller—Fred Miller to you."

She took his arm. The mink made a soft cushion. "Let's walk. Hear me out. Do you have a gun?"

"Yes, I have a gun."

"Good, so do I. A Luger. I stole it from Tash. He's got so many he'll never miss it. Come on, I'm wearing low-heeled shoes, I can walk in the sand."

She was right about the moon glowing behind the fog. The wind gusted off the ocean, full of mist. It blew her scent. She seemed to be all around him, circling him, like the fog.

"My husband," she said. "He's the key to this deal for me. The German is the key for you. Let me tell you a couple of things about my husband. He is not what he appears."

"I'm not so sure. He appears to be a perfect asshole."

"I need hardly tell you that nobody's perfect. However, he is among other despicable things a Nazi sympathizer."

"I know. His name is Brian Sheehan and he goes all the way back to Sir Roger Casement. You don't have to tell me your husband's story."

"You *are* a detective, Mr. Cassidy. I'm impressed."

"Look, I'm sick of sitting around that stupid motor court. Now start talking and make it worth my while. I'm a patient man, but I'm not a saint."

They were moving slowly across the sand, leaving a perfect trail for any henchmen abroad in the night.

"My husband is making a considerable fortune these days acting as the middleman for a group of Nazi mucky-mucks who not only got out of Germany but managed to commandeer a U-boat or two that arrived during the spring and summer—" She took a breath. It was a long sentence that had turned against her.

"Relax." He squeezed her arm. "You're beginning to interest me."

"I'll bet I am. The U-boats, I gather from what I've overheard, were carrying art treasures. They landed in the Gulf Coast, along the Florida coast and in the Keys, the islands off the Carolinas, even up in New England. The paintings were considered highly negotiable, a means of financing these Nazis as they began their new lives in the New World. Once the art gets to the States it's easily funneled to California. . . . The stuff is being sold in the movie colony where questions are only infrequently asked, if at all. Studio heads, producers, directors, stars, their doctors and dentists and lawyers and their pool men, for all I know—they're buying this stuff. Tash is acting as the conduit and he's taking a very large cut. He runs the auctions. The prices are high, Cassidy. Very high."

"What does Tash do with the take?"

She shrugged. "That's his business—"

"You must have picked up something. You seem awfully well informed. Hasn't he ever spoken about people in it with him?"

"V. He's referred to someone called V. I've seen notes on his desk, things like that. That's all. Vincent, Victor . . . I don't know."

"All right. V. I know what V means. Go on."

"The man you want from me is somehow involved. Don't ask me how because I don't know how."

"The man you know as Fred Miller," Cassidy said. "Same fellow who stayed with you at the castle the past six months—"

"How do you know all this? Wait, no, I don't care. You know and that's plenty. Fine." She stopped and stared out at the surf rolling up the sand and dying ten feet in front of them. "I want to keep this as uncomplicated as possible, just you and me and Tash and the German." The wind was tugging at her hat. She bowed her head against it, hands plunged deep in her pockets. "You want the German . . . and in return you can do something for me. That's the deal. Take it or leave it."

"You haven't told me what you want me to do."

"I've found out a few things about you, Cassidy. Football player, now you're a detective with this ex-cop Leary, you were involved with the wrecking of the Max Bauman gang. . . . All of which tells me that you just have a chance against my husband . . . a chance, mind you. No more than a chance, but you're the only chance I've got—"

"Mona," he said, turning her by the shoulders, "what do you want me to do? And try to remember, this isn't one of your goofy movies. I'm not in this alone. This is a government operation. They're not people you bargain with—"

"All right, all right. I give you the Germans, you free me of Tash . . . that's all."

"How? Why don't you just leave?"

"Leave him? *Leave* Tash Benedictus? You don't leave Tash. . . . You run the risk of his reverting to form, becoming Brian Sheehan again. You don't know the kind of man he is. He kills people just to stay in practice . . . and he's worried, Cassidy. Nervous. He's up to his neck in Nazis and it's getting out of control. The German this summer was a little too much. Tash knows he's being used; he keeps fuming that they're using him, that they've gone too far—"

"They? Who are they?"

"I don't know. The Nazis, I suppose." She shook her head impatiently, the black eyes glittering, the scarlet mouth curling down at the ends. Her face was white in the eerie glow. "If not the Nazis, well, who else?"

"I don't know. I wonder." Cassidy shrugged. "So what do you want me to do for you?"

"Tash has told me that if I try to leave him he'll kill me. I've been his prisoner for so long. . . . But now, now I have a wonderful offer to go back to work!" She looked up at him and all the jaded ennui had dropped away. Her face was animated, hopeful, as if the young woman from years before were shining through. "It's a solid offer, starring role. With Preminger directing. He's lining up a new picture, like *Laura* or *The Woman in the Window* or *Phantom Lady*. Ty Power is set to costar. This funny little man, Ray Chambers, or Chandler, he's supposed to be good and he's writing it. Do you understand, Cassidy? I want this job. I want to work again, I want to be a star again . . . but Tash knows I'll never come back to him once I'm out there—he knows I hate him. So he keeps me tied to him, keeps threatening me, keeps telling me he'll go to the papers with the story and you can believe me, he's got some of the columnists in his pocket, they'll print it, the bastards!"

"What story?"

"Look, I was a drug addict. I had a bad habit. I did anything I had to do to get the stuff. When Tash found me I was fucking anybody they wanted me to, the guys running the studio, they'd use me as the centerpiece for their parties, I'd put on a show and then I'd be dessert. And being moviemakers they put it all on film." She laughed harshly. "You think Fatty Arbuckle got a raw deal? If you'd like to see me with three black cocks inside me, why old Tash can just set up reel seven for you . . . always good for a laugh. Watch the movie star scream! Or reel twelve where I entertain some of my girlfriends. He's got enough to destroy me a thousand times over, believe me! And he'll use it—"

"How can he? You must know he killed the men who made you do that stuff. He'd be in dangerous water—"

She stepped backward, almost staggered on the sand, gave him a look.

"You know that, too?"

"So, leave him or blow the whistle on him. Get 'em to reopen that case—"

"Forget it. That's the way L.A. was in those days. And my God, he'd kill me. First he'd discredit me and whatever story I'd tell . . . and then, I promise you, he'd kill me. They'd never find my body. That's why I need you."

"To take you away when we take the German?"

"Oh, no. No, no. That wouldn't stop Tash. You've got to kill him for me."

"I'm not a killer—"

"Oh? That's not what I hear." She began slowly walking back toward the car. He followed. The wind was up, whipping sand into his eyes.

"Then you have been misinformed."

"Oh, don't play the lord with me." Her laughter was swept away on the wind and surf. "You're a brute of a footballer underneath that coat of varnish."

"Flattery will get you nowhere."

"You puzzle me, Cassidy. But you are serviceable between the sheets, I'll say that for you."

"A testimonial," he murmured.

"Will you kill him for me?"

"I might."

They had reached the car. He held the passenger door for her.

"I suppose that will have to hold me."

"It's the best offer you'll get from me."

"There'll be a party Sunday. I'll tell Tash I ran into you while shopping. He knows you have a connection to the picture business. So I'll tell him you're here on business."

"Quite a coincidence. Will he swallow it?"

"I really can't say. But I am an actress—so he might. Don't miss the party. Lawn bowling, croquet, movies in the screening room, beautiful woman, rich and powerful men, the catchpenny barons of our tawdry little world."

He closed the door, went around to the driver's side, and got in. It was a relief to get out of the wind. "Potential customers for the Nazi treasure?"

"Some of them. But only those Tash can trust. Or believes he can trust."

"He's taking big risks."

She nodded. "That's the way he likes it. You're not afraid, are you?"

"I'm always afraid of men like your husband." He started the car, turned on the lights and the yellow spotlight.

"But you will come to the party?"

"One thing—I won't be alone."

"That's all right. I don't intend for you to gun him down on the spot, in full view. Mustn't leave him floating in the punch bowl."

"Not and spoil the punch." He swung the car in an arc across the sand and poked its nose into the narrow road leading steeply to the highway.

"I'll have him on view, then. For inspection."

"Hmmm."

"My part of the bargain. I'll have your German, your quarry, on view. Whatever you do then is your business."

"I'll look forward to it."

The lights of the café were out but those on the gaudy sign burned on forever, as if they pointed the way to the underworld. Cassidy pulled up beside the Rolls-Royce.

Mona Ransom remained seated when he'd cut the engine and extinguished the lights.

"I believe," Cassidy said, "our revels now are ended."

"Not necessarily. Not if you want me to stay with you. For a little while?"

"I'm afraid not. I'm in training for Sunday."

"Said with a smile and therefore just acceptable. But just."

He helped her into the Rolls. She started the huge engine and glanced at him through the window. She rolled it down, smiled reflectively. "I'll bet you never sleep with a man's wife before you kill him."

Cassidy returned her smile. "Good night, Miss Ransom."

"Until Sunday, Mr. Cassidy."

He watched her go and very soon the fog swallowed her and he was alone again.

# CHAPTER TWENTY-THREE

The dinosaurs were still there and he supposed they shouldn't have taken him by such surprise. Hollywood was full of dinosaurs of one kind or another but, still, these came out of his own past and he hadn't thought about them in a long time.

Cassidy hadn't been to a Hollywood party since before the war when Karin had gone out to make her movies and he'd caught up with her once the football season was over. Looking across the undulating lawn from where he stood by the pool, he saw that nothing much had changed. The style was apparently permanent. C. Aubrey Smith, who had looked ninety then and looked ninety now, wearing whites and a club tie that flapped outside his blazer and a floppy sun hat, was lining up a croquet shot while Ronald Colman watched, a bored look on his finely shaped face.

The crowd was splashed decoratively about the terraces, spots of color like party favors against the jade lawn. Mess-jacketed waiters moved here and there with trays of canapes and drinks with fruit in them. By the pool a group of several perfectly tanned, young, and hopeful contract players lounged in bathing suits, swam, and made having-fun noises. The studio had sent them over, decorating the set. Nobody would speak to them except in the never-ending search for a quick lay. It was a meat market but at least on a Sunday afternoon in Hollywood everybody's cards were on the table and there was always the chance you could make a deal.

Karin and Terry Leary were standing on the veranda that ran across the back of the *faux* hacienda. Heavy-beamed rafters projected over their heads like the guns of a battleship. Red ceramic pots of bright flowers hung from the hooks and gourds were stacked in corners like pyramids of cannonballs in the town square. They were talking to Mona Ransom and a man in a dark suit who had the look of a New York banker. Sam MacMurdo was wearing his colonel's uniform with a chestful of medals. He was talking to an actor called John Wayne, who'd won the war more or less single-handedly on Hollywood's backlots. Wayne seemed genuinely interested in MacMurdo's decorations, maybe because MacMurdo was a lot bigger than he was. MacMurdo seemed genuinely interested in a young blonde in a low-cut sundress. She, however, was eyeing John Wayne, whom Cassidy had known for years as Marion Morrison. Morrison had been a football player in college on the West Coast and Paul Cassidy had brought them together for dinner one night on the basis of shared interests. It was odd how two such fine physical specimens had not wound up in the real war. Cassidy wondered fleetingly what Morrison's excuse was.

Back before the war Nat Olliphant had been running Monarch Pictures, but that was history, back before Nat had the big heart attack and dropped dead playing doubles on Ikey Shapiro's court in Silver Lake. Olliphant had thrown quite a shindig for Karin and you had to hand it to him, he'd had a hell of an idea about that big swimming pool that lay at the bottom of his lawn, down three rambling flights of steps set into the earth. He naturally thought he'd fill this huge pool and freeze the water. Then he'd throw the first ever ice-skating party in Beverly Hills in the middle of August—all in honor of Karin Richter at the inception of what was sure to be a glorious film career.

Well, it was a real Olliphant production. You had to hand it to Nat, all right, or you would have had to, but the portable refrigeration unit he'd sent over from Effects blew itself out fighting the ninety-five-degree heat. The pool wound up full of cold slush, very cold slush, you had to give Nat that much. It was tremendously cold but it definitely wasn't ice. Nat stood there looking at the wilting peaks of slush, then he paced back and forth, short and hairy and bowlegged, then he looked up at Karin, then back at the slush. Finally he looked back at Karin. "Karin, honey, my lamb, you're gonna tell me you can't skate on this, right?" Through the slush you could see all the dinosaurs Nat had had painted on the walls of the pool—the brontosaurus looking back over his shoulder, the *Tyrannosaurus rex* with teeth bared and looking to take a bite out of somebody like Vic Mature, the triceratops, the stegosaurus. They seemed to be drowning in an Ice Age that hadn't quite worked out.

That party came back to Cassidy like the memory of a song, words you'd never forget. He could still see the white middy sundress with the blue piping Karin had worn, how tan she'd been, how she'd stood talking with Ruby Keeler and Fred Astaire and how Miss Keeler had taught her some tap steps beside the pool . . . how the slush had melted and everybody had started giving the dinosaurs names. . . .

There had been a war since then and Nat Olliphant had served his last double-fault, but the dinosaurs were still there. Nat had put them there to publicize a caveman picture with Mature and some girls in skimpy mastodon hides. The picture finally got made by somebody else, but the animators from the studio had already painted the dinosaurs in the pool so they were Nat's forever and now Nat was at Forest Lawn for the duration. Still, his dinosaurs and his pool hadn't changed at all. But now it all belonged to Tash Benedictus.

• • •

"We can talk now. Tash took some of his clients down to the wine cellar. He'll show them a list of available investment possibilities. That's what he calls them, 'available investment possibilities.' It's a list of paintings." Mona Ransom was wearing a dress with a bare midriff. "The art won't be on view until the auction. Tash may be a wild man, but he's not entirely crazy. Now he's dropping hints about preemptive bids in the right ears." They were standing in the shade of a palm, looking down at the pool where the kids from the studio were frolicking and casing the crowd.

"Do you ever get a look at the list?"

"It's just names of artists . . . Tiepolo, Hals, Rembrandt, Raphael, Monet, Bonnard, Van Gogh. The names of the pictures or drawings mean nothing to me. What difference does it make?"

"You never saw a listing of a piece of sculpture, did you? There's a piece called the Ludwig Minotaur. Does that sound familiar?"

She shook her head. The black hair shone in the sun as if it had been oiled and polished. "It's a long list. I saw it on his desk. I didn't pay attention. What difference does it make? You're after a man, not a statue." She put a cigarette to her lips and handed him a gold lighter. "Please?"

He lit the cigarette. She was so pale she seemed almost on the point of disappearing. "Where's Moller?"

"Hanging about somewhere. You'll see him. But Tash is very upset that you're here."

"I'm not altogether surprised."

"I told him I ran into you while I was shopping with Kay Westerby. I blamed the invitation to the party on Kay. Tash said he didn't know who he wanted to kill first, Kay or me. We can trust Kay. She's been a good and discreet friend for years. But Tash, well, he's going crazy, he's got too many balls in the air at one time. If his first reaction wasn't always to kill everyone it would be a farce—but he's so serious. Now he's got you turning up, he doesn't know if it's a coincidence or not. But he knows you were looking for the German the last time he saw you and now he's got the German in the pantry or the greenhouse and you drop in out of the blue—he's not a mathematical genius but he's reasonably adept at two plus two. So, I'm scared, Tash is scared . . . and you should be scared, too."

"I'm scared, I'm scared. What are the other balls he's juggling?"

"Well, he's worried about the Feds. He thinks they *know*. I can see it in his eyes. And he's waiting for some damned Brit to show up and help out with the auction and he's not here yet and Tash doesn't know where he is. . . ."

"What's so important about this Englishman?"

"*I* don't know. Tash needs him to run the auction. Frankly, I wouldn't be surprised if the Brit is bringing in half the pictures. I mean, why else would Tash need him so desperately?"

"I just ask the questions," Cassidy said. "Any little tidbits about this V character?"

She looked at him obliquely, as if she were afraid he might be outsmarting her. "What do you know that I don't know? No, don't answer. I don't want to know. I just want out."

"I'm innocent as the egg, that's me. Just trying to help out. I keep telling you that." He kept trying to pick people out in the crowd, but it wasn't easy. There were too many familiar faces but none he knew. No MacMurdo, no Terry, no Karin. Jean Arthur and Billy Wilder and Veronica Lake were talking, then Lake strolled past and smiled shyly at Mona Ransom. Cassidy watched the blond star with the peek-a-boo hair wander down toward the pool.

"You like Moronica, do you?" Mona Ransom smiled very slightly.

"What?"

"Moronica Lake. That's what Tash calls her." She blew smoke at the retreating actress. "Somehow V is connected to this Englishman. I heard him on the phone. He doesn't even know when I'm in the room anymore. He acts like I don't exist these days. He doesn't have a single use for me anymore. Not one. But he can't stand to be left alone and he knows he'll never get another woman who's willing to put up with him . . . and he knows I owe him my life. And he knows I'll never leave him because I'm afraid—but he doesn't know one thing about me, he doesn't know I have enough guts to have him killed. . . . Oh, I know V's name. I'll bet you don't."

"Vince? Van? Victor? How about Vulkan?"

"How did you—"

"But that's a code name, you see. I'll bet you don't know his real name."

"No. I don't."

"Well, neither do I. Now what about my German?"

"It's complicated. Hard to explain."

"Since your future depends on it—try."

"Well, Tash knows you've never seen Moller, so that calmed him down. And apparently Moller is good at disguise—"

"He is. I have met him once. He tried to kill me. And he was someone else at the time."

"Yes, Tash said Moller can become many men. Isn't it perfect, an actor moving unrecognized among a lawn full of actors? Maybe that really isn't Charlie Laughton over there, maybe it's your German in a padded suit. Look around you, Lew Cassidy, he could be almost anyone, anywhere." She smiled a shade glassily. Cassidy hoped she wasn't on anything.

"Does Moller know my friends and I are here?"

She shrugged her broad, square shoulders. "I don't know . . . but if Tash told him, I promise you he wouldn't hide." She looked away quickly. "He'd want to see the hunting party."

Cassidy was impatient. She was getting on his nerves. She was too flighty, having too good a time. "Don't forget our deal, Miss Ransom."

"Have I made a deal with the Devil? Are you the Dark One, Lew Cassidy?"

Cassidy stared into her black eyes. Odd, hearing that expression again so soon. Karin had said it to MacMurdo.

"It's Moller in return for your husband. Not Charles Laughton, not Ronald Colman. It's Moller, no one else."

She looked at him, shading her eyes. The sun had moved. "You know, I think you are the Devil." She laughed bitterly. "And all these years I thought it was Tash."

"Just tend to business and everything will be all right. There'll be a happy ending."

"Don't be silly. That's strictly the movies."

• • •

Cassidy stood near the bar that had been set up near the end of the swimming pool. The day was searingly hot, the sun bright and angry. Los Angeles lay roasting, somnolent, beyond the hedge, far below, seen through a thick, smoggy haze. It was too hot to think clearly. Unfortunately he had the feeling that clear thinking was precisely what was required. He sipped the gin and tonic and squinted up across the terrace toward the hacienda, which lay in shadows as the afternoon crested and headed down the slope.

He didn't want to see Tash Benedictus, for a start. He was too erratic: what if he wandered in drunk and in the mood for a scene? What if his case of nerves got the better of him and he started yelling? But so far Cassidy had been lucky.

And what was he going to do—assuming he escaped having to deal with Benedictus—if he came up against Moller?

He and MacMurdo and Terry Leary had hashed it through. Obviously it would have been infinitely preferable if Mona could have maneuvered him out of Tash's reach, could literally have delivered him into their care. But you couldn't blame her. She'd done more than her part. Because of her the game was still afoot. If, of course, she could be trusted.

MacMurdo had wondered about that. Maybe it was all a setup. Maybe Benedictus had told her to send that wire. Maybe Moller was behind it, maybe Tash had told him that G-men, Army men, were on his trail . . . and maybe Moller wanted to get them out in the open.

MacMurdo could see a hell of a lot of problems. Maybe Vulkan was behind the telegram. . . .

MacMurdo was smart and he had a good mind for duplicity. He'd spent the war honing it. But Cassidy was pretty good at cutting through the bullshit himself. Sure, we want Moller. But at bottom *you* want Moller. *Your* masters in Washington—Dulles and that bunch, they want Moller. "Well, Sam," Cassidy had said, "let's just go get the sumbitch. What are they gonna do, Sam? Kill us? Hell, everybody dies." This was Hollywood and where else could you talk like a movie? If only he'd felt the bravado that lay in the words.

MacMurdo had given him a game-day smile. "You're right, pard. This ain't no time for the faint of heart."

Leary had laughed aloud at that. "You guys," he said, "who writes this shit?"

"You don't like it?" MacMurdo frowned.

"Like it? Hell, I love it!"

"Damn good thing," MacMurdo said. "It's how we prove we're not afraid."

• • •

"Broke what they call this sound-barrier thing. As I understand it and stop me if you've heard this, if I yelled 'Fuck you!' at Benedictus from down here poolside just as this plane, this X-1 jet, flew overhead, the plane would reach him up on the veranda before my 'Fuck you!' Does that sound credible to you, Frank?"

Frank Capra, the director, fingered his ascot for a moment. "I guess I wouldn't be surprised. It's a new world with new things in it. *Glamorous Glennis* he calls it."

"Who calls what, Frank? I don't follow you."

"This Yeager guy. The pilot."

"Glamorous what?"

"Glennis. It's his wife's name, I gather. Named the plane after her. Glennis. Odd name."

"Faster than sound," the other man mused. "Progress."

"There'll probably be a movie in it one day, Charlie."

"That'll be the day. Hayseed flies faster than sound. Still, why not? We got a history of hayseeds. Wilbur and Orville. Maybe you're right."

"Bio-pix," Capra said and they began moving away. "Take Coop, he's the man for the role. Or this new fella, Greg Peck. Good-looking boy. Dad's a druggist down in San Diego."

Cassidy strolled among the guests, watching, waiting, wondering about the bartender or the man in the polo kit or the chap with the tennis whites, wondering if Moller was near. Terry Leary and Karin were sitting in lawn chairs in the shade. Terry waggled his fingers at him impishly. It was insane. Somehow they were no longer the hunters. The advantage had mysteriously passed from them.

He kept overhearing bits of conversation. Someone was buying up land out in the Valley, making a good thing of it. Somebody else was quoting Groucho Marx. "Miracle Pictures. If it's any good . . . it's a Miracle!" A famous actress was having all her teeth out, prompting obscene jests. A producer was determined to make his whore a star. On a bet. "I'd say it's a safe bet. The old fart's done it before. Twice, actually." That was Laughton, his jowls wobbling beneath a cigar, sweat streaking his famous ugly face. Bogart stood talking to a somewhat owlish-looking man with black hair and round horn-rimmed spectacles. Bogart was smoking a cigarette, the owlish, tweedy man a pipe. Bogart was short, compact, his eyes world-weary, and he wasn't wearing his hair. There was something about him, hair or not. He was a star. He looked as if nothing devised by man could surprise him. The man with the pipe said something and Bogart laughed.

Cassidy had his drink freshened. Terry Leary was gone, but MacMurdo had taken his place. C. Aubrey Smith dropped his croquet mallet and tottered off in search of strong drink. Barry Fitzgerald pointed at him and began to cackle. A beautiful dark girl handed him the mallet. Fitzgerald looked at her as if she'd presented him with a dead fish.

"Don't you hate these parties? Well, I hate the bloody things." It was the owlish man who was looking up at him through the round horn-rims, smiling pleasantly. "I don't know about you, but one doesn't despise the upper classes because they take baths and have money and always want your share, too. One despises them because they are phony. And they encourage one to drink too much and stand about hoping for a spot of shade. Don't you agree? Well, I suppose it's all a matter of opinion." He was still smiling gently, faintly amused. "These people . . . they do pass for the upper classes hereabouts, believe it or not, as you choose."

"Well," Cassidy said, "you may be right."

"Ah, I've found one. Saints be praised!"

"One what?"

"A thinking man. Rara avis. This is no place for a man of culture. Do you pretend to culture, sir?" He'd probably had too much to drink but it didn't seem to bother him. He blinked hazily behind the horn-rims. He calmly puffed his pipe, regarding Cassidy with good-natured curiosity.

"No. I used to be a football player."

"Ah. The natives would call that typecasting. What would you say I used to be? A clue—I was not a football player."

"Damned if I know. Studio head? Night security man?"

The man chuckled. "I was in oil. An oil man. Not a rich man, just a sort of glorified paper pusher. All in the long ago. What are you now, you ex-footballer?"

"Well, just between the two of us, I'm a detective."

"You're kidding me!" Delight sparkled in his eyes. "Cop?"

"Private."

"Do tell, do tell. An actual shamus at a Hollwood party. Mr. Bogart would have enjoyed this. Could you be among us on a case?"

"Just old friends."

"No such thing in this town. Just ins and outs, no real friends."

"Mona Ransom's a friend of mine."

"When the fleet's in you chaps outnumber the rest of us. I understand she's an interesting woman. Now listen—"

"Wait a minute. If you used to be an oil man, what are you now?"

"A scribbler. A wordsmith. A writer."

"Screenplays?"

"Sometimes. I'm not proud of it. I've just finished one. *The Lady in the Lake*. There's nothing to this writing business, of course. You just fill yourself with gin, sit down at the typewriter, and open a vein. Now, being a private eye, perhaps you can tell me if I've got an idea here. . . . Maybe it's all just nonsense but I've heard a word or two, a rumor of deviltry—you will be utterly candid with me, won't you? I require that. So, here's the story. I have this detective, grand fella, we'll call him Phil, shall we? Now, you won't believe this, but remember it's only a story, based on only a rumor . . . but I've heard there's an active market in Nazi loot right here in Beverly Hills." His soft voice had dropped to a whisper. He was speaking with the pipe in the corner of his mouth, obviously a long-standing habit. Cassidy's mind went into a sudden skid as the words dropped quietly between them.

Was this yet another incarnation of Manfred Moller? His appearance as Brenneman's assistant in Boston had contained an element of humor:

maybe this was his idea of a joke. The owlish man was going blithely on. "Sound too nuts for you? Well, I'm not kidding. Lots of Nazi loot being sold right in the middle of an industry owned and run by Jews! The irony is nearly overwhelming. . . . Still, I suppose it depends on who's selling the stuff, where the money goes. Supposedly paintings for the most part, some jewels because they're easier to move from one country to another. Hedges against inflation, so I've heard people say. The art market's going to go crazy in the years to come, art and real estate. . . . Well, speaking as a man whose writing has been more admired for characterization than plot, this strikes me as a great plot. Trot old Phil out for another case, see if there's life in the old chap yet. Or is it all too preposterous? Tell me, as a professional detective, do I have the beginning of a story?"

A rotund black cat had strolled across the grass and taken to rubbing himself against the writer's leg. He knelt down with a sharp knee crack, stroked its neck, then looked up at Cassidy, waiting for an answer.

"Sounds crazy to me," Cassidy said. He felt like a man, Harold Lloyd maybe, clinging by his fingernails to the top of a well, frantically trying to keep from falling in. He was losing his grip. Who was this man? How could he have heard such a story? Of course, his father had always told him that in Hollywood every secret was an illusion. The land-of-no-secrets, Paul Cassidy had called it.

The cat purred into the quizzically smiling face. "Sure, you're probably right. Crazy story. Well, it was just a rumor I heard at lunch a couple weeks ago. Over at the Paramount lot. Overworked imaginations. Full of details for a rumor. Well, I'll write something else. What's your name, if I may be so bold?" He frowned, stood up. "Or are you the latest new phenomenon of the silver screen, too? Am I supposed to know your name, for God's sake?"

"Lew Cassidy. I'm from back east. You wouldn't know me. I didn't catch your name."

"Mmm. This is where John Wayne would say, 'I didn't throw it, hombre.' My name's Chandler. Ray Chandler. Oh, Christ! Do you see that strutting nitwit over there doing the bad Von Stroheim impression? Director. Preminger. German. I've already been through a picture with an Austrian. Wilder. That's as close to the Germans as I want to get. He—Wilder, that is—kept telling me, *ordering* me, to do things. Shut the door, Ray. Open the window, will you, Ray? I had to get him to put it in writing, no more peremptory orders. Damnedest thing. But I may wind up writing the picture for Preminger. Your friend Miss Ransom, he wants her for the lead." He tapped his pipe against the brick wall, beyond which lay Los Angeles. "Well, Cassidy, ignore the story I told you. I'm a little tipsy. Only way to get through these bloody awful parties. Wish me luck, I go to face the fearful Hun." He nodded, waved a little shyly as he turned the corner of the pool. Somebody screamed in the water, splashed him, and he flinched, walked away.

• • •

Another hour spent wandering the grounds, catching looks from Terry and MacMurdo and Karin, none of which told him anything, another hour of sipping gin and tonic while the ice melted, while the sun sank lower behind the hills of Beverly, another hour of hoping Benedictus didn't jump out from behind the bougainvillea and confront him or kill him—and Cassidy was working on a major-league headache and losing his faith in Mona Ransom's big deal. The first lights were flickering on down below in the city. The smog was darkening. The sky out toward the ocean was still brilliant white-blue. He wanted to take Karin, tell her the truth, tell MacMurdo to go win some other war, take Karin and go home. Instead he stood in the slanting rays of sunshine, looking at the party from a safe spot by a phony wishing well from a long-forgotten and probably idiotic movie. A wishing well a foot and a half deep. It was about as good a definition of Hollywood as you were going to get. A place where the dreams were shallow and the realization of them just plain fake. Hooray for Hollywood . . .

"He's over here, Lew. He's standing over there. The man in the white suit."

Karin had come up behind him quietly and it took a moment for him to see what she was looking at. A man standing alone in the fringe of shadows cast by the thickly forested hillside that rose abruptly from the lawn.

"Man in the white suit," he murmured.

"He's my husband," she said softly. She was staring at him, her face expressionless. The sight of her husband, the man she needed to find more than she needed anything else in the world—seeing him didn't produce any visible reaction. He had never seen Karin's face so blank. "He's the man you're after, Lew. It's all over."

"I wish it were all over."

"Just take him," she said. "Where's MacMurdo?"

"But, Karin . . . don't you want to—I don't know—"

"I don't want to do anything," she said. "MacMurdo wanted to find him. That's what all this was about. I knew that. He was never finding him for me." She turned to Cassidy. "Did you truly believe that I thought the dear good Colonel was trying to find my husband for *me*?"

"Yes, I guess I did."

"I knew at least that much. I was just the means of getting what he wanted. Now he's got it." She looked back at the lone figure, standing in the shadow, smoking a cigarette. Waiting.

Then Cassidy caught at least a passing glimpse of the truth. Just a quick peek and it hit him hard, the way Bennie the Brute once had, long ago.

Karin didn't love Manfred Moller.

She never had.

Maybe it was the other way around. Manfred Moller loved Karin. That was it. MacMurdo hadn't been finding Moller for Karin, not even as an illusion, not even as the lie. He had been counting only on Karin to lure Moller out. It was never for Karin. She'd never wanted her husband back. Never.

Karin didn't give a goddamn about her husband, about Manfred Moller.

So why was she going through all this?

If she didn't love Moller, what was in it for her?

She looked up at him as if she'd read every thought.

"Are you disappointed in me?"

"No. I just don't get it. Why put up with all this if you don't want Moller?"

"He has something of mine."

"Moller?"

She shook her head. "No, no, not him."

"Karin, please."

"MacMurdo."

Cassidy stared at her but she'd closed up. *MacMurdo* . . . What the devil did he have of Karin's? Would he ever understand what was going on? He was having doubts. . . .

# CHAPTER TWENTY-FOUR

The four of them stood by the wishing well. Cassidy, Karin, Terry Leary, and Sam MacMurdo. Their shadows had lengthened all the way to the retaining wall that held everything in place, kept it all from sliding away.

The man in the white suit had drifted down the terraces and was leaning on the wall, looking out across the darkening city. Searchlights were slashing at the smog in the name of some new movie. If the retaining wall gave way, it was goodbye old kraut, old pal. The man in the white suit lit a cigarette. He was moving very slowly. Waiting. Mona Ransom had told him: Cassidy knew it. She'd told him *something*. But what? She wanted to make her deal. She wanted Tash Benedictus dead by the side of the road and she knew she had to deliver to make it so.

He thought she'd told Manfred Moller one hard thing. Meet some friends of mine, hear them out, and just maybe they won't kill you. She'd made a lot of movies. She knew how to cut the dialogue, cut the crap, and get right down to the threat. In the movies you had to lay it on the line. Mona Ransom was a Hollywood baby and she was desperate.

"Okay," MacMurdo said, "this is your moment, sweetheart." He gently placed a hand the size of Guatemala on Karin's shoulder. "You're what's going to make this a piece of cake. He can walk away from the rest of us, tell us to go to hell if he's got the nerve. He can duck back into this fucking hacienda and do his damnedest to get away from us . . . and we might chew up poor Benedictus and his art deal like a bunch of rabid guard dogs . . . and Manfred Moller might get away with his minotaur and what's left of his Nazi network and wind up flying down to Rio. And that could happen, sweetheart. But . . . but not once he sees you. When he sees you—that's when we catch the lightning in the bottle. All you do, Karin, is just stand there. Fucking piece of cake. Let him see you." His hand slipped from her shoulder. He looked at Cassidy, then at Leary. "Let's move out."

"Sure."

"Did you lay on the First Airborne for this? Where's the air support? You don't expect the three of us to handle this guy on our own, Colonel?"

"Leary, sometimes you try my patience. Just the least bit. I'm not a good man to push."

Cassidy said, "Who needs air support? Let's go."

Karin's eyes were blank. They seemed to say, Let's just get it over.

• • •

When it came to faces Cassidy knew that he would for all time carry the memory of Cindy Squires's face in his mind, embedded in the pain in his heart, the last time he lost himself in her eyes, the look in her eyes, the sweetness and love and hopelessness she knew even before he did. The good-bye look, the last instant of her existence. He would never forget the look until in the end, in the last moments, his consciousness was blotted out and his own life was over.

He wouldn't remember the look on Manfred Moller's face quite so long, perhaps, but it was right up there when it came to faces, reactions, looks on kissers. He might one day forget but at the moment he recognized the emotions detailed in Moller's face. It came just after he turned, just after MacMurdo said: "Herr Moller, we'd like a word with you. But first here's someone you may have thought you wouldn't be seeing again."

Moller turned. He was a tall man with short, pale brown hair, clear blue eyes, a high forehead, an open, solid set of features. He looked like a man who could will his composure. He looked like a man who would regret the need to be ruthless, merciless, but would nevertheless do what needed to be done. His eyes lingered on the immensity that was MacMurdo, then slid slowly to Cassidy. Recognition flickered briefly, memories of Boston, the death of Henry Brenneman.

Then he saw Karin. The composure developed a fissure. A bolt of lightning seemed to have caught him, pinning him to the moment. His eyes widened, his lips parted slightly, his jaw tightened. "Karin." It was a whisper. "My darling . . ." He put his hand out to touch her.

Karin remained motionless. Her face showed nothing.

Moller kept reaching for her. He wasn't seeing the lack of a response: he saw only her face, what he hoped was love, but it was only the reflection of his own consuming love for her.

MacMurdo shook his head and brushed Moller's hand away.

"Your wife is well. She is in no danger from us. It looks to me like you'd probably like to speak with her, see her alone . . . well, hell, why not? She's your wife, you're entitled." He shrugged, smiling widely. "All this can be arranged, Herr Moller. But you know how these things work. You're an old hand at all this. You don't want anybody to get hurt. Neither do we. So we begin . . . with a word in your ear. Just a moment of your time and we all get out alive." He punched Moller lightly on the shoulder, an act of joky intimacy that took the German off guard. He was vulnerable. He barely heard what MacMurdo was saying.

Cassidy saw Moller's pain, felt it, watched it form in his eyes, on his features, in the set of his shoulders. The pain, the longing, the loneliness, the yearning for a woman he loved. It had all begun slipping away, this world that held the woman who had come back from the rubble of Cologne, the woman he'd seen come back to life as he fell in love with her, it had begun slipping away when Göring had given him his last set of orders. It was as if Cassidy were seeing a montage. Berlin in flames, so many comrades in their graves, Karin waiting in the mountains with Rolf, then the summons to meet with Göring. . . . Karin had become a memory for Manfred Moller, as she had for Cassidy. Maybe it was the role she'd been born to play, again and again.

The lost love, the poignant memory . . .

Karin stared hard at MacMurdo for a long second or two, then turned and walked away without speaking. She didn't look back.

Mona Ransom was watching, standing by the bar near the pool and the cabana. The lawn was dark emerald, cool, shady.

MacMurdo nudged Moller along the wall toward the forest.

"Let's go for a walk, pard."

• • •

There was a small, dainty, manicured clearing in the trees where a gazebo stood, freshly painted. It was like another movie. Thumper and Bambi and Goofy and Mickey had to be in the woods somewhere. Baskets of flowers and vines and creepers hung from the gingerbread arches.

Manfred Moller was smoking another cigarette, listening to MacMurdo, wondering how he was going to get out of this nasty business with his minotaur and his wife and his life. Cassidy could read his eyes, couldn't stop reading them. Moller was the sort of man who'd spent a lifetime learning how to weigh the options, make allowances, come out on top. Right now he was trying to factor in the unexpected—Karin.

MacMurdo wasn't wasting time. He was sketching out a scenario that Moller could live with.

Cassidy saw them for what they were: two professionals at work. They both knew the outlines of the playing field, the basic rules.

• • •

"You, my fine German friend, are a very lucky man. Your team was wicked and then lost the war to boot. I have little time for losers, not much time for the wicked. And I'm not even going to hold your SS background against you. I'm a generous man, see. I'm not going to take you in as a spy and let them stick those live wires up your ass until you tell them everything you've ever known. Hell, boy, I'm not even going to put a bullet in your gut for the pure simple joy of it. You've killed two men we know of for sure since you've descended on our happy land and you tried to kill this gent here and a friend up Beacon Hill way in Boston—"

"Excuse me, Colonel MacMurdo, but may I ask what accounts for all this generosity of spirit?" Moller was calm, still thinking it through, trying to peer into the machinery of MacMurdo's mind. "And let me assure you that if I had intended to kill this gentleman, he would be dead. I placed him in a maze. He found his way out. My intention was to slow him down so I might escape. I do not kill except to save myself and my mission, when it's unavoidable. Had this man died, he would have died of his own incompetence." He smiled quickly at Cassidy. "Obviously he has demonstrated his competence. How he and you have come to this place I would very much like to know. It seems on the face of it that I have been betrayed—"

"Or we are very smart guys."

Moller shrugged. "That is always a possibility. What do you propose to do with me?" He sounded increasingly confident. Moller knew what he was doing.

"Anything I goddamn well want to do, boy. That's the unvarnished truth of it. But you've run into me on a good day. I figure the war's over. 'Fore you know it we'll be gettin' ready for the next one and we might be fightin' on the same side." His laughter must have scared hell out of Thumper and the guys. "You and I, we've had tough wars. Your pretty little wife, she may have had it worse than either of us . . . so I'm proposin' to let you live, boy."

"You are quite right about my wife. She is a brave woman."

"You love her," MacMurdo mused.

"I do."

MacMurdo smiled genially, turned his broad back on Moller and leaned forward on the railing, looking into the gathering darkness of the forest. "We know about the Göring network."

"More than I do, I'd say. In any case, he won't be needing it."

"And, of course, we know about the minotaur."

"Ah."

"What else was there? The minotaur and what else?"

Moller shook his head. "Originally there were some plates for counterfeiting dollars. Some money. I left the plates on the U-boat. I took about a hundred thousand dollars, all counterfeit. Very good fakes. I left the rest of the money. The minotaur was what mattered. Americans could finance the rest of the network. Göring had plans to reclaim the minotaur from me when he got out."

"How big is the minotaur?"

He held his hands eighteen inches or so apart. "The Reichsmarshal gave it to me in a specially fitted-out suitcase."

"I want the minotaur." MacMurdo turned around. "Give me the minotaur, I give you your wife and your freedom." He smiled engagingly, acres of gleaming teeth. "Can't beat that deal with a stick."

"Won't your superiors be unhappy with you?"

"My superiors would have trouble finding their assholes if Rand and McNally personally drew the map for them."

"And *their* superiors?"

MacMurdo's smile grew even wider. "Those big boys might just offer you a job, old son."

Moller nodded. "Like Gehlen. I hear your spymaster Dulles has hired him—"

"You got good ears," MacMurdo said.

"It was known he'd make a deal. You need us to help you face the Russians. We could have told you that years ago and saved the trouble of this war."

"You get no argument from me, pal. My superiors, all the way to the top, will be very happy with me if I deliver you to them as a brand-new friend . . . and also hand them Benedictus and his nest of Nazi art smugglers. What more could they ask? And naturally I come out a hero. As usual." He took out his little black pipe and packed it, applied a match in the silence. The whole ceremony had the aspect of a celebration. He was telling Moller the heat was off and it hadn't been so bad, had it?

"What if I want out entirely?"

"Where's your gratitude, pal?"

"I've had a long war. What if I don't want to work for any government? What if I want to live my own life with my wife?"

MacMurdo puffed and cogitated, an involved process.

"Well, hell," he said at last. "I guess it's nothing to me, one way or t'other. I was just offering you a job, good pay, nice retirement program—"

"If they didn't just use me and then kill me, you mean."

"Who knows? I'm the first to admit you can never trust the men behind the desks. You don't want to take the job, don't take the job. You can take Karin and do whatever you want. You must have a good deal of money left. Unless Tash charged you rent this past summer." MacMurdo chuckled. Smoke plumed out of his mouth and nose.

"What will your report say if I disappear?"

"Fortunes of war. You got killed in the infighting. I didn't stop to pull your bleeding corpse to safety. You can go to Buenos Aires or Rio or Paraguay, anywhere you want. You'll find plenty of old chums. Sit around on long summer nights and tell yourselves it was that fart Hitler who lost the war and exterminated the Jews and the Gypsies and the rest of you were just following orders—"

"That's the truth, actually."

"As you wish, pal. Anyway, take your money and your wife. Head for the hills. You've got money. You'll find a way out. I know a guy here in the City of Angels can make you a passport good enough to get you past the beaners and into deepest mañana-land. Like I say, I'm a hero and you're gone."

Moller's eyes narrowed. He looked from MacMurdo to Cassidy to Leary and back to the Colonel. "Who are these men?"

"Mine. It doesn't matter." MacMurdo tamped the ash with a nail.

"Why? Why are you doing this for me?"

"Because we're alike, old pal, you and I. All around me I got civilians. But you and me, we're company men. And I'd want to be given the same chance if our places were reversed. We're not just soldiers. And we're sure as hell not war criminals. You know what we are, you old German bastard, we're fuckin' warriors! Out of goddamned mythology, my friend!" He was pointing the pipe at Moller, prodding his chest as if he'd suddenly realized he had tied one on, a proper snootful. "And a warrior deserves respect. Simple as that. Your war is over. You followed your orders, you conducted a perilous mission in a foreign land—hell, you've earned the right to your own life. The right to die in bed."

Moller stared into MacMurdo's face, searching for his eyes behind the veil of smoke. He wanted to believe. More than anything else, he wanted to believe. The Brotherhood of Warriors. "I see," he said at last.

MacMurdo rubbed his hands together, the pipe clamped in his powerful jaw. "Well, goddamn! We need us a plan. How we gonna make the switch, then? The minotaur for your wife? Hell's bells, now we're gettin' somewheres!" He grinned at Cassidy and Leary. He was at his down-home best. "We doin' bidness with this here old boy."

"The art auction."

"When? Where?"

"I don't know. Benedictus, it's his show."

"We'll find out. Are you gonna have trouble with old Tashkent?"

"I think not. I'll handle it."

"You think he might like to get his hands on your minotaur? Bring a nice price—"

"There isn't enough money, Colonel. And *he* doesn't know where it is."

"He sure as shootin' has got ways of finding out."

"Don't worry, Colonel. Now . . . you asked me nothing about the Göring network."

"Oh, hell, you don't know anything about it. Why would they tell you? You were a delivery boy, pal."

"I wanted to make sure you knew that."

"I do have one question, though. Who the hell is Vulkan?"

"Who?"

"Vulkan. Code name. Who is he?"

"I never heard the code name Vulkan. I'm sorry."

"You wouldn't be pullin' my leg, would you? Old warriors and all?"

"I simply don't know. The word has never come up."

"Well, ain't that somethin'. I do declare!" MacMurdo looked at Cassidy. "Somebody's havin' fun with us, pard. Ain't that the dickens!"

• • •

Cassidy and MacMurdo had the house in the Hollywood Hills to themselves that evening. Terry Leary had taken Karin out to see a movie, Gregory Peck and Ingrid Bergman in *Spellbound*. "It'll do her good," Terry said. "It'll do me good. You and the Colonel can settle the hash of the Nazi swine and we won't have to listen."

"I'm not sure it's the picture for her," Cassidy said. "Peck's an amnesiac who may have killed somebody—his doctor, for Christ's sake! Ring any bells? Karin? And her doctor's been murdered—"

"Relax, Lew. It's only a movie."

Now Cassidy stood alone on the deck overlooking the twinkling lights of the city, each pathetically striving to be seen, like the faded starlets of yesteryear.

Mona Ransom had set Moller up for them. Betrayed him. Did he know how it had worked? Would he kill her if he found out the truth? Would it be one of his necessary killings? Did Moller even know his brother was dead? Well, he did if he killed him. . . . But no, he wouldn't have, Karin said he wouldn't have. And what would have required the killing of Rolf? But he didn't kill himself, so who did it for him?

And what was going on between Manfred Moller and Benedictus?

Benedictus had been the safe harbor, the contact, his goal when he set off in that crummy little plane from Nova Scotia . . . from the Reich in the U-boat, for that matter. What nerve it all must have taken, the Reich in flames, Göring going crazy, a one-way U-boat and an airplane stuck together with chewing gum. . . . How could Moller never have heard of Vulkan? Or was he lying? If it wasn't Benedictus, then who? It was as if Vulkan were a ghost ship, a foghorn echoing, always just out of reach. . . .

And what was the story on Karin and Manfred? She certainly hadn't seemed to care a damn about him. Could she have been faking her concern all along? But she'd been desperate. Lew, please help find him, it's all that matters, we must find him. . . . So why didn't she care once he was found? Was that part of her deal with the Devil? MacMurdo. Because the Devil had something that belonged to her . . . therefore she had to help MacMurdo find Manfred Moller. It came down to that. Had to come down to that. He had something of hers. Something.

Manfred, on the other hand, was smitten by her still. He'd insisted on his love for her in that strong silent way no doubt commonplace in the brotherhood of warriors.

Where was the truth, anyway?

Terry in the Kansas night, with the lights shining on the tarmac, had warned him that there was something funny going on, that Karin was giving him a performance, that the amnesia was an act. Impossible . . .

But what if he'd hit on something? Was it possible?

But why would she fake it?

No, she couldn't.

Still, she'd given quite a performance as the distraught wife worried about her poor lost Santa Claus of a husband. But maybe *that* was the truth and the current attitude of indifference the performance. . . .

And if it came to mysteries, as it seemed to all the time now—

How the living, enduring hell had Tash Benedictus come to be expecting them at the castle? He'd been sitting up there getting stewed every night *waiting for them!*

Impossible.

Maybe Mona had it all wrong.

Cassidy hoped so. If she'd had it right, if he'd been waiting for them, then it was all a whole lot worse than his nastiest nightmare.

• • •

He heard a heavy tread on the redwood deck behind him. MacMurdo stretched mightily, yawned. It was thundering out in the direction of Santa Monica. The hillside around the house was wild country. Where the lawn ended the animals would come to watch, their eyes glowing faintly in the darkness. Up above Mulholland Drive was quiet, dark as a coal mine with cloud cover smudging out the stars. MacMurdo yawned again and shook himself like a Great Dane coming out of the water.

Something in the shadows reacted to MacMurdo's huffing and puffing. There was a sudden rustle in the leaves. MacMurdo turned in the dim light spreading outward from the house and planted his feet; the .45 had appeared in his hand.

A deer stepped out of the darkness, stood still, looking at them in some wonderment.

Slowly MacMurdo lowered the gun and exhaled.

"Relax, Sam."

The deer came tentatively toward them, obviously the next thing to tame, a picture of gentle curiosity, head cocked.

"Easy, boy," Cassidy said, grinning at the warrior.

"We're down to the short strokes," MacMurdo said. "Worst time in the world to relax. You just can't be too careful. We're dealing with what you could call unsavory types, in case it's slipped your mind." He smiled slowly, slid the automatic back inside his belt. He sat down in a slatted wood chair and put his feet up on the edge of the table. He was wearing ancient cowboy boots, the leather cracked and ingrained with dust. "What are you doin' out here, pard?"

"Trying to think. Driving myself crazy."

"Don't sound so down in the mouth. Thing like this, you never can figure it out till it's over. Hell, pard, you don't even know for sure who the good guys and the bad guys are, not yet, not till it's over. So . . . soon we'll know." He laughed in the dark. "Sometimes you've been thinkin' I was one of the bad guys, right, Lewis?" He laughed again.

"You were very convincing with Moller today. I was impressed."

"I was supposed to be convincing, and that's the God's honest truth."

"Too damned convincing, Sam. You set me thinking. I don't trust you, Sam."

MacMurdo laughed again. "Oh, Lew, Lew. Like I said, you won't know who's who till it's over. But don't you think I've proved myself yet? You're a hard judge, pard. What is it you're thinkin' about?"

"I'm thinking about how I wish you'd drop the cornpone, hayseed bullshit. And I'm thinking about what I'll have to do if it looks like you're going to give Karin to him."

This time the laughter shook the deck. "Well, if that ain't your looniest idea yet!" The deer nosing at the grass jerked its head up, figured enough was enough. The laugh boomed; there was a flash of white tail. Then it was gone. "Jesus, pard," he rumbled, massive shoulders shaking, "if I can make you believe that load of road apples, the poor kraut bastard must think I'm Santa Claus and the tooth fairy rolled into one! Now pull yourself together, Lew, and listen up. I'm taking the minotaur and Herr Moller back to Washington with me and I'm gonna turn him inside out, shake him till he's empty . . . unless we settle for the minotaur and kill the bastard. I don't think he knows shit from Shinola—and one way or another the kraut's a goner. Now don't you worry about your little missus—you know in your heart you can trust your goddamn life to Sam MacMurdo. And that goes for Karin, too. You get Karin, pard, I put my word on record." He had begun smoking a cigar. He was enjoying himself. The sound of his own voice always had that effect. The cornier he got, the more he ladled it on, the happier he was.

"I wonder," Cassidy said, "why Karin, with her amnesia and all, ever consented to do all this—since she made it clear to me today that she's not interested in what happens to Moller, one way or the other. Now, I had to ask myself, Sam, if she isn't here to try to get her husband back . . . then why is she here at all? And I can't come up with a satisfactory answer. Something tells me you'll have an answer, Sam."

"Oh, you know women. Why do they do the things they do?" He shrugged. The aroma of the cigar filled the night. "Maybe she changed her mind. Maybe she started out wanting her husband, then she met you and her subconscious went to work and she decided there was something wonderful about you, something she couldn't explain, you were her white knight riding to the rescue. . . . How the hell should I know? I'm a simple soldier."

"You are so full of shit! It's funny, but it scares hell out of me. Lying comes naturally to you, you're a genius at it. Such a good old boy and you can't tell the truth to save your soul—"

"You better stop insulting me, pard, or I'll have to plug you." He didn't sound offended. He might have been speaking to an unruly child.

"I think she's gone through all this because of the deal she made with you. Remember? A deal with the Devil . . . She says you've got something of hers."

"She say that? Really?"

"What have you got, Sam? Better level with me."

MacMurdo dropped his feet to the deck with a resounding thud. "Look, sonny, I'm gettin' your wife back for you. Just what's givin' you this big hard-on about me? What have I ever done to you? What more do you want from me? Are you sure you want to dig into all the reasons behind everything? What difference do they make?" He snorted grumpily. "You're mighty damn intent on making everything complicated. Ignorance is bliss, truest damn thing ever said. Why don't you just take your wife, you can go home, pard, and hang up your machine gun, call it a war—"

"But you have something of hers. What is it, Sam?"

"Well, maybe she's thinkin' about what I've got *on* her. Now there's a distinction to be made there."

"Tell me what you're talking about, Sam."

"I want you to know this is against my better judgment."

"Yeah, yeah—"

"I've got some documents that prove she's a . . . well, hell, she's a war criminal. Maybe that's what's been on her mind, what convinced her to come along on our little adventure."

Cassidy couldn't find his tongue for a moment or two, finally got it all pulled together. "Karin? A war criminal? That's insane, you can't believe that—"

"Well, think about it. I had to have something to make her do this, didn't I? She didn't know you from third base and she'd never been in love with Manfred Moller. He was nuts about her, that's all true. So I had to have her to bait the trap. You follow me? I might have done it without her but, hell, I had her in my hand. Of course, she wasn't enough. This is where God was my copilot, as they say in Hollywood. Proves I'm on the side of right. She wasn't enough . . . but she'd been married to you. The main trap was to get you involved, somebody with a real good reason to lead this scavenger hunt—and you'd do any goddamned thing I wanted once you found out your beautiful, long-lost wife was back from the dead. You were a perfect example of what is known in certain circles as MacMurdo's Luck. Once you found Manfred Moller, then I had the second trap to spring. . . . Karin, who drew you into it, would draw Moller out of his hidey-hole. When the Good Lord puts so many of the pieces in your hands it's a crime not to solve the puzzle."

"Okay, you're lucky and you're a genius but what's this war-criminal routine? I'm gullible, but I'm not crazy—"

"It's a cruel world out there, pard. You ever notice that? For instance, Dr. Rolf Moller was not quite the Boy Scout he may have seemed. How do you think he was able to keep his little mountain clinic so spick-and-span and free of all the pus and crud of the war? He had all the drugs and supplies and equipment he needed. He wasn't off treating gut-shot soldiers in some field hospital right in the line of fire—hell no, he was on a war-long mountain holiday! Just lucky? Bullshit, my friend. Dr. Moller was doing some special work for Himmler and the SS and the Gestapo. He was working on British and American prisoners of war. Drug experiments, truth serums, some brain operations with particular attention to memory and willpower . . . the micro-control of pain to elicit information without killing, hypnosis, trying to turn prisoners into double agents . . . lots of very interesting stuff and it wasn't the worst kind of experimentation—not the kind of things they were doing in some of the concentration camps. But it was still way outside the rules, people were sacrificed, that goes without saying. It was scary, not cricket at all if you happened to be on the losing side. I figure we had doctors doing some of the same stuff, but we won, see. So Rolf Moller's a war criminal if we choose to make him one. . . . So that's why he was a willing member of our mission, taking care of Karin, keeping her calmed down, all that drill. Karin served as his aide at the clinic once she'd recovered from her own wounds—she kept the records on the various experiments, served as a makeshift nurse, ran the ward, helped out with anesthetics, administered drugs, made herself useful. . . . Look, I wasn't going to tell you all this, there was no need to, but since you suddenly don't trust old Sam anymore, hell, you're a big boy, you deal with the truth. We could make all this as tough on Karin as we choose: the German skating champ who marries an American and then becomes a movie star, goes back to Germany and spends the war torturing American prisoners . . . Now, the fact is this old girl probably didn't do anything so godawful, but it's up to us to how bad it looks. We could turn her into the Beautiful Angel of Death and stage quite a trial. You know how all that works. So, sensibly, she decided to lend us a hand."

Cassidy didn't say anything for a while, waited for his heart to stop racing and the dryness in his throat to recede. Waited for his legs to stop shaking. Finally he spoke very softly. "You really are a bastard."

"Jesus H. Christ, man, I'm saving her from all that! How I wish I could get you to stop worrying so much! Let's just grab hold of reality, pard. Karin's okay, you're getting her back, we aren't going to try her for war crimes. I've saved your life and you've saved mine, we've faced the enemy together. Ease up. We get through this week, we can shake hands and go home."

"You really are a bad man, Sam."

MacMurdo stood up, threw up his hands in a mixture of impatience and disgust. He marched back and forth across the deck, cigar glowing like hellfire.

"No," he said finally, "no, I ain't, old pard. What I am is a patriot. I love my country. I owe her the best I've got in me and I'll do what I've got to do for her. You say I'm a bastard and a bad man and all I can see is that I've been puttin' my life on the line for the Stars and Bars. Well, I guess it all depends on where you're standin' when you take a look at me—"

"Stars and stripes," Cassidy said. "Not bars."

"But I'll tell you one thing, my friend, I'm a good man to have on your side when you're pinned down in no-man's-land and the rats are chewing on your buddies and the barrage has started. Look, I'm gonna have Moller. You're gonna get Karin. Life could be a lot harder on you, Lewis."

"Who is Vulkan?" Cassidy was still having trouble talking. "Tell me if you know."

MacMurdo shook his head. The red glow of his cigar moved back and forth like a trainman's swinging lamp telling you to stop if you valued your life. "That's the problem," MacMurdo said. "I have no idea."

# Chapter Twenty-five

Cassidy lay on the strange bed in the strange room trying to sleep and having a tough time of it. The rolling thunder hung on in the night sky and a cool breeze played at the curtains. He could smell the wild hillside and half thought he heard animals in the underbrush. He closed his eyes but knew sleep wouldn't come. Finally he threw the covers back and went to the window, stared out into the darkness.

It was the war-criminal thing.

He couldn't get it out of his mind. Was it all a lie? What about Rolf? What was the work he'd done at the clinic? How many of his patients had died as a result of his work? What role had Karin played? Unanswerable questions. Unaskable questions, with Rolf dead and Karin . . . the way she was. He couldn't imagine how he'd ever be able to ask her, for fear of driving her back into her shell, for fear of the answer.

Terry had brought her home from the movie and they'd all been tired, worn down by the stress of the party and the confrontation with Manfred Moller. Karin had gone off to bed almost at once. The rest of them soon followed. Lew hadn't told Terry what MacMurdo had told him: he didn't know if he ever would. Now he stood at the window knowing full well that any attempt to order things more clearly was bound to stretch the night, make it unendurably long. But he was awake. There was nothing else to do. His mind would go its own way.

All the deals in the air . . .

One, his own deal with Mona Ransom, the deal to kill Tash Benedictus in exchange for Manfred Moller, seemed unreal by night. A deal of convenience. He'd have agreed to anything if it meant finding Moller. Now, was he going to bring MacMurdo in on it? And just how was he going to kill Benedictus? For that matter did he have any true intention of carrying out his end of the bargain?

My God, it was absurd! He wasn't going to kill Tash Benedictus. He felt as if he were losing his grip, raving inside his head.

He had never intended to murder Benedictus. He was simply going to get Mona out of there and Benedictus was going over in MacMurdo's tender grasp, probably to prison for trafficking in Nazi loot. Cassidy's mind was sluggish, not working well enough to survive in a high-speed game. He'd actually been worrying about having to murder Benedictus! There was too damned much going on, he couldn't keep it all straight.

And now he knew the truth of Karin's deal with the Devil. *War crimes*. What had they really done at the clinic? How bad had it been? Had men been murdered? Had Rolf been an honest-to-God war criminal? Was MacMurdo powerful enough to spring such a man for a mission like this one?

The questions were driving him crazy.

What was true?

Were any of them what they seemed?

Cassidy was lost, back in the wilderness of mirrors.

Or was it all a single strand of lies, carefully manufactured by Sam MacMurdo, strung on a wire, ready to yank tight around someone's neck . . . but whose? And to what end?

Well, there was no getting inside the Colonel's mind. It had all begun with MacMurdo, in that gamesman's fertile brain. Would it end with him? Let's see, Dr. Rolf Moller and Karin, two war criminals. And Rolf wasn't around to defend himself anymore. . . .

He climbed back into bed and was just drifting off to sleep when something swam toward him from his subconscious, something he was nearly able to recognize. . . .

Something about who might have murdered Rolf Moller.

• • •

They sat on the deck having breakfast beneath a hazy sky. The sun floated like a rumor over Los Angeles. The fringe on the umbrella over the white wooden table flapped lazily in the soft damp breeze. They were alone, just Leary and Cassidy, two old pals.

"When's Harry due in?"

Cassidy put down his coffee cup. "Any minute, I'd think."

"I never thought I'd say it but I miss the old bastard. The three of us, like the Hole in the Wall Gang. The Wild Bunch. That's what he calls us. . . . Do you realize, Lew, he can remember some of those guys. Knew 'em, talked to 'em. And Bat Masterson." He sighed.

"Listen, Terry. You know what you said about Karin back there in Kansas? Said there was something funny going on. I've been thinking about that. You know what? The more I think about it the less I like it. In fact, old pal, I don't like it a goddamn bit, not if I got your drift right. Now, what the hell were you implying? You've known her damn near as long as I have, you *know* her—so you'd better make it pretty clear just what you were implying—"

"Hey, come on, Lew. It's me, Terry Leary. We're on the same side here. I'm trying to look out for you—"

"Sure, sure. Amigos. Now get on with it."

"Jeez, keep your shirt on, Lew. You're not thinking so clearly here. You're forgetting who your friends are—"

"And I'm tired of this conversation already. You're beginning to sound like MacMurdo, and that worries me."

"MacMurdo's the one guy we can trust, you'd better get that straight—"

"Trust MacMurdo," Cassidy repeated. "But don't trust Karin. You're losing me, Terry."

"Listen to me, amigo. There are a few things you'd better get straight in your mind while there's still time. Everybody's playing for keeps—"

"Spare me this, Terry."

"Damn it, Lew! This woman is *not*—get it?—is not *your* Karin. Once, a long time ago, she *was* your Karin, but not anymore. She's led a whole new life, there's been a war, it's a whole new world. And she's become this new Karin . . . and you don't know a single goddamn thing about this new woman. You really don't. Think about it. A man you've never seen before shows up with this Karin, he tells you this amazing story about what happened to her in the bombing of Cologne, about her amnesia and her doctor who saved her and this SS man she married—so what can you do? You're stuck with the story he tells. You believe him, you damn well believe *her* and all these haunting little dreams she has about her past with you, you're so glad to have her back you'd believe any damn thing . . . and then all of a sudden guns and grenades are going off, people are dying all around us, we've got quite a body count and it's on the rise, y'know? And you're off in the snowy woods at some castle and movie stars are screwing you and crazy one-armed, one-eyed Irishmen are pretending to be people they're not and all of a sudden you've got an emerald from the Nazi treasure and we're scraping the good doctor off Park Avenue and now we're fucking around with more Nazi loot and all these movie types. . . . Well, I mean, Jesus, Lew!"

Terry Leary sank back in the chair and stroked his mustache and gave his coffee cup a severe look.

"Well," Cassidy said, "all that goes to show you've been paying attention. You haven't missed a beat. But what I asked you was what are you telling me about Karin? My Karin, your Karin, everybody's Karin . . . the only Karin we've got? You think she's faking amnesia. . . . You think she's part of some dark plot. Hell, you're accusing her of God only knows what, and I want to know why."

"Look, Lew, I've spent a long time being slightly twisty but damned good at my job. With damned good instincts. And I'm just about perfect at surviving. And the one sure thing I've learned is not to trust anyone. I don't trust anybody . . . but you and Harry Madrid and me—"

"Don't forget your pal MacMurdo."

"You and Harry and me, that's the lot. Harry and I have had our differences, but all that's past. He's a stand-up guy. And you? Well, if I had a brother I wouldn't trust him the way I trust you. But Karin? Who the hell is Karin? I sure as hell don't know. You knew her for a few years . . . then she was gone. You knew her, amigo, but you don't know her now, that's all I'm saying."

"But I do *know* her. I've loved her and I still love her and she's not part of some crazy plot. You've lost your bearings, Terry. You're outsmarting yourself and when it comes to Karin I resent it like hell!"

"Fine, you resent it," Terry Leary said. "But you will see Popescu, right? What can it hurt?"

"We don't even know if he still lives here, Terry. He's probably back in Seattle or Portland or some goddamn place, and anyway he was a crazy man, he was an actor—"

"He was among other things a perfectly legitimate hypnotist. Come on, let's give the guy a break."

"I wonder just how legit—"

"Well, we'll soon know. I found him. He's living in what might be called reduced circs in Santa Monica. He occasionally does his act in a club or at USO shows. He's alive and kicking, amigo. I told him we've got a job for him."

"I don't like it," Cassidy said. "He's a quack."

"But he can't do any harm, Lew. Just let him talk to her."

"I'm going to have to tell her. You know that. Rolf said it could be dangerous for her, she's got to know what we're getting her into—"

"Of course, that's the point. We're putting a little pressure on her *if* she's faking it. If she's not, she'll be game. She'll want to dig into this past of hers. That will be the Karin you love and remember, amigo."

Cassidy sat watching the sun burning through the morning haze. What was happening? Somehow life had been turned inside out.

He felt as he had when his father and Terry had come to break the news that Karin was alive and coming home. With her husband.

He was back to having no idea of what the hell was going on.

• • •

MacMurdo and Cassidy were watching Karin swim. It was the middle of the afternoon and the sky over Los Angeles had turned flat gray. Karin moved easily in the water, swimming methodically, building up laps.

"She is one beautiful girl." MacMurdo was speaking with uncharacteristic softness.

"For a war criminal."

"It's nothing to joke about."

"My view exactly. How do we take Moller and Benedictus?"

"At the auction. The art will be there. This Englishman who's in on it will be there. We'll have everybody in one place. But it's your job to find out from Mona Ransom the time and place."

"So we're going to take Benedictus, too. That's sure?"

"Why not?" MacMurdo smiled.

"I just want to make sure there isn't some other game going on that I don't know about. I made a deal with Mona and I'm making sure we keep it."

"Well, you made the deal. Not me. So it's your problem. Mercy, you should ask me about those things." MacMurdo was chuckling. "Look, pard, you got yourself a case of divided loyalties, that's your problem. You're thinkin' about Mona Ransom when you should be thinkin' about Moller and Karin. Mona Ransom's nothin' to you—"

"She's plenty. To all of us. I made the deal with her and she led us to Moller, gave him to us on a platter. We owe her, Sam. Not just me. All of us."

"Well, she's gonna be all right, so don't get yourself in an uproar. You gotta keep your eye on the main chance—"

"Mona is the main chance. She's the buffer between us and Benedictus. She's the one keeping his mind off us."

"Okay, pard," MacMurdo said soothingly. "Okay."

"Mona's the key, Sam. If Benedictus catches on and spooks, then there won't be an auction. Then it'll be every son of a bitch for himself—"

"Relax. We've made our deal with Moller . . . now we shut up and wait. Moller isn't going to grab his minotaur and run for it, because he wants his wife. And we've got her. Remember, Lew, Benedictus is just a by-product of the Moller investigation. A bonus. My masters will, of course, be delighted. . . . You know me, once a hero, always a hero." He slapped Cassidy on the back. "Cheer up, pal."

"Just so Mona gets out of this free and clear."

"Right, right."

"We owe her," Cassidy said again.

# CHAPTER TWENTY-SIX

Cassidy saw the man step down from the bus a block away and start walking toward them. He was tall and broad and wore a flowing cape that caught the breeze and furled out behind him. He was carrying what seemed to be a conical object that didn't look like much of anything Cassidy could identify.

It was late evening for Santa Monica, about ten o'clock. The street was a four-block cul-de-sac with scrawny palm trees and uneven paving. The bungalows were small and plain and looked as if the next quake would be the last one for them. The people in the houses were on their way down or had maybe never gotten much of anywhere. It wasn't a happy block. It was just a block.

They waited beside the car, smelling the salty night winds. The house was a two-bedroom job with cream siding and some stucco, a screened-in front porch with a swing, a stoop with three steps, and a muddy lawn. There was a sandbox with a length of garden hose curling into it from around the corner of the house. The source of the water, thus the mud. There were tin shovels and buckets in the sandbox, the remains of a rudimentary sand castle. What had once been a lawn gave the impression of having been grazed to death. A rusted tricycle lay on its side, along with a red wagon, a doll, some toy soldiers, a tank with a gun turret that needed repair. The funny thing was, no children lived in the house.

The man from the bus had taken the conical shape and put it on his head. A sorcerer's cap with astrological symbols pasted on it. He was whistling the song about the Buffalo girls dancing by the light of the moon. He stopped suddenly at the sight of Cassidy, who was standing in the middle of the sidewalk.

"Lewis, Lewis, it's you! It *is* you. Leary said you were out here." He came forward, took Cassidy's hand so vigorously that the wizard's cap toppled off his head. He had a full head of thick curly hair.

"Popescu," Cassidy said. "You old fake!"

"Not Popescu now, you fool. Don't you read *Variety*? I am the Great Magnetico these days. Don't blame me. My agent, the abominable Silberstein, thought of the name. A reference to my magnetic powers of understanding—"

"You don't have to convince me. You taken to playing with toy trucks and little soldiers?" He nodded at the sandbox.

"Camouflage. I've made peace with my neighbors, they think I'm weird, but I leave all this crap out for their kids to play with. They can screw up my yard as much as they want to. Makes me a nice old fart. I don't grab their sorry little peckers, their folks are happy. My yard's a playground. Live and let live. Terry, how the hell are you? And Karin, for God's sake, it's been years, you were just a kid in skates . . ."

Karin looked at him, a shy smile on her face, hesitant. "I'm afraid I just don't remember. I'm sorry."

"I understand. I hear you've been through your share of troubles. A little memory difficulty. Well, we're going to see what we can do about that." He picked up his funny hat. He took Karin's arm and started picking his way through the rubble on the cracked sidewalk leading up to the stoop. "Let's see what the Great Magnetico can do for you. You should all come and see my horrible little act at the famous Club Crummy. God, you'd have a laugh with old Popescu. A little magic, a little telepathy, I damn well do have the second sight, you'll never convince me I don't, so don't bother trying. A little hypnotism, of course, and I'm not bad at that. Magic's my weak spot, I'm afraid. I have trouble making a hamburger disappear. Come on, come on. Look out for that Blondie doll, Terry. My, you've got a copper's big flat feet. Come on in, come on in."

He led the way into his house, which was somewhat overheated and full of birds in cages, chattering away, hopping about on their little crooked claws. The living room was antiseptic, compulsively neat. Except for the birds, which the Great Magnetico utterly ignored. Cassidy stood by one cage, transfixed by the colors of one of the birds, soft pastels, clearly demarked from one another, purple and baby blue and yellow and lime green. The bird bounced along its little trapeze, brainless, quite unaware of its own beauty and quite possibly the better off for that. After all, it was stuck in the cage. It wasn't going anywhere. What good was beauty there in the cage?

The lights were dim. Dance music played faintly on a radio in the kitchen. Popescu went to the kitchen and kept up a steady stream of chatter about magic and his days in the movies and how he taught Orson Welles card tricks. When he came back he brought steaming tea for himself and Karin, a plate of dried-out sugar cookies, a bottle of tequila with a worm floating in the bottom, two bottles of Tecate. Cassidy was sweating but couldn't quite work up the desire for a beer. Terry Leary took one, dropped his hat on the end table, wiped his forehead with a napkin, and sucked up half the bottle. It was too hot in the tidy, lifeless room that itself was so unlike Popescu.

Popescu gave Karin her tea, made sure she could reach the cookies, then reached up, sank his fingers into the thick curly hair and pulled it off with a *thwupp* sound. A shining bald dome was revealed, startling to behold, as if Hitchcock had lit it from within by means of a hundred-watt bulb. "*Voilà!*" he said softly, flipping his hair onto the end table next to Terry Leary's hat. "You like the cueball look? Well, I went through a spell of hard times couple years back, I took up the wrestling game. Shaved my head so they could call me Barak the Turk. Now I keep it shaved just in case Barak gets a gig." He stroked his long mustache which curled up on either side of his nose, nearly touching the nostrils. It was strange, the way he didn't look laughable—even with the absurd mustache and the bullet head. He simply wasn't a laughable man. He believed in himself, much in the way that Winch believed in himself. Laughter was thereby short-circuited. His hands were hairy, as if to balance the gleaming head. His muscles were huge. Beneath the cape he was wearing a tight T-shirt with horizontal stripes.

He sat down on the chair across from Karin, who sat on the davenport, watching, transfixed. He sketched out in a few sentences what he understood the position to be regarding her memory loss. "Now, my dear, you've had some shock and some cranial damage." He took her hand and patted it. A wizard, all right. "Either of these, or both, may have occasioned your memory loss. You do want a peek at that past of yours, Karin, is that right?"

She nodded.

"Because if you don't, if you resist this experience, we're all just wasting our time, right?"

"I do want to know," she said. "I'm not afraid, if that's what you mean."

"Good. There's nothing to be afraid of."

"I know."

"So, I understand you've been having dreams, dreams or memories, we don't really know which. Is that about right?" He sipped his tea, looked at her expectantly with eyes as black and gleaming as Mona Ransom's.

"Yes. I have had dreams. Standing by an ocean liner on a pier. I think I recall a man I'm with in the dream." She was looking down at her hands folded in her lap. "Walking down Fifth Avenue to Washington Square. There's a huge Christmas tree under the arch, snow falling, I hear children singing carols. . . ."

Popescu nodded, stopping her. "All right, fine. Is the tea all right? Cookie? Are you comfortable, Karin? Are you feeling relaxed?"

"Yes. I'm fine."

"Good," Popescu said. "Well, this is all lovely, isn't it?"

She nodded. She wanted to get on with it.

"I'm just going to ask you to look at the old wall clock over there. An old Regulator. Schoolroom clock. Just relax, Karin. Don't worry about getting hypnotized, don't try to get hypnotized, just keep watching the pendulum and listen to my voice, listen to what I'm saying, I'm going to describe some of these scenes of yours, the way the gulls swoop down and float back and forth, back and forth, like the pendulum, swooping and gliding, think of the arcs of their flight, the sound of the waves lapping at the hull, just steadily lapping and slapping at the liner's hull . . . and the lights of that huge Christmas tree under the arch, the way the lights twinkle through the falling snow, the sound your boots make crunching in the snow, you're so happy, it's Christmas, a brisk night, a clear night, the snowflakes drifting slowly down and they catch in your long eyelashes, the snow is so cold and clean. . . . Do you recall that night, Karin?"

"Oh, yes," she said, sounding very tired. "The snow, yes, I remember that. Yes."

"And were those happy times? Very happy times?"

"The happiest days of my life, yes, they were, so very happy. . . . The Christmas tree . . ."

"That's fine, Karin. That's a lovely happy memory. Was it nice being in New York? Were you alone? With somebody? What made you so happy, Karin?"

"I was with someone. . . . That's why I was so happy. . . . Someone I loved . . ."

• • •

Cassidy squatted on the sidewalk and pushed a rusted toy car back and forth, making a road in the mud. It was a cast-iron car with chipped green paint. It was going to last longer than the Chevy Cliff Howard was working on at the Ocean View Motor Court. Terry Leary leaned against the rented Plymouth smoking one cigarette after another. The evening thunder was rolling in off the Pacific and you could almost feel yourself corroding from the salt on the wind. A bottle of beer dangled from Terry Leary's free hand. A train rattled along the tracks somewhere, a clattering, lonely sound just like in a movie. The lights of Los Angeles had turned the sky pink to the east but it was dead quiet in Santa Monica.

*War criminal . . .*

The idea was like a drop of acid, burning at his brain. And Terry Leary's insistence that she was a fake, that she wasn't his Karin anymore. And the empty, blank look in her eyes when she looked at Manfred Moller. It was as if she'd dropped him by parachute into an arctic waste and flown away, never to return. *War criminal . . .* What had she done at the clinic? What? Or didn't it matter in the brave new postwar world?

And who killed Rolf? The thought that had crossed his mind earlier . . .

One of the survivors of the little clinic in the Hartz Mountains.

Some POW who had survived.

Who'd have a better motive?

He looked up at the sound of the screen door creaking open. He'd lost track of time and there she was.

Karin stood on the porch with the rips in the screens and looked out at him, stood staring as if she were trying to memorize the night, the moment, his face. She held on to the railing, came down the two steps to the sidewalk. Behind her Popescu loomed up, took shape in the doorway to the house. He was still holding his teacup.

She came toward him, looking at his face with an expression he couldn't immediately identify. But he knew he'd seen it before. Then she touched his face, ran her fingertip down his cheek.

"Lew," she whispered. "You should have told me. What is it they say? You should have refreshed my memory?" She smiled. "We've got to start making up for lost time. Another movie cliché." She took his hand. "You should have told me. Someone should have told me."

"You remember?"

"More will come back to me now. But I remember what I was doing on that pier . . . who I saw the Christmas tree with that night in New York. . . ."

She blinked at the tears streaking her cheeks.

"My husband." She leaned forward, pressing her face against his chest. "Lew Cassidy."

"Karin."

"It all makes sense now, Lew. Everything I've been feeling about you . . . it's natural, it's the way it used to be. I've fallen in love with you, I've been falling in love with you all over again. . . ."

"Are you all right?"

"I want to start living my life again."

"When do you want to begin?"

She grinned and took his arm and Terry Leary held the car door.

• • •

She lay in his arms for a long time before they finally made love. First they talked in low whispers and lay quietly and shared a sense of wonder at what had happened, how they'd been brought together, how she'd survived the war, how something like Fate had led them to this moment. She was full of questions about details of her past, of their life together, and now he was free to tell her everything. And with every story she came further toward him through time, everything he said triggering more memories in her, until she was completing sentences for him. He told her of how he'd heard of her death during the raid on Cologne. She said her memories of that event were mostly a jumble of impressions, vague pictures of fire and heat and crumbling walls and a steady cascade of incredibly racketing, overpowering, calamitous noise. And heat. It was all a blur and she whispered that she hoped to God it stayed that way. She talked about their wedding up at Lake Placid, the banks of flowers Reichsminister Goebbels had sent, the movies she'd made . . . the life they'd lived.

"It was all so close to the surface of my mind," she said. She rested her head in the crook of his arm, stroked his fingers while she talked. "It was right there, waiting, and that strange, gentle man just let it come out. Remember how I got in the car that day and somehow knew the way to your apartment? Well, it was all just sitting there waiting for me to reach in and get it. . . . Lew, I remembered where you lived because I lived there, too, I knew that place. . . . Do you know what that means to me? I remember you, I remember everything about you, everything we did together. Now we have the whole world before us, Lew, we've got another chance, we get to live our life together again. It's hard to believe, I don't even begin to grasp it yet, but we're both here, together . . . a miracle."

"And the war is over," Cassidy said. "Karin, I lived with the fact that I'd never see you again. Night after night I felt the panic, knowing you were gone forever . . . and now here you are."

"But the war isn't over yet," she said. "Our war won't be over until MacMurdo's war is over. . . . We've got to get him out of our lives. We won't be free until he's gone—"

"What is it he has of yours?" He couldn't bring himself to ask more than that.

"Later, my darling. Later."

She was ready to make love and they took a long time, an act of love and of cherishing, of thanksgiving. You knew that you never got a second chance. But sometimes the laws of nature went awry. Sometimes you did get a second chance. There was nothing more valuable in life than a second chance.

And when she slept, her hips pushed against him, her face calm and untroubled, he lay back and watched the light of morning come. When it was over, when MacMurdo had wrapped up Moller and Benedictus, when he could stop thinking about Karin working in Rolf Moller's clinic—then he had an emerald he wanted to give her, green and full of their new life.

It was amazing how Popescu, the Great Magnetico, had done it.

His gentleness had brought it all back so easily.

# Chapter Twenty-seven

Harry Madrid didn't look right in Los Angeles. Almost impossibly he'd looked much better, much more at home, in Maine. Now he was squinting in the hazy sunshine, his skin pale and parchment dry. He was digging in his ear with a little finger trying to dislodge wax. He needed some work done on the crop of white bristles in the ear. He was glad to be off the train at last but he wasn't happy about being in Los Angeles.

Cassidy was filling him in on Mona Ransom and the party and Manfred Moller and the way the deal was working out. He told him about Ray Chandler seeming to know what was going on and Benedictus seeming to have notes regarding V, which would make you think that Benedictus might be Brian Sheehan all right but he certainly wasn't Vulkan, which left them back in familiar territory—not knowing who Vulkan was. He told him about the Englishman Benedictus was waiting for and he told him what they were waiting to find out—the details of the auction.

And finally he told Harry Madrid about Terry Leary's warnings about Karin, told him about Popescu and the results of hypnotizing Karin. Harry's seamed, impassive face cracked into a broad smile. "That's swell, son," he said, "that's just damn fine news. So she's all right, she's back . . . damn fine news, Lewis. Now you've got something you'll fight to keep from losing. That's the way life should be. You lost that after Miss Squires got killed. Now you've got it back."

"Harry, I fought to keep from losing Cindy. I did what I thought I had to do. . . . Hell, Harry, it just wasn't enough. I couldn't stop her from dying . . ."

"Well, you got a second chance at that, too."

"I don't want to lose her," Cassidy said.

"I know, son, I know."

• • •

When the telephone rang that afternoon it was Mona Ransom at the other end. She was whispering, her voice insistent, edged with the filigree of something like hysteria. She was teetering and he had to strain to keep her coherent, to keep her under control. He heard it all in her voice: it was all beginning to come apart. Or maybe it all just beginning. Sometimes you couldn't tell if the signs were good or bad. You just found out later.

"I'm afraid," she whispered. "It's Tash, he's so tense, and I think he's onto something. He knows something is going on that he doesn't know about. He hates that. He's very suspicious of me, he accused me of having an affair with you. . . . I acted halfway guilty, I'd rather have him believe that than the truth. Now he's getting ready to head up to the place in the mountains." She stopped and took a drink of something.

"The mountain place," he said. He knew the story, how Tash Benedictus had killed the men who were using Mona, had burned down their lodge, and had built one of his own on top of the ruins. "Go on."

"He's loading the car now. We're all going. Your German, Tash, and me. He's making the German do the driving."

"How's Moller? Has he given any of it away?"

"No, he's the same as ever." Ice cubes rattled in her glass. "He hasn't even mentioned his meeting with you to me. He's a solitary man. He acts like he doesn't need another living soul."

"Well, it's an act. There's one person he needs."

"And the Englishman Tash has been waiting for, I think we're expecting him tonight. At the mountain place."

"Mona, this Englishman, could he be Vulkan? Have you picked up any hints?"

"Look," her voice with that sharp edge of fear, "I don't have any idea about that—"

"It's okay, Mona. Now, when is the auction taking place? And where?"

"It's not decided yet. Listen to me, Cassidy, listen—I'm afraid. Once Tash gets me up in the mountains I don't know what he'll do. He's worried, he'll be drinking, I'm afraid of what he might do to me. . . . Do you hear me? I'm afraid he'll kill me. I'm afraid he'll get loaded and start thinking about my screwing Moller. . . . He doesn't trust me, he never did trust Moller. . . . What if he kills me? Or Moller, if he's the one you care about? What then?"

"Calm down, Mona—"

"No, no, don't tell me that. You've got to come and get me, you have to." She was almost in tears. "I held up my end, I did everything you wanted, I got Moller for you. . . . Now I'm afraid, I don't want to die, I know Tash, I know what he can do when he gets crazy. . . . You've got to come and get me tonight, I can't wait any longer, he's going to be waiting for the Englishman, he'll be thinking about the auction. . . . He can be taken by surprise, you can kill him, you said you would—"

"Mona!"

"The Englishman is coming tonight." She began repeating herself, working herself up again. She was almost out of control. "They'll all be busy looking at what he brings, the loot, oh, Christ, come and get me, kill him, kill him. . . ." She was sobbing. *"Kill him!"*

"Mona," Cassidy said. "Tell me how to get there."

# Chapter Twenty-Eight

The rain that finally burst out of the days of threatening thunder was already washing out some of the canyon roads by the time Terry Leary and Cassidy left for the mountains. The rain blew across the highway east of San Bernardino and the shoulders were running muddy and soft. The radio said that a storm was building up in the higher mountain elevations. Terry smoked quietly, staring past the thumping windshield wipers. Finally he said: "I'm glad about Karin, amigo. I'm glad I was wrong. . . . She's the real thing. She always was. No hard feelings?"

"Without you we'd never have gone to Popescu. I might never have gotten her back." He grinned at his partner. "No hard feelings."

"Are we crazy to go after Mona?" Leary laughed shortly. "Not that it makes much difference now."

"We owe her. Anyway, maybe you don't, but I do."

"Whither thou goest," Leary said. "But I don't much like it. These are crazy people. You know that?"

"I know it. Benedictus, anyway."

"Come on, Lew. They're all nuts. They're the kind of people who use up other people's lives. They make their problems and their craziness everybody's problems. People die when that goes on."

"Nobody's going to die. We're going in under cover of the storm, we're going to rescue Mona because . . ."

Leary said: "Why?"

"Because we're the heroes, dammit. Then Tash won't be able to go look for her because the meter's running on him and his little enterprise. He's got the auction to run. And then MacMurdo and the Feds take over. They put Tash away, recover the minotaur and the art, Moller either goes over to our side or he disappears, Mona makes her movie, and Karin goes home with me. Music swell, up and out, roll credits."

"Sounds easy. We'll do it blindfolded."

"Don't be sarcastic. It doesn't suit you, cutie."

"I'm not a hero," Terry Leary said. "That's my problem."

"You'll always be my hero."

"Shut up."

• • •

The storm had finally broken all along the coast and in some ways it was worse than the snow in Maine. This was rain but rain with teeth in it. It blew, it stung, there was nothing of the peace of Maine in it. It soaked through his clothes, drenching and freezing him, as he climbed the rocky, slippery, steep mountainside toward some dim lights glimpsed through the trees.

The road surface had been on the narrow dividing line between bad and worse. The rain was turning to slushy ice when they stopped to take on oil at a wide place in the road called Delmer. The station's REO tow truck was just pulling out to fetch somebody from a ditch. The afternoon had landed with a crash at about five o'clock. Night came on hard, like part of the storm. The road clung to the mountain, winding upward through the black firs and pines, a black ribbon disappearing in the night.

Mona had given good directions and he spotted the lodge a couple of hundred feet above through the rain and heavy foliage. Lights were showing dim yellow. They seemed very far away. There were six or seven cars already stuck in mudslides and abandoned on the road below. From where they stood, on a clear night you could probably have seen the glow of Los Angeles, a premiere at Grauman's Chinese.

"Looks like a long climb," Leary said doubtfully.

"She said if we drove any farther we might alert Tash. She said she'll come back down the hillside with us, a couple of minutes rather than twenty minutes of walking by the road. She knows the mountain." Cassidy was winding his scarf around his mouth and chin to keep the deluge out. The gale whined at the car. The motor was still running, for the heat.

They checked their guns, then jammed them deep into their trench-coat pockets. "I don't like this, Lew. The weather aside, it's too easy."

"She's waiting for us. She told me which window to go to. She'll come out and we take off. Benedictus will be wrapped up with the Englishman and Moller—"

"Two bits says the Englishman never got through."

"Two bits says we're on our way home in an hour."

"Well, we better get to it."

Cassidy cut the engine and the wipers stopped. Immediately rain flooded the glass. Together they headed across the slippery road and into the gully that was a muddy river, then up the side, wet stones and underbrush and scrub underfoot. He was suddenly on his knees, breathing hard, grabbing at sharp-edged rocks, feeling his palm slit by an icy point, hearing Terry swearing. "Dammit to hell," the voice came to him, "I've torn my pants! Shit!" He kept pushing upward, holding on to ropes of underbrush, trying to convince himself that it was all a snap.

He was licking blood off his hand, staring at the windows of the lodge, trying to keep the rain out of his eyes. The sharp edge had cut through the leather of his glove. Terry arrived panting. He'd lost his hat on the climb. "Brand-new Dobbs you owe me, amigo. How's your leg?"

"My leg is killing me. Make you feel better?"

"A little. So where is she?"

He was yelling to be heard above the screaming wind tearing up from the canyon. Cassidy shook his head. "Inside somewhere. She's waiting for us. She said she'll come to this window. So we wait."

They huddled in the overhang of the roof. It was a very modern building, a Hollywood Frank Lloyd Wright adaptation. Slabs of rough stone and redwood, plenty of glass, low-slung, stone fireplace chimneys, very elegant, perfect for Cary Grant and Irene Dunne. A fancy house with two cold men soaked to the skin waiting to rescue the leading lady. But she was missing her cue. It was like waiting after the director calls for action and nothing happens.

"Lew, we'd better find her. I'm half frozen. This fucking wind."

They lifted themselves up onto the balcony running across the rear of the lodge, facing out across the slope of the mountainside. The night was flat black with rain whipping in all directions at once. They moved slowly, carefully, hoping the storm would cover whatever sound they made. Rain was dripping from the timbered balcony.

Through the window Cassidy could see the warm, comfortable room. The walls of stone softened by paneling and heavy nubby curtains, huge throw rugs over polished wood, logs burning in the fireplace, a bottle of champagne in an ice bucket, large slipcovered chairs and couches . . . Not a living soul.

They worked their way around to the front of the house where the rain made jumpy puddles in the forecourt. A single set of muddy tire tracks was filling up with water, leading to the six-car garage that matched the house. There had to be somebody home. But there was no movement, only the sound of the wind like a single endless shriek. And the rain lashing the night. Two men with guns in the shadows wondering what to do, both of them already knowing that this wasn't the way it was supposed to be.

"Let's get the hell out of here," Terry Leary said. "We did what we were contracted to do. . . ."

Cassidy took the .38 from his pocket. His leg hurt and he limped through the rain to the house. Terry Leary was saying something but the wind blew it away. Terry's hair was plastered to his head like a skullcap. Cassidy stood under the eaves and tried to listen for any identifiable sound but there was nothing, only the storm. He turned the handle on the door and pushed it open. The warm air came like the breath of life. They went inside.

It didn't take them long once they started looking.

They were too late.

They found the body hanging by a chain thrown over one of the exposed beams in the kitchen. The chain had been wrapped tightly around the wrists, then the body hoisted up so that it hung swaying in the center of the kitchen. The tile floor was slick with blood, a lake of it. A constant dripping from above, like a metronome. There was blood on the refrigerator and the stove and the cabinets and the walls. The throat, wrists, chest, and abdomen had all been slit open.

Cassidy stood looking at the frayed remains of Manfred Moller, taking it all in, the thick, sickening smell of blood and waste. The caked butcher knife lay on the floor by the wall. In the blood on the floor, tiny and pathetic, lay his penis.

Cassidy slipped in the blood, nearly fell down, vomited into the sink. Terry Leary stood staring out the window where the rain was snapping at the glass. Cassidy washed his mouth out at the faucet, stood up, tried not to look at the mess. "This is insane," he said.

"It's torture," Leary said.

"You don't say." Where was everybody? This job on Moller was warm and fresh. He caught a glimpse of the blood-streaked legs, the sodden trousers pulled down to the ankles.

"Why would Benedictus torture Moller? Weren't they in cahoots, Lew?"

"Moller had been sleeping with Mona, that's one thing. But it's the minotaur. . . . Moller was holding on to it, it was his hole card. He could trade it for Karin—that was what it had come down to. He couldn't let Benedictus have it . . . then he would have lost everything."

"So Benedictus wanted the minotaur. He knew about it from the time Moller arrived in Maine."

"And he must have played a part in getting it to Brenneman in Boston. Benedictus, Karl Dauner, that bunch." He kept hearing the dripping blood. Something was mixing with the smell of blood and death. Something was making him sick again. "I think he did this to him to get information—not for revenge. He's crazy, Terry. This is all crazy. . . . It's like it was with Max Bauman, when everything went out the window and there was nothing left but the craziness—" He sniffed. "What the hell is that smell?"

"Did Moller tell him?"

"If he did, it was because he wanted Tash to finish him off as a favor."

Cassidy turned his back on the scene and went back down the hallway to the living room. The door still stood open. The fire crackled.

"They're still here," Cassidy murmured, staring out into the storm. The single set of muddy tire tracks was barely visible now. "Nobody's left. No fresh tracks." He led the way outside, lurched against the wind, almost blinded by the downpour until he reached the right angle where fifteen feet away the garage building stood. He turned and ran back toward Terry Leary, who was halfway between house and garage, standing like a statue in the expanse of gravel and mud seeping down from the hills.

"They're in the garage," Cassidy called.

Terry Leary turned, cupped a hand to his ear.

Cassidy thought: *Gas, it was gas. . . .*

He was flat on his face, skidding full length in the wet, engulfed in a rumbling explosion that shook the ground. Pain shot through his ears. Wooden beams, aflame, cartwheeling through the blowing rain, bouncing, skittering like drunken skaters in the mud puddles. Glass shattering, filling the air. The house was gutted, the roof gone or hanging inward like something melting. For a moment, through the framework and the leaping yellow flames, Cassidy saw the body of Manfred Moller twisting below the beam. Then with a roar and a crash the kitchen ceiling collapsed, sparks rose in a massive bright bouquet of red and yellow and blue and the body was gone.

Cassidy rolled over, got to his knees, felt his bad leg collapse, crawled toward Terry Leary, who was on his back. A flaming piece of wood had struck him a glancing blow, knocked him down, and he was struggling to get into a sitting position. He stared past Cassidy to the house. "So much for the evidence," he gasped. Rain and gritty, acrid smoke swirled everywhere.

"They're in the garage," Cassidy said. The wind choked him. He pulled his gun from his pocket.

He looked from the house to the garage.

Suddenly, without time to realize that one set of doors had opened, he was blinded by the glare of two huge headlamps. There was another explosion in the wreckage of the house. The car surged to life, burst out of the darkened garage, smashed through the sheets of rain, swerving as it came, then slanting toward them. It was the big Rolls-Royce Mona had driven out to the motor court. From where he knelt in the mud the grille seemed high as an iron gate, the tires bore down on them like the great grinding wheels of a tractor, the Rolls moved sluggishly and quickly all at once, swerved and skidded, roaring, gears grinding, mud spitting from beneath the wheels. . . . It came skidding toward them, tons of coachwork, the lights cutting at the rain and the night, two people inside, a voice screaming over the wind and the fire reaching for the trees and the roar and the grinding, *run for it, run for it,* her pale face behind the window, eye sockets like black holes in a death's head, the car turning, now moving slowly, swinging around, the driver's side across their path, a hand at the window, the car floating on the mud, the muzzle flash once, twice, the crack of the gun lost in the wind, water spurting up in front of Terry Leary, the second shot hitting him, Terry stumbling and falling to his knees in the mud, pitching sideways, the son of a bitch only has one hand, how can he drive and shoot at the same fucking time, and the Rolls was straightening out, the target practice was over, that one goddamn hand back on the wheel, foot to the pedal, water spraying, Terry Leary sprawled bleeding, feet kicking, the headlights picking him out, a cop is down, a cop is down, Cassidy on his knees, fumbling to get the gun free with his wet glove, losing precious moments, the Rolls turning, determined, evil, bearing down on Terry Leary—Christ, the first shot, it hit some metalwork, flew away with a twang, too fucking late, the wheels crossed the fallen body, grinding Terry into the gravel, his legs kicking wildly, reflexively, the life being ground exceeding small, coming at Cassidy, swerving again, her face like goddamn murdering buggering empty dark death at the window, he felt the rush of power as it swept past and he fell backward, felt the heat from the underworld, the scorching fiery furnace that had been the house, and some of the wet black trees were shriveling and burning and the Rolls was headed away, lights poking ahead at the night. . . .

Terry Leary lay badly twisted, his trench coat torn, crisscrossed by tracks, blood soaking through, blood on his face. Cassidy knelt over him, peered into his face, saw eyelids flutter, the beginning of a wet bloody grin. "Where's the happy ending? Shit, amigo . . . take my gun. . . ." He coughed, blood bubbling. "I don't feel so hot, amigo. . . . Take the fucking gun. . . . Make the bastard pay. . . ."

Cassidy took the gun, jammed them both into his pockets, and turned without a good-bye, began to move without thinking. Two minutes to get down the hill on foot, two minutes the hard way, two minutes through the rain and mud and past the sharp icy rocks, and he was staggering, running past the crackling conflagration, feeling the flames hot on his face, slipping and falling, trying to slide feet first down the hill, scarf ripped away by an unseen branch, hold on to the guns, asshole, the miserable fucking mick bastard killed Terry back there and he's about to wish he hadn't. . . .

Cassidy slid down to the road, gasping for breath, saw his sad little Plymouth drowning where they'd left it. He steadied himself on the fender, tried to breathe like a human being, tried to get his hands steady, took both guns in his cold bare hands, stepped out into the road, the wind smashing him like a giant fist across the chest, shaking him. He stood in the blowing, raving wind and rain, staring into the night, straining to see the powerful headlights of the Rolls curving around the mountain road, waiting, seeing her white mummy's face behind the glass, seeing the tires ripping Terry's trench coat, the blood, the pink bubbles looking black at the corners of his mouth, in his pencil-thin mustache. . . .

The Rolls took the turn at the crawl on the slippery road, slid toward the abyss, straightened out, gathering speed as it came toward him, oh, Terry, my old amigo, here goes nothin' and he raised the two guns, waiting for the Rolls to come close, waiting until the lights had caught him so Benedictus could see him like Grim Faceless Fate waiting in the road, and then he began blazing away, firing into the great black beast, aiming as best he could between the massive round headlamps, unable to tell if he was hitting a goddamn thing, but his soul and his anger and his pain were in every bullet, like driving a knife home again and again, for Terry and Karin and old Pilkers and the Brothers Moller and the poor dead Gypsy in the road, not an end to killing but an exclamation fucking point, and he blew one of the headlights out and he knew the Rolls was going to run him down, and as it closed on him, visible in the reflections of its last cyclopean headlamp against a billion raindrops, as it closed on him one door flew open, a body swung out into the road, was yanked back as if it were on a spring, the Rolls skidded, spun slowly, almost gracefully, to the edge of the narrow road, hung suspended in space like a nightmare that might come true, and then slowly plummeted over the edge. . . .

Cassidy stood at the side of the road, staring into the darkness, following the descent by means of the one sturdy headlight, spinning, poking now at the night sky, now at the darkness below, and then the light went out and the wind shrieked at itself and above it all the sky was bursting with the colors of the fire raging up the mountain, in the rain.

Cassidy's arms were sore from absorbing the kicks, his legs were shaking, but by God he was the last of the gunslingers, which just went to show you: Hollywood could turn a man into a hero of its own.

# Chapter Twenty-nine

The mountainsides pressed in around him. He couldn't see the Rolls anymore. But in his mind the gunfire racketed on, trapped, and he wished it would stop. But it just kept roaring and he kept seeing the Rolls fishtailing and skidding and spinning, the blur of the body dragging along, bouncing on the road like a rag doll, the door slamming on it as if it might be cut in two. . . .

He went back to the Plymouth, took the flashlight from the glove compartment, and went over the edge where the Rolls had skidded off the road. It was no damn different than the last hillside he'd slipped and fallen down about ten minutes before. He dropped the flashlight twice, fell, skidded, slipped, swore, and finally came to a stop with the enormous car nose-down in front of him. It was wedged against a tree, standing almost on end. It was a lot like poking around the airplane in Maine.

He wanted to see Tash Benedictus dead.

From below, wailing on the mountain road, he heard the siren, saw the red glow of an ambulance, then a fire truck from the village. Of course. The explosion, the fire: hard to ignore, storm or not. They'd find Terry. They'd do what they could. They wouldn't leave him there in the mud like another piece of wreckage. The sky was aglow, angry. The ambulance and the fire truck were pushing steadily up the road. He saw them dimly, in outline, through the rain.

He found Mona Ransom first. She was no longer entirely recognizable. Her mink coat was torn, hanging in furry matted shreds, and her body was hopelessly broken. She was still handcuffed to the hand grip on the door panel, unable to free herself. Tash hadn't been taking chances. Maximum agony for everyone. She'd been held in place, dragged and beaten and smashed to pulp. He shone the light on her and it was like seeing Manfred Moller hanging from the timber all over again. Her face was gone. He hoped to God he'd shot and killed her before the door had flown open. He hoped he'd saved her from that at least.

Shining the light across the car's interior he saw no trace of Tash Benedictus.

He must have been thrown free. Maybe he was somewhere in the mud, suffering, dying. Maybe Cassidy could find him and watch him die. Help him along the way. He clung to the framework to keep from falling, worked his way over the freezing stones and brittle, cutting branches, around to the other side of the car. The driver's door hung open. He was thrown clear, all right.

He searched the area looking for any signs but found none. In the darkness and the cold and the rain there was no Tash Benedictus, no one-armed, one-eyed Irish bastard . . . just a dead woman and a wrecked car and the wind and the sound of sirens.

How could he have survived?

Well, he could have. He did.

But where could he have gone? Alone, banged up, on the mountain, in the storm?

Exhausted, Cassidy climbed back up to the Plymouth. The road below was empty. They must have reached the blazing house by now.

They'd found Terry by now.

There was nothing Cassidy could do, not for Terry, not for Mona. But he could still put paid to Benedictus. He could avenge Terry, avenge Manfred Moller, avenge Mona Ransom.

But he had to find him first.

• • •

Even while it was happening he knew he was in shock, knew that his thought processes were gummed up, moving sluggishly, so he just hung on, trying to get things done. He kept seeing the faces. Manfred Moller, teeth clenched, tongue bitten through, hanging by a string of gristle . . . Mona Ransom with her exquisite features obliterated, a pulpy mask . . . and Terry Leary, trying to smile at the end, the blood at his mouth, just like the movies but it wasn't chocolate sauce . . . It was

Terry's face he couldn't shake, his oldest, best friend, friend to the death. . . .

The Plymouth needed gas. He coaxed it down the twisty road to the village. The gas station was an oasis of light and activity. A snowplow was getting ready to attack the mud on the mountain road. A young man in a yellow slicker was talking to the driver of the plow. "All hell's broke loose up there at the Benedictus place," he told the driver. "I heard it, woke me up, sounded like one of them blockbusters going off—"

"You hear quite a few blockbusters, d'ya, Ned?"

"You know what I mean." He laughed. "Helluva noise. Like when I was a kid and they had the big fire up there, you remember that one? Place must have a curse on it. Ambulance radioed down to Jerry at the police station, they found a body out in the driveway. Stranger."

"Anybody see Benedictus or that wife of his? Were they at home?"

"Well, that's funny. I seen 'em go up before the storm really got to goin' hard, both of 'em in the Rolls—"

"So they're up there? Christ, they didn't have much of a chance then. . . . Musta been a gas leak, like over at the Timmons place 'bout five years ago—"

"Well, here's the thing. I ain't so sure they're still up there, got ourselves a mystery here. There's gonna be hell to pay, see, 'cause Benedictus's other car, that Bentley, the two-door, damn thing's gone. I had it in here for new plugs, and when I came down here 'bout ten minutes ago the damn thing's gone! So did he take it and go back to town? Or what?"

Their conversation bounced along and Cassidy looked at his watch. Tash had an hour's lead. If he'd been thrown clear of the Rolls, if he'd been able to walk, if he'd reached the village . . . an hour, yes, an hour had passed, maybe even a little more. Poking around the wreckage of the Rolls had taken forever. Yes, an hour, maybe even two.

The Plymouth was gassed and he was paying the bill when the attendant shook his head. "You ain't gonna try gettin' down the mountain, are you? Not tonight?"

"Thought I would." His own voice was far away, unreal, and he couldn't stop thinking about Terry Leary.

"State cops are out there. It may be blocked. Mudslides and they say you can't see a damned thing. Say, where you comin' from?"

Cassidy nodded vaguely.

"You see the fire up there?"

Cassidy shook his head. "I better get going." He took the change from a five and left the gas station.

The road was invisible under the carpet of shifting silt and the storm itself acted like an immense mirror. He was struggling along at ten miles an hour when he saw the state highway patrol up ahead. Red flares like smudgepots burned, whipped by the wind. The patrol car was parked at the side of the road. The patrolman waving him to a full stop had a red face and a mustache and was shaking his head. He wore a broad-brimmed hat that was tied under his chin and dripping steadily. His ears were red as earmuffs.

"I don't reckon you oughta try this road tonight," he said.

"Believe me, I wouldn't if I had a choice. This is an emergency."

"What's the problem?" The wind yelped at his voice.

"My wife's having a baby in San Berdoo."

"You don't wanna get yourself killed going down here—"

"I'll sure as hell be careful."

"Yep, I guess you will. Okay, pal, but for God's sake, take it easy. You got the best reason in the world to stay alive."

Harry Madrid had said something like that, about having found Karin, about how life was supposed to be. He nodded to the patrolman, rolled up his window, and moved onward.

It was a scary ride because you couldn't see the road, you couldn't see anything. It was like flying through fog. A bumpy flight, but it gave him time to think.

Benedictus was on his way to pick up the minotaur.

He'd killed Manfred Moller to find out where it was. Cassidy figured he'd found out. If not from Moller, then from Mona. She'd probably have done just about anything to end what Benedictus had been doing to Moller. Yes, Mona had known where the minotaur was, it was the hole card she'd hoarded to save her life if she needed it. Well, it hadn't worked, it hadn't saved anybody's life. . . .

Cassidy figured he knew where the stupid fucking minotaur was.

All he had to do was get off the mountain alive.

# CHAPTER THIRTY

The rain softened once he was halfway down the mountain. The cold was gone; it was warm and muggy and you had to open the window to breathe and even then it was a chore. It had taken a long time to get off the mountain and by the time he could see the lights of San Bernardino it was two o'clock in the morning. He couldn't imagine when he was going to get any sleep.

The rain just kept coming, rushing in the gullies, sweeping across the road now and then, overwhelming the windshield wipers. He reached the coast and followed it northward, occasionally hearing the roar of the surf. In Malibu part of the cliffs had collapsed. The highway was strewn with dirt and boulders and he followed the flares and the highway cops signaling like semaphore men, their slickers glistening in the red glow.

He turned on the radio and listened to dance music through the small hours and wondered how he was going to tell Harry Madrid about Terry. If he'd been killed on a battlefield, you'd write a letter. But it hadn't been that kind of battlefield and he was going to have to tell him, face to face. He turned the radio up, trying to drown out what was going on in his mind. Like everything else, it seemed to be a losing battle. He was used to it by now.

It was still raining when he pulled off the highway in sight of the three bright lights shining on the sign that said Ocean View Motor Court. You could still just make out the old name. El Dorado.

It was dawn, barely, and there was a light in the office. He pulled the Plymouth up to the door and got out. It felt like somebody was pouring a big bucket of water down on his soaked hat. How had his hat survived crawling up and down that moutainside? Terry's Dobbs hadn't made it. Terry hadn't made it.

He went into the office and hit the bell on the desk. He heard a sudden cough, a man coming out of a catnap in a state of confusion, and then Cliff Howard came out of the other room. He took a bleary look at Cassidy, squinted, then broke into a wide, toothy grin. "Well, you couldn't stay away, could you?" He laughed quietly. "Place kinda grows on you, don't it?"

"You always stay up all night?"

"No, Mr. Sheehan, to tell you the truth, I'm normally sawing wood at this time of day. Or night, that is. But tonight's been a short one—"

"Let me guess, Cliff. But first, I smell coffee. I'm about out on my feet."

"No sooner said than done." He ducked back through the doorway, reappeared with a thick chipped cup full of the hot and black.

Cassidy sipped, burned his mouth to prove he was still alive and at his post. "I'll bet a fella in a Bentley coupe has been here tonight. Eye patch, one arm, you couldn't miss him, Cliff."

"Damned if you're not a quick one! Showed up here," he yawned, looked at the Big Ben alarm clock on the counter, "three, four hours ago."

"You were holding something for his wife, sort of for safekeeping, was that it?"

"No, no, not like that. I was as ignorant as a newborn babe . . . but there *was* somethin' here he wanted, you got that right."

"Just tell me, Cliff."

"Well, whoever he was, he rolled in here, gave me a hunnert-dollar bill, just the one bill, for the use of a spade, no questions asked—"

"Where did he do his digging?"

"Well, he couldn't do much with just the one arm, so he gave me another hunnert, honest to God another one, and asked me to go out there with him. Back of cabin eleven. Rainin' like a bitch it was, mud ass deep, water runnin' down the hill there, damn Dakota gullwasher, real turd floater, y'know? So I started diggin' where he told me to, dug this hole like a tiny grave, fillin' with water fast as I could dig it out. . . . All it was, somethin' wrapped in a gunnysack—was it a head or what? Like that move, *Night Falls*?"

"*Night Must Fall*," Cassidy said. "No, it wasn't a head." He could see it in his mind, a gunnysack soaked with mud, a treasure beyond the telling, buried where El Dorado had once been. "Did you know the man in the Bentley?"

"Nope, never saw him before, but I sure seen that car, that Bentley, we don't get many of them, you know, that Bentley's been here before, six, seven times—"

"Who was driving it then?"

"Woman, real pale, black hair, I never got a really good look at her face, she'd drive in, go to cabin eleven, prob'ly for immoral purposes, y'know, but we're in no position to be choosy. What can you expect from foreigners, anyway? She'd visit this guy, you knew damn well what they was doin' in there, and if you didn't she'd let out a yell every so often, damned embarrassin' but the wife said we needed the bidness and she was right about that—"

"The pale woman was no foreigner."

"No, not her. *Him*. The man. He kept to himself, stayed here a week or so, just before you got here, now I hate to say it of anybody but I think he was a German, kinda talked like a German but he had this funny accent, sorta English, but there was German underneath it, like that actor, Helmut Dentyne—"

"Dantine. Helmut Dantine." Cassidy swallowed more coffee.

"Yep, that's the fella. Dentyne. Anyway, this one-armed fella showed up—he wasn't lookin' so sharp either, had some blood on his face, like he'd had a fight, blood under his nose, little cut on his forehead."

Cassidy peeled off five twenties but Cliff Howard shook his head. "No, no, you're practically a friend of mine by now. Can't take your money. Two hunnert bucks in one night's plenty for me."

"Take it, Cliff. It's not my money anyway. If that makes you feel any better." He put the money on the counter.

Cliff Howard left it there and walked to the door with Cassidy. He went outside and popped an umbrella open, stood in the rain while Cassidy got into the car. "Listen, Mr. Sheehan," Cliff Howard said, "tell me one thing. What the dickens was in that gunnysack?"

Cassidy thought it over. "The stuff that dreams are made of, my friend."

Cliff Howard leaned back and laughed. "That's a good one. Just like the movies, right? Stuff that dreams are made of."

"Exactly."

"Say, you got somethin' to do with the movies, right? Am I right or am I right?"

"Sure," Cassidy said, starting the Plymouth. "We all do. Every damn one of us, Cliff. We all have something to do with the movies. We can't help it. Am I right or am I right?"

"Well, I guess you are at that." He stood in the rain and waved, smiling at the departing Mr. Sheehan, wondering perhaps what had happened to his own dreams.

• • •

He stopped at a diner outside Malibu and had breakfast. Then he went to the washroom and splashed cold water on his face, a face he barely recognized. He looked like hell, but then it had been a long night, a hard night—all night long.

So Tash had the minotaur. Moller had buried it behind cabin 11 where Mona Ransom had visited him regularly before he showed up officially at the Benedictus house. And now Tash had killed them both.

Of course, trusty Lew Cassidy was climbing over the bodies in hot pursuit.

But there was always one more question.

The auction.

Cassidy knew neither when nor where.

But by the time he was back on the road all he could think of was Terry Leary dying in the rain. He couldn't wait to kill Tash Benedictus. It was, in the end, very reassuring to know who the villain was.

# CHAPTER THIRTY-ONE

Cassidy called the police station across the road from Ned's service station and learned that the man found at the Benedictus place had been alive. The cop was young and talkative and didn't question Cassidy's story that he was calling from the *Los Angeles Times*. The ambulance staff and the local sawbones had treated the injured man as best they could but the cop didn't think he'd regained consciousness. There had been blood transfusions right from the start but they'd had to get him to a hospital. His name was Terry Leary, he was from New York City, and no, they didn't know what he'd been doing at the Benedictus place, but he'd somehow gotten himself shot by somebody. No, they hadn't been able to investigate the remains of the house. "Funny thing," the young cop said, "it's the second time a house on that spot has burned to the ground. I guess this one blew up first, though. Heck, we don't know who was even in the house, if anybody. But they wouldn't of gotten out alive. Still red hot up there. In the summer, the whole darned mountain would be on fire. Look for the silver lining, I always say." Obviously they hadn't yet noticed the wrecked Rolls among the trees on the mountainside. They had an interesting day or two ahead of them.

"Do you know where they took the survivor?"

"Just a minute." Cassidy heard him asking Margaret and he could see the whole scene. The chief was up at the site of the fire. The all-purpose secretary/dispatcher, Margaret, was at the desk pretty excited about the whole thing. She'd know where this Terry Leary, gunshot victim, would have been taken. The young cop, Jerry, came back on the line. "Livingston Memorial in Los Angeles. What did you say your name was, anyway?"

"Walter Burns of the *Times*."

"Walter Burns. Well, Walter, the chief wants me to get my fanny up the hill. I'll tell him you called."

• • •

He didn't want to go back to the house, not yet. He didn't want to tell Harry Madrid the story and he didn't want to get into a wrangle with MacMurdo. The Colonel wouldn't understand what had happened, would remind him that if he'd let Mona Ransom fend for herself Terry Leary wouldn't be in the shape he was. The Colonel's sympathies would be brief and when he found out that the whole plan had disintegrated he'd go through the roof. Mona was their agent inside, she was the source of information. Without her, they wouldn't know where the auction would be held and when. Now she was dead and Moller, the man they had the leverage on, was dead. Everything was shot to hell and Benedictus could make a run. He had the minotaur and he might not even wait around for the auction. Take the minotaur and make a run for it. MacMurdo had worked hard to win this war of his and a civilian had just about lost it for him. He wasn't going to like it.

But now Karin, at least, was out of it. Out of it and safe. With Manfred Moller dead she was excess baggage. Thank God.

He called Livingston Memorial and tracked down someone from the emergency room who could tell him what was going on. Terry Leary was in surgery and he had not been conscious at any time since he'd reached Livingston Memorial. There was nothing else to find out.

He called the house. Harry Madrid answered.

He told Harry what had happened. Harry took it in like an old cop. "You just can't stay out of the shit, can you, son? Well, Terry's the main thing. He's a tough son of a gun. Colonel MacMurdo is off on yet another of his little missions. Karin is siting in the kitchen staring at the rain. And I'm about to perpetrate breakfast for the two of us. Lew, you gotta stay cool. Why don't you come here and get a couple hours of sleep?"

"Not quite yet, Harry."

"You want me to tell Karin about Moller?"

"Sure. Look, Harry, what are we gonna do about the auction?"

"You'll think of something." Harry Madrid chuckled softly. "The auction is soon, Lew. And I think Benedictus will be there. It's his nature, he sees it through. Then he's going to run for it. Soon. He wouldn't have done what he did up there on the mountain if it weren't time. He's killed a bunch of people, now he's ready."

"I'm up against the wall, Harry. I wish I knew who killed Rolf Moller, y'know? Where the hell does *that* fit into all this? Whatever happened to the Englishman Benedictus was waiting for yesterday? Vulkan . . . who is Vulkan? See what I mean? We don't even seem to get any closer . . . Harry, how did Tash Benedictus know we were coming to Maine?"

• • •

He found Dr. Langworthy in the Livingston Memorial coffee shop dunking a filled doughnut in a cup of milky coffee. A Camel was burning down in a glass ashtray. The rain was drumming at the window, palm trees struggling to stand upright in the gale. Langworthy's bushy gray eyebrows drew together and he took a sloppy bite of doughnut. His eyes were set in dark circles on either side of a beaky, hooked nose.

"I was in charge of the ER last night, this morning, when they brought your friend in." His voice was tired. He'd had a long lousy night, too. "Pretty bad shape. He's still in surgery. He's going to be in surgery for awhile. He's a mess. I have to tell you this. Shot in the chest, lots of blood loss, lungs full of blood. What ran over him? A truck? A bus?"

"A Rolls-Royce."

Dr. Langworthy shook his head. "Hollywood. Shit. Well, the Rolls left him a lot flatter than a human being is supposed to be. Crushed pelvis, legs, internal organs shot to hell. The physical body can only withstand so much punishment. I was in OR for a while watching them try to put Humpty Dumpty together again—your friend has led quite a life. We found another bullet in him, lodged near his spine. Looked like he's been carrying it around for several years. . . . What's the story there?" He munched some more doughnut and lit another Camel.

"He was a cop in New York. Got shot four years ago."

"What a life! So you're a close friend of his?"

"I am that."

"You a religious man?"

"My mother was a Catholic."

"You ever pray? As a kid?"

"I guess I did."

"You remember how?"

"I suppose so."

"You'd better start. Your friend needs all the prayers he can get."

"Do you think he might make it?"

Dr. Langworthy sighed, rubbed his eyes. "Oh, anybody's got a chance, things being what they are. He might make it. That's what I'm afraid of. Don't pray for him to live, see. Pray for him to die. Trust me on this one." He looked at his watch. "Christ, I'm tired. But right now I gotta go practice some medicine. I'm gonna practice until I get it right."

• • •

He made a few more calls from the lobby of the hospital. He was casting about for any information he could get about the auction. There weren't many angles to play until he remembered something he'd heard. It was a long shot. It was crazy. But it was the only shot on the table.

He placed a call to Teet Carle, who ran the publicity department at Paramount. "Lew Cassidy? You New Yorkers come out here, it starts to rain! Howsa boy, Lew? How's your dad?"

"He's fine. Still working the Army gig. Look, Teet, I got a question for you."

"Shoot."

"You've got a writer under contract at Paramount, little guy, big glasses, looks like an English professor, name of Ray—"

"Chandler. You gotta mean Raymond Chandler. He's a pretty big hitter, Lew. Sweet guy but, let's face it, a little prickly. He's one of the *writer* writers we got out here. O'Hara, Faulkner, Chandler, prickly guys. Ray, you couldn't find a nicer guy but . . . oh hell, you know what I mean. Writes like an angel, been known to have a drink now and then. Jeez, the stories I could tell you, last spring when he was writing *The Blue Dahlia* for Ladd, Johnnie Houseman producing, wooh! The stories, damn near the end of Houseman! But you didn't call to hear all this. So, what's the deal with Ray?"

"I need to talk to him. I thought he might be at the studio today—"

Teet Carle laughed. "Ray's a little pissed off at us just now. We want him to become a writer-producer, like Billy Wilder. Hell, we'd even let him produce his own pictures. But Ray takes the view that he's a novelist, he doesn't want to get his hands dirty with this movie Shinola. So he claims we've broken his contract, tells everybody we suspended him; well, it gets a little murky . . . which is a long-winded way of saying no, he's not at the office these days—"

"Damn," Cassidy said. "How can I get hold of him?"

"You're in luck, Sunny Jim. I know exactly where he is. He and Joe Sistrom—he's the only guy at Paramount that Ray's talking to right now—he and Joe are right across the street, right here on Melrose, at a joint called Lucey's. At this very moment. Drinking lunch. They'll be there awhile, Lew."

"I owe you one, pal."

"Hey, don't be a stranger, Lew boy. Hey, go Fordham!" He was laughing when he hung up.

• • •

Chandler was smoking a pipe and drinking a highball. He displayed the same owlish expression, the quizzical smile, that had been in evidence at the lawn party. He wore a tweed jacket and looked like a man about to dash off to deliver a lecture on the Lake Poets. The man across the table had thick black hair, bushy, as if it had just exploded from within his skull. He was peering through immensely thick glasses at Chandler, smiling soothingly. That was Joe Sistrom. The crusts and pickles from a couple of club sandwiches sat before them and Sistrom was drinking a cup of coffee with the determination of a writer who had to go back to work.

"I can't work with people like Wilder, I can't work under such conditions." Chandler's voice was soft, not angry, merely final. "It was impossible."

"I remember, Ray," Sistrom said. "But for *Double Indemnity*, who knows, maybe it was worth it."

"Maybe," Chandler said ruminatively, not quite sure. He looked up, squinting from behind his spectacles, through the pipe smoke. "Do we know you, sir?" He blinked. "Damn it, I *do* know you from somewhere . . . not an actor, not an agent, not a studio flack. . . ."

"The party at Benedictus's," Cassidy said.

"Ah yes, the football-playing chap! Well, it's a small world, or so I've been told. Say, Joe, did you hear the radio this morning? Benedictus's house up in the mountains—"

Sistrom nodded. "They don't seem to know if he and Mona were inside or not. Nobody can find them. Well, frankly, I'm not all that surprised, the company that bastard keeps. Latest thing I heard, so help me God, had something to do with the Nazis." Shaking his head, he picked up a bit of pickle and gnawed at it.

"Benedictus is alive," Cassidy said. "Mind if I sit down for a second? I'm hoping you can give me an answer to just one question."

Chandler nodded at the empty chair. Cassidy sat down. Sistrom's eyes floated behind the thick glasses, staring at Cassidy. "What have you got to do with Benedictus?" he asked.

"I was up there last night. This is just between us, you guys. Agreed?" They nodded, suddenly alert. Cassidy knew he had them hooked. "Mona Ransom's dead. Another man, a German called Moller, is dead, too. Benedictus tortured him to death and then blew up the house to cover his tracks. And because he's not going to be needing the house anymore. Ray, remember the rumor you told me you'd been hearing lately . . . the selling of Nazi loot here in town? Benedictus's connection?"

"I figured it was just a crazy story," Chandler said very quietly. "You're about to tell me it's—"

"It's true. Tash is running the show—"

"So what's this got to do with you?" Sistrom had grown cagey. "Is this a rib? What is this?"

"There's a long version and a short one. The short one is this. I'm a private investigator from New York. My partner and I were here working on busting this ring open and last night Benedictus took care of my partner. We were so close to nailing him—but now Benedictus is on the lam, but he's got one big score to make first. One more auction. Soon. Very soon. Ray, I have no idea where he holds these auctions. . . . Mona was going to tell me but it's too late for that now. He kills everybody who gets close. I'm convinced he's gone right off the edge. He's crazy now. . . . He'll do anything. You hear what I'm saying?"

"Yes, I hear you." Chandler looked at Sistrom. "Too bad I'm such a pipsqueak, Joe. This sounds like a case for Philip Marlowe—"

"I'm Marlowe this time around," Cassidy said. "I've got a gun that says so."

"Jesus," Sistrom said. "Guns make me nervous. What do you want from Ray? Exactly?"

"Where do these auctions take place? What have you heard?"

"Oh hell, Cassidy—those are just rumors." Chandler's pipe had gone out and he tapped the edge of the bowl gently against the ashtray.

"Remember, I'm Marlowe—"

"Well, I can only tell you what I've heard—"

"Where," Sistrom said, "do you hear this stuff?"

"Writers' Building here on the lot."

"Where will it be, Ray?"

"Officially the studio owns the place. Pinnacle, I mean, not Paramount. But I hear Tash really owns it, little spread in the mountains behind Santa Barbara. Pretty secluded, I was actually up there one time. Cissy, that's my wife, took rather a liking to Mona. Felt sorry for her, I think. It's a nice layout, there's even an airstrip. . . . Let's see, I think I can tell you how to make the trip. . . ."

# Chapter Thirty-two

"Too bad about Leary."

MacMurdo was driving a Cadillac he'd commandeered somewhere among his connections. The sun had appeared for a few late afternoon hours but it had already dropped behind the lush green hills into the Pacific. It was supposed to rain again later, but for the moment the evening was wet and clean and smelled like Eden must have smelled once, wherever and whenever Eden was. MacMurdo looked over at Cassidy, then back to the winding black ribbon of road. *Too bad about Leary.* That was all MacMurdo had said on the subject.

Cassidy stared ahead. He barely remembered sleep. Chandler's rumor said it was all happening tonight and Chandler's rumor was all they had. Cassidy hadn't revealed his source to the Colonel, certainly not that it was a rumor. He supposed those things they were driving among were mountains of some kind but after last night he looked at them and decided they weren't worthy of the name. Green hills, just moist, lush green hills turning black as the last of the light went quickly westward. It smelled like life out there.

Harry Madrid and Karin sat in the back seat. She'd insisted on coming. There was no dissuading her. Cassidy hated her being there. He didn't know what was going to happen but he knew he didn't want her there.

Benedictus, the enemy, was going to be there and he was, simply put, Death. One thing he did know, only one thing, for certain. Benedictus was dying tonight. Cassidy looked upon it as a cleansing process. He shook his head, fought off another yawn. You had that kind of thought when you hadn't slept for a long time. But nothing made any difference. It was dying night for Tash Benedictus.

"You're too tired for this tonight," MacMurdo said. "You'll pardon my saying so, pard, but I don't want my life in your hands tonight."

"I don't really care what you think, Sam. As far as I'm concerned, you're just my driver tonight. Do what you want. I'll do what I need to do. We're not exactly a team anymore. I signed on to help you find Moller. Moller's dead now and I'm a tourist."

"What you are," MacMurdo said softly, "is a loose cannon rolling around *my* deck. My ship. That's the thing, pard. That's why you worry me. I'd just as soon you got out of tonight alive."

White wooden fences lined the road now and some horses were moving in the twilight. Over the trees an old biplane painted bright blue and white swooped down and disappeared.

"Reminds me of Kentucky," MacMurdo said. "Those fences. Fresh white. It's all mighty clean up here. Rich folks. You gotta love rich folks. They've got so much money. Damn, but I always wished I could be rich for a time. See what it's like. Y'know what I mean, pard?"

"You'll never get rich in the Army," Cassidy said.

"That's the truth." MacMurdo smiled. "You are a truth-telling man, God love you."

• • •

They followed a cream-colored Bugatti through the low white wooden gate. No guard on duty. Nothing out of the ordinary. A rumor made real: only in Hollywood, Cassidy, only in fantasy land. Would Hedda and Louella be on hand? The idea just added to the insanity of it all. It was just like a movie. Hell, everything was just like a movie.

There were maybe twenty very grand cars parked before the ranch house, Cords and Continentals and Pierce-Arrows and a Riley and a Jaguar and the cream Bugatti. Beyond the lawn, stretching away toward the hills, was the airstrip Chandler had remembered. The blue-and-white biplane was rolling to a stop near the hangar. Something struck a chime of memory . . . the hangar. And he remembered the glass-enclosed tennis court, Karl Dauner's tennis court, remembered it crashing down, the glass twinkling like falling snow. . . .

There were several planes on the field, buyers who had flown in for their share of Nazi plunder. There was another biplane, a Ford Trimotor painted bright red, a big two-engine job Cassidy couldn't identify, which sat on its haunches looking like a small version of the DC-3 with a twin tail assembly and a fuselage sloping back to a tiny toy wheel mount.

MacMurdo parked the Cadillac in the deep shadows next to a black Pierce big as a hearse. He turned to look at Harry Madrid and Karin in the back, but he spoke to Cassidy. "Now, you're an angry man, pard, I realize that. And you've got all sorts of ideas about Benedictus and I can't say I blame you. But you're just gonna have to behave yourself. No walking in and opening fire, you got that? We're going to take this old critter by surprise, we're the last people on earth he's going to expect. So we just go in, we know nothing about last night, everything's fine as far as we're concerned. He may not have recognized you guys last night, what with rain and wind and trying to drive with one arm and shackling Mona to the car and arranging to blow up the house and finishing Moller—well, hell, he had a lot on his plate. So let's just figure we're mysterious buyers and old Tash thinks we're all in the dark about his various excesses. . . . You got that, Lew?"

"Let's just get on with it." Cassidy got out and opened the door and helped Karin out. "I wish you weren't here—"

"No place for a woman? Believe me, Lewis, I've seen worse." She squeezed his hand. "I've got to be here."

"I don't understand. You're crazy." He brushed her hair with his mouth, felt the scar at her temple. The war lay within that scar, Rolf's clinic, all of that.

"It's almost over," she said. "Let's finish it."

• • •

Inside the house there was a low murmur of conversation, as if it were somehow just another casual gathering of friends looking for a convivial evening. No music, no hilarity, just ice clinking in glasses, quiet chatter, overlaid with an air of expectation, the discernible whiff of tension. The women were wearing slacks, the men cashmere jackets or bush coats and ascots and suede boots for the Hollywood touch. It was thundering again outside as if the storm were waking up and getting ready. Unlike the lawn party, Cassidy saw only one famous face. Errol Flynn was talking to a man and a woman who were finding him most amusing. He was wearing a beret tipped at a rakish angle, polished riding boots, and smoked a cigarette in a holder. As he spoke he seemed instinctively to strike a series of poses. The rest of the crowd was composed—at least the men—of people who struck deals for a living, not poses, and their eyes moved quickly, deep in their sockets, searching out the deal, the risks, the rewards. They weren't men who were catching glimpses of themselves in mirrors. They didn't know they had profiles. They didn't care.

Benedictus appeared, came in through the French doors from the patio, alone, stood calmly observing his guests. He wore a taupe gabardine jacket with western stitching. The empty sleeve was tucked carefully into the jacket pocket. The picture was complete. The eye patch, the hearing aid, the sandy hair, the faintly mocking style. Meet Evil, Cassidy thought. He no longer wanted to torture the man until the man's heart stopped. Now he just wanted to rid the world of him, execute him. Get it over with. He felt as if there had been a Tash Benedictus waiting for him ever since Karin had gone away before the war. There had been something bad waiting for him, an awful job that had to be done. It had turned out to be some dark figure, a stranger, a one-armed Irishman, Brian Sheehan, a killer whatever the hell his name was.

Benedictus—Brian Sheehan—wore a strip of sticking plaster on his forehead. That's all it had cost him, a bump on the head, and Manfred Moller had been gutted, Mona Ransom had been battered to death, and Terry Leary had been shot and run down by six thousand pounds of Rolls-Royce. He'd fixed it so Terry Leary would damn well be better off dead. Maybe he was dead by now. . . . Maybe it was already over for Terry.

And there was Tash Benedictus, one eye shining like firelight, that crooked smile in place, sipping at a glass of Irish whiskey. There was Tash Benedictus straight from Hell, carrying Hell with him wherever he went. He should have trailed wisps of smoke, some kind of warning, but he just smiled and smiled and was a villain.

"Ballsy little bugger." Harry Madrid was smoking a cigar, holding the wrapper in his hand. He dropped it into the base of a potted palm.

"I'm going to kill him, Harry."

"Of course you are, son."

MacMurdo said: "Everybody just stay calm, damn it. He's got the minotaur. Y'know, I'm back to thinkin' he may be Vulkan after all. I mean, who else? Runnin' the whole bloody business . . . Now, let's just not get anxious, gentlemen."

Karin stood beside MacMurdo, watching him.

"He sees us," Harry Madrid said softly.

Benedictus came toward them, a welcoming smile on his face, and what was so frightening was the simple truth that he didn't strike a false note. "Well, of all people," he said. "Mona mentioned she'd seen you and I was terribly sorry to miss you at our little Sunday afternoon. I was bloody rude but it was one of those days, business and pleasure, business won out and I missed my own party. Now, let's see, if it ain't Harry Madrid! And Mr. Cassidy, the search for the downed airman—it all comes back to me! And you, sir, a new face . . ."

"MacMurdo."

"Welcome. Mi casa, su casa, and all that. And this lovely lady?"

"I'm Karin Cassidy."

"Well, howdy-do, howdy-do." He smiled raffishly, as if it were all just

Hollywood junk, bottom half of a twin bill. "I hope you've brought your checkbooks."

"Somehow," Harry Madrid said, "I'd think you're more in the cash-and-carry business."

"Merely a turn of phrase. You are quite correct in your assumption."

Cassidy said: "I was hoping to see Mona."

"Were you?"

"Will she be joining us this evening?"

Benedictus made a sad face. "I'm afraid not. We had a spot of bother up at our mountain place. Fire, gas line exploded, house went just like that. Well, she's upset and trying to oversee the mess. . . . It's been on the radio all day, I'm surprised you haven't heard. So, no Mona. But, on to the business at hand—are you planning to bid on some of our little pieces? I expect Mona filled you in on things." He waited, all calm expectancy.

"Very briefly," Cassidy said. "Mr. MacMurdo here represents an anonymous investor—"

"I always keep an eye out for the odd bargain," MacMurdo said.

"Well, I hope you find one, sir." Benedictus turned to Karin. "Will you excuse me? My associate is getting things ready. Can't leave him to do all the work. He's the chap who'll do the auctioneering. Until later, then."

They watched him mingle with the crowd, the good host, as if the Nazis and their victims and all of his own victims were abstractions, not worth remembering.

"He's a swine," Harry Madrid said, "but there's nothing wrong with his nerve."

Cassidy spoke tonelessly. "He's not going to see the morning, Harry."

Karin was speaking intently while MacMurdo, enormous, attentive, leaned forward, listening, his eyes raking the crowd. Cassidy strained to hear what she was saying but failed. *War crimes* . . . What was so important all of a sudden? Was he still working on her, holding it over her? What more could he want from her?

• • •

The paintings and drawings were arranged on easels in a long room with hooked throw rugs, wagon-wheel furniture, and a few Frederic Remingtons that decorated the walls and weren't for sale. None of them even registered on Cassidy. He prowled the room alone, watching the doorway, scanning the faces, but in his mind's eye seeing only Tash Benedictus. Harry Madrid had linked his arm through Karin's and they were among those viewing the art with an eye toward purchase.

MacMurdo came to stand beside him.

"No sale on minotaurs," Cassidy said.

"Tash is keeping that one, pard. It's his ticket out of here. I'm inside his mind."

"If I were you, I'd get outa there. I'm about to cancel his ticket and you don't want to get in the way. I don't like this place; I want to go home. Is that clear, Sam?"

"We're almost there. Just hang on. These folks are going to start spending lots of money. They're the cultural underpinning of Los Angeles. But we're going to take Tash, the minotaur, and all his records. We'll let the Feds roll up the buyers later. Or not. It's up to them." He smiled, a good old boy. "Might put a crimp in the picture business for a while."

Harry Madrid and Karin made their way through the crowd and were standing beside them when Tash took his position behind the podium at the far end of the room. He picked up the gavel, rapped it a couple of times.

"Ladies and gents," he said, smiling with invincible aplomb, "my friends, thank you for coming. As you may know by now, it takes more than a cloudburst and a fire to keep this cheeky chap from his appointed rounds." There was applause and cries of *Atta boy, Tash!* and *Stout fella!* "And now it's time to separate you from your hard-earned money." More good-natured laughter. "Rather than put up with a one-armed auctioneer"—he lifted his hand with a glass in it—"who might spill his whiskey, let me bring on my associate, direct from London, who will do the honors this evening." He stepped back, clearing the way for a short, stocky man with a round, innocent face who came in from a side door and went directly to the podium, picked up the gavel.

MacMurdo said: "Well, damn me if I ain't seen it all now."

The auctioneer smiled benignly out over the crowd. As he smiled, the monocle on the black ribbon dropped from his eye.

It was Not Me Nicholson.

# CHAPTER THIRTY-THREE

Not Me was handling the bidding like an expert, but none of it was making any sense to Cassidy. Not Me and Tash Benedictus? There was no connection. There were no cards showing that mattered yet.

MacMurdo watched Not Me knock down a Franz Hals to polite applause. Then a group of drawings by Van Gogh. "The twisty little shit," MacMurdo murmured. "Gizmo. Little fella saved my life that time. . . . Who'd of thunk it, pard? Your old pal."

"I don't get it," Cassidy said.

"That's the thing about this kind of operation. All the cards in the deck turn out to be jokers. Pack of wild cards. You just never can tell, pard." He stroked his hair back from his forehead, as if checking to see if it were still there. You couldn't be too sure. The white scar where the Nazi had shot him lay like a brand on his scalp. "Nothing makes sense until the very end. I've seen it happen a thousand times." He shrugged. "That's the way people are. But what the hell? We're damn near there. One lesson in all this, pard."

"Oh?"

"Never trust a man wears a monocle."

Karin was standing close to MacMurdo, her eyes bright, listening to his every word. She smiled at Cassidy, the strain tightening the corners of her mouth. She nervously brushed her hair back. She was wearing a gold locket he'd never seen before. A gold heart on a gold chain against her black turtleneck sweater. It had been covered by the magenta scarf. She stroked it for a moment with her fingertips. Her nail polish matched the scarf. "Don't worry, darling." She took Cassidy's hand.

A Monet, a Dürer, a Tiepolo, a Fragonard . . . People made their purchases, there were smatterings of applause, and they carted them out to their cars or airplanes. It struck Cassidy as absurd. A war had been fought, innocent people had been murdered by the cattle-car load, their homes plundered, museums sacked for the collections of Göring and the rest of Nazidom, yet no one in the room seemed to have noticed it. Nobody had been reading the papers much since '39.

Harry Madrid caught Cassidy's eye. "A picture is just a picture, Lewis. Neither good nor evil, just a lot of paint daubed on a canvas a few hundred years ago. Generations have lived and died, the art endures. I guess it's a good place to put your money."

"It's all stolen. They leave trails of blood and pain—"

"Appropriated," MacMurdo said. "Not stolen. Spoils of war. Don't get worked up about it."

A Vermeer was sold.

"I hope they're fakes. Worthless."

"With Gizmo in the deal, hell. He probably painted the goddamn things himself." MacMurdo looked at the room again. Benedictus was standing off to one side watching Not Me Nicholson drive up a bid.

MacMurdo said: "I think this shindig is just about over. Now's the time for us to make a fairly obvious departure."

"What are you talking about? I'm not leaving—"

"Relax, pard. We're coming right back."

• • •

MacMurdo pulled the car off the road a couple of hundred yards from the gate. Cassidy turned to his wife: "Karin, I wish you'd—"

"I'm coming with you." She got out of the car and slammed the door, stood waiting. "Don't you understand? I can't let MacMurdo out of my sight. . . ."

The rest of them got out and joined her. Together, MacMurdo and Cassidy in the lead, they walked back to the house. The last of the buyers drove past them. MacMurdo raised his hand like John Wayne halting the cavalry. They moved deep into the shadows.

Not Me Nicholson was standing in the doorway under the light. He was talking with Benedictus, who had changed clothes. Now he wore lace-up boots, jodhpurs, a leather flying jacket. A costume for every occasion.

What, Cassidy wondered, was the occasion? Another opening, another show.

Not Me went to a black Packard, backed it around, and drove out through the gate. What did that make him? One of those peculiar supporting players, never out of work, on his way to the next picture, fitting smoothly into the next story? Maybe on another soundstage he'd be the lead's best friend . . . or did Ronnie Reagan get that part? Well, there'd always be a part for Not Me. . . . The taillights blinked out of sight, like a dream ending.

It began to rain. Softly. Cassidy heard it, the big soft drops, plopping onto the leaves. The front door was shut. Just behind the rumble of thunder there was the whirring grind of an airplane engine turning over.

"Time to go," MacMurdo said.

They followed the edge of the driveway as far as the corner of the house, then cut across the wet grass until they reached the patio. The French doors stood open. It was raining harder. Across the landing strip the fog was beginning to form at the tree line, rolling slowly toward them.

The plane Cassidy couldn't identify, the one with the twin tail assembly, was feathering a prop. The pilot was barely visible in the cockpit.

Tash Benedictus came out of the hangar. He was carrying something in a gunnysack, swinging it from a clenched fist. A fistful of minotaur.

"Tash, old boy! Going somewhere?"

MacMurdo stepped out of the shadows, huge, like an animal with mayhem in mind.

"Why, yes," Benedictus said, calling through the rain spattering the leather jacket. "I'm going somewhere."

MacMurdo slowly shook his massive head, the light shining on the dark blond waves. "No, my friend. You're gonna have to change your plans."

Cassidy felt Karin tugging him back. "Stay here," she said. "Let him do it—"

He yanked free of her hand, stepped out of the shadow, the backup man. That's what it said on the walking stick Terry Leary had given him. . . . Terry Leary. Cassidy's hand was on the butt of the .38 in his pocket. It always came down to this. He hated it. It was enough to make you swear off the movies forever.

"Can't, old boy. Can't change these plans."

There was a movement; Cassidy caught it just at the corner of his vision, a man coming out of the black mouth of the hangar. He raised his hand, another bit player, who came on at the end, pointed his finger in their direction.

MacMurdo said, "Shit," a long hiss of irritation, a regret, an inconvenience, and he was falling backward, landing on his back. As he hit the ground his automatic appeared in his hand, he rolled toward the gunman, braced his elbow on the ground, and squeezed off one shot.

The man in the hangar's mouth flopped over backward, his heels beating on the ground as he died. Only then did the two shots explode in Cassidy's head. He'd recognized the man in the instant his face was in the light. Porter. The man from the castle in Maine, the man who'd wakened them that night in the woods, in the snow.

"Same fucking leg," MacMurdo said. There was blood staining his pants, a shredded hole in the fabric. He took a deep breath and stood up, waving Cassidy's hand away. "Stop that bastard!"

Benedictus was running for the plane. One propeller was only a silvery blur, the other cranking slowly. Suddenly he stopped, turned, set the gunnysack down, hampered by having only one arm. He drew the Luger. He fired at MacMurdo. Cassidy heard the slug smack into MacMurdo, saw him driven backward. Karin screamed and Harry Madrid pulled her down, sheltering her. Five, six, seven seconds since the first bullet had found MacMurdo.

Cassidy had his automatic in his hand. One part of his brain wanted to slow it all down because he was going to enjoy this next bit.

He fired once at Tash Benedictus, hit him. He fired again, missed, fired again, and chopped him to one knee.

MacMurdo took two steps, staggered, his face white with pain, dripping rain, fell, crawled to a palm tree, leaned back against it, breathing deeply.

Benedictus was leaking blood that looked black. A chest wound was soaking through his shirt. The leather jacket hung open. Somehow he forced himself upright. He was half dead and fresh out of hope, but he didn't seem to know there was no coming back now. Cassidy watched, sickened, disbelieving, as he lifted the Luger, drew a bead on the gasping MacMurdo.

Cassidy shot Benedictus again, watched his face disappear. He was blown backward, the gun flying away, the body sprawling awkwardly, doubling back on himself.

The plane was edging around, both props whipping the rain, the first wisps of fog, the pilot coming into view again.

MacMurdo was on his feet again, somehow indestructible. From the shadows Karin broke away from Harry Madrid, grabbed at MacMurdo. He swiped at her as if she were yet another irritation on what had become a tough night. His paw knocked her down.

MacMurdo hobbled out toward the body of Tash Benedictus. The rain had turned to blowing sheets, bouncing hard off the fuselage and wings, forming a blowing spray as it was caught in the propellers.

MacMurdo was picking up the gunnysack, cradling the minotaur. What was going on?

Karin was on her feet again. Harry Madrid was pointing at something. Cassidy turned, looked.

A black Packard was moving out of the shadows at the edge of the airstrip.

What the hell was going on? Who was in the car?

Karin had run out toward the retreating figure of Sam MacMurdo. He was moving away from her, holding tight to the minotaur. The gunnysack was smeared with blood. The plane was broadside to them now, the door banging open midway down the length of the fuselage.

Karin clung to MacMurdo; she was screaming at him, clawing at him, all the words drowned out by the roar of the plane's engines.

The Packard slid forward and as it rolled to a stop the door swung open. Not Me Nicholson hit the ground running. In the back of the car, almost hidden, was someone else, a man wearing a homburg, a shadow.

"Lewis!" Not Me was shouting. "Stop him! Stop MacMurdo!" Not Me was holding a gun. Everybody had a gun these days.

MacMurdo's voice came from far away, near the froth blown back from the props. "Get back!" he screamed. "Get back!"

Cassidy could barely hear anyone. He looked at Karin, caught in a tableau with MacMurdo. Was he trying to keep her out of the thrashing blades?

"Stop him!"

Rain sweeping across, bearing fog.

MacMurdo, yanking away from Karin, turned and fired wildly at Nicholson. The slug spun off the radiator and smashed the Packard's windshield.

Nicholson returned fire.

Cassidy screamed. "You'll hit Karin!" He threw himself at Not Me, knocking him sideways.

MacMurdo hurled Karin to the ground again and ran, hobbling painfully, limping and stumbling with an insane strength and will toward the plane, the beckoning door. He was close to it now, clutching the minotaur, ten feet of wind and rain to go.

Nicholson fired again, drilled a hole in the fuselage.

MacMurdo had reached the doorway, the hatchway; with a great swinging arc he threw the wrapped minotaur into the plane. Then he lifted himself with the power of his immense arms halfway into the plane. As he pulled himself aboard Nicholson fired again and put another hole in the fuselage.

Karin slipped in the rain, fell, was on her feet again, running blindly toward the plane as it finally began to move slowly away from her.

MacMurdo looked back almost casually from the doorway as if he were about to wave. Cassidy was running after Karin as the plane taxied away toward the fog. He heard Nicholson panting behind him, heard the explosion near his head as Nicholson fired again at the plane.

It was moving faster now and MacMurdo, for some reason deep in the folds of his own psyche, turned and took one final careful shot.

Karin stumbled, fell in the mud.

Harry Madrid puffed past, following Nicholson, both of them still firing at the plane, hoping for one lucky shot. The rain was pounding down and the plane was gathering speed. Cassidy could hardly see it in the fog now.

The moment he saw her face he knew it was all happening again. He was going to lose her. She was dying. He had seen it all before. The good-bye look.

He held her and kissed her in the tears and the rain and she whispered into his ear. "I'm almost out of time, Lew, it's getting dark. . . . I'm so cold, so wet, hold me, and listen. . . . Elisabeth, Elisabeth . . . the locket . . . MacMurdo hid her from me. . . . That's why I had to stick with him, that's what he had of mine, listen to me, I've got to tell you this, Lewis, it's important, it's more important than my life. . . . It's all up to you now, you have to find her now. . . . That's why he tried to kill me, he didn't want me to tell you, he knew you'd never stop looking. . . . That's how he made me do all this, he said it was the only way I'd ever see her again. . . . Now it's up to you. . . . It's all right now. . . . Don't cry, Lew, I'm so tired, Lew, and we did find each other again. . . . It's all right now, I love you, you're alive, you'll find her, I'll be with you, promise me you'll find her and you'll tell her I loved her. . . ." She lapsed into exhaustion, dead weight, Cassidy held her, knelt rocking her in his arms, feeling the life and the blood pumping out of her.

"Can you hear me?"

"Yes, yes," she sighed. "Take my hand."

"Elisabeth? Who is she?"

Karin smiled, eyes closed. "Our daughter, my darling . . . Elisabeth is our daughter. . . . I couldn't tell you then, you'd have tried to come to Germany and you couldn't. . . . She's yours and mine, Lewis. . . . Now hold me, Lew, help me get through this last part, you're not losing me, we're together, now just hold me while I let go. . . . Kiss me, Lew. . . ."

He kissed her and got her blood all over his mouth, tasted her, tasted her for the last time as the strength left her and by the time he realized Not Me Nicholson and Harry Madrid were kneeling beside him she had slipped away, she was gone, Karin was gone, truly dead and gone at last. . . .

And Lew Cassidy was alone.

But not quite.

As she'd left, Karin had passed him another life in trust. A reason to live. A reason to try to understand what it was all about.

Elisabeth.

Their daughter.

Someone, the man in the back of the Packard, had come to stand beside them. He was offering a blanket, shyly, diffidently. "Here," he said. "For your wife, Mr. Cassidy." He handed the blanket to Cassidy, who spread it over Karin's body.

"Who the hell are you?"

Cassidy blinked at the rain and tears. Somehow he had come to hold the gold locket in his hand. He looked at Not Me. "Who is this guy? I'm on the wrong goddamn page."

None of it made sense, but none of it mattered, not anymore. Elisabeth. She was all that mattered now. "Who are you, pal?" He looked up at the man in the homburg and the shapeless gray topcoat. He couldn't see any face at all.

"For the moment," the man said, "think of me as a man called Vulkan."

# CASSIDY

Another New Year's Eve. The last hours of the last year of the war. 1945.

The clock was running out and the brave new postwar world was waiting and later on that night someone was dropping by with a message for me. It seemed to me that I had to prepare myself. I wanted to be ready.

I'd better be ready.

The rest of my life, such as it was, depended on my being ready.

• • •

It was snowing again. It wasn't Maine and it wasn't a Connecticut country house with the bad guys coming through the snow crust with guns. It was Manhattan this time and it wasn't a blizzard. It was just a soft, thick snowfall on a crisp December night. I was looking down at Park Avenue, watching the headlights probe at the snow and the streetlamps growing exquisite, fragile halos. It was very pretty.

I'd given up my place in Washington Square. It was full of memories of Cindy and Karin and besides old Terry needed me. Oh, sure, Terry Leary made it. I should have known he would. He lived through the operations and got out of a couple of the casts and we flew him back from Los Angeles, got him home on Christmas Eve.

Dr. Langworthy's fears came true. I said my prayers but I prayed for him to live. I couldn't pray for him to die. Not Terry. I prayed for him and he lived: I loved him and I didn't want to go on without him. There's a moral in there somewhere. Probably something like *Don't Screw Around with Prayer Unless You're Prepared to Be Right*. It would make a good sampler for out at the county home.

He wasn't going to be winning any dancing contests. He wasn't going to be standing up much anymore, for that matter. But maybe, in time, we could get him into a wheelchair. If we were lucky.

For now we'd turned the Park Avenue apartment into our place again. The hospital bed was set up in the sunken living room with its fancy mirrored bar and the chrome-rimmed stools and the complete and total complement of ghosts. Ghosts. Everywhere ghosts, waiting in the shadows, longing to come out for the night's haunting. Some nights we had quite a party.

The radio was on. The lights were on low. Terry's eyes were closed. The nurse, a large and extremely strong, motherly sort in her robust fifties, was in her room, where Karin had once slammed the door in a rage and where I'd gone to tell her, somehow, that I loved her. It was the same room where I'd once kissed Cindy Squires and Max Bauman had sent Bennie the Brute to find out what was going on. Cindy and Max and Bennie and Karin were all dead, but the nurse taking care of Terry Leary didn't know anything about the ghosts. She said she had no time for New Year's Eve but she enjoyed listening to the football games on New Year's Day. She couldn't understand why I didn't care about the football games. I tried to make her see that football had been my job, not my fantasy. I told her that playing football hurt. Baseball was my fantasy. She said that so far as she could tell I was a perfect example of the perversity of the human psyche. I told her she was probably right.

Once back in New York Terry had begun to come around. He hadn't said much for a while out there in Los Angeles. He told me he wished he were dead and he pretty much left it at that. He wasn't kidding. But the past week he'd begun to come to grips with things. He was a cripple. He wasn't going to change that. But he wasn't a quitter, never had been. He was beginning to be glad he was alive. He was reinventing himself. We'd sit and listen to the radio and I'd read and he'd doze and we let Harry run Dependable Detective. Most days I'd spend an hour or two at Heliotrope with the books, making sure the waiters washed their hands when they went to the john. What the hell, the world could stagger along without us. And I was pretty low myself.

The master of understatement. I was pretty low. I'd managed to preside over the killings of the two women in my life I'd loved. I'd buried Karin in the same cemetery where Cindy Squires lay, which was no doubt sappy but it was the way I wanted it. I visited them on Christmas Day and it was bleak and gray and cold and I wanted to give in to my grief, I wanted to go to sleep with them, just get out of it, slip off into the endless peace and silence of forever.

Sometimes Terry and I'd get to talking about the ghosts and sometimes we'd both wind up crying and we'd look at each other blubbering like idiots and him with two useless legs and me with two dead women and then we'd get to laughing because it was so sad, and it was so ungodly damn sad it was funny because we couldn't do a damn thing about it. Nothing. Those things clawing at the bars were our lives and we were stuck with them.

One night Terry said: "Jesus, we got this way staying home. . . . Think, amigo, what mighta happened if we'd gone to war!" And we damn near went into hysterics at the thought because we couldn't quite figure out how it could have been a whole lot worse. I mean, we *knew* how much worse it was for those guys invading Europe and taking South Pacific islands one at a time, but we'd made a fairly bloody hash of the home front, too.

We'd sit there, or in Terry's case he'd lie there, complaining that his legs hurt when we both knew that was impossible, and they'd come for us, the ghosts. We'd see Cindy Squires with that ash-blond hair swinging forward while she sang "The White Cliffs of Dover." There was fat Markie Cookson, sweating, drinking champagne, his great hulk quivering with self-satisfaction, unaware of a last appointment on the Jersey shore. . . . And Max Bauman back in the days before he went off the deep end when he sat in the living room and told us how his son had gone down with his ship . . .

The past would creep up on us and we'd see Karin and Rolf Moller and big Sam MacMurdo and we'd get to thinking about the night Rolf got killed but then we'd get to laughing when I'd tell Terry stories about Harry Madrid out in the Maine woods . . . and then Harry would show up and tell Terry how much better off he, Terry Leary, was stuck in bed where he couldn't do himself any more harm. . . . We'd all get to laughing and then we'd make the mistake of thinking about things and Terry would take his pain pills and his sleeping pills and Harry and I would sit up late listening to Duke Ellington and Sinatra and Bing and Artie Shaw and Benny Goodman and Terry would snore in his drugged sleep and we'd smoke some of Max Bauman's Havanas and then Harry would slap me on the back and shake his head and go on home and I'd be alone in another long night. . . .

That's when I'd start going over everything again.

That's when I'd get back to Not Me Nicholson.

• • •

Not Me was the one who knew the whole story. Or, at least, the only one who knew more was Vulkan. And Not Me worked for Vulkan.

Vulkan turned out to be a man named Allen Welsh Dulles. That's right. Allen Dulles, the spymaster, the total insider. He was fifty-two and he'd been a charter member of Wild Bill Donovan's Office of Strategic Services, the OSS, since its formation in 1942. He'd spent the war based in Bern, Switzerland, running a spy network in Nazi-occupied Europe. As the war wound down he'd run Operation Sunrise, which involved the surrender of German forces in Italy.

MacMurdo had worked for what he'd referred to as Army Intelligence—in Not Me's view an oxymoron, whatever the hell that was—but in fact he'd also been part of OSS, too, and had been working for Dulles when he'd gone deep into Berlin. So MacMurdo and Dulles were old comrades-in-arms. They knew each other well. As it had played out, Dulles had known MacMurdo better. Though when MacMurdo rode that plane away into the fog Dulles and he both knew the game wasn't over.

Not Me told me some of the story, nowhere near all of it, and he helped me get through the Karin thing and the truth of Terry Leary's condition. He came back to New York with me and we buried my wife and he explained how Allen Dulles had eased all the red tape we'd have run into in Los Angeles. There were a lot of corpses and not enough explanations to go around.

From New York, Not Me took me down to Washington to have a talk with Mr. Dulles at a huge house in Georgetown set in a vast expanse of lawn speckled with beautiful dead leaves.

Dulles had a squarish mustache on a long upper lip and he was to smiling what Terry Leary now was to walking. He stood in a book-lined study looking like my old headmaster. He wore a very dark suit with a vest, a white shirt, a dark tie. His face was pale and he looked permanently tired. He watched me from behind a fancy globe in a wooden frame over by a French door leading onto a stone veranda with this huge lawn stretching away. It reminded me of my first meeting with Sam MacMurdo, when I'd looked through the windows and seen Karin walking beneath the willow tree with the purple storm clouds building up in the sky.

"I'm deeply sorry about your wife, Mr. Cassidy."

"Thank you. I know you are."

"She was a noncombatant. But I've gone over this with you before. Now, normally in events involving civilians such as yourself—particularly since we never had the slightest intention of involving you in any of this—you do realize that that was all Colonel MacMurdo's doing, of course. . . . Normally we don't talk with civilians. I am reminded of Wellington."

"Wellington?"

"The Duke of Wellington said it. 'Never explain, never apologize.' For a man in my line of work, not a bad motto."

"Then why am I here?"

His eyes flickered to Not Me. "Nicholson here has convinced me that you're quite sound. You can't have a better reference than Mr. Nicholson. Let's go for a walk, Mr. Cassidy. Let me tell you a story."

• • •

It began in January of 1945 when Dulles in Bern learned from an agent he was running within the crumbling German High Command that Reichsmarshal Hermann Göring was setting up an American escape route that would be activated by an SS/SD officer, Manfred Moller, whose brother Rolf owned and operated a mountain clinic for the care of party bigwigs and the "special treatment" of certain prisoners of war.

Dulles knew also that Manfred Moller had been informed only of his first destination in the United States. Dulles knew the destination, too. So he set about doing an intense background study of this Tash Benedictus who'd be receiving Moller. And he learned that Benedictus wasn't a Nazi sympathizer; rather, he hated the English, which put him in bed with the Nazis, with whom he'd been working during the war raising money. Anything to damage the English. Benedictus's share of the money was going to the IRA. He had his own agenda.

Dulles began formulating a plan for using Göring's network, the Moller fellow, and Tash Benedictus. With these elements in mind he looked at what he wanted to accomplish.

In the first place, he wanted to employ many officers of the Third Reich in the rebuilding of Germany and, in particular, the German intelligence system. Toward this end, he had been working with the enigmatic Admiral Canaris who had run the Abwehr, the German armed-forces intelligence service, until the time of Canaris's arrest, July 23, 1944, for his part in the plot to assassinate Hitler. With Canaris held in Gestapo headquarters in the Prinz Albrechtstrasse, Dulles turned his attention to Reinhard Gehlen, who was directing all German intelligence relating to Russia and Eastern Europe. His offer to Gehlen was simple: Gehlen could direct all West German intelligence operations following the war. Gehlen would effectively become one of the most important players in the dawning anti-Communist era. Gehlen liked the idea. No punishment, no war-criminal status, a secure post with prestige and the backing of the United States, a world in which he would indeed be appreciated. Hitler had not appreciated him; again and again Hitler had refused to accept Gehlen's dead-on analyses of Soviet strength and plans, with disastrous results. Dulles wanted him precisely because of his expertise in Soviet affairs. Gehlen was forty-two years old. He was contemplating twenty-five or thirty years of worthwhile work to come . . . but he'd had another offer.

The other offer had come from an unexpected source—a field man on the other side, an American. And this offer differed from Dulles's in two significant ways. There would be risk . . . but there was the chance to live the rest of his life as a very rich man. Probably in South America. The American suggested the creation of a privately run intelligence operation, with information-gathering and action branches. It would be targeted on Eastern Europe to begin with but would have worldwide potential as more survivors of the war were signed on board. The service would be available to governments, to individuals, and to the newly emerging industrial firms that would be impervious to the old rules of national boundaries. The American used to tell Gehlen that the new world was going to be a very different place. "Forget Germans, Brits, Japs, Yanks, Chinks, Russkies—that's the past. From now on it's dollars, marks, pounds, yen, rubles. And the one thing everybody will need is information. They'll pay anything, do anything to get it . . . it's the edge. They'll pay us. We're the wave of the future, pard."

Sam MacMurdo's plan for the future.

Sam MacMurdo was a rogue, an adventurer, who had moved through World War II like a kind of crazy corsair. Daring, brazen, impossibly useful—and most important, *charmed*. Gehlen almost went for it, at least for a moment or two. Then his careful nature reasserted itself. The plan was full of holes. Sam MacMurdo was the kind of man who could get you killed pursuing his dreams rather than your own. Reinhard Gehlen thought he should, as evidence of his good will, tell Mr. Dulles what this brigand MacMurdo was up to.

In the second place, Dulles wanted to bring MacMurdo down. But he didn't want to waste him. Dulles hated waste. "Use every part of the pig," he used to say, "including the squeal." Somehow, he would *use* MacMurdo before deciding what to do with him in the end.

So Dulles added MacMurdo to the mix. Manfred Moller, the Göring network with its Ludwig Minotaur, and Benedictus. MacMurdo was a natural fit. The plan Dulles developed was about as elegant as things got in Allen Dulles's world.

Dulles first contacted Benedictus, told him he knew Göring was sending Manfred Moller and that he, Dulles, had a proposition that would keep him, Benedictus, out of prison on a treason charge. Benedictus would be able to continue his activities raising money for the anti-English forces he supported in Ireland; he would work for "Vulkan" rather than the Nazis. It required only a slight recalibration of his mental set. It was easy. Done. Since Moller had no instructions from Göring beyond reaching Benedictus, Bendictus's job was to keep him at the castle while telling him that it was taking time to get the network in motion.

With Moller having arrived in Maine, Dulles had two elements in place. He then arranged for MacMurdo to learn of the Göring network, of Manfred Moller's part in it. . . . And it was then that he, Dulles, realized that Manfred Moller's brother Rolf owned the clinic, had access to inside information of a sensitive nature about some of the Nazis he wanted to install in the new structure of West Germany. Tracking down Manfred Moller, MacMurdo had gone to the clinic and once there drew Rolf and Karin into the plot to find Manfred and the minotaur and the Göring network in America. All this was fine . . . except for the existence of Karin. She was the wild card. Dulles didn't know who she was and he'd never heard of Lew Cassidy. And MacMurdo told Dulles only that Rolf Moller was going to help locate his brother.

The rest of it was MacMurdo's plan: recognizing Karin as the former skater and actress who'd married the football player; discovering that Cassidy was a partner in a New York detective agency. He began building his own plot to get away with the minotaur; at least that was what Dulles believed in the aftermath of the mess in California. "MacMurdo was fresh out of wars and he was tired of being poor," Dulles said. "He could keep himself busy if he set himself up somewhere with a nice little private information-gathering agency—and he wouldn't ever have to worry about money again."

Watching MacMurdo, Dulles's mind kept ticking over. MacMurdo was a rogue, that was a given. This show was getting very complicated and the more complicated it got, the likelier it was that MacMurdo could turn it around, make it work for him. Dulles tried to make sure MacMurdo had plenty of other responsibilities and he himself had more to do than he could handle. So he needed a number two, someone who could go inside the gears and wheels of the plot and *make it work*. That would be Not Me Nicholson. Dulles had him seconded from MI5 to MI6 or some more arcane branch of British intelligence and briefed him, turned him loose as the art supplier for Benedictus. Once again, the fact that Not Me and Cassidy knew one another was coincidental, not crucial but useful.

MacMurdo had told Dulles that Harry Madrid was in Maine looking about for signs of Moller, that Cassidy was sure to follow. Vulkan had then warned Benedictus; but Moller had made a break for it after learning of the destruction of Karl Dauner's end of the network, stopping to pick up the minotaur on the way. Moller had simply reacted like a soldier.

It was then that Dulles's plan skidded into a kind of crack-up. The only control he had any more was Nicholson: Benedictus needed Nicholson to provide the art to sell in Los Angeles.

And it was then, when Manfred Moller had disappeared and Nicholson was waiting to hear from Benedictus as to what in the world was going on, that Rolf Moller decided to make a move. He was scared. People were getting killed wholesale. He hadn't counted on this. He wanted *more*. More assurances, more money, more power in the Brave New Germany To Be. He simply overplayed his hand. He threatened to go to the newspapers, particularly to Nazi-hater Walter Winchell, with the story of the plan to use Nazi war criminals in the rebuilding of postwar Germany. . . .

Dulles had gotten almost all he wanted from Rolf Moller. And he couldn't run the risk of having everything blown to bits. Rolf had to be eliminated. On the night that Cassidy and Madrid got back from Maine and met Not Me at Heliotrope, Not Me had just killed Rolf Moller.

• • •

"The rest you know," Dulles said.

"Did any of it work?" I asked.

"What a remarkably straightforward question," he said. "We seldom hear them in my business, you understand. Did any of it work?" he mused softly. "Well, let me think. In the first place, the use of some of our German friends to rebuild their country . . . I suggest you keep your eye on Germany, Mr. Cassidy. Pay attention to Germany. Yes, that part of it worked and to a certain small extent Dr. Rolf Moller played a part. We had two programs running, Paperclip and Haven. Yes, they seem to be paying dividends. The Göring network didn't produce much for us, largely because you destroyed the heart of it one night in Karl Dauner's tennis court—well, the fortunes of war. You did what the moment required, I daresay."

"Kind of you," I said.

"Think nothing of it." Dulles plodded on across the lawn, kicking his way through the leaves. "We were able to use Mr. Benedictus to achieve some of our aims and you saved us from having to settle his accounts. And finally there is the case of Colonel MacMurdo. . . . What shall we say? Unfinished business, I suppose. He's up to mischief somewhere. Unless he died of his wounds—"

I laughed. "Not MacMurdo."

"No, of course not. We both know MacMurdo. Sometimes I think he is immortal."

"Where is he?"

"We're looking for him. He'll surface. He'll want to go into business. We'll find him."

"I don't want you to kill him," I said. "I need him."

"Kill him? Good heavens! We'll be more likely to *hire* him."

"I want my daughter," I said. "He's my only hope."

Dulles looked at me appraisingly.

"I will do anything to find my daughter. Do you fully understand? *Anything*."

"I fully understand."

Mr. Dulles was doubtless already constructing a plan.

• • •

So, it was New Year's Eve of 1945.

Since I'd seen Dulles it had been reported in the papers that seven Nazi agents in South America had eluded deportation by various writs and transparent ruses.

On December 21 General George Patton, who'd made no bones about his belief that ex-Nazis were needed to rebuild Germany, who wanted to invade Russia while we had the strength and the atomic bomb . . . General Patton died from injuries received in an accident. He was run down by a wagon or a truck . . . an accident. Not Me had a good laugh at the explanation. "The most predictable accident in history," he said.

I wondered what condition the world was in now that the war was over. It didn't look so hot to me. I sure as hell wasn't for invading Russia. And I could see the reasons for needing some of those Nazis to help run the country. But Not Me was saying that Patton had been murdered for his views, and that struck me as cruel and unusual punishment.

Terry had drifted off to sleep again.

It was eleven o'clock.

I was sitting alone waiting for our guests. I did what I was always doing these days. I took it from my pocket and placed it on the table before me.

A gold locket. Heart-shaped. Nothing unusual.

But when I opened it I saw what mattered to Karin.

There is a picture of me, the way I used to be. I'm happy in the picture, smiling spontaneously, just a snapshot. The picture has been in the locket a long time. Did she know who it was from the beginning? When she saw me did she already know who I was? Had Terry been right, had the amnesia been a pose? Had she been so afraid that I'd have gone after MacMurdo to make him tell us where she was? Had she been so afraid that she couldn't risk it? Well, we'd never know now.

There is a picture of our daughter. Her smile matches mine. Her hair is straight and blond and held in place by a tortoiseshell comb. I suspect she'd been about four when the picture was taken.

I will find her.

And there's only one man on earth who can tell me where she is. . . .

• • •

Harry Madrid arrived about eleven thirty. He brought a bottle of champagne. He took off his hat, shucked off his coat, and put his hand on my shoulder.

Terry woke up and said something funny and Harry Madrid laughed.

Winchell came by. He brought a bottle of champagne, too, and said he couldn't stay long. "I've got a blonde waiting for me," he said.

I looked at the locket. "Me, too, Winch," I said.

He went out onto the terrace and popped a cork out onto Park Avenue far below. "Blondie's waiting for me," he sang to himself.

Winch came back in and poured champagne and lifted his glass. We all did—Terry, Winch, Harry, yours truly. Winch proposed a toast.

"To Elisabeth," he said.

We all drank to that.

Then the bells were ringing outside and horns were honking and sirens going off.

It was 1946. Soon I'd be thirty-four years old.

Winchell was gone when Not Me arrived. He'd called earlier that day and told me he was hoping to stop in. He was wearing evening clothes and a velvet-collared chesterfield. The locket was open on the table and he looked at it.

"Remember Sam MacMurdo?" he said, his monocle in place, a small smile playing on his round face.

I stared at him.

"I've just talked to our old friend Vulkan about the Colonel."

Harry Madrid looked up at him. Terry Leary put down his glass of champagne, waiting. "Yes?" he said.

Not Me looked my way.

"We've found him," he said.

It was my turn to smile.

Elisabeth . . .